BETTER
IN THE
DARK

BETTER IN THE DARK

Chelsea Quinn Yarbro

A TOM DOHERTY ASSOCIATES BOOK
NEW YORK

BETTER IN THE DARK

Copyright © 1993 by Chelsea Quinn Yarbro

All rights reserved, including the right to reproduce this book, or portions thereof, in any form.

Maps by Chelsea Quinn Yarbro

This book was originally published as a Tor® hardcover in 1993.

This book is printed on acid-free paper.

An Orb Edition
Published by Tom Doherty Associates, Inc.
175 Fifth Avenue
New York, N.Y. 10010

ISBN: 0-312-85978-3

Printed in the United States of America

0 9 8 7 6 5 4 3

for
ROBIN A. DUBNER
Attorney-at-law
Saint-Germain's staunch defender

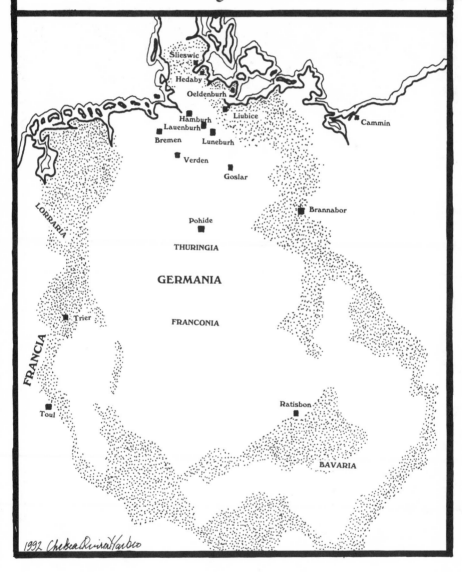

OTTONIAN GERMANIA
940 A.D.

Slieswic

Hedaby

Oeldenburh

Liubice

Cammin

Hamburh

Lauenburh

Bremen

Luneburh

Verden

Goslar

Brannabor

LORRARIA

Pohide

THURINGIA

GERMANIA

FRANCIA

FRANCONIA

Trier

Toul

Ratisbon

BAVARIA

1992 Chelsea Quinn Yarbro

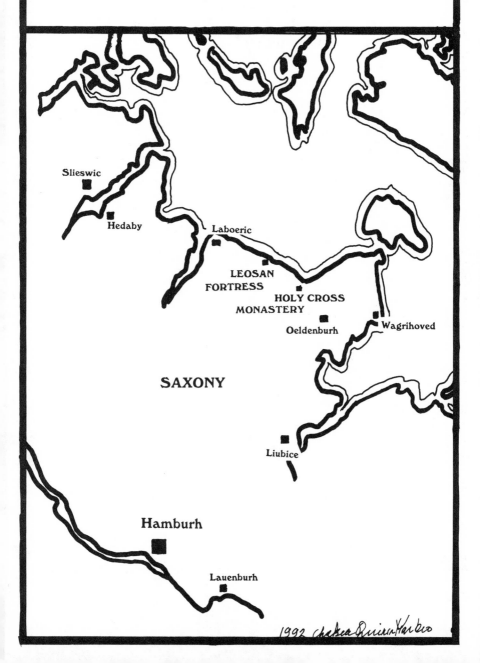

UPPER SAXONY

Slieswic

Hedaby

Laboeric

**LEOSAN
FORTRESS**

**HOLY CROSS
MONASTERY**

Oeldenburh

Wagrihoved

SAXONY

Liubice

Hamburh

Lauenburh

1992 Chelsea Quinn Yarbro

BETTER
IN THE
DARK

Author's Notes

There is a reason they are called the Dark Ages, and not the least of it is that they are hard to identify; historians are divided in opinion as to when they begin and end. Most prefer to establish the onset of the Dark Ages at the fall of Rome, although that date, too, is open to debate, since it can be interpreted as:

a) the splitting of the Roman Empire under the sons of Constantine I, in 340 A.D.,

b) Alaric's sack of the city in 410 A.D.,

c) the German barbarian Odoacar's execution of the last Roman Emperor and his subsequent assumption of the title King of Italy in 476 A.D.,

d) the coronation of Clovis I, who defeated the Roman Governor of Gaul to become the first King of France in 486 A.D.,

e) Totilia the Ostrogoth's triumph over and expulsion of the Byzantines from Italy in 540 A.D.,

f) and so on.

For convenience, I put the beginning of the Dark Ages around 500 A.D.; the end came roughly between 1130 and 1220 A.D., depending on what part of Europe is in question, for these changes happened slowly, and their effect took time to be felt. At this period, a regional lag of a century or more was not unusual. Architecturally the Dark Ages are often called the Romanesque and come before the great changes of the style called Gothic, heralding the beginning of the Medieval period.

Architectural styles, as all things in human culture, do not exist in a vacuum; the gradual development in building mirrored many other social developments. Too often it is generally assumed that European societies went from Imperial Roman to Medieval in a flash consisting primarily of King Arthur, Vikings, and Charlemagne, forgetting that the flash lasted nearly seven hundred years, years that also embraced, to touch on a few highlights—along with King Arthur, Vikings, and Charlemagne: the Byzantine Emperor Justinian and his wife, Empress Theodora; the life of Saint Benedict, who established the Rule of monastic life that is still followed today; the rise and fall of the Lombards in northern Italy; the rise and fall of the Visigoths in Spain; the halt of barbarian invasions in Europe; the rise and fall of Persian dominance in the Middle East; the life of Mohammed and subsequent rise of Islam in the Middle East, Asia, Africa, and Spain, as well as the attempted expansion into France and the Mediterranean islands; the work of the English monk-historian the Venerable Bede; Saint Boniface and his attacks on German paganism; the establishment of Ambrosian and Gregorian chants in European Christian churches; the colonization of England by Vikings, Angles, Jutes, and Saxons; the life of Alfred the Great; the establishment of Novgorod and the conquest of Kiev by the Viking Rurik and the resultant founding of the Russian state; the arrival of the Magyars in Hungary; the plays of Hroswitha of Gandersheim; the founding of the Holy Roman Empire; the first official canonization of Christian saints; the writing of *Beowulf;* the reigns of Ethelred I the Unready and Canute in England and Denmark; Robert II of France and the institution of "The Peace of God"; the life of Ruy Gomez y Díaz de Bibar, called El Cid; the Norman conquest of Sicily and southern Italy and the subsequent massacre known as "Sicilian Vespers"; Macbeth's reign in Scotland; the Norman conquest of England; the First Crusade; the establishment of the Republic of Florence; the lives of Peter Abelard and his mistress/wife/student Héloise; the rise of the troubadours, Minnesingers and Meistersingers; and the Stephen-Matilda war in England.

Hard as it may be to identify the beginning and end of the Dark Ages, the years 937–940 A.D. are clearly smack in the middle of them, and demonstrably not part of Medieval culture. The language is markedly different than that spoken anywhere in Europe today, just as modern English is not very much like Old or Middle English. Because of language "drift," names that are common to us look strange in their earlier forms: Giselberht instead of Gilbert, Walderih for Walter, Culfre for Colin, Ewarht for Everett, Rupoerht for Robert; a few, like Karagern and Ranegonda, are no longer popular and have disappeared. Place names, too, have altered. For example, in 940 A.D. Lorraine is not yet Lorraine: it is Lortharia or Lorraria, depending on which source is being used. And the countries are different shapes than the ones we know today—although the shapes have changed several times in the twentieth century and are continuing to mutate as I write this in 1992. The customs are not those of the great Medieval states, and the conceptions originate in a different mind-set than the predominantly empirical one that was standard in Imperial Rome and is again in our time. This period produced an intensely subjective cosmology, laden with omens and symbols and codes. Although not caught up in the fatalism of the doctrine of predestination, the people of the tenth century often saw themselves the target of a complex series of tests, with often their very survival depending on the successful completion of these enigmatic tests, or the correct interpretation of omens.

At the time of this novel, Saxony was in a more northern part of Germany than it is today; in the tenth century it occupied most of the southern end of the Danish peninsula and much of the territory south to the forests of Thuringia. On the west it bordered Lorraine and part of Burgundy; to the east, Warnabi, Nordmark, and Lusatia, roughly the same boundary as the recent border between East and West Germany. The north-eastern section of Saxony along the Baltic Sea had only recently been subdued; German-founded villages were isolated and had to be protected and self-sufficient to survive. The nearer the villages were to the newly established border with Denmark, the more hazardous the life there was: Danes often raided south for goods and slaves, and outlaw bands controlled large sections of the vast forests that covered most of the region.

In 937, the new King of Germany, Otto, later called the Great, undertook a lifelong and vigorous campaign to expand and unify the various German duchies and cities as well as to develop a German presence in the border areas of his Kingdom. He managed this so successfully that he conquered Italy as well as most of Germany and became the first Holy Roman Emperor. His reign is sometimes referred to by historians as the Ottonian Renaissance, but that seems going a little too far to me. Many of his achievements were the out-growth of earlier attempts to strengthen the German state, and his greatest attainments were military, not academic or artistic. His father, Henry (or Heinrich or Haganrih) I, had annexed the Schleswig marches in 934. Or to put it more accurately, he took the land and kicked the Danes out. From that time on the German settlements in the region, once marginal at best, became strategically important, and as a result were subject to all the advantages of enhanced attention—more armed troops, regular inspections, reinforcements, preferment in allocation of supplies, an increased presence of the Christian church—as well as all the disadvantages—greater military risk, higher taxes, increased obligations to other Germans, an increased presence of the Christian church.

While the fortress and its inhabitants in this story are fictional, they are in many ways representative of the various German coastal installations which were established along the Baltic Sea from about 890 to 1050 A.D. The monastery of the Holy Cross is also fictional, but based on accounts of such institutions at the time and in the general geographical region of the story. There are more historical ingredients in the tale: the outbreak of ergot in 936–940 is recorded from central Lorraine to Pomerania (northern Poland); the sack of Bremen by Magyars occurred in 938; the harbor city of Hedaby (or Haithebu or Heidabai), slightly south of the modern city of Schleswig (Slieswic in 950) near the German-Danish border, was about the most important commercial port on that part of the Baltic coast—neither Keil nor Lubeck was in business yet, beyond local fishing, and were not known by the names they bear now; the institution of deputizing a female relative to serve for a male, while uncommon, was legal and did happen occasionally; there were Orders of monks who followed the Cassian Rule and chanted prayers around the clock in shifts called Choirs; paganism was still very powerful in northern Europe and the Christian church would need another two hundred years to finally get the upper hand; poor and unmaintained roads made travel arduous, while bandits, pirates, and local warlords made it extremely dangerous. Journeys overland usually moved in 15–20 mile-per-day increments in good weather, as little as five miles per day in bad weather. Voyages were equally chancy and were undertaken only by the hardiest and most determined, who were willing to assume tremendous risk for the possibility of tremendous profit. Most profitable of all was the spice trade, which included dyes and glazes; in Europe, ginger and pepper were especially prized, and the merchants who succeeded in delivering these were often set for life. These adventurous merchants also tended to be held for ransom if they were unfortunate enough to fall into the wrong hands. What laws there were in effect were often harsh and arbitrary, and the punishments attached to wrong-doing look excessive to our eyes. Few countries had a uniform code of laws, and those that did were subject to regional variation and the prejudices of the presiding official. In tenth-century Germany, or Germania as it was then, most of the regional government, such as it was, was under the direction of a Gerefa who had authority over a castle or fortress and as much of its immediate environs as could be policed. This title, while inheritable, was generally appointed; eventually it became Graff, or Count in German and Sheriff in English. The Gerefas were under the supervision of a Margerefa (or Meirgerefa), an administrative office determined by the King, usually awarded to relatives and powerful regional landholders. The office and the title eventually became Margrave.

Technology was not very advanced, and many of the engineering feats of the Imperial Romans were thought to be the work of magicians in the Dark Ages. Intellectual curiosity was not regarded as a virtue and occasionally resulted in persecution. Yet there were some developments, and a few rediscoveries that improved the lives of many of the people in the tenth century. Four innovations proved to have the greatest impact in the average person's life at about this time: the invention of the horse collar, which allowed oxen to be replaced by the stronger, faster horse as an agricultural animal; the three-field crop rotation system; the floating mill, built on rafts and rising and falling with the river so that grain could be ground year-round; the standardized horseshoe and horse-shoe nail, which proved to be of enormous military importance.

Provisions of all sorts were in chronically short supply, whether cloth or metal or rope was wanted, in large part because methods of production were inefficient and slow. Food and foodstuffs were not often plentiful, and nutrition was more a matter of getting enough to eat than maintaining a balanced diet. For all but the privileged it was a fat-deficient diet, which led to less physical growth in youth as well as to a reduced birth rate because of the difficulty of carrying a pregnancy to full term. Life spans were short and infant mortality high, and although this story predates the arrival of Bubonic Plague in Europe by a few centuries, epidemics of several sorts regularly claimed many lives, for medical treatment was primitive at best; in some instances it was worse than the illnesses it purported to treat. A stonemason who lived to age forty with all his limbs intact could count himself lucky—if he made fifty, he was considered remarkable.

The center of the European world in the Dark Ages was Constantinople. The Greek-speaking Christian state there dominated the western world for about eight hundred years. From the fall of Rome, whichever date you choose for that event, to the founding of the Holy Roman Empire there was no rival of Byzantine power in Europe.

There are, of course, some thank-yous to add, along with the assurance that any errors in fact or historicity are mine and not made by these helpful people: as always, thanks to Dave Nee for yet another tremendous bibliography, this time of tenth-century material, as well as musical references for that period; to William Brown and Paul Howard for pointers on European language development and literacy in the tenth century; to Doris Weiner for access to her vast collection of European pagan anthropology; to G. G. Gerhart for advice regarding historical maps; to Paula Hill for her knowledge of Dark Age cottage industries and general domestic history; to Edward Smith, S. J., for information on the state of Christianity in tenth-century Germany; and to my editor, Beth Meacham, and the rest of the Tor staff for their continuing interest in things that go chomp in the night.

Chelsea Quinn Yarbro
Berkeley, California

PART I

RANEGONDA OF LEOSAN FORTRESS

*T*ext of a dispatch carried by a messenger of the Holy See to the King of Germania, Otto. Delivered June 28, 937.

To our most puissant ally and worthy ruler of the Germanian people, our Kiss of Peace upon the first anniversary of your reign for which we in Rome have cause to be grateful to Heaven in this 937th Year of Grace:

Too long have we seen the world torn by envious strife that can only find condemnation in the sight of God. We have seen the struggles of the people given little or no heed while the great concern themselves with the honor of killing. We must ask that such battles be directed in the cause of our faith, and that the long tradition of revenge which has brought a never-ending cycle of destruction be abandoned as unsuitable to Christians.

Your father most valiantly brought many pagan souls to God as he fortified his realm, and this is most worthy and favored by Heaven. We are informed that you have elected to continue this vigorous pursuit, and we are willing to endorse your expansions, but only as long as you are bringing grace and the true God to those people still worshiping idols and carrying on practices that Christians cannot name. It is fitting that a Christian King use his might to the glory of God and the advancement of the Church. We will praise all advances you make over heathen people.

We say this in the full realization that the codes of fighting men do not lend themselves to the ways of peace, but the day is coming swiftly when Christ will come again to judge the living and the dead. Surely the ferocity of the Magyars is only a foretaste, a timely warning that many of us will stand living at the Throne of God, and at that time none of us will wish to have the sin of murder or other treachery on his soul. We would be lax in our duty if we did not seek to end all earthly strife, and bring all souls to the Mercy Seat, for the battle for the souls of men must be won in the cause of Christ if we are to sing with the blessed and fly with the angels around the Trinity in Heaven.

While we are aware that there are many dangers impinging upon you, we must ask that you bring nothing to your reign that would prolong the deprivations of war. It is one thing to repel the invaders from the Hungarian plains or force back the pagans in the forests, but it is another to drag your brother Christian into endless battles over the Lorrarian territories of what was so recently Austrasia. It would better serve your purposes for Germania and Francia to be resolved in your minds to end this dispute, for Lorraria is not worth the damnation of your souls and the ruin of your Kingdom. An alliance made by you with Francia would be most welcome to us, and to the Christian people of the world God has entrusted to us until His Son comes again to rule.

Content yourself with turning the Magyars from your land and extending your borders into the regions of the pagans: do not waste your men and your arms in strife with your Christian neighbors. Settle the dispute of the Lorrarian territories before you have depleted your land and are unable to withstand, let alone push back, the assaults of the heathen warriors from the East. The conversion of pagans is always pleasing in the Sight of God, but oppression of fellow-Christians is forever a sin. We make this demand of you as Christ's messenger on earth, and pray hourly that you will turn from your disastrous course and once again rule as the great King you are destined to be as the Last Days come upon us.

We wish you to recall that God is a righteous judge and that no secrets are kept from Him, Who commands the course of the stars and the rising of the seas. Bear in mind that you may escape the wiles of your enemies on earth, but no man is the least part of the majesty of God. Therefore let us hear swiftly of your intention to put an end to your rivalry with Francia. We will dispatch our own Bishops and Archbishops to you to negotiate the agreement if you do not have men of your own you wish to entrust with such a task. For those peoples beyond your borders who are not yet children of Christ, we pray that you will bring them the Light of the World.

You are mandated by God Himself to show Christian charity to all those who have suffered at the hands of the marauders from the East. Let no door be closed against those who come for protection and comfort. As it befits a vassal of the King to honor his edicts, so it is fitting for Christian to receive Christian in the name of Him Who died for your sins. We admonish you to conduct yourself with proper humbleness of spirit. We want to hear nothing of peasants abandoned or villagers left to wander and starve. We do not wish to learn that the daughters of such parents have been sent into concubinage, or that their infants have been left alone in the forests. Moreover, we do not want to hear that you have permitted their children to be sold to the heathens in the north as slaves, as has, lamentably, been tolerated in times past. Slavery is misfortune enough for those born to it, but for a Christian to be a slave to a pagan is abominable. Also we abhor those who treat with thieves and robbers to steal from those fleeing destruction, and we utterly condemn the reeves, comites, and captains who participate in this practice. We instruct all Christian leaders to punish any of their vassals who so abuse their Christian dependents. We order you and all your vassals to preserve the lives of Christian travelers in these difficult days. If you must have ransom, then so be it, but we will excommunicate any who indulge in slaughter. There are those who will not wish to do these things we require, but they are the ones who will howl in Hell when Christ comes to raise the living and the dead, and all things will be known to Him.

In the fervent belief that God will guide you aright and that Christ will favor you in your magnanimity, I embrace you as the hope of Europe, and sign with the Seal of the Fisherman, on this first day of Lent,

Leo VII

1

In the smaller of the two graves lay the swaddled bodies of three children, none of them older than five; in the other, set apart from the rest of the little churchyard, the body of their mother sprawled in the sodden garments she wore when they drowned her that morning. A restless, biting wind blew off the sea and scattered sandy earth onto her wet hair.

"A pity," said one of the monks at the side of the grave as he looked down at the mother.

"She was an adulteress," said his superior, Brother Haganrih, in a quelling tone. "She died as she deserved to die."

"It is still a pity," said the first monk. He was taller, younger than his superior, and in spite of his recent vocation he had not rid himself of his attitude of command, a fault for which he was often chastised and which he prayed daily to be rid of. He could not easily bow his head even now.

"She should not have done the sin. That is the pity, that she was weak," said the superior. "She let another man than her husband touch her."

The first monk sighed. "She said she was forced."

"What woman does not say that when she has been found out? It is the way of women to lie, especially about their fleshly passions. Eve said a similar thing to Adam and to God, that the Serpent forced her to eat of the apple, not that she wished to have forbidden knowledge. Women are ever thus." The superior stared into the grave once more. "Best to cover her up. There's nothing more we can do for her in this world."

The first monk Signed himself and reached for the wooden shovel. "May the White Christ have mercy on her and upon all Christian souls," he said as he began to fill in the grave.

"The father will have to pay for killing the children," the superior reminded the first monk. "He will have to give forty pieces of gold."

The first monk nodded as he worked: Brother Giselberht was aware of the law of King Otto; it was not so long ago that he would have been the one to enforce it. He could not deny the justice of the sentence on the woman or the wergeld for the children. Still, as a man who had killed his first wife, he had the uncomfortable knowledge that such acts lingered and ate at the soul. He added his own petition to Heaven along with prayers for the repose of the dead woman and her children.

By the time he was finished, the wind had become fiercer; the sea was now a deep grey-green, rolling heavily like entwined sleeping monsters, whitecaps showing as far as the monk could see. Somewhere, beyond the horizon, a storm was gathering, the first gale of winter, he suspected, and coming almost a month earlier than usual. All the signs warned of hard times ahead: at dawn he had observed a fox-cub attacked and carried off by an owl as night came to an end. It was an evil omen, one he had pondered through his recitation of morning psalms. He took his shovel and started along the low headland toward the squat wooden buildings surrounded by a stout log fence that housed the Aceomataec or Cassian Benedictines and was dedicated to the Holy Cross.

This place was not so much a change from the fortress Brother Giselberht had commanded two years ago as it first appeared: both were isolated, both were less than sixty years old, and both had been established when the Danes had been pushed back and the Wagrians and Obodrites had been brought under the rule of the King of Germania. Life in one was hardly less austere than life in the other.

In the monastery church the None Choir was chanting their prayers, part of the continual song of worship that rose from this place without ceasing. The monk stopped long enough to kneel at the entrance and prayed to be worthy to enter this holy ground. He was still new enough to the Order that he said none of his prayers by rote, but invested each with emotion and fervor. As one of the Vigil Choir, he would enter the chapel to chant to the glory of the White Christ from the middle of the night until dawn.

Brother Giselberht returned the shovel to the tool shed and then made his way to his cell, one of four cubicles in a cabin of standing logs. There were seventeen such cabins, all in a row, and all but five of the seventy-three monks lived in them: only the warder-Brothers stayed always in the gatehouse except during their Hours of chanting; Brother Haganrih had a cell at the rear of the church, where he could protect the altar with his life.

It was Brother Giselberht's hour of personal prayer, and he set about his devotions with the fervor and determination that were the mark of the depth of his conversion. He Signed himself, lay prostrate on the plank floor, and began to recite the Psalms, starting with the Sixty-first; Benedictine Rule required that he complete a recitation of the Psalms each month, but such was Brother Giselberht's dedication that he doubled the requirement regularly. Between each verse he asked God to forgive him for the murder of Iselda, reminding God and His Son that he had been in the right when he did it and that the reduction of the wergeld required by her family exonerated him from all wrong-doing. But these protestations brought him no peace and he felt as if his words were being drawn into a vast emptiness, which was a failure of faith.

When he left his cell he was exhausted, more ready for sleep than for the weaving he had been assigned to do. The bell for supper rang as he crossed the central court of the monastery, which afforded him some relief, although he longed for a slice of lamb or pork instead of the fish and bread and thick pea gruel that was their daily evening fare. Meat was one of the many things he had given up when he had renounced the world and his title. He lowered his eyes to the bare ground and noticed that a half-dozen dark feathers tipped with brilliant red were scudding along the ground, driven by the wind created by the hem of his habit as he passed. Another omen, he knew, but one that was mysterious to him. With the image of the feathers hot in his mind, he knelt at the door of the refectory and Signed himself, asking God to make him grateful for the food provided.

There were long plank tables set up along three of the four walls, and the monks gathering there did so in complete silence, taking their places and bowing their heads over the wooden platters set before them. Aside from the shuffling of their feet and the scrape of the benches the only sound in the refectory was the distant chanting of the None Choir.

Two of the new Brothers served the meal, offering bread trenchers to each of the seated monks before putting the bowls of baked fish and pea-and-barley gruel on the long table. Large flagons of mead were put on each of the tables, and the monks filled their wooden cups with their contents. As soon as this was done, the two new Brothers prostrated themselves in the middle of the room and waited while the seated monks recited the prayers of thanksgiving. Then, as they returned to the kitchen to prepare a meal for the None Choir, Brother Haganrih came to the center of the room and began to read the Lesson for the day: the ordeal of Jonah in the whale. He was accorded the attention of every monk as the austere fare was eaten with as little attention to the food as possible in order to avoid the deadly sin of gluttony.

As soon as the Lesson was finished, the meal was over. Whether or not the monks had eaten their fill, or had tasted more than a sip of mead, they had no recourse but to rise and go to the ambulatory—in this case, a wide pathway around the inside of their walls—for meditation and preparation for Confession, which was carried on communally just before sunset, when the Compline Choir replaced the None Choir in their church.

Brother Giselberht was pondering the meaning of the omens of the day when Brother Olafr came hurrying toward him, swinging his crutch and hopping, making a signal to him to stop. The other monks in the ambulatory took great care not to listen to what passed between the two. "Good Brother, may God keep you ever in His care," he said ritualistically.

"And amen say all good Christians," answered Brother Giselberht, but with reservation, for he did not often see a warder-Brother except to learn of misfortunes. "What has God brought to this place?"

"Your sister wishes to speak with you," said Brother Olafr.

"My sister?" he asked, because this was not time for her scheduled visit; he Signed himself, anticipating something terrible and hoping God would spare him in the same instant. "Did she tell you what the cause was?"

"She said only that it was urgent," replied Brother Olafr.

In a day beset with worrisome omens, this was the worst. "Where is she?" he asked, trying to do as the Order required him: to use as few words as possible.

"We have her at the gatehouse, in the reception room. She apologized for interrupting our Offices." Brother Olafr ducked his head, though his expression was more disapproving than humble, and he went on with resentment, "I did not look at her but to identify her."

"God will reward you for preserving your chastity," said Brother Giselberht distantly. "I will have to go to her."

"Brother Haganrih will not approve. You will have to Confess your disobedience." He frowned as he pulled his habit more closely around him, trying to keep out the freshening wind.

"I will do so," said Brother Giselberht, and started across the central court of the monastery toward the gate-house where visitors were received.

There was a single lamp in the gate-house reception room, and it was placed to illuminate a painting of the White Christ risen in glory; He was dressed in Byzantine splendor and the wounds in His hands and feet emitted rays of light. Smoke from the lamp was already fading the colors.

Ranegonda was wrapped in a long, hooded mantel dyed the color of pine needles that concealed her russet bliaut and pale blue chanise as well as her long, fair braids. She was kneeling before the painting, her head bowed, but rose as soon as her brother came into the room, her hand on the hilt of the dagger she wore at her waist. "God preserve you from all evil, Giselberht," she said, lifting the hem of her garments as high as her knees in recognition of his former status; her heuse were made of heavy leather with thick soles, and reached to her calves. She was much like her brother—slender, sinewy, tall, and grey-eyed—but at twenty-five she was showing the first signs of age that had not yet touched him.

"May the White Christ also keep you, Ranegonda," he said as he Signed himself, unwilling to look at her because he was embarrassed that she still insisted on treating him as if he commanded the nearby fortress. "It is not your day to be here."

"I know," she said, "and I apologize for intruding, but there are two circumstances that bring me." She watched him to see if he would permit her to continue. "First is that King Otto has sent word that he will not be able to supply the fortress with the requested additional soldiers until next spring. He has had other battles to fight and he cannot spare the men for a short while yet. I have the letter, if you want to read it?" She indicated the heavy leather wallet that hung from her belt along with a massive ring of keys.

"It is not fitting for me to read what the King has written; I am out of the world." He motioned her to move back from him, as if the very presence of the letter could contaminate him further. "You may tell me what it says if you think I must hear it, but otherwise, it is yours to deal with."

Ranegonda stepped away from him, limping a little, for her old injury was paining her today. "I will have to write to him, then. He will have to know that his dispatch has reached us and that the fortress is taking measures to prepare for the winter without his assured help. Margerefa Oelrih will expect some account of our plans, and King Otto will demand an acknowledgment of his orders. But I will have to tell him that you have been informed or nothing I say will be heeded."

He nodded once, showing his understanding of her situation. "You have my permission to use my seal for this letter. You may write to the Margerefa and the King that you have informed me and that I continue to leave such concerns of the world in your hands. Say that I repose my trust in you, and beg that the King will do so as well." He waited for her to continue, and when she did not he reminded her, "You said there were two things."

"The second is the more difficult," she said, unwilling to look at him.

"Tell me what you believe I must know," he ordered her. "Since you are reluctant to speak of it, I must suppose it is about Pentacoste."

"I fear it is," said Ranegonda, her pale skin flushing.

"What is it this time?" Brother Giselberht asked, feeling very weary. He did not like having to turn his mind to his second wife, let alone talk about her.

"She has been permitting Margerefa Oelrih to visit her, as her own guest, not as the King's magistrate. He was at the fortress but two weeks since and stayed for ten days doing nothing but paying court to your wife. I have said that it compromises your honor and the honor of the family, but she says that there is no impropriety, and with you withdrawn from the world and your marriage to her, she is entitled to seek some consolation in the company of those whose rank is equal to her own. She has no desire to enter Orders and will not return to her father unless she is ordered by the King himself." She said this very quickly, as if she had been afraid that if she faltered she would not be able to finish. "I don't know what to do. She will not listen to my objections."

"No," said Brother Giselberht. "It is not surprising that she . . ."

"It makes no difference who speaks to her," Ranegonda went on. "She pays as little attention to Brother Erchboge as she does to me, and none at all to the other women of the fortress, not even her two attendants, who have been at pains to accompany her at all times." She looked away from him suddenly, her certainty fading. "She told Brother Erchboge that you deserted her for the White Christ, and that shows to her that the White Christ does not accept her, or He would have kept you together as man and wife."

Before he became a monk, Brother Giselberht might have thrown a tankard or a platter across the room had he been told of such intractability, had his wife dared to challenge him so flagrantly. Now he mastered himself to click his tongue in condemnation. "It is pettiness and the frailty of women that makes her do this thing. As the master of the fortress in my stead, you may send Margerefa Oelrich away at any time he comes for business that is not the King's. Inform my wife that he is not to come again except in the discharge of his office. Tell her to pray for inspiration that she may be worthy to be one of those women who forsake their sex to leave the world behind for the glories of Heaven." He Signed himself and waited until Ranegonda had done the same.

When Ranegonda had Signed herself, she watched her brother with concern. "You're thinner," she said at last.

"It is fitting for a man with my sins to fast," he answered.

"Still," she said.

"I am grateful that God has given me time to seek redemption before ending my life. That it cost me a little flesh is nothing if it preserve my soul." He was not quite three years her junior, and most of the time held her in affection. But there were times when she spoke as if they were still children and she tasked with guarding him at play or providing his meal for the afternoon, and such instances irked him.

"The signs are for an early winter, which could lead to a lean harvest; I know you have noticed them," she said. "I do not like to see anyone so thin when food is plentiful, for those are the ones who starve when food is scarce, as it is likely to be this winter. You will fast more than God could require before spring comes." It was a lesson they had heard from their mother all through their youth, before she had died ten years ago giving birth to dead twins in another hard winter.

"The White Christ provides for us here, Ranegonda," he reminded her sternly. "We are told to trust in Him."

Ranegonda gave him a somber look. "Your crops are like all the others, and they will yield less grain because of winter arriving early. The storms will destroy the crops, and there will be only the early harvest to salvage. You know that as well as any farmer does. So I tell you once more, eat while there is bread or you will not live to celebrate the Risen Christ again."

"If Brother Haganrih allows it, I will." He met her glare with one of equal force. "Is that all?"

She was about to say yes, and then she hesitated. "I found spiders in the muniment room yesterday, in the old chest, not the new."

"With the deeds and the gold?" he asked, horrified by the omen.

"Yes," she said.

This time he Signed himself without thinking. "Sweet, White Savior Jesus," he whispered, using the old soldiers' oath; he would have to atone for it later. "How many?"

"Five that I could find. There could be more." Her face was grave. "I haven't mentioned it to anyone, not even to Brother Erchboge."

"I should hope not," said Brother Giselberht with feeling. "Five! With the gold and the deeds. Lord of Salvation! And there could be more. You believe there could be more?"

"I looked but could not see them, but—" She broke off, then stared at him. "I will look again if you want."

"No," he said at once. "Leave it is as it is. You have seen the omen and told me. That's sufficient." He wanted to ask her if she had discovered anything else, but the dread that she could tell of things still worse kept him silent. He tucked his arms into his sleeves. "Well, you have told me. Is there anything more?"

"A minor thing." She gestured to show that it was not urgent. "It concerns Captain Meyrih."

"Is he well?" asked Brother Giselberht.

"It's his eyes. They're starting to fail him. The moon is on them. He does not wish to give up his command, but he tells me that he cannot see well enough to perform his duties. He is afraid that he cannot protect the fortress as he must." She tried to look reassuring. "His children are all but grown, and he has your vow of protection, but he does not want to become one of those old, blind veterans who sit in the sunny corner of the barracks and drone on about the great battles of the past." She shared his sense of indecision. She lifted her skirts to her knees again. "Let me know what you would like me to do when I come again in four days' time."

Brother Giselberht nodded slowly. "This is unhappy news," he said. "Captain Meyrih taught me half the skills of war."

"He is nearly forty. What else can he expect?" Ranegonda did not wait for an answer. With a quick movement she was at the door, tugging on it to get it open.

"I will pray for an answer," said Brother Giselberht, watching as she closed the door behind her; he went and secured the stout wooden bolt before returning to the monastery grounds and his interrupted meditations.

Ranegonda hitched up her skirts and climbed back into the saddle on her feisty dun, saying nothing to the two armed men who escorted her. She clapped her heels to the dun's sides and started him cantering away from the monastery, signaling to the men to come with her. Her features were set, showing none of the emotion that gripped her; it was not for her to reveal to these men how little she had gained from speaking with her brother, who was becoming a stranger to her. It was more than their growing alienation; she was upset by Brother Giselberht's reticence and his indecision.

Reginhart, the younger of the two armed men, spurred his horse to catch up with her, calling out "Mädchen! Mädchen!" as he went. The older, Ewarht, held his distance.

Slowly Ranegonda pulled in her horse, letting him fall back to a slow trot. "I ask your pardon," she said to Reginhart as he caught up with her. "It was unwise to do that." Her eyes sharpened. "But I am called Gerefa, not Mädchen."

"It was a fine race," said Reginhart, patting the neck of his bay and ignoring her correction. "I like a good run now and then."

To the north the Baltic Sea stretched out, more restless than it had been an hour ago. Ranegonda pointed to the horizon. "By tomorrow there will be rain."

"The harvest isn't complete," said Reginhart.

"We will have to work tomorrow morning, as long as we can, to bring in as much as possible," she said. "The men will have to go to the fields with the farmers or we will not have bread after the Nativity Mass."

"Some will refuse," Reginhart predicted. "It is not mete that fighting men should work like peasants."

"It isn't fitting that they should starve, either, but that will happen if they will not help the harvest," said Ranegonda sharply. "You need no bad omens to see in what plight we stand. We have less grain in storage now than is prudent, and if we lose any of this harvest, it will go hard for us." She looked to the right once more, studying the sea again. "The storm is a bad one."

"You're certain," said Reginhart. "The season for them is a month away yet."

"All the signs point to it." There was also the throb low in her leg, which was more reliable than all the signs together. "We will have to be ready."

"How can we be, with most of the rye still standing in the field, and half the wheat?" He sounded angry because he was frightened and unable to admit it. "You are a woman, and you are taken with odd notions."

"I am Gerefa of the fortress," she said in a tone that permitted no argument. "And I tell you that we will have to work like the lowest slaves if we're not to starve this winter."

Reginhart wanted to protest this, but as Ewarht was now just a length behind them, he kept silent; it was not his place to question what

Ranegonda said as long as her brother kept to the monastery. Ewarht was a stickler for correct form and he would not look favorably on Reginhart if he thought the younger man was challenging their Gerefa. He squinted into the sun ahead of them. "We will not be at the fortress much before dark." It was true enough, and safe to say.

"We can push the horses," said Ewarht.

"No," said Ranegonda. "We can't afford having one go lame, or risk a fall. If we keep moving we will arrive while there is still light, and we'll be safe."

There was a vast expanse of forest reaching along the wide lowland where they rode, and within that forest there were rumored to be bands of desperate men. To venture through the close-growing trees was hazard enough in daylight—at night it was egregious folly. Reginhart pointed toward the first of the trees. "Keep your sword out," he recommended to Ewarht, who had already drawn his.

Ranegonda reached for the scabbard that hung from the high pommel of her saddle. She drew her short-sword and said to the others, "Good. We're prepared."

"The road is poor," said Ewarht as if they had forgotten since they rode over it half a morning ago.

"Be careful, then," said Ranegonda. The sword felt heavy in her hand, and she had to keep from balking at its purpose. Twice in the past she had been forced to fight off robbers, and both times had left her shaken and nauseated. She did not want to have another such encounter.

"You should take a larger company of men with you," advised Ewarht as they entered the cover of the trees. It was darker here, and the sunlight, by contrast, more brilliant and red, making their eyes water when they moved through the slanting rays.

It was hard to pick their way along the narrow, rutted path through the trees. For the first quarter of their passage they went without speaking, each of them listening for inappropriate sounds, staring into the green darkness for the flash of metal. They were forced to ride in single file, which increased their vulnerability to attack from the side. Reginhart used his sword to swipe at the bushes as they passed, making sure that no one lurked within them. As startled birds rose in loud cries there was a constant rustle as animals moved away from the intruders.

"If winter is coming early," said Ewarht from the rear after they had gone some distance, "it is time to start hunting. There are boars and stags to bring to earth."

"That there are," agreed Reginhart from the front. "We can hunt boars later, but if we're going to chase stags it had better be while the ground is still hard." He coughed once. "And before the wolves get them."

"I've already considered that," said Ranegonda, trying not to permit her nervousness to show. "After the first storm will be time enough for stags."

They went on a way with only the smacking of Reginhart's sword and the fall of their horses' hooves to mark their passage. Then Ewarht said, "If you can read the signs for early winter, surely the wolves can, too."

"Very probably," said Ranegonda, thinking that the forest was much larger and deeper than she remembered from earlier that day. "Creatures have learned these things of old, and their knowledge is vast."

"I saw scraps of red cloth tied to the branches of the oak tree in the field to the west of the fortress village," said Ewarht.

"Some of the peasants try to serve God and the old ways," said Ranegonda, who had occasionally left yarn tied to the branches of trees when she was younger. "If they want the oaks to carry messages for them, we must pray that God will show them His Mercy in their ignorance."

"Brother Erchboge won't like it," Ewarht predicted, listening intently as they continued on. "He says that those who leave tokens for the old gods will suffer for it when they have to answer to the White Christ when He comes. There is no place for the old gods where the White Christ lives. The White Christ forgives all sin, but only the sins of those who believe in Him."

They were almost at the edge of the trees now, and beyond was a stretch of fields, then a gathering of stone-and-thatch houses and a fenced yard of cut trees at the foot of the only real promontory on the coast for several leagues in both directions. It was there that their fortress stood, taking up most of the high ground, an irregular oblong surrounded by a stone parapet and guarded by two towers instead of the usual one, the taller by the landward gate, the shorter on the highest point of ground above the beach; it was there in the uppermost chamber a huge brazier burned night and day to guide ships at sea.

"We were lucky this time," said Reginhart as the last of the sun's rays struck his leather-and-scale armor. "At another time we might have to battle our way out of there."

"At another time, we will be hunting," said Ranegonda, determined not to appear frightened. She returned her sword to its scabbard. "If we catch more than stags or boar, it will be the misfortune of the outlaws we find." She wanted to force her dun to canter, but she knew the gelding was tired, and so allowed him to continue to trot. She said to the others, "We do not have to go in single file here." The road was a fairly straight track, wide and rutted from the constant traffic of wood-cutters with carts who ventured into the forest to cut trees. Today it was dusty, gritty with sand, but once the rains came, it would quickly become a bog.

They reached the village and passed down the only street. Those few villagers who were not yet within doors stopped and went down on their knees as Ranegonda went by, though one of the men held up a talisman to ward off evil; the old gods did not like women commanding the fortress.

When they started up the hill toward the massive wooden gates, Ranegonda could hear a wooden horn sounding, marking her return. Just as they reached the gates, they swung ponderously open, permitting Ranegonda and her two armed men to pass inside. As they drew up in the courtyard, grooms with slave brands on their foreheads came running out to take charge of the horses.

Because of her skirts it was an effort for Ranegonda to swing her leg over the saddle as she dismounted, and she set her jaw in the hope that her weak right ankle would not buckle as she put her weight on it; she managed the chore well enough and handed the reins to the nine-year-old boy who had charge of the horses and the dogs of the fortress. "Make sure they have grain tonight," she told the boy.

He bowed, his knees slightly bent. "That I will, Gerefa," he said, and took the reins of Ewarht's and Reginhart's mounts as well.

The fortress was ugly, utilitarian in the extreme, with two blunt towers and little windows which were covered with parchment in winter when it was often colder inside the stone edifice than outside. Wooden buildings occupied most of the eastern half of the courtyard, housing for the men-at-arms and their families; the stables, kennels, coops, and slaves' quarters were on the west side, with a wooden Common Hall in the middle, the stone kitchens, baths, and bakehouse behind it. In summer the place remained dark and held the dank heat with tenacity. But it gave protection and safety, and that made it beautiful to Ranegonda. A second call on the wooden horn informed all the inhabitants of the fortress that Ranegonda was inside the walls.

"Mädchen," said the monitor as he approached her, his head lowered to show respect to the office she held. "The White Christ be praised for your swift return."

"And my escorts be praised, as well," said Ranegonda as she Signed herself.

"Yes. Most certainly," said the monitor, who wore an owl's claw on a thong around his neck. He lowered his head still further, knowing that what he told her next would not be welcome. "Your brother's wife would like to speak to you. She is waiting in the sewing chamber." Ranegonda heard this out stoically. "All right," she told the monitor. "I will be with her as soon as I have set my cloak aside. Tell Pentacoste that I do not want to come in a dusty cloak smirched by the stains of travel." It was nothing more than a delaying tactic, but it was plausible enough, and the monitor accepted it without reservation. As he backed two steps away from her, Ranegonda steeled herself for her necessary conversation with her sister-in-law.

Text of a dispatch from the customs officer at Hedaby to Hrotiger in Rome; carried overland by a party of merchants bound for Salz in Franconia, transferred to another company of merchants and taken as far as Constanz in Swabia, and transferred there to a courier of the Bishop of Milan bound for Rome. Delivered December 19, 937.

To the factor and agent of the Excellent Comites Saint-Germanius, Hrotiger in the city of Rome, greetings at the end of September.

This is to inform you that the first of five ships bound from Staraya Ladoga has landed. The cargo consists of furs, amber, silk, brasses, and spices. The taxes have been paid upon the value of the cargo, but it cannot yet be released until the other four ships have arrived or been accounted for, as the full value of the goods cannot be assessed until that time. We will hold this cargo in our warehouse, and when all parts of the shipments have been received, we will arrange for their shipment to Rome, in accordance with the orders of the Comites Saint-Germanius.

The Captain of this first ship to land, the West Wind, *has informed me that the Comites sailed aboard the* Midnight Sun, *which is the largest of the other four ships. It is expected that the rest will arrive shortly if they have not been damaged or sunk because of the tempests. There have been four storms in the last ten days, and many ships have put in to port to find shelter. Many of the sailors newly arrived in Hedaby have said that other craft were in grave danger from the storms. Therefore we are hesitating to state more than that we have not received confirmation of any wreckage from the Comites' ships. We are just now seeing ships in the harbor that were expected more than a week ago. These have brought word of two of the Comites' ships, the* Savior *and the* Golden Eye, *which have been sighted on the water and bound for this port. We have not yet received any word about the* Harvest Moon *or the* Midnight Sun, *either to the good or the bad. In duty to your master, we must tell you that there have been* reports of other ships sunk, although none of the sightings have been part of the Comites' ships we have already mentioned, nor have we been informed of jetsam discovered belonging to him.

It is also possible that pirates have attempted to seize the cargo carried in those ships, and if that is the case, it will be some time before we will know of it, for pirates carry their plunder far from these harbors, the better to conceal their deeds. It is possible that if pirates have taken the cargo they may also demand ransom for your master, in which case you will know of it before we do at Hedaby. We pray that no such misfortune has befallen the Comites, but pirates are desperate men who care nothing for their own safety, and will venture onto the waves when prudent men search for safe harbor.

Should there be reason to send another report, it will be dispatched to you as soon as possible, in order that you can act upon whatever information is given before the first of the year. Your master has provided instructions in the event of any difficulty arising from his voyage, and we will act upon them if it becomes necessary. If we have not received the cargo of all five ships by the end of the year, we will release those portions of the cargo which have arrived and arrange for them to be carried south to you.

With the wish that God favors you and the cause of your master and brings you health and prosperity, we vow continuing service to you.

*the sign of the customs clerk
by the hand of Brother Thimofei*

2

For the first time in four days the sky was showing patches of blue amid the scudding clouds and the waves had ceased to maul the shore; this was a welcome relief from the ferocity of the storms that had ransacked the Baltic, and those who emerged from their houses to examine the destruction left behind also saw the splendid sunshine.

Ranegonda ordered half her men out of the fortress to assess the damage, and she herself led the small party down the steep trails to the beach, to see how badly the cliff below the fortress had fared in the relentless battering of wind and water.

There were tangles of debris on the beach, some of them driven up the rough sands to the base of the cliff beneath the seaward tower, a formidable testament to the fury of the sea.

Aedelar shaded his eyes and looked at the mess. "At least we can burn it, once it's dry."

"An excellent notion," said Ranegonda. "Tomorrow I want parties sent down here with sledges; load them up and carry the wood up to the fortress." She shaded her eyes as she looked westward. "Today we have more urgent work. I want each of you to ride for an hour along the beach, some to the east and some to the west. The tide will be at its ebb in an hour." she said. "Be diligent. If there has been other damage, I will know about it."

The men ordered to accompany her glared but did not defy her order. She looked at the small group. "I know you don't like this duty. It is probably going to be for nothing, and the work is tedious. At the same time I know it is a risk as well as you do, for there may be those seeking to reap what harvest they can from the storm, and they will want to drive you off from their discoveries, which cannot be permitted. Be certain your swords are at the ready and go no faster than a trot. Keep a watch for traps on the beach, as well. Stretched ropes, pits in the sand—you have seen the tricks that are played. You do not want to lose your horse to these carrion." All but one of them heard her out with respect, for in the two years she had acted for her brother they had come to realize she had a most unwomanly good sense. The one who resisted was recalcitrant by nature and his behavior surprised none of them. She decided to improve her position. "I will ride with you, so that you will—"

Captain Meyrih, whose eyes were clouding over with white, shook his head. "It isn't necessary, Gerefa." Like most of the soldiers, he was not quite certain what title to use for her, and chose to call her by her administrative title than her military one, which Ranegonda herself preferred.

"It is my obligation," said Ranegonda in a tone that accepted no argument.

The storm had robbed the beach of some of the finest sand that had smoothed it through the summer; there was coarser sand more evident now, and by the end of winter the storms would wear the beach down to pebbles. With the spring and calmer weather, the fine sand would return. Right now there was enough fine sand left to make walking awkward, but the coarse sand contributed scratches and minor abrasions where it rubbed at the skin, and once inside boots and leggings, it was a minor but persistent torment, one that would be paid for later in scrapes and blisters.

"It's hard walking," complained Reginhart.

Ranegonda did not answer him directly. "Aedelar," she said to the man nearest her. "Fetch the horses. They should be saddled and waiting. Take Ewarht with you."

Aedelar touched his leather cap and looked back up the slope. "We'll have to bring them down on the east, beyond the stream. It'll take a while, but it's safer. The footing isn't good enough here." He indicated the rocks on the face of the promontory. "It could crumble if we bring the horses this way. And it's a hard climb."

"You're right," said Ranegonda. "Don't take any unnecessary risks. We haven't horses to spare."

"I know," said Aedelar impatiently. "And just four mares in foal, too." He looked toward the path up to the fortress. "It's the only high ground for leagues. Right now that seems unjust."

The others laughed, and Ewarht cocked his head toward the cliff. "We'd best go get the horses."

"They're not going to come of their own accord," said Aedelar in concession, and trudged off through the damp sand, Ewarht walking slightly behind him.

Ranegonda had hitched up her skirts so that she could walk more easily through the sand; she envied her men their short bliauts and thick leggings—skirts were the very devil in sand, or scrambling down the trail, and with her weak ankle they were doubly treacherous. "I want note made of any wreckage we find. Arrange to bring lost cargo to the fortress. There will be a commissioner from King Otto arriving before the end of the year and he will demand an accounting of ships lost off this coast."

Reginhart lifted both his arms to show how much beyond them such an investigation would be. "If King Otto wants to know that, then he ought to build another fortress somewhere between us and Laboeric; the one at Wagrihoved is useless, nothing but—" He shook his head emphatically. "Two days east and two days west! We can't patrol the sands that far."

"An effort must be made," said Ranegonda firmly. "You are as aware of that as I am." She did not fold her arms but there was an unmistakable authority in her stance, and none of the men wanted to defy her. "Ride for an hour to the east and to the west. Unless there are parts of a ship to be found, or other signs of a wreck at sea, there is no reason to go any farther. I will answer for any questions the commissioner may have."

"And if another storm comes in?" asked Reginhart.

"Then return to the fortress, of course, though there will be no more storms for some days if I read the signs right," she said, losing patience with him. "You're not a fool, Reginhart."

The others laughed, but Reginhart looked annoyed. "As you say, Mädchen." Of all the titles she could have, "Mädchen" was the least pleasing to Ranegonda, for she hated being reminded of her unmarried state. Reginhart sensed this and took full advantage of her dissatisfaction.

"If I learn that any of you has been lax in your search, there will be a price to be paid, I promise you." She put her hands on her hips and looked around at her men. Satisfied that there would be no more resistance for the moment, she went on. "If there is treasure found, notify me at once and the treasure will be placed in the muniment room to wait for the commissioner. At that time, it will be decided how much of the treasure will be given to the finder."

"King Otto will keep the lot for himself," said Berahtram, who had lost an eye in battle with Otto's father.

"King Otto has not done so dishonorable a thing," said Ranegonda. "He will see that the finder—if anyone finds anything—is given his due." She pointed to the west. "You can lead the men in that direction, Berahtram," she went on. "Make sure that you check the inlets and the places where streams fall. I will lead the rest to the east."

"Be careful of the edges of the marsh," said Captain Meyrih. "It is not safe to venture too far toward the marshes."

"I know," said Ranegonda with kindness. "And I thank you for your concern for the welfare of us all." She started away toward the swath of wet sand where the spent waves came. The footing was more secure and provided a better view of the fortress above them. "I want everyone to be careful. If you suspect danger, take no chances."

"A few peasants picking over the bones of a ship, what is that to us?" said Reginhart.

"It could be a great deal if the peasants carry arms, or if they are not peasants but pirates," said Ranegonda. "It was not so long ago that you were set upon by just such a group." Her reminder was pointed, and all of the men knew it: Reginhart's recklessness had almost cost him his life a year ago.

"I was foolish then. I will not be so now." Reginhart cocked his head, making the movement a challenge to the others.

Ranegonda paid little heed to him but continued toward the sea. "I am expected to account for all the men at this fortress. If anything befalls you—any of you—I will have to answer for it in my brother's stead." She looked back over her shoulder at them. "You will follow my orders, like them or not." Just as she said this, her skirt slipped from the hitch in her belt, and she tripped over the hem, falling forward with her hands straight out in front of her. They struck the end of a black, broken beam poking up from the sand, and a long, shallow wound gashed the inside of her left arm. Ranegonda swore as comprehensively as any trooper, damning her limp and her weak right ankle; she wiped the welling blood away with her skirt. She sat up, refusing to be embarrassed by her fall. "This is just what I meant when I warned against mishap. Any one of you could be injured in this way. Including a horse; such an injury as this could lame him or destroy a hoof, and that would be the end of him."

"The scrape looks bad," said Berahtram, coming toward her.

"It is not enough to bother with," she countered, getting to her feet as she said this. "It will scab over before we are back at the fortress."

"You will have to see the herb woman," said Reginhart.

"If there is any cause, I will," Ranegonda answered.

"Are you fit to go on?" asked Captain Meyrih, trying to peer through his blighted eyes to make out what was happening.

"Of course I am fit," said Ranegonda in exasperation. "It is little more than a scratch. Let everyone take it as a lesson, and be careful as you go." She glared around the sands, wondering inwardly what the injury meant, what omen was it?

"Let me look at it," Reginhart volunteered.

"It's nothing," Ranegonda snapped, rubbing her arm against her skirt and leaving a red smear. "Do not be distressed." She looked away from him and regarded the waves while she brought her temper under control.

The men waited silently while Ranegonda paced a short distance away from them, then came back. Captain Meyrih said in an undervoice, "That was badly done, Reginhart. Badly done."

Reginhart did not try to defend himself, knowing it was useless.

As Ranegonda returned, her face was unreadable. In the harsh sunlight the scars on her cheeks and neck were starkly visible, reminders that she had survived the Great Pox. Her long braids were knotted at the back of her head, the way long-haired soldiers went into battle. She looked at the men. "I want no one taking loot for himself. Is that understood? If anyone is caught doing such, he is banished from the fortress. The nearest Saxon holding is Laboeric. It will take you two or three days to get there, if you think you can reach it on your own, on foot. If the wolves or the bear or the brigands don't kill you before you arrive. Your wives will have to remain here until the King's commissioner decides what to do with them and your children." She looked at each of them in turn. "I will not hesitate to banish any of you who loot. The King's commissioner will expect it of me, and my brother will demand it."

Berahtram answered for all of them. "Banishment is better than having a hand struck off."

"God's Truth," said Captain Meyrih, and Signed himself.

Ranegonda folded her arms. "I want no faithless men fighting beside me."

"May God preserve you," said Berahtram promptly. "And keep you in His vision." He glanced at the others. "We all say it."

There were mutters and nods, which Ranegonda accepted without too much inner questioning. She came closer to them as she knotted her skirt and tucked it into her wide leather belt, checking to be certain it would not come loose a second time. "All right. Be alert and watch around you. Have a care of what you do and take no chances. Those of you who carry horns, keep them to hand, in case you need to summon aid."

"It might not arrive in time," said Reginhart with ill-concealed eagerness. "Better to fight and be done with it."

"And risk more men, who would have to search for you without warning? Put the outlaws at the advantage? That is not bravery, it is foolishness, is it not?" Ranegonda inquired in great politeness.

Reginhart sighed, resisting capitulation. "It is a coward who sounds his horn for a skirmish."

"Then the great Roland was surely a coward for sounding his," snapped Ranegonda, tired of these protestations. Her ploy worked, for Reginhart looked away, his face darkening.

Any further animosity was stopped as Berahtram pointed to the east; at the crest of the first rise to the fortress there were horses. "There," he said. "We'll be at it soon enough. A good omen."

Ranegonda was relieved to see them, and motioned to the men to come with her. She went silently, concentrating on walking without limping. She did well until they reached the place where the little stream made a glittering swath through the rocks and sand, and there she lost her footing again. Her arms flailed as she strove to recover herself without falling.

"Take my arm, Gerefa," said Berahtram, coming up beside her. "These streams are tricky."

"My thanks," Ranegonda muttered, and kept doggedly on to where the wide path from the fortress came to the beach.

Ewarht offered reins of the dun gelding to Ranegonda first, in respect for her position as Gerefa, and did her the courtesy of looking away as she struggled into the saddle, her skirt catching on the tall cantel as she swung her leg over. Then he let the others select the mounts they preferred as he climbed into the saddle of a raw-boned blood-bay mare. "May I ride with you?" he asked Ranegonda.

"If you like," she replied as she gathered in the reins while the gelding, restive after three days in his stall, scampered and curvetted. As she brought the horse to order, she called out, "Berahtram, you and Aedelar lead them to the west. Take half the men. The rest come with me." She pointed into the east, realizing that beyond her sight stood the Monastery of the Holy Cross and her brother and the White Christ. Quelling the anxiety that filled her, she started her dun moving to the edge of the spent waves, where the footing was best, and with an effort held him in to a trot.

Coming up beside her, Ewarht remarked, "Away in good time, Gerefa; it isn't much past midday."

"Yes," she agreed. "That gives good time until sunset." She had her hands full with the dun, but still managed to watch the beach for signs of wreckage. Behind her rode Karagern, Faxon, Amalric, Rupoerht, Ulfrid, Walderih, and Culfre, all men who were not on watch, as were the half-dozen men now mounting up to go west with Berahtram and Aedelar. The oldest of the seven with Ranegonda, Ulfrid, was thirty-one; the youngest, Karagern, was fifteen.

"Do you expect to find anything?" Ewarht asked when they had gone a short distance along the beach.

"The sea alone knows that," said Ranegonda, pulling her dun in more firmly. The horse tossed his head in objection, then settled down with a huff.

"He wants to run," Ewarht observed. His own mare was more mannerly, settling into her pace methodically.

"And then he'd be too tired to be of any use on the way back," said Ranegonda. "He'll be fine once he works the knots out of his legs."

When they had gone a bit further, Ewarht commented, "There have been more raiders on the beach, these last few years."

"There have been," she said, not wanting to reveal how deeply this troubled her. She looked toward the land, where a few straggling trees hovered at the edge of rocks and sand, offering protection to anyone waiting there. She stared into the green darkness as if by will alone she could discover the presence of the outlaws known to live in the vast forest beyond. "If they come, we will fight them off."

"Certainly," said Ewarht.

There was driftwood piled up at the high-water line, most of it worn and weathered. The mounted party paid little attention to these ancient veterans, looking for new wood and scraps of cloth from torn sails, or bales and chests of lost cargo.

"That's a strange place," said Faxon behind them, pointing to a tangle of old, water-twisted tree-trunks. It was said that those who wanted to appease the old ocean god came there at the full of the moon to leave offerings, and that to find it empty during the day could bring ill-fortune to the finder.

"Best to stay clear of it," advised Ewarht, who knew the rumors as well as anyone. "Day and night."

A few of the men laughed, but most of them took the precaution of Signing themselves as they went by; Culfre averted his eyes for greater protection.

"Tell me," called out Rupoerht once they were safely beyond the dangerous place, "how much longer do we ride this way?" He pointed to the right, where the trees were nearer.

"I ordered an hour in each direction," said Ranegonda. "There is a way to go yet." She swung around as far as her saddle would allow. "If you are troubled, draw your sword."

None of the men did that, although three touched the hilts, to be certain that the blades could be drawn quickly; their occasional conversations ceased.

Gradually the horses' trot slowed to a jog, steady and easy to ride, covering distance at twice the speed a man would walk. Their shadows, which had been beneath them and toward the sea, were now beginning to move to the front of them as their search went on; when the heads of the horses could be clearly made out in the shadows, they would turn back. The wind out of the north was hard, slapping at them as they rode, keeping the sun from warming them.

They were almost at the limits of their ride when Amalric spotted something drifting a little way out in the water. He rose in his stirrups and pointed. "There! At the last waves."

The others reined in, and Ranegonda pulled her dun around to face the sea.

"It looks like a chest, a big one. I'll try to reach it." Faxon swung out of his saddle, handed the reins to Karagern, and waded off into the water, yelling back, "It's heavy. Locked, too."

"Bring it ashore," Ranegonda ordered, and rode a little way into the water. "Is that all?"

The others were looking more closely now, Amalric shading his eyes. He pointed again. "There's another one. Over there, near the cove."

"And something else," called Faxon. "It looks like a merchant's bale. I don't know if it's cloth or what."

"Ah!" Ranegonda exclaimed. "Retrieve them all as well, if you can. We'd best search there." She signaled to Ewarht. "Help bring them ashore and rig a sled to drag them back to the fortress. If they are left on the beach overnight, we will not find them in the morning. There's rope on Faxon's saddle. Use that if you need to."

"Yes, Gerefa," he said, riding into the water to help Faxon drag the chest away from the sea. "We'll tend to it." He waved her away.

"Gerefa," Karagern shouted, "there's a seal on the lock. It has wings."

"Then perhaps we can learn who owns it," Ranegonda answered loudly. "Make note of them all." She swung her arm, gathering the others. "Walderih, Culfre, Rupoerht, Ulfrid, come with me," Ranegonda said, leaving Amalric, Faxon, and Karagern with Ewarht. She set her dun trotting more briskly again as she headed for the cove beyond the low outcropping of boulders.

The others rode after her, keeping to the edge of the water as she did.

Ranegonda drew her sword as she rounded the boulders, half-expecting to confront thieves scavenging for flotsam and jetsam. But there was nothing waiting for them but a half-dozen bales of furs, a few more bound-and-locked chests, and what appeared to be part of the bow of a trading vessel and a section of mast, some of it already buried in sand. She drew her horse in and raised her sword so that the rest would stop.

"There was a wreck," said Culfre, for all of them.

"Two days ago, judging by the sand," said Ulfrid. He sheathed his sword and looked at Ranegonda speculatively. "Well?"

She returned her sword to its scabbard, making up her mind. "Walderih, stay mounted and hold the horses for us. The rest of you, dismount and come with me. Keep your hands free and your knives ready."

The men did as she ordered, only Rupoerht hanging back as he came out of the saddle. "It could be a trap," he said.

"There would be signs of it," said Ranegonda. "The sand hasn't been disturbed since that wreck came ashore." She started toward the portion of the mast that thrust into the air. "It looks as if the ship broke apart, and drifted here afterward. We will be finding pieces of the ship for months to come, I would guess." She pointed to a section of steering oar. "See that? It is from the rear of the ship, and this"—she indicated the portion of bow—"is from the front."

The men with her looked, and Rupoerht Signed himself. "There will be bodies."

"Probably, unless the fishes got them. Or the outlaws have been here already. Look down the beach, one of you, to see if there are any dead," said Ranegonda, refusing to be shocked by what she saw. Was there an omen here, she asked herself, and if so, what did it mean? She studied the wreckage more intently, seeing here a spar, and there more remnants of sails.

"Or the old gods," added Culfre, also Signing himself.

They went closer to the water-logged sections of wood, Rupoerht murmuring a few words for protection. "The ship . . ." He made a short gesture at the destruction they saw. "It could not be saved."

"We had better find some identification, if there is any," said Ranegonda, deliberately stepping over the broken mast. "The King's commissioner will demand we show him tokens of the wreck. Otto has said he will have full accounting of all losses in his waters." She made a sweeping motion with her arms. "Search this cove. Search it well." Taking her own order, she went directly toward the splintered bow, approaching it carefully.

The bowsprit was shattered, standing up from the sand with the bow below, held in place by the few remaining ribs. The nearer Ranegonda came to it, the more it seemed to be a cupped hand with a single finger pointed skyward; she felt herself go cold, starting with her wet feet and ending near her heart. There was a riddle in this ruined ship, but she was unable to guess what the answer to it might be. Reluctantly she stepped inside the curve of the ruined hull.

"Gerefa!" called Rupoerht from a short distance behind her.

Ranegonda did not answer him at once; she stood in the shadow looking down at the motionless figure lying beneath a few pieces of deck planking, his side-turned head half buried in sand. He was pale where he was not bruised, and his few scraps of clothes were in tatters. Only his upper chest and shoulders were visible above the planking; the rest of him lay under the rubble and sand. One arm was extended beyond the smashed planks; a small hand, swollen and discolored, at the end of it was limp. "God of the Ravens!" Ranegonda whispered, and stumbled toward the motionless figure, reaching out as she did to lift the wood off him, steeling herself for the damage she was sure she would encounter. As she struggled with the heavy planking, the gash on her arm opened with her effort, and began once again to bleed.

"Gerefa!" shouted Rupoerht, louder and nearer.

"Be quiet!" she ordered over her shoulder as she levered a second section of deck off the still form, revealing more of the torso, which was crossed with old scars but was mercifully undamaged but for bruises. She turned to motion the soldier back from her and almost fell as her ankle gave way. As she reached out to steady herself, her injured arm brushed the face of the body, leaving a bloody smear across his mouth.

Rupoerht had reached the curve of the bow, but he came no farther. He Signed himself and moved back. "Do you need help, Gerefa?"

"Not yet," she said, continuing to work to free the body. "But we will need a way to carry him. Go. Tell the others to prepare a sling for . . . for him." She had a dread of calling the dead dead in their presence, and never more so than now.

Once again Rupoerht Signed himself, glad for a reason to move away. "All right. I'll tell them."

Ranegonda ignored Rupoerht's departure and knelt down beside the man, trying to clear away the sand from around his head, working steadily until she had succeeded in freeing him from the sand. She touched his face and was surprised that the flesh was not colder; she brushed the dark, loosely curling hair back from his brow and studied his beaten features, trying to discern what he might have looked like before the storm savaged him. Then she started to rub her blood off him.

The fingers of his out-flung hand moved, closing weakly on her wrist.

She could not scream, so great was her fear. Her voice stopped in her throat and she gasped as if the breath had been knocked out of her. As she watched in petrified amazement, his battered head turned, the eyes open marginally. When she tried to move away, his hand tightened. She whispered a prayer and put her hand on his chest, above the scars, searching for a heartbeat, or breath.

His hand moved again, and though he seemed to have no force in him, he carried her arm inexorably to his mouth, pressing her wound to his lips; she stared in fascination. There was no pain, only a mild tingle and a suggestion of warmth.

Walderih and Ulfrid appeared around the curve of the ship and froze, seeing Ranegonda bending over the supine figure, her body blocking from their view most of her strange interaction with the man she had thought dead.

"Make a sling for him," Ranegonda ordered without taking her eyes from the stranger's face. "He's alive."

"Gerefa?" said Ulfrid, seeing omens of death all around him. "How? No one could live through such a wreck; how could he?"

Ranegonda had no answer for that question; she did not want to think about it herself. "Make a sling," she repeated with determination. "Now. Come back when it is ready, to help me move him."

The two soldiers hurried away, grateful to be out of the shadow of the broken hull.

Some moments later, as he released her wrist, his dark, pain-dazed eyes opened and fixed on her. "I know you," he murmured, but in a language that had not been spoken for nearly three thousand years.

Text of a report written by Brother Desidir for presentation to the King's commissioner.

May it please God to show favor and honor to King Otto and to those who serve him, and may each come to God with a clean heart. Amen.

We of the Monastery of the Holy Cross, ever obedient to the Rule of our Order, have provided burial outside the walls of the monastery to nine bodies washed ashore after the recent storms. Only one of those unfortunate dead recovered carried any identification, and that was one Mordicar, a carpenter from Huy in Lorraria. It is supposed that he was the carpenter for the ship itself, or built cargo cases. The rest are without identification.

We have taken into protection fourteen bales of furs and cloth, most of which have been ruined by the sea-water. We have saved what seals we could in order for a record to be made of the cargo, in the hope of finding the identification of the lost ship or ships from which these men and the goods came.

We have been informed that there are chests being held at the fortress, on the cause that they are too heavy to carry here easily and would present too tempting a target to those dire men who prey on travelers for the purpose of taking slaves and treasure. We are told that there are seven in all, each closed with bands and locks, and the locks identified with the same seal. It is the opinion of the Gerefa that these all belong to the same merchant; she has given her Word to hold them until such time as the owner is found or until it is decided by the King what is to be done with them.

It is thought that some of those things we have at this monastery should properly be taken to Hedaby for taxation, but the weather is too severe to undertake such a difficult and long journey at this time. We will be at pains to preserve what we can of the furs and cloth, and the rest we will consign to the midden before they are too rotted for use. We will prepare an accounting of what we cannot save so that the King's commissioner will know how much has been washed ashore.

We must mention that there have been men seen on the beach during the night. We assume that they are nothing more than outlaws coming to try to find anything of value that we may have overlooked. It may also be that these are misguided souls who are leaving token for the old gods in the mistaken belief that such acts will appease them and cause the storms to cease. We have admonished all those peasants who live around us that such actions will serve only to anger God, Who will visit plague and famine upon them for their impiety.

There is also the injured man at the Saxon fortress near this monastery. He was found with the wreckage and was taken to the fortress to have his wounds dressed. We have been told that the man had a money-belt secured around his waist and that it contained twenty-three gold coins. The monastery has been given four of them, to pay for our care of the goods that may be his. If it is learned that they are not his, then the coins will be returned, assuming he lives. We are told that given the severity of his wounds, it is likely that mortification will result, and from that, nothing but the Hand of God can save him. We pray for his recovery, but we fear that he is beyond the reach of our faith. Whether he lives or dies, we will make every effort to find his people and either arrange for his return or inform them where he is buried.

We have discovered, also, the body of a boy, clearly not a sailor for his hands were not rough and callused in the manner of those who live on the sea, who has been identified as a child missing from Oeldenburh. His father died during the summer, but there are others to care for the boy. His brothers have said that he was carried away by the outlaws of the forest, who were demanding ransom for his return. It is supposed that the boy wandered off or tried to escape and became lost, and was caught in the storm, although some of the peasants think that he was drowned to honor the old storm god, which may account for the severity of the weather. The body has been given to his brothers for proper burial. We have offered prayers for the repose of his soul.

There are other discoveries, less easily identified, that are being kept here for your inspection. We swear by God and the Trinity that nothing has been taken or tampered with, and the articles are as we found them.

May your service to King Otto be the equal of your service to God; we pray for you on this day, October 17th, 937, and for all days to come until Christ returns and summons all to Judgment.

Brother Desidir

3

"Is he dead yet?" Pentacoste asked her sister-in-law as Ranegonda emerged from the chamber where the stranger lay. Her chanise smelled of saffron and had something of the precious herb's color; the bliaut over it was the red of old wine, adding color to her splendid features. Her lips were parted, smiling a little, and her lovely eyes shone with anticipation.

"Not yet," said Ranegonda shortly, displeased that Pentacoste should ask. She carried a basin with a crumpled cloth in it, but no sign of its use.

"And no rot?" Pentacoste urged. "I saw him when he came. I cannot believe that his hurts are not mortal, not as pale as he was, and with such marks on him." She fingered the heavy cross that hung around her neck. "He has not wakened today, has he? He lies there in a sleep that is more than sleep, and you haven't been able to rouse him." She licked her lips. "Has he broken his back? I saw a knight die of that, once. He howled like a starving wolf before he it was over. Or is there worse than broken bones? Does he bloat from inner rot, instead? Perhaps he should be physicked, to draw out the poisons." She brushed a tendril of dark auburn hair back from her brow and ran her hand down her long braid; it was a sensuous movement, graceful and provocative, and it was wholly wasted on her husband's sister.

"Pentacoste!" Ranegonda admonished her in an undervoice. "He might hear you."

"Then would he thank me," she said, her softness becoming hard in a moment. "He would know that he must prepare to die. You could send for my husband to attend him." Her single laugh was edged with fury, and though her mouth was square with ire, her face remained beautiful.

"You are not to speak this way; I forbid it," said Ranegonda, reaching out with her free hand and taking Pentacoste by the arm in order to draw her away from the door. "It is wrong to urge Death to come."

"When it brings an end to suffering, where is the wrong?" she asked innocently. "You have not understood my meaning, Ranegonda. I wish your dying man no harm, only the end of his pain, and the quiet of the grave." She tried to pull away from Ranegonda's grip and could not. "Let me go."

"When you are away from this corridor, I will," said Ranegonda, propelling Pentacoste toward the next level above them, where the women of the fortress gathered to spin and weave; it was in the seaward tower with a broad window that faced the courtyard as well as a narrow one facing the Baltic. In the winter the windows were covered with parchment that protected them from the rain but not the cold. Just now they were still open but the room was draughty and chilly enough to make wool-working pleasant. "I do not want you to go near the stranger again, not until he leaves that chamber. Do you understand me?" She forced her sister-in-law to look at her. "Do you understand me?" she repeated.

"I understand what you say," answered Pentacoste, her smile growing wider.

Ranegonda decided not to argue the matter. "Then I warn you: keep away from him, Pentacoste. I will not brook any contest about this."

"So you can have him for yourself?" Pentacoste asked with counterfeit sweetness, which changed to egregious and spurious concern. "That is what you want, I can see it in your eyes. He is your only chance to have a man of your own. You cannot help that you are unmarriageable. My husband would say it is the will of the White Christ that you should have scarred cheeks and a weak ankle. So you have decided to take your joy where you can, and the gratitude of that man is better than nothing at all. How hard it must be, to know that you will lose him, in spite of everything you are doing to keep him alive. Though you will not have to endure his spurning you if he dies; I suppose a dying man is all you can hope for. What whole one would be satisfied with you but for pity?"

"If that is so," said Ranegonda, refusing to be dragged into their old disputes, "then respect my position if you can respect nothing else. Keep away from the foreigner. If he dies you will know of it soon enough." She indicated the loose bale of raw wool. "Tend to your spinning, my brother's wife, and let me care for the wounded, since that is my purpose."

"The dying," Pentacoste corrected her.

"Thus far he is alive," said Ranegonda firmly.

"And for how much longer? Two days? A week? He takes no food, they say, and he lies insensate for most of the day. What is to prevent his death? Your desire that he live?" Pentacoste shook her head, lowering her splendid eyes in the assumption of modesty, and probed again at Ranegonda's most vulnerable place. "But I discern your purpose. We all do. You have no one but this man, and you must be content with your hope that he will live. You must cling to that until he is in the ground. Very well, make the most of your foreigner; I won't begrudge him to you. But I think it wrong that you will not permit me to have the company of proper men simply because all you can have is a dying man who will never—"

"That's enough," said Ranegonda, her tone more level than she expected it would be. "You are married and it is not fitting for you to have any man court you." Anticipating Pentacoste's next objection, she went on, "You disgrace your husband's name if you do; it does not matter that he is my brother, but that you are inside these walls. You are in my charge in his stead and I must answer for your conduct, and well you know it. Tell me no more tales of your father's court—he is no example of proper behavior if even half the tales of him are true."

When Pentacoste looked up there was scorn in her countenance. "You imagine too much, Ranegonda, but I suppose I must expect it, given how you are. I have done nothing to disgrace you or this fortress. Ask my women if you cannot believe me." She motioned to the high, narrow window that overlooked the sea. "How am I to do anything imprudent in such a place as this."

Ranegonda held back the sharp words that she longed to speak, for it would only make their dealings more difficult. She stared at Pentacoste until she knew she could contain her feelings. "In the name of my brother who is still your husband, bring no evil to this fortress. Be content in your fortune. Do your work here, and pray for wisdom."

"From the White Christ?" asked Pentacoste angrily. "It was that wisdom that stole my husband from me."

"Then don't pray," said Ranegonda, and stepped back. "I will send your women to you."

"How kind you are to prisoners, and the dying," Pentacoste accused.

Again Ranegonda bit back a hasty retort. "I will do what my brother obliges me to do, Pentacoste, and if that does not suit you, so be it." She turned away before Pentacoste could offer her any more jibes. Much as it galled her to admit it, she knew that some of Pentacoste's accusations were accurate, and that caused her serious qualms. A woman in her position could not afford to compromise herself, and her care of the stranger was beyond what was required of her. There were those who would infer the same things Pentacoste had. She refused to dwell on her predicament now; there was too much to do. She hurried across the flag-stone courtyard to the women's quarters in the landward tower, pausing long enough along the way at the kitchens to authorize the cooks to kill two goats for the next day's midday meal.

Daga and Genovefe were with the wives of the officers of the fortress, all of them busily stripping flax as they discussed their children and the coming winter. They agreed that the omens were ominous, indicating that the weather would be more severe than usual, and would require more preparation than the previous year. There were other signs of misfortune that filled them with unease. Two of the women were noticeably pregnant, one of them radiantly, the other already showing signs of illness.

"Your mistress needs you," Ranegonda said to Pentacoste's two attendants without any greeting. "She is in the cloth room."

Genovefe sighed and set the flax aside; Daga was less accommodating. "I haven't finished my work here."

Ranegonda was not willing to endure any more defiance this day. "She is waiting. It isn't fitting for her to spin alone."

"It's not," said Daga, and rose, brushing the front of her bliaut with a fussy thoroughness that matched her finicky temperament. "Our duty is clear. You need not remind us, Gerefa. The cloth room, you say? Spinning wool for mantels or planning how to find another suitor?"

"You have no right to claim that of her unless you can show good reason for your assumption, and thus far you cannot. Pentacoste is not discreet but she is not wanton, either. She is in the cloth room. Where she waits for you even now," Ranegonda said with determination and although she was not willing to admit the same misgiving Daga had, she added, "She has been left alone too often, and she indulges herself with idle dreams."

"She sent us away," protested Genovefe. "This morning she told us to come here. We did as she ordered us; if we had stayed she would have become angry, she said so. She wanted time to herself, and so we left her. We are supposed to obey her—we are her attendants, not yours. She rules us. Last week she threatened to have me whipped."

Ranegonda was not surprised, but she said, "Your father has not granted her that right. Only my brother may do that. Or Brother Erchboge."

There was a titter in the room, and a hushed embarrassment at the mention of the absent Giselberht; the monk who served the fortress was regarded with too much awe to invoke such a response. Njorberhta, whose pregnancy was ill-omened, Signed herself and touched the elder sprig hanging from a cord around her neck to protect herself from possible harm brought about by this reference to those who had withdrawn from the world, for such a withdrawal could influence an unborn babe to remain in the womb too long, or to die before birth.

"And these days the Gerefa only whips himself," said the grey-haired wife of Captain Meyrih. Unlike many women her age, she still had half her teeth and of them only two were blackened. She smiled merrily, her blunt, chapped hands moving industriously.

"These days, I am Gerefa," Ranegonda reminded them sharply, and signaled to the two waiting-women. "Go to your mistress. See that you remain with Pentacoste for the rest of the day."

"If that is your wish," said Daga as she lifted the hem of her bliaut above her ankles in marginal respect.

"You know your task: that she is guarded," said Ranegonda, paying little attention to this casual discourtesy. "If there is any lapse in your service to her, it will not go well for you."

Njorberhta seconded this, her sallow face tense. "It is wrong for her to behave as she does, and you must see that she does not shame us."

"What are we to do to stop her? We are not armed men. It is not our place to restrain her if she seeks company. When she has visitors we remain with her, of course, but that is all we can do. We would fail in our duty if we refused to guard her," Genovefe said uneasily.

"Come to me if there are any questions," said Ranegonda, and stood aside to permit Daga and Genovefe to pass. "You may not compel her, but I can."

"Do you think so?" said Daga over her shoulder as the two women hastened toward the dark stairway in the seaward tower.

Ranegonda offered no answer; she watched the other women work, a quick pang of nostalgia passing over her, remembering how she, too, had stripped flax when she was a girl; it had seemed a chore then, and now she thought of it as a welcome diversion from the weight of her responsibilities. Had there been signs when she was a girl that she had missed? As often as she recalled her youth to mind, she could find nothing that pointed to her current position in the world. This worried her, and often she mixed her reflections with her prayers, though she knew that Brother Erchboge thought such matters were trivial and therefore possible means of damnation. So great a change of station must have been hidden in unread portents. Surely there had been a warning that she would be her brother's deputy, yet somehow she had not seen it. She put these troubling ruminations from her mind.

It was almost dark when she returned to the stranger's room in the seaward tower, a later hour than she had visited him on previous days. Had the man not been so desperately ill, she would not have entered his room alone for fear of bringing scandal down on herself and the fortress. Brother Erchboge had blessed the man earlier in the day, as he had every day since the man was found, but to no effect. Nor had the strip of parchment with the Paternoster on it, laid on his pillow, been any help to the stranger. Though she knew it was a fruitless gesture, she carried a tray with a trencher and a cup of broth; so far the man would not eat.

"Foreigner?" she called as she came through the door, expecting no response.

"Yes?" came the answer.

She had to grip the tray with both hands to keep from dropping it. It was only the second time she had ever heard him speak, and the sound of his voice, light and rich at once, held her attention. "You're awake?"

"Yes."

She stood very still, looking at him in the thin slice of light that came from the brazier outside the door. "Did you speak?" There was slight, exhausted amusement in his answer. "I did." Ranegonda knew she ought to summon one of the women, but to her own inner astonishment she closed the door, blinking once to accustom her eyes to the gloom. "You *are* awake? At this hour?"

"Yes." This time the voice was a little stronger, certainly not the whisper of one at his last strength as it had been when she found him on the beach. "It is night."

"It is." She recovered her sense enough to start across the room to his bed.

"I am better," he said to her, and there was another note in his voice, a second tone, deep, almost unheard. "In the dark."

His words hung between them, and then she gave herself an inner shake. "I've brought you food," she said, not daring to sit beside him as she had when he was unconscious.

He took a short time to respond. "That is kind of you." He spoke Saxon Germanian well but with an accent she had never heard before.

"I have bread and broth," she said eagerly, coming the last two steps to his bed and bending over him. "So you can eat."

"Ah." There was disappointment in his tone, and something more, though she could not place it, something like the lower note in his voice, something that came from the dark.

"What is it?" she asked him anxiously as his dark eyes met her light-grey ones. "Is there something else you want?"

His smile flickered and was gone. "Regrettably there is," he said, more to himself than to her, though his eyes did not leave hers.

She had never experienced such a look before; those enigmatic, compelling eyes reached into the heart of her. She tried to speak sensibly and ended up babbling. "There are other things in the kitchen. It was mutton today, still on the spit, and I know the cauldron isn't empty; the stock is rich with turnips and onions and thistles. We have only salt beef, and one goose hanging. I could tell the men to get a rabbit or a duck, if that—"

"No," he said very gently. "But I thank you."

"We have beer," she went on hastily, as if the speed of her suggestions could improve him. "There is some mead, as well, and a little wine."

He shook his head. "I do not drink wine."

"What then?" she asked, feeling suddenly bereft.

At last he looked away. "I wish I knew how to tell you," he said after a moment. It had been centuries since he had been in such a predicament, and this pale-haired woman was a far cry from the marauding Huns with whom he had last experienced this deprivation. He reached up and rubbed his face, feeling stubble under his fingers; he would have to shave soon, he realized, or someone might notice how slowly his beard grew. "This is difficult," he said to her, holding her gaze with his once more.

"What is it?" she urged him. "Are your hurts worse? Is there rot in your wounds?" This was her greatest fear—that he had injuries she could not detect or treat. She hated Pentacoste for wishing it on him.

"I am improving," he said. "I need time." He smiled at her once more, this time long enough for her to venture one of her own. He gestured to her to come closer.

"But you must eat, to regain your strength." Without intending to, she sat down on the bed, facing him, the tray providing the only barrier between them. She wanted to touch him, to assure herself that this was no dream.

"Truly." He agreed, then hesitated, looking around the night-filled room as if he could see it clearly; when he spoke again it was on another matter. "The ship was lost, I suppose."

"Yes," she said reluctantly. "We found pieces of her, but . . . you are the only one washed ashore. If there were others, we have not found them."

"That's unfortunate," he said, frowning, his expression distant. "How many of them went down?"

She looked puzzled. "How many?"

"Of the ships," he prompted. "Was it just the *Midnight Sun* or were the other four lost, too?"

"We found no wreckage but of the one ship, or so we suppose," she said, continuing carefully, "If other ships sank, their wreckage did not land here, and I have heard of nothing found between here and Laboeric to the west. Aside from two letters from my brother at the monastery east of here, no dispatches have come from that direction since before the storm." She looked toward the narrow window. "The land is disputed, east of here."

The foreigner accepted this with a single nod. "Then what did you find? Other than me?"

"There were bales of fur, all ruined by the water and rotting when we came upon them," she went on, searching for the thing that might take the inner pain from his face. "Some shreds of sails were found along the beach. There were two cases filled with cloth, but the salt of the water has ruined the colors. Still, we saved the larger one, and I said nothing of it to the monks, though it is in my records here. And a leather book, but it was ruined as well."

"Nothing else." He sighed once, hard, convincing her that he had lost whatever cargo he had aboard.

"Only a few chests," she said. "Banded and locked."

"Chests. How many?" he asked sharply.

"Seven. They're in the landward tower, in the muniment room." She realized that she had his full attention. "They are unusual chests, strapped with iron and made of wood covered in black leather. There is a sign on the locks."

"The eclipse—a black disk with raised, displayed wings," he said at once.

"Yes," she confirmed, for the first time feeling she had done something that brought him ease. Some of the pervading sense of insufficiency left her. She set the tray on the floor beside the bed. "We haven't opened them. There was no key and I will not permit the men to break the locks."

"Seven of them saved; better than I feared," he said, and his frown faded. He regarded her for a short while, and then he asked her, "Could you have one carried here?"

"To this chamber?" she asked, reminding herself that foreigners often did very strange things. "One of the slaves could carry the smallest chest."

"Would you order it done?" He paused once more as he anticipated her next questions. "They are mine, if that gives you any reassurance. There is a merchant's agent in Hedaby who can provide proof, if you want to have it; send word there, or to the customs magistrate at Slieswic. My seal is on record in both places, and in Hamburh as well. In my money-belt there are keys to open the locks, I hope. I've brought those chests a very long way. They were carried in the hold where I slept." Again he gave her a chance to speak. "What they contain can help me."

"And what is that?" asked Ranegonda, more curious than apprehensive.

"Earth," he said at once, and offered her an explanation that was the truth but not all the truth. "I need it for my work. I am Franzin Ragoczy, Comites Saint-Germanius; I am an alchemist, and a smith, for that matter. I use earth for ores, among other things."

"I am Ranegonda, Gerefa here." She fought the impulse to rise and lift her skirts above her knees.

"Gerefa?" He was startled; it had been many centuries since he had met a woman in such a position of authority. In these times only Olivia strove to keep to the old Roman ways. "You have no father or uncles or brothers?"

"My brother put me in his place when he became a monk of the White Christ," she said, aware that he could find this out from anyone inside the fortress. "He has no children and our two brothers are dead."

In the darkness his features were as concealed as if he wore a mask. "If your care of me is any indication, you have shouldered your duties admirably; your brother is a blessed man."

She stared at him in growing surprise, for such praise was foreign to her. "I cannot . . . there is no . . . How can you . . . You are a foreigner and you know nothing of . . . You were on a merchant ship," was all she could bring herself to say.

"Of course. How else should I travel?" He was growing tired but strove to conceal it. "And you are right; I am a foreigner." There was too much he needed to learn; sleep was a luxury now. Later he would rest, but now there were questions he had to ask. He pressed his lips together in order to keep alert. "I own ships, if any of them rode out the storm."

"It is permitted?" asked Ranegonda, her confusion scrambling her thoughts so that all her questions blurred.

"Who would deny me?" he responded calmly as his exhaustion increased; his eyes started to close and he forced them open.

"King Otto," she blurted out. "This is a Saxon fortress, the only one for two days' ride in either direction along the coast. King Otto licenses all Germanian ships in these seas."

"But I am not Germanian, in spite of my name," he said wearily and sensibly. "I sail in ships of all countries; the ones for this voyage are . . . or were Italian ships, with the license of the Pope as well as the King of Francia. They have brought cargo from Visegrad and Staraya Ladoga in the last year, and farther before that, when we brought spices and dyes from the East." Now his fatigue was making his voice rough and he apologized. "I fear I am growing inattentive."

"Those are the places of stories, where omens cannot be recognized, and there are dangers no man can resist," said Ranegonda, not quite willing to believe him. "Merchants arriving at Hedaby speak of many lands that cannot be, but then there are no questions asked on the origin of their cargoes. Pirates present themselves as foreigners from distant places, in order to sell their booty without hindrance. It was said that there were men who came there who had—"

His yawn was nearly a sigh. "Your pardon."

Ranegonda rose at once. "You need to rest; I will leave you until morning." She looked down at the tray once more. "And you must eat. Here. Let me give you food before I go."

They had not escaped the trouble, after all, he thought as he turned in order to watch her while she leaned over him. They had come back to it, and he knew they would continue to come back to it until he explained or until his esurience drove him to take what he needed while she slept; persistence was in her blood. "I would not benefit from the broth, Gerefa, nor from the bread. But I thank you again for the kindness of bringing them to me."

"Then tell me, what do you require? If it is here, I will bring it to you," she said, this time with conviction.

He shook his head a little, hating what would come once she understood his nature. "It . . . may be loathsome."

"Many remedies are loathsome," she said, thinking of what she had seen the farrier do to men wounded in fighting. Some of them had lived, she remembered, but not all.

He lay back, weighing the matter, and decided circumspectly. "Can you bring a shoat to me? A live one, in good health?" It was not the best source, but it was better than rats, and created fewer questions than his greatest need would. "It need not be the largest; a runt will be enough."

"What will you do with it?" she asked, knowing how rambunctious young pigs could be.

"I will feed," he said very quietly.

Ranegonda considered his answer, and offered, "We can slaughter it for you and bring you the parts you want."

"No," he said, his voice dropping again, but this time not from enervation. "It must be alive."

She Signed herself, growing nervous. "A shoat, you say?"

"Or a lamb or a foal," he said. "But I suppose you have more shoats than the others. Losing one will not rob you of too much."

"The gold you carried will pay for it," said Ranegonda, and then faltered. "We did not know what was in the belt when we removed it. I hoped it would show who you are. The gold is being kept for you, except for the donation to the monastery."

He regarded her with renewed interest and a trace of ironic humor. "It sounds as if you are keeping my bond. Tell me, Gerefa, am I being held for ransom?" The question was more amused than angry, and for that reason alone she answered him candidly.

"If there is someone who is willing to pay for you, yes. Otherwise we must deliver you to the King's commissioner when he comes here, and you will be sent to Otto for his judgment. You will have to deal with

him for the terms of your release." She smiled uneasily. "Is there
someone who would pay for your return?"

"Yes," he said, thinking that there were two he knew would send
gold to free him—Hrotiger and Olivia—as well as half a dozen others
who would gladly pay to have him back within their grasp once again,
a notion that sickened him more than the bruises and long hours in icy
seas had.

Ranegonda smiled. "Then the money will keep you until the ransom
is paid. You had a good amount with you. You need not fear that you
will have to work with the slaves." Mischief was foreign to her, but she
felt it now, and indulged the amusement he had awakened in her. "Of
course, as I am Gerefa, it is for me to decide how you will be received
here."

"And how will that be?" Saint-Germanius asked, matching her ban-
tering tone, though he felt misgivings. If he were not so tired and his
body sore, he might have done more to try to influence her; she was
honest and determined and filled with a fire she could not acknowledge,
he knew from the single taste of her blood he had had on the beach.

She cocked her head to the side, letting the decision come without
reflection and without regard to the omens. "We will begin with the
shoat."

A dispatch from the Margerefa Oelrih to Gerefa Ranegonda, carried
by courier from Bremen.

*To the sister of the former Gerefa Giselberht who governs at his behest
at the Saxon Fortress Leosan, this notice of arrival from the King's
commissioner, written on the 14th of October in the second year of King
Otto's reign.*

*As the King's commissioner, I wish to inform you that yours will be the
third fortress on my inspection of all Saxon fortresses along the Baltic at
the start of spring. I will bring forty men and their families to reinforce
your fortress. They will require housing and food, which you will want to
prepare before my visit.*

*It is the wish of King Otto that the number of logs cut in your forests
be increased. You have done well for so small and remote a fortress, but
there are pressing reasons why every one of the King's vassals must be
more active in the King's cause, and no group has more reason to know
this than those of you who are the outposts of the Kingdom. If this means
that you must bring more woodcutters to your fortress, then do so. You
are permitted to build a stockade wall around your village if this is
necessary to protect the people and the logs cut and the planted fields from*

raiders. However, the logs needed for such a stockade wall must be reckoned separately from the logs required by King Otto, and the King's need must come before your own. You will have to make your preparations to permit you to accomplish both the increase of logs for the King and the raising of the stockade walls as well. If there is any conflict in these goals, then primary consideration must be given at all times to the demands of the King.

An accounting of all crops and logs for the last year will be expected upon my arrival, such accounts to be scrutinized by Brother Ernust, who will accompany me and serve as my scribe. If there is any question concerning your figures, the matter will have to be resolved by the King's magistrate at Slieswic. We command your diligence in preparing your reports.

There are reports of Danes raiding the coast, and if such come as far south as your fortress, you are to repel them and to take what prisoners you can. These are to be kept for King Otto, to be used in bargaining for the release of Saxons held beyond the Danish borders. You are to kill as few of them as you can so that their ransoms may swell the coffers of King Otto and give him power with the Danes. Those Danes who refuse to be captured are to be killed without torture, so that there will be no reprisals.

In the matter of other raiders and outlaws living in the forest, such precautions are not required. If your fortress sustains attacks by such as these, let your men-at-arms kill as many of them as they can. There is no need to show any weakness to these outlaws, for they would show none to you. If any of your woodcutters are injured or seized by these bands, you are authorized to use all your force to rescue the woodcutters and dispense saddle-bow justice to the marauders. They deserve no greater mercy than a swift hanging, and to fail in this task would damage the reputation of your fortress. Such desperate men have put themselves beyond the King's law, and for that they must suffer the fate of all traitors.

You are reminded that you must provide protection to the Monastery of the Holy Cross in time of need, not only for the honor of Gerefa Giselberht, but to protect those pious men who are out of the world and who are not permitted to arm themselves against any but the pagans. Their safety is in your hands, and you will answer for their lives. When your reinforcements are established within your stockade, you will be expected to supply regular guards to the monastery just as you will supply guards for the woodcutters. Failure to do this will bring harsh judgment upon you and your removal from your position.

Any of your vassals taken as slaves or captives must be reported to Slieswic and to Hamburh as soon as possible so that ransoms may be arranged. If demands for ransom are presented directly to you, pay those you can and send escorts to bring the ransomed back to Germania. Those sold away from the Danes may be lost, but there are certain to be others who can be brought back to this Kingdom; you are authorized to reclaim all those vassals of King Otto who have been stolen from his lands. If any other misfortune befalls Fortress Leosan, word is to be sent at once, informing the King's magistrate of the nature of the trouble and the fatalities which have resulted. If reinforcements beyond the ones already being provided to you are required, state the number and the reason for your request. Only an outbreak of disease is not to be reported, so that the miasma will be contained. Any breach of this order will result in the immediate killing of the courier as well as your own quartering should you survive the plague. You must mark the gates of your stockade with yellow flags to warn all travelers away, and you will not provide any charity or trade while the miasma is upon you. When the plague has passed, then prepare an account of the dead and dispatch it as you would any other notification of trouble. At that time, it will be decided if it is wise to send more men to guard you, or if the danger remains, in which case we will wait until the miasma has dissipated. There are signs for plague in Saxony, so be alert to all illness, even the most trivial.

Any disputes regarding ships on the sea are to be taken to Hedaby or Liubice for settlement, and you will abide by what the Comites of either harbor decides. It is not for you to question the rights of those at sea. Those who profit from shipwreck will be treated as the thieves they are.

For the honor of King Otto and the preservation of Saxony, I commend myself to you and to your vassals, and pray all comes safely through the winter. Those who defend the outposts of the Kingdom perform a great service to the King that will be rewarded. Most especially I entrust your sister-in-law to your particular care, for her own sake and the sake of her father in Lorraria; with her husband out of the world, her care must be your most stringent concern.

Margerefa Oelrih
(his sign)
by the hand of Brother Ernust

4

It was the third day of rain and all efforts to put up new houses in the little village had come to a halt. Stacks of logs lay in the mud while the inhabitants huddled around their fires and cursed the old gods who had brought such bad weather to them. The woodcutters were more bitter than the farmers, but both groups resented the rain, and left small bones tied with string at the crossroad and the well to inform the old gods of their dissatisfaction; a few left holly and hawthorn sprigs as well, in the hope that the old gods would relent and stop the rain long enough to raise the walls of the new houses and make necessary repairs on the old. A few of the thatchers continued their work, but it went slowly and one of them broke his leg when he slipped from a wet beam and fell to the floor below.

Those in the fortress did not fare much better, and though their stone walls kept out the wind, they remained stubbornly dank, impervious to the smoky fires that blazed in the main hall and in the central rooms of both towers. The men put their time to cleaning and sharpening their weapons, repairing their armor, and rubbing their tack with beeswax. The women did what they did most of the time: they spun wool and wove it on the two large looms in the cloth room, or worked at preparing flax for linen. In the stable the farrier inspected the horses, physicking two of them with hot gruel mixed with oil and mustard, to kill the worms that brought bloating and death. The cooks laid down beef and venison in salt against the coming lean months, put the remaining fruits in the dark cellar on beds of straw, and dried peas to cook later in barley water. Barley and wheat and rye were ground into flour and put in barrels beside the shelves where the new cheeses were ripening. Slaves were set to work securing parchment over the windows and fueling the braziers with charcoal; others carried loads of wood to the hearth in the Common Hall.

Brother Erchboge kept to his place in the chapel, spending hours on his knees, fasting and praying. He was already gaunt from his austerities and after two days without food he began to look cadaverous and to lapse into light-headed exaltation as he recited his prayers. The men-at-arms regarded him with suspicion and awe, and the rest took the lead from him, expressing admiration for the monk without showing much inclination to emulate him. Yet, from time to time other denizens of the fortress would come to pray with him, and at those times his fervor increased and his voice rose in sing-song cadences as he rocked back and forth on his knees.

"He's feverish," said Pentacoste to Ranegonda.

"He is inspired. God reveals Himself to Brother Erchboge at those times, and everything is clear to him," Ranegonda said. "Or so he claims." They were at the foot of the stairs in the seaward tower, and from outside the sound of hammering reminded them that the preparations for winter were not yet complete.

"He is becoming mad," said Pentacoste more emphatically. "It is the White Christ. He makes men mad." She looked hard at Ranegonda as she delivered this condemnation. "And some women, too. There are women who become monks, you know that there are. And there is much talk about them, in Lorraria." She pressed on, making certain that Ranegonda was displeased with what she was saying. "It is not the same as the women who are in their own monasteries, not at all. It is completely different when women have their own establishments. You know of many such, doubtless." Her eyes widened as she Signed herself. "Surely you've heard of these women, these Prioresses who are holy women? But you must have. They are spoken of throughout the whole of the Kingdom. Word of at least one of them must have reached this place." She was enjoying this reminder that Leosan Fortress was isolated and without any true court, or musicians, or jongleurs, or much news of the outside world. "But I mean the other monasteries, the ones housing men and women together. In my father's domain women as well as men enter the same monastery, sometimes living side by side, working as comrades and praying in the same chapel. They say there is no sin."

Ranegonda watched her without expression, then said, "That is how you do it in Lorraria. Here in Saxony we do not permit women to enter monasteries with men. It leads them to temptations." She paused. "Who knows if they sin if they remain within the same walls as men, but all suppose it is possible; if they live apart they save themselves much pain."

"So the White Christ does *not* banish all sin from his serfs," marveled Pentacoste, showing her fine teeth. "Does my husband know that yet?"

Ranegonda realized she was being baited and refused to be drawn into the game her sister-in-law delighted in playing. "If you wish to learn the answer, ride with me and my men when we take four barrels of salted goat to them; ask him yourself. We go in two or three days' time." It was an offer that Pentacoste would never accept; she was terrified of the forest that lay between them and the monastery and rarely ventured into it, even when escorted by a company of armed men.

"No," said Pentacoste with a grim angle to her jaw. "It isn't fitting for me to enter the monastery, not with my husband inside it, since I am not willing to live there without touching him. If he prefers the White Christ to me, then there is nothing left for me to do." She turned on her heel and started up the narrow stairs toward the cloth room. Several steps up she stopped and turned back. "You think I am deceived by you, but I am not."

"I have no intention to deceive you, Pentacoste; I never have," said Ranegonda, feeling worn down by her brother's wife. "You may believe that or not as you wish. It is the truth." She Signed herself to show her sincerity, then started away toward the heavy door.

"You don't deceive me!" Pentacoste insisted, and fled upwards.

As she stood watching the place where Pentacoste had stopped on the stairs, Ranegonda frowned, for the omen in their confrontation was not good. She was about to go across the broad inner court to the kitchens when she heard a voice at her shoulder.

"She doesn't understand," said Saint-Germanius softly. "And I do not think you could explain it to her."

Ranegonda swung around, and cursed as her ankle betrayed her. She thrust out her arm to brace herself against the wall only to find Saint-Germanius there to steady her. She was startled by his assistance and by the surprising power in his arm. Color mounted in her face making the pox scars stand out more than they usually did. "What do you mean?" she demanded harshly, more from embarrassment than offense.

"Why, nothing but that she does not have your sense of honor." He said it easily enough, which relieved her worst suspicions. "It has nothing to do with you, Ranegonda. She does not doubt you, she doubts honor itself. She does not think that such a thing exists, that it is only something men talk about, not something real. She understands duty, and does it grudgingly, if this was any example. But honor?" He made sure that Ranegonda had recovered her balance and took a step back from her.

It was not fitting that Ranegonda should speak against her brother's wife but to Giselberht, but this foreigner had caught her sufficiently off guard that she nodded her acknowledgment. "Did you hear it all?"

"I think so," said Saint-Germanius carefully. He was dressed in a simple black-wool bliaut and chausses leggings which he had purchased with gold from his money-belt just over a week ago from one of the women in the little village below the fortress who was not afraid of the omen inherent in black sheep. His chanise was fine, pale linen, made by the wives of the men-at-arms. He had ordered tall Roman boots from the saddler, but of so strange a design that they would not be ready for several more days; for the time being he had borrowed a pair of heuse from Ulfrid, whose feet were almost as small as Saint-Germanius's. A week ago he had purchased a dagger, honed it himself to an edge he could trust, and shaved. He still looked exhausted, but most of his bruises had faded, and those that remained were a parchment yellow, easily ignored in the muted interior light. Since he had left his bed, he had spent most of his time in the seaward tower, in the large storage chamber at its base, although he sometimes walked in the large court-yard at dusk.

"It should not trouble me that she is . . . as she is, and I pray for wisdom in dealing with her, but she still—" Ranegonda said with a slight frown. "My brother has said that he does not expect me to change her. He was warned that the women in her family are . . . flagrant."

"Strange that he should marry her," said Saint-Germanius carefully.

"It was the proposal of Margerefa Oelrih; he arranged it all. The alliance is a good one, and as her father did not insist that Giselberht take Pentacoste's sisters as concubines, the bride-price was affordable. Lorrarian nobles need timber and the King needs friends on the border. And Pentacoste is so beautiful." She sighed once. "I wish Giselberht had not killed Iselda."

Saint-Germanius had heard little about the death of Giselberht's first wife, and though he was curious, he was also circumspect. "How long ago was that?" It was a safe enough question and his dark eyes met her grey ones with such calmness that she was able to answer him without alarm.

"It was just over five years ago that she died; it was not quite mid-summer," said Ranegonda. "If the baby had not been born dead . . ." She caught her lower lip between her teeth, looked away from him, then went on resolutely. "It was a son. If it had been a girl, then he probably wouldn't have had to kill Iselda."

"He killed her for having a dead child?" Saint-Germanius asked, so appalled that he could not disguise his emotions.

"They say she strangled it in the womb. Mothers do that sometimes. The cord was around his neck when he was born, and he came feet first. His little face was almost black, with the tongue out." She Signed herself; by the time she looked at Saint-Germanius, his features were composed. "I saw the omens myself, but I could not believe that Iselda was so cruel. If you had known her, you would have thought she was all devotion. And she suffered so with the birth, they say for the sin of killing her child. What else could Giselberht do?''

"He was required to do it," said Saint-Germanius, thinking how savage the world had become once again.

"The day he drowned her was the worst day of his life. Not even when our father died did he have such grief. He was distracted, and Brother Erchboge feared that he would become possessed. He was like a man dreaming terrible things and unable to wake up, or afraid that, if he woke, the demons of his sleep would follow him into the world." She shook her head slowly. "It was so sad. He beat her unconscious so that it would be over quickly and she would not have to struggle too long—the Margerefa and the Bishop allowed him that much—but even then it was hard for him to throw her into the sea. There was no wergeld, of course. There is never any wergeld when justice is done."

"Because of the dead child?" Saint-Germanius guessed.

"Her babe accused her with his birth, and her family could not say otherwise, not that they would have, given how the baby died. No one could defend her, not after the birth that was a death," Ranegonda told him. "And there were omens: a fishing boat ran aground on the beach and the month before the baby was born a white sow ate her piglets."

Saint-Germanius took a little time to think about what she had said, and to remind himself of other practices in other times that were no less arbitrary than this; when he spoke his voice was carefully neutral. "Tell me, Ranegonda, what would have happened if the sow had not eaten her piglets or the ship not run aground? Would anything have changed?"

"There would have been no warning," said Ranegonda very somberly. "We put rue under her pillow, and mugwort, and she prayed three hours every day on her knees and Brother Erchboge whipped her twice to drive out her evil, but it wasn't enough."

"I see," said Saint-Germanius, remembering many acts of cruelty, his own and others'. He looked past her, through the door to the feeble, rain-dulled daylight. "There is another storm coming."

"The signs are for it," agreed Ranegonda, becoming calmer as she spoke. "There may be snow soon, but not yet. In a week, but not before."

"Probably not," said Saint-Germanius.

"You are almost recovered." She stared at him silently for a short while, then turned abruptly, pulled the hood of her mantel over her head, and hurried out the door into the steady afternoon drizzle.

Saint-Germanius watched her go with a pang, for he sensed her distress; when he tasted her blood he forged a link with her that only he was aware of, one that he knew because of the link would add to her feeling of apprehension. He was about to return to the storage room when he noticed that Pentacoste was standing on the stairs above him, her gaze directed down at him; there was a knotted length of yarn laced through her fingers.

"Foreigner," she said, her voice low and slightly breathless. "Foreigner. Look at me."

He said nothing, but he moved slightly so that his face was in shadow.

"She has kept us apart." Pentacoste let the yarn drop, smiling as it fell. "Now it will change."

Saint-Germanius made no attempt to catch the yarn, but he noticed where it landed. He still said nothing. Only when Pentacoste had returned to the cloth room did he go to examine the yarn, though he did not touch it: it was rough-spun and knotted in several places, forming a pattern like small buds on a bare branch. At one end of the yarn there was a twig of hawthorn with yellow dye on one side. In this place where everything was regarded as omens and signs, Saint-Germanius wondered uneasily what this length of knotted yarn presaged.

The storage room contained much of the equipment that was used to build the fortress some sixty years before. At one time the chamber had also served as the armory, but now that there was a farrier, the armory had been moved to the log building behind the smithy, and all that remained here were the builders' tools. Stacked at one angle of the hexagonal room were massive ropes, a few simple counterweight cranes, a number of large blocks-and-tackles, four sledges up-ended against the wall, most with runners worn. Saint-Germanius had become familiar with them all in the last few days, and he regarded them with a certain affection. And he regarded the rest of the stone room with a degree of hope, for if he could persuade Ranegonda to let him use it as his own, he might begin to make his stay here more tolerable; he had realized a week ago that it would take many months to arrange for his ransom, and in the meantime he was resolved to make the most of his predicament.

"At least," he said to the musty air, "I have a little of my native earth; that is some solace." He had feared at first that he would have to live on blood alone, an idea that had long ago become repugnant to him. The water had weakened the potency of the earth, but not vitiated it entirely; he could still draw strength from it for a while.

By the time sunset came, the guard in the light room of the tower had changed for the second time that day, and Karagern was outside the storeroom, swearing at his assignment to guard the lamp until midnight. Saint-Germanius heard him through the door protest his duty again. "I don't mind keeping watch, Gerefa, I just want to do it while the sun is out."

"I've given you the assignment," said Ranegonda, standing far enough inside the base of the tower that her voice echoed through it.

"Ask Ulfrid, or Ewarht, or one of the others. They don't mind being up there at night, but I do." He sounded worried, and his voice rose. "It isn't right, watching the sea at night. There are things on the sea then that it is ill to know of."

"It's your assignment until mid-winter. The duties will change then." She was stern and not prepared to permit Karagern to argue with her. "If you are not willing to do your work, you will be turned off. You might be able to reach Holy Cross before morning, or Laboeric in three days."

"Wolves and Ravens!" he swore. "Think what you are asking me to do. I would not live long enough to go ten leagues."

"I am asking you to keep guard over the light that guides ships," she said at her most reasonable. "The King has ordered that we keep the light burning, and so we shall; it is our duty."

"You don't understand!" Karagern's tone was higher, more frightened.

"But I do," said Ranegonda. "You and Walderih are afraid that the light will draw ghost ships to the shores. I have heard the tales, too, but I will not defy King Otto because of them. If they come, we must pray that God will protect us from them."

This time Karagern's outburst was obscene. "You want us all to be driven mad! You are summoning up demons," he exclaimed, his voice cracking. "You are already one of them!"

Ranegonda was soft-spoken, but there was no question of her command. "If you do not start up the stairs now, you will go immediately to your quarters and pack your things."

"Swine-woman!" he bellowed at her just as Saint-Germanius opened the storage room door.

"Is there a problem?" he asked at his mildest.

Ranegonda shifted her hard-eyed stare to him. "What are you doing there?" she demanded.

"Looking for a place where I might be able to work, as you gave me permission to do the day before yesterday," he answered, glanced toward Karagern and added calmly to Ranegonda as if he were not intruding, "If you need someone to keep the light, I'll do it."

Karagern rounded on him, his regular features distorted with fury and made grotesque by the flame of the oil-lamp he carried. "You! You have already come here! You are already within the walls instead of at the bottom of the waves. You were drawn out of the sea by the light. Everyone knows it. You're worse than the ghost ships. You think you are unmarked, but for those who can see— You have brought misfortune to this fortress. From the time your ship was found, there has been nothing but suffering here! And now you say you will keep the light. The ghosts will be on us, and we will be without protection." His young face grew crafty as he watched Saint-Germanius. "Or you were never in the sea at all, and made a pretense to gain our charity, in which case you will have other intentions. This is part of your craft, isn't it, to make us lax in our task. When we are wholly slothful, you will signal your pirates to come, and we will be slaughtered like sheep, or sold to the Danes to be their slaves, and this fortress made a stronghold for your murdering comrades." He showed fists to Saint-Germanius, his brow lowered and his voice growing rough with ire and dread. "This is your doing, isn't it? You brought the owls, and you brought the dead seals."

Saint-Germanius refused to be provoked, regarding Karagern with a trace of amusement. "If I did plan such destruction, I certainly took my time about it, didn't I?"

"Only to convince the Gerefa that there is no danger," said Karagern with contempt. "She is a woman and thinks that if she nurses a man, he will do her no ill."

At this Saint-Germanius bowed slightly to the young man-at-arms. "If you fear that is my intention, then keep the guard, and prove yourself right. Otherwise, withdraw your accusations." Then he looked steadily at Ranegonda. "I repeat my offer: I will watch the light, until dawn if you want."

"It is duty given to Karagern," said Ranegonda, her face set. "He is sworn to do it, or he is a traitor."

Karagern had gone too far to retreat now without bringing shame on himself. He set the oil-lamp on the stairs as a sign that he would not do as she ordered. "I leave in the morning."

"You will sleep in the village tonight," said Ranegonda in disgust and resignation. "Those who will not protect these walls may not remain within them. Go pack your things. Take everything that is yours and nothing that is of this fortress. I will meet you at the gate shortly."

"I am pleased to leave here. Yes. Let me be quit of Leosan Fortress." Karagern cocked his head and when he moved it was with a vainglorious swagger; suddenly he seemed far younger than his fifteen years, like a child playing at being a man. "You will see. This place will be cursed, if it isn't already."

"If it is, it is my concern, not yours," said Ranegonda sharply, and stood aside to let the young soldier pass. When he was out into the courtyard, she met Ragoczy's enigmatic gaze and was filled with confusion about him. She spoke with difficulty. "You don't have to . . ."

"To mind the light?" he asked kindly. "But I meant what I said: I am willing to do it."

"You will have to keep the watch alone," she warned him.

"So I understand," said Saint-Germanius without apprehension. "If you fear that I will sleep, I remind you that I am more . . . restless at night." He had never admitted to her how little need he had for sleep, for he feared she would think the omen a bad one and his presence dangerous.

Ranegonda nodded uneasily. "I have noticed that you more often sleep in the day." She coughed. "I thought it was because of your injuries, and because many of the soldiers here distrust you, and you didn't want . . . But Brother Erchboge says that this could have other meaning and the men—"

"If you will forgive me," Saint-Germanius interrupted, deliberately keeping the heat out of his words, "Brother Erchboge is the one who has planted those angry notions in Karagern's thoughts, and in the minds of your other men-at-arms. He may mean only the best for this place, but he is creating disruption."

"It is his devotion to the White Christ," said Ranegonda quietly. "He is so . . ." She gestured to show the depth of the monk's dedication. "For him it is all fasting and prayer and exultation."

Even five hundred years ago Saint-Germanius might have challenged her, and the monk, but now all he said was, "Many another seeks the same thing, and faints instead of finding rapture. Any man who fasts for seven days might do so."

"That is pride," said Ranegonda, repeating the thing she had been taught. "Brother Erchboge is one of those who has known ecstasy." She Signed herself. "I have seen him when the power of God is on him, and I know he is then unlike the rest of us."

"Perhaps," Saint-Germanius said.

There was another brief silence between them, this one less hectic than the first had been. Then Ranegonda clapped her hands once, decisively. "The light is in the room at the top of the tower, on the fifth level. There are buckets of charcoal to keep it lit. The brazier is not to be moved except to keep the fire from going out. You are to guard it until Faxon relieves you. If you see a ship making for the coast, or any other danger, ring the bell that hangs there."

This time when Saint-Germanius bowed it was in respect rather than irony. "It is my privilege, Gerefa."

She regarded him steadily for a long moment, as if to satisfy herself that he was not mocking her. "I thank you for this, Comites," she said at last, giving him his rank. Then she swung about and started across the courtyard toward the heavy gates where Karagern would have to meet her.

Saint-Germanius bent and picked up the oil lamp Karagern had set on the stairs, and began the climb to the fifth level. As he passed the cloth room on the third level, he paused and glanced in, aware that no one worked there after sunset but sensing something in it that caused him disquiet. After checking below to be sure he was unobserved, he stepped into the room and quickly looked around.

The two looms were webbed and wool-loaded shuttles carrying the woof of the fabric hung on pegs at the side of both of them. Carding paddles were laid atop a large basket filled with the last of the summer shearing. Four empty spindles stood near the pile of carded wool, the produce of each of their day's use carefully wound between two long pegs in anticipation of being transferred to shuttles. On the third of these long-pegged spokes the wool was not as even as on the others; Pentacoste had worked a pattern of knots into the yarn, a pattern that repeated regularly. Turning, Saint-Germanius moved closer to the second loom, and discovered what he had half-supposed he would find: the same knotted wool woven into heavy fabric. There was a holly leaf and a short length of faded red ribbon tied at the top of the loom.

As he continued up the next two levels, Saint-Germanius considered what he had seen, and wished he had a greater understanding of this place. Just before he reached the fifth level, he called out his name, alerting the guard.

"Where's Karagern?" came back the response, sharp and distrusting.

"He does not want to watch at night," answered Saint-Germanius as he reached the small stone chamber at the top of the stairs.

Amalric clicked his tongue in annoyance. "He's a silly child. It's that monk," he said as Saint-Germanius came into the light. "He has half the men thinking that the Devil himself is lurking in the forests, and that all the monsters in Hell are hanging on the steering oars of every ship on the sea, each determined to come to this fortress and pillage it for treasure and souls. I say it is a poor demon who takes this fortress when it can have Hedaby or Cammin." He Signed himself in case God was offended by his opinion of Brother Erchboge.

Saint-Germanius knew better than to show too much agreement or to condemn Amalric for his opinion; he chose a remark that Amalric could endorse without discomfort or anxiety. "Devout men do not concern themselves with a soldier's worries."

"May God and the White Christ remember that and us at Judgment Day," said Amalric with a slight chuckle as he motioned to Saint-Germanius to approach. "What has the Gerefa done about Karagern, then?"

This time Ragoczy's answer was as direct as possible. "She has ordered him out of the fortress."

Amalric Signed himself. "That is an ill thing," he said, all amusement gone out of him.

Saint-Germanius set down the oil lamp. "What else could she do? If she permitted him to remain after he refused such an order—"

"I know, I know," said Amalric impatiently. "It is what any Captain would have to do. In her place I would do the same thing. My oath to the King would require it if good sense did not. But it is still an omen, and a bad one at that. The rest of the men aren't going to like it."

"And given the circumstances, would they like it any better if she permitted Karagern to remain, given what he has done? Would not that omen be equally ill?" asked Saint-Germanius reasonably.

"No, they wouldn't like it. Not unless he were punished for it. She'd have to have him flogged and branded before they'd be satisfied," said Amalric as he slapped his hands on his thighs he brushed the palms together. He sighed once, short and hard. "Well, it would have come to this, I fear, if not now, then before too long. Since the Gerefa's brother went to the White Christ, there have been those who resent her, and they balk at her orders. They say it is an ill omen to be led by a woman."

"Was it Karagern who said this?" asked Saint-Germanius, taking care to make the question unprovocative.

"I have heard him speak of it," answered Amalric. "But so has Brother Erchboge. Many of the men here are troubled by what has become of us, with Ranegonda serving for her brother. If we were not so far from . . . from the King, there are those who would ask for another Gerefa."

"So if it was not Karagern who broke first, it would have been one of the others?" suggested Saint-Germanius.

"Of four or five, yes," said Amalric, lowering his eyes. "The others are sworn to this fortress, and will defend it against whatever comes against it, be it soldiers or Danes or pirates or demons."

Saint-Germanius's smile was more in his dark eyes than on his mouth. "Do you number yourself with them?"

"Certainly," answered Amalric, continuing with pride, "My grand-father served here when the fortress was first built: he and my father lie under the stones of the courtyard, and so will I, one day, next to my woman." He suddenly gestured to the tub of charcoal in one angle of the room. "You use that for fuel. Make sure the flame is always at least a handsbreadth high. The alarm bell is there"—he indicated another part of the chamber where a large metallic tube hung from a heavy beam—"and you strike it with the mallet there beside it. It probably won't be necessary, but you ought to know."

"I agree," said Saint-Germanius.

"Lift the parchment and look toward the sea frequently," Amalric continued, demonstrating how to do this without endangering the fire. "On a night like this you won't be able to discern much even if there are ships on the ocean. The rain makes it impossible to see any distance, and what you do make out could be anything from ships to islands to anything at all."

Saint-Germanius's night vision was better than most others', and the rain less of an impediment, but he said only, "I will look regularly, as you've shown me." He noticed Amalric conceal a yawn, and went on, "Unless there are other things I should know, why not leave me to it? I think there is still bread in the kitchens."

Amalric nodded vigorously as if the movement would restore him. "Yes. I want my fried pork and bread before I take my rest." He started across the room, then stopped and gave Saint-Germanius a careful scrutiny. At last he said, "I don't know what you are, foreigner, but I begin to hope you are not the bad omen we all thought you were when we found you."

"For the sake of your Gerefa, I trust that others share your opinion of me," said Saint-Germanius, caution under his amiable manner.

"There are some who are inclined to consider you an ally of sorts," said Amalric. "The rest, well, in time they may be persuaded. I think you show wisdom and courtesy to dine alone, and you have behaved well to the Gerefa. Many foreigners are not so respectful. The men notice such things." He nodded once to Saint-Germanius and then left him alone in the light room.

Beyond the parchment windows the rain continued, growing in intensity as the hours lengthened into night. Shortly after darkness enveloped the Baltic coast most of Leosan Fortress was secured and silent. Only the few sentries walking the parapet and the lingering scent of roast pork from the kitchens revealed the presence of the fortress tenants—the sentries, the smell, and the light burning high in the seaward tower.

Text of identical letters from Hrothiger in Rome to merchants' factors Bientuet in the Market of the Fur-Sellers at Quentovic in Francia, and Huon in the Street of the Foreign Traders at Ghent on the border of Brabant. Carried by the courier of the King of Burgundy and delivered March 14 and March 29, 938.

Worthy factors, my greeting to you at this holy time of year and my thanks for your diligence.

Now winter is quite upon us and the roads impassable, but as soon as the passes are clear, this will come to you with all speed, and I ask that you do not delay in dispatching your answer.

I wish once again to discover any news you may have received concerning my master, Franzin Ragoczy, Comites Saint-Germanius, whose ships the Midnight Sun *and the* Golden Eye *have been missing since early October. His others, the* Harvest Moon, *the* Savior, *and the* West Wind *are at Hedaby where they are being refitted and repaired. The* Harvest Moon *may not be salvageable, I have been informed but three days ago.*

I need not remind you of the rich cargo my master carried, for you were provided copies of his inventory when I first wrote to you in October, when it was not yet known that the ships were missing. You were then authorized to begin preparing his markets in your cities, and therefore I ask that you be ready to receive the portion of the cargo which is now being held at Hedaby. I am going to arrange its release before the end of April and should have it in your hands before summer.

Any information you may come by regarding the current location of the Comites Saint-Germanius would be welcome and worth a handsome consideration paid in gold. I am not interested in sailors' rumors, for I can hear those at Ostia. I want to know what has become of the ships and my master so that I can do what I am bound to do, and see that his interests are correctly served.

If there is any demand of ransom set by pirates or by those with the mandate of their rulers, inform me of it at once. I will pay for the fastest courier you can find, and any expenses incurred in bringing the news directly to me at this villa, Villa Ragoczy, which is on the east side of the old city walls. With frequent changes of horses and clear roads, word from you should reach me in no more than forty days.

I will expect a full accounting of your dealings with the cargo as you dispose of it. Your share shall continue at the same rate it has in the past: twelve percent of the price paid for the goods. We are agreed the amount is generous and the cargoes of the first quality and that our dealings in the past have been equitable and to our mutual benefits. Therefore I am certain that you will be able to realize a fine profit for yourselves and for the Comites.

My messengers and their armed escort will visit you at the beginning of August to collect the monies you will have waiting, and will bring them here to me to be waiting for the Comites upon his return. Any failure to comply with this instruction will be heard in the courts, for in withholding money due my master at this time is not only theft but treachery, for we must assume the Comites is in danger, and that he may be in urgent need of these funds.

Written by my own hand and signed on December 29, 937, at Villa Ragoczy of the Comites Saint-Germanius in Rome.

Hrothiger
bondsman to Franzin Ragoczy

5

To celebrate the Mass of the Nativity, Brother Erchboge had ordered all the plank tables and benches moved back to the walls of the Common Hall and the fires banked the better to mortify the flesh. Then he summoned everyone but the sentries, the slaves, the light-keeper, and the foreigner to worship there at the dawning of the third day after the Winter Solstice. At his insistence the inhabitants of the fortress had fasted the day before—only the very young and the ill were excepted—and now they were cold as well as hungry as they knelt through the long ritual.

It had begun not long after dawn, with chanting and the recitation of prayers to the White Christ giving thanks for His birth. Then Brother Erchboge had launched into telling the story of how it happened that the Savior was born in a stable and why the shepherds came to do Him honor before anyone else. He spoke of the companies of angels that filled the sky and carried a tailed star to show the way to the stall where the White Christ lay. He described how the shepherds left their flocks in the field, and upbraided those doubters who said that no one grazes sheep in the field in the middle of winter.

"It is wrong to think that these shepherds were unaware of the risks to their flocks, for surely the wolves raven in Judea as they raven here. But the angels remained to protect the sheep and drive off the wolves and bears that would otherwise prey on them." He nodded twice, very decisively. "We are taught that angels protect the things of those who believe in the White Christ."

At the culmination of the Mass, each of them was given a small loaf of bread and the entire contents of a chalice of wine, for all Christians were to partake of the Body and Blood of the White Christ twice in the year: at the Nativity and the Paschal Masses. The wine was part of the bounty provided by Pentacoste's father for the use of the servants of the White Christ, and it was thought to be the rarest luxury by those who lived at Leosan Fortress.

"Drink. Eat," intoned Brother Erchboge as he filled the Chalice with wine again, and held it out to Ranegonda's lips; as the Gerefa she was entitled to be the first to take this, but as she was also a woman, she was relegated to the position of the first of the women, just ahead of her brother's wife.

"Praise and thanks to God," murmured Ranegonda as she Signed herself when the Chalice was empty and the Blood of the White Christ started to sing within her. She took the small loaf in her numb hand and wondered how she would get to her feet without staggering; her head rang and her vision was wreathed in wavery brightness. It is the wine, she thought distantly as she used her good left leg to try to rise.

Beside her Pentacoste was smiling, and although she never glanced in Ranegonda's direction, there was enough mockery in her eyes to shame the Gerefa. As she allowed Brother Erchboge to tip the wine down her throat, she managed to dampen the corner of her veil with the wine. "Praise and thanks to God," she said as the monk handed her the loaf.

The shuttered windows made the Common Hall dark as a cave, and the hanging oil lamps dispelled little of the oppressive closeness. A slight ruddy glow still showed on the hearth, but for the most part the Mass was carried on in an artificial dusk that bore in on all of them.

The men, who had taken the Supper of the White Christ first, were also feeling the impact of the wine. Ewarht had righted one of the benches and was sitting on it, smiling and looking slightly sick at the same time. He had already taken a bite out of the loaf and was chewing with determination. Not far from him Walderih teetered as he walked toward the door, one arm held out for balance. Rupoerht, standing near the massive hearth where the last vestiges of heat could be found, was consuming his loaf, wolfing it down as if it were good meat and not simple bread. Faxon was sitting, back to the wall of the Common Hall, his knees drawn up and his face blank, his small loaf held untasted in one limp hand. Ulfrid had reached the door and was standing in it, contemplating the raddled snow in the Marshaling Court, paying little heed when Aedelar wandered up beside him.

The monitor for the fortress watched the door to be certain that no one left before the monk dismissed them, for that would dishonor the fortress and the White Christ at once. Although he was getting old, he was still a force to reckon with, and no man who had received the White Christ wanted Duart to speak against him to Ranegonda, or to complain of his conduct to Brother Erchboge. For this occasion the monitor had removed the owl's claw from the thong around his neck and had in its place a little silver fish.

"Is Brother Erchboge going to celebrate the Mass for the villagers?" asked Genovefe in an undervoice as she approached Ranegonda. "Or is it only for us?"

"Later," said Ranegonda. There was a shattering brightness around her, she thought, that had nothing to do with the dim oil lamps; she decided that it was the power of the White Christ, or the wine, for she had not tasted the dark red wine enough to be certain which.

"Today?" Genovefe blinked and held up her loaf, saying to herself, "I wish we had some porridge as well as this."

"In the evening," said Ranegonda, not trusting her tongue to manage much more than that.

"Will they have wine as well?" She touched her head and giggled. "Is there enough wine in the fortress to give them each a Chaliceful? How will they work in the morning if they drink so much wine?"

"They will have mead," said Ranegonda.

Genovefe nodded several times, as if once started she found it difficult to stop. "I wonder what they make of this?"

"The villagers?" asked Ranegonda, feeling stupid because she could not follow Genovefe's remarks.

Pentacoste was on her feet, but she made no effort to join Ranegonda and Genovefe; instead she sauntered toward the hearth, smiling serenely at each man she passed, and at last choosing a place an arm's length from Rupoerht. She lingered there, occasionally glancing toward Ranegonda, but more often staring at the soldiers. Her mantel hung open enough to reveal the embroidery at the neck of her bliaut.

"The souls of the White Christ, and the wine," said Genovefe, and put her hand to her mouth in shock. "I don't question the—"

"I often wonder about it, too," said Ranegonda, cutting Pentacoste's companion short. "They say that there is rapture in Heaven. Is it this, the lightness, or something else?"

Genovefe nodded several times again, and waved vaguely in the direction of Daga, who had just levered herself up from the floor. She would have called out to her, but that was not appropriate at Mass. "We are to have a difficult time with Njorberhta, I fear," she observed to Ranegonda. "She complained yesterday of shooting pains in her belly."

"It was the fasting," said Ranegonda, but with so much doubt that she could not pretend she did not share their worry. "She has been ill since she conceived."

"They say it will be a hard birth." Genovefe Signed herself. "May the White Christ protect her, and the old gods, too."

"May they all watch over her," said Ranegonda, and copied Genovefe's Sign. "And our women as well. Be sure that Culfre's wife has her herbs ready."

"Winolda says she lacks a few things she must have," said Daga with a frown as she gestured to the young woman kneeling, patiently waiting for Brother Erchboge to give her wine and bread for the banquet of her soul. "But she is ready to do all she can, though that may not be much."

Captain Meyrih's wife struggled to her feet, and then came toward Ranegonda, her wrinkles emphasizing her smile. "The Nativity Mass. It is always a joy."

Ranegonda did her best to nod in agreement, though the movement made her head swim, and her foreboding for Njorberhta dimmed the glitter at the edge of her vision. "Brother Erchboge has been very eloquent today."

"The birth of the White Christ," enthused Genovefe, her face flushing as she spoke, her emotions only partly engendered by the wine. "It is a great occasion. It makes the winter fair as summer."

"Like other fine times," said Captain Meyrih's wife, placing her hands together with the loaf between her palms. "A pity we could not continue to gather holly for the Solstice, but I guess it is a small price to pay for the wine. There is always holly in the forest and we can find it if there is need, but wine is a gift from afar." Her chuckle was warm and contented. "There is holly above the bed, so what does it matter if we do not hang it in the Hall?"

"Or in the chapel," said Genovefe, who referred to the small building tucked into a corner of the eastern wall. Dark and draughty, it had been built just twenty years ago and already it leaked in a dozen places despite attempts at repair.

"Well, Brother Erchboge has declared he will remove all tokens of the old gods," said Captain Meyrih's wife. "It is fitting that we let him decide what will please the White Christ best."

Ranegonda wanted to say something about the old gods, but her thoughts were turning sluggish and she found that she could not shape them into words; it was worse than trying to unfasten knots with gloves on. At last she managed to say, "If the old gods came to the White Christ, we could have the holly again, and Brother Erchboge would not complain of it."

Daga joined them, attracted by the laughter Ranegonda's words inspired. "It is a fine day," she said. "But it will be better once we eat."

The other women agreed, and a few of the men asked what the fuss was about as Brother Erchboge glared at them.

"We're hungry," explained Genovefe. "The Mass feeds our souls, but our bodies are famished."

"You have not yet surrendered to the White Christ," Brother Erchboge declared, his voice loud enough to bring the Hall to silence. "When you do, you will be replete with His presence and worldly food will not nourish you half so well."

Ranegonda looked over at the rail-thin monk. "We have not your calling, Brother, and our flesh is weaker than yours; surely the White Christ will forgive us our hunger," she said, hoping to forestall another long sermon; two years ago Brother Erchboge had talked for more than three hours at the conclusion of the Mass of the Nativity, and two of the roasted pigs had been burned dry as he held forth on the glory of withdrawing from the world.

Duart approached the door, his stooped shoulders bowed forward, prepared to keep everyone within the Common Hall until Brother Erchboge decided to release them. The doors were partially open now, letting in the frigid wind and wan light.

"It is my failing that you do not yet turn from earthly needs," said Brother Erchboge. He finished his service of wine and bread, then once again went to the west end of the Hall. "I must blame myself that you are not more moved by this glorious time."

"It is the snow," said Reginhart. "If we had not had so much snow, we would be more joyful." He indicated the door. "There is going to be snow again before nightfall. Look at the sky. It is like pale slate."

"It is a hard winter," added Culfre. He stared at his wife before he glanced in the direction of Pentacoste.

"All the more reason to take refuge in the protection of the White Christ," said Brother Erchboge, his sunken eyes brightening. "He is the guardian of the world, and He will receive all who come to Him in penitence and grief. He is all-merciful. There is nothing in Him but Spirit, and the rewards of the Spirit are His. If the world treats you cruelly, turn from it and embrace the White Christ, for He will take away your sin and the world will no longer have power to hurt you."

"The snow will still be able to freeze us, however; the White Christ is not proof against the cold," said Amalric, who had just finished his loaf of sacramental bread and was looking about for something more to eat. "And my stomach growls whether I pray or not."

"There are those with faith who could sit naked in the snow and feel nothing but the warm breath of Paradise," said Brother Erchboge with quiet passion, and added, "I am not yet worthy for such faith, but I pray that in time I will show you this mystery."

"It would be a mystery," muttered Rupoerht, just loud enough to be heard. "Only a fool goes into the snow naked."

"A fool or someone who is holy," corrected Brother Erchboge. He paused to cough, a long, gagging sound that made those who heard it uncomfortable. He spat and then regarded all those who waited around him. "Perhaps you have listened enough for one day."

A few of the men-at-arms were openly pleased to hear this, but most of the rest behaved more cautiously. Ewarht motioned to them all to remain where they were, for he did not want to be detained for anticipating their dismissal.

Duart watched Brother Erchboge closely, his short-sighted eyes straining to make out any gesture that the monk would give him. When he saw none, he asked, "Is the Mass complete?"

Again Brother Erchboge coughed before he could speak. "Yes. It is complete."

Had Brother Giselberht still been Gerefa, he would have had to leave the Common Hall first, but since Ranegonda ruled in his place, it was the monitor who led the way out of the doors and summoned the slaves to place the tables and benches back in their usual locations.

Ranegonda reached the door at the head of the women only to find Pentacoste already out the door. She bristled at this casual insult but would not take her to task on the day of the Nativity Mass. There would be other occasions, she thought with weary conviction, when Pentacoste's contempt could be challenged. To avoid creating more shock, she turned back to Genovefe and said, "You had better be ahead of me, since your mistress has—"

Genovefe blushed as she grabbed the edge of Daga's mantel and pulled her with her through the door out into the snow. "It isn't fitting that we linger, with her carrying on as if she were a child."

"You don't bring children to Mass," said Daga.

Ranegonda watched the two women hasten after Pentacoste and tried to think of some way to convince her brother to speak with his wife, to remind her of her place in the world and the need for her conduct to be more appropriate. But as she reasoned it through, she realized it was useless to hope for such a thing; Giselberht swore when he entered the monastery that he would never see his wife again. Nothing Ranegonda could say would change his mind. Whatever was to happen between Pentacoste and her, she would have to be the one to decide it. She permitted several other women to leave the Common Hall ahead of her before she stepped through the door herself, leaving after Winolda and Sigrad.

"You are being very good to her," said Duart to Ranegonda as he watched Pentacoste hurry toward the seaward tower. "Better than she deserves."

"I am doing as my brother bade me," said Ranegonda.

The monitor continued to stare after Pentacoste. "I suppose she meant ill, leaving as she did."

Although Ranegonda was convinced that Duart was right, she said, "Oh, I doubt that. She is like a willful child, deprived of what she wants most and determined to make everyone sorry for it."

"A good beating would end that," said Duart bluntly.

"But my brother will not allow it," Ranegonda reminded the monitor; she was speaking more freely than she usually did, and decided that the wine was responsible for it. "I must abide by his orders where his wife is concerned." She continued beside the monitor a short distance, then turned to look down the alley between the soldiers' quarters. "I should see if Flogelind is improving," she remarked. "For her to keep away from Mass is a bad sign."

"Truly," said Duart at once, and inclined his head to her, stepping to the side so as not to show any intention of impeding her progress.

Ranegonda made her way through the slush to the door of the apartment assigned to Ulfrid, his wife, and three children. She paused long enough to Sign herself against the powers of disease, then rapped sharply. "It is Ranegonda," she said when she heard a soft cry from inside.

The oldest boy—a child of seven—opened the door and stared at Ranegonda for a moment. "My mother is sick," he said.

"I know," said Ranegonda, doing her best to deny the fear those words inspired. "I want to see her."

"She is sick," the boy repeated as he stood aside. Beyond him his younger brother sat on the floor playing with a little cart, and beside him his three-year-old sister sniffled because she was not permitted to touch the beloved toy.

The room was like all the other family quarters: a single large chamber divided by a partial wall, with the children's beds in the loft above their parents' on the smaller side of the division. A stone chimney rose in one corner, the hearth shared with those in the family chamber next to this one. In the part of the room facing the chimney there was a table and two big chests containing their clothes and few possessions.

Flogelind was still in her bed, a single oil lamp providing light for her. She was wrapped in two woolen blankets and a rug of patched fur. She was pale but for two bright spots on her cheeks, and when she spoke her breath hissed like water in a closed cauldron. "Gerefa."

Ranegonda leaned near the woman, wishing already she could leave. "How are you faring?" she made herself ask, trying not to think of the miasma that rose from the sick woman's body.

"I . . . I am praying I will improve, and Culfre's wife has given me a poultice for my chest." She gestured to the strip of bark laid next to her pillow. "My man brought this to me, for strength."

"A powerful token," said Ranegonda, certain that the virtue of the tree was too little to banish the fever. "With protection and Winolda's herbs, you are going to recover. By the time the buds are on the trees, you will be weaving linen again." She wished she could believe her assertion.

"And Brother Erchboge has come daily to bless me," she said, her voice becoming raspy. "I have asked the White Christ to make me well."

"Good," said Ranegonda. "It is sad that you are not able to attend the Nativity Mass." She was glad of the wine in her veins now, for it gave her the appearance of courage where she actually felt dread. "I will tell the cooks that you are to receive an extra portion of goose today, to give you more strength."

"I hope it is not wasted," Flogelind whispered. "Forgive me. I . . . I cannot . . ."

"No," said Ranegonda, moving back from the bed. "Rest. One of the slaves will bring food for you and your children."

It was a terrible effort for Flogelind to speak, but she said, "You are good to me."

"I am Gerefa," said Ranegonda, moving toward the door. "It is my task."

Flogelind was not able to answer her, and the children were too distressed to respond with more than silent stares.

Once outside, Ranegonda leaned against the door, doing her best to keep from running away from the place. It was clear to her that Flogelind was going to die. Her fever was increasing and her strength ebbing, a disastrous combination that would certainly leach the life from her before many more days went by. To die at the dark of the year was very bad. She Signed herself and started back toward the open court where those who had been at Mass were milling about enjoying the headiness of their sacramental wine. As she stepped out of the shadow of the rough wooden buildings she saw Pentacoste leap into the air to catch the wreath of pine boughs one of the men-at-arms had thrown; whoops and shouts accompanied her. Concealing a sigh of despair, Ranegonda limped toward the edge of the group of men-at-arms, hoping to stop the display.

Daga hurried toward her, the edge of her mantel raised to cover half her face. "I am sorry, Gerefa. We told her it wasn't wise, but she was determined."

"I hardly thought you'd encourage her," said Ranegonda, and noticed that Daga was nearly weeping; she went on more gently. "You are not obliged to stop her, only to protect her when she is wild."

On the other side of the Marshaling Court, Pentacoste flung the wreath high into the air, calling aloud for one of the men to catch it before it fell. Half a dozen of the men-at-arms rushed after it, sliding and tumbling in the snow.

"How are we to—" Daga asked, surreptitiously wiping her eyes.

"You aren't," said Ranegonda. "It is her doing, not yours." She continued to watch her brother's wife cavort with the men-at-arms, battling the sense of foreboding these revels evoked in her.

"If you could stop her—" Daga began, only to have Ranegonda interrupt her with an impatient gesture.

"If I could stop her, it would make it worse, not better. As it is she resents . . . me, this place, my brother. This is what she does to show her contempt. I am grateful that so far it is all she does, and that it appears that she is playing. If I kept her from this, she would claim injury. She would look to be the one who was deprived of winter amusements, not the kind of careless, frivolous woman who compromises her family and her husband." She had not meant to speak so bluntly, but now that she had done it she felt a degree of satisfaction that surprised her. She was about to go on when she felt a snowflake land on her face.

"Snow," said Daga, turning her face toward the sky.

Pentacoste gave a low, disappointed cry before she gathered up skirts and started toward the landward tower and her own quarters.

"Catch this!" shouted Culfre, who had snagged the wreath and now flung it with all his might after Pentacoste. His face was flushed and there was an eagerness in him that came only in part from the wine; he pointedly ignored the wounded stare of Winolda, who watched him from the shadows of the Common Hall.

"Get inside, whelp," called Captain Meyrih to Culfre, and shook his head as the wreath dropped into the snow as no one attempted to grab it; his eyes were not yet so bad that he could not see the ill-omen in that. "Remember your wife. Have care for the things that matter, and be wary of snares," he admonished Culfre as the young man-at-arms stared after Pentacoste.

Ranegonda motioned Daga to follow Pentacoste, then fell silent in response to the omen of the snow, and was pleased to watch the others in the courtyard seek shelter in under the eaves of the buildings. What troubled Ranegonda, and had always troubled her the most about snow, she reflected as the flakes came in ever greater numbers, was that it made no noise. Rain, hail, sleet all announced themselves, but snow crept in more stealthily than a thief, and wrapped everything in gelid mystery. She drew her mantel closely about her and wished that she had one lined with fur; for the last year all the furs taken in the forest around the fortress had been commandeered by Margerefa Oelrih for his own use and the pleasure of the King.

Many of the others were retreating from the snow, going into their quarters and the landward tower for shelter and warmth. The hilarity of a moment ago was behind them, and some of the giddy merriment of the wine was fading, routed by the cold.

"Best get inside, Gerefa," said Rupoerht as he passed Ranegonda. "It's getting worse."

"Yes," she said, distantly. "I should go . . ." Her words faded as she started toward the seaward tower, telling herself that she was going to speak with Berahtram to be certain that no more charcoal needed to be carried up to the fifth level to fuel the light, as it was her duty to do.

Yet as she entered the seaward tower she paused, and as if drawn by an invisible cord, started toward the door of the storeroom.

Saint-Germanius had made many changes in the chamber over the last four weeks. While the old building supplies were still there, they were set aside in well-ordered stacks, and now took up less than a quarter of the floor space. From the woodcutters in the village he had purchased planks and built shelving along one of the angled walls; his trunks of earth were set against another, and a pallet of quarried stones left over from the building of the fortress lay in the center of the room, where Ranegonda found Saint-Germanius studying each of them in turn, occasionally marking one of the chiseled faces with charcoal. He raised his head as the door opened, no appearance of surprise about him.

Ranegonda stood with her back against the door. The rush and roar of the sea were audible here, caught and magnified by the walls. She stared at him, taking care to hold her mantel-hood around her face, for the cold made her scars stand out.

"Gerefa?" Saint-Germanius said when Ranegonda did not speak.

"It's snowing," she said abruptly. "Just at the end of the Mass, as we left the Common Hall, the snow came."

He nodded, then set down the stone he held. He was dressed much the same as he had been since he purchased his clothing from the village weavers, but now he wore his foreign-design boots, high and stained dark with thick soles and a horseman's heel on them. "Is something wrong?" He could sense her turmoil and waited for an answer.

She touched her forehead with her free hand. "I . . . I never . . ."

He came toward her, stopping little more than an arm's length away. "Tell me: what is the matter?"

"There is too much snow," she said, speaking slowly and Signing herself with care. "No one will be able to travel the roads, not even to Holy Cross. We are cut off." It was the first time she had admitted her fear aloud, and she shuddered suddenly as she realized the enormity of what she said.

"You are afraid of being cut off," he said as if he were talking about the color of a block of wood.

"Yes," she said. "There have been raids along this coast before now, Danes coming to take food and slaves. My father was killed in the last raid . . . three days after they left, his wounds rotted and he died." She shook her head, this time feeling queasy. "We have men here, but not many weapons."

"I can make quarrels for your crossbows," said Saint-Germanius.

"We have no extra metal," she said, putting her hand to her mouth. "The smith has a few old horseshoes, but if we have to fight, he will have to cast them afresh for the horses." She sighed. "There are one or two old kettles we could melt down, if the forge is good enough to do it."

"Let me build my athanor and it will not be difficult to use the kettles," he told her, his calm certainty gaining her attention. "I can make you arrowheads and caltrops. And I can make other things as well, including medicaments to treat the sick and the injured."

Ranegonda heard him as if he were far away. "I dream about raids at night. There is nothing but carnage in my dreams, and I pray that the omen is not what I fear. This cannot be prophecy, can it? I will not live to see this place become a charnel house, will I?" She stared at him, but would not let him answer her. "I think I see the Danes come, by land or by sea, and there are so very many of them, and so few of us. They come in hundreds, and each one is twice-armed, with axes and bows. They swarm over the walls like insects over dead sheep, and all that they leave behind are slaughtered men and ravished women with their bellies cut open." She put her hands to her face. "I am shamed to dream such unworthy things."

"You cannot help what you dream," said Saint-Germanius, knowing it was not quite true. He studied Ranegonda's eyes, his own revealing little.

"The dreams are always with me. I cannot escape them; they pursue me. Sometimes, when I am walking the parapet, or checking to be certain that the light is burning, the vision comes over me again, and I beseech the White Christ to banish such things from my mind. There are ruined bodies everywhere." She paused, horror making her pale more than the cold. "And other times, I see us all gaunt, more like Brother Erchboge than . . . The children have hollow faces and they are like dry husks. Everyone within the walls is weak, and the famine is so great that no one has the strength to hunt, and all the sheep and goats and geese and horses are gone; the soldiers fight over a starving dog. In a hard winter, it is possible this could come to pass, isn't it?"

"It is possible," Saint-Germanius agreed softly. "But you have taken measures to be sure that it does not happen."

"I want to stop it from happening," she said distantly. "I want it to be something we never suffer again. We starved here once, and fifteen of our men died. I was only ten, but I have not forgotten what I saw." She made a gesture of futility. "If the winter is longer than we think it may be, what then?"

Saint-Germanius regarded her with compassion as he gave her the most practical answer he could. "You have laid meat down in salt. You have stores of peas and grain. You have flour in barrels. There are cheeses in the village, and enough livestock to keep you through the worst months."

"And if there are raiders who take it all from us?" She wondered how she dared to admit so much to this foreigner when she was unable to speak of it to anyone else within the fortress walls, including Brother Erchboge. "What if the outlaws come out of the forest, or the King's men-at-arms are posted here? How will we survive such things, given our . . ." She let the words fade.

"You are stalwart, Gerefa. You have come this far. Trust yourself to complete your task." This time his compelling eyes held hers, and his voice was lower, a soft resonance that reached deep within her. "You have great burdens here, but you have carried them alone. If you will permit me, I will share the load with you."

For several heartbeats Ranegonda stared at him, feeling that she had never before truly seen him. Her mouth was dry as she asked, "Do you mean that you . . ." It was unimaginable that someone wholly unallied to the land should make such an offer.

"My land is long conquered," Saint-Germanius said to her. "My only ties are the ties of blood."

She made a sound between a laugh and a cough. "Then how—?"

"I offer you my help, in whatever way I may be of use to you, Gerefa." His dark eyes became more intense. "I will be your vassal if that will aid you. You have my Word on it."

"My vassal," she repeated, now bemused. "But why?" There was a catch in her voice now.

"You gave me back my life," he said simply, remembering the taste of her blood and the grit of sand. "With that gift there is a bond."

"Your wergeld?" she suggested, not ready to believe him. "You are proposing to meet the price in service?"

"There is no price for such a gift, Gerefa, but what is paid in kind." He continued to watch her, aware of her doubt and her hope.

She tried to look away and found that she could not. "You offer me your life?"

"If you will have it," he said, a slight, enigmatic smile touching the corners of his mouth.

"Even if I fail to defend this fortress?" Just speaking such damning words aloud agitated her; she swallowed hard against the constriction she felt in her throat. "Even if all the omens are true?"

"Yes," said Saint-Germanius steadily, and held out his arms to her.

It had been years since anyone had offered this simple comfort to her, and before Ranegonda could check her impulse, she sought the haven of his embrace, moving to him as if drawn by a lodestone. She was only half a head shorter than he, so it was easy to rest her head on his shoulder, her face turned away from him so that he would not have to look at what the pox had done to her. Tears she had refused for months to shed now filled her eyes. "What will become of us?"

"Winter will be hard," said Saint-Germanius very gently. He felt her desperation and her courage as he held her, as he had felt it through the stones of the fortress, the bond that had been forged on the beach. "And you will have to make decisions that you will not want to make." He laid one small hand on her head, the rough wool of the mantel's hood pressing his palm.

She tugged at the shoulder of his bliaut, biting a fold of the garment in order not to scream. In spite of her efforts to stop, she continued to weep, her anguish increasing, though she made almost no sound but a high cry like a distant hawk. Her hands tightened. "Protect me," she whispered, speaking to the White Christ and the old gods.

But it was Saint-Germanius who answered, his voice low and steady. "I will."

Text of a letter from Berengar, son of Pranz Balduin, to his father. Carried by messenger from Bremen to Gostar by official courier. Delivered March 16, 938.

In duty to my noble father, my greetings as the ancient Romans made them on the first day of January, bringing my prayers for your success and health throughout the coming year from a hospice near the Monastery of the Angel of the Resurrection, and by the hand of Brother Audvarht.

I have returned to Germania from Lorraria, although I am well-aware that in so doing I am acting against your wishes. I regret that I must refuse to obey you, for it is rebellious of me to turn from your way. I know that my disobedience may well be rewarded with death if you are unwilling to forgive me or to permit me to do as I have determined I must.

It is my intention to seek out the daughter of Dux Pol. I have not forgotten that you forbade me to seek this woman, that the abduction of a married woman would result in war between our families. But Dux Pol has said that his daughter Pentacoste is wife no longer, and that although her husband lives, he has withdrawn from the world and is now a monk. This being the case, it is the same as if she were a widow, or so the Bishop in Lorraria told me, and the lady may marry again if her father permits her to do it.

I am aware of Dux Pol's reputation, and I do not deny that he has made whores of two of his daughters and used them for his own purposes, but it is not so with Pentacoste. She is unlike the others, as I attempted to tell you before she was sent into Germania to marry that Gerefa chosen by Margerefa Oelrih. You would not believe me then, and you would not believe that it was Margerefa Oelrih's intention to have her as his own, though I warned you it would happen if she was not given to me. You complained of the bride-price and you said that she would prove to be as debauched as her sisters, but this is an error.

As soon as the roads are clear and it is possible to reach this Leosan Fortress where she lives, I intend to go there and learn for myself what is her wish. I have already reached this place, but half-a-day's ride from Bremen, and I will venture north as soon as the first couriers take to the road. I will travel with one man-at-arms only, and pray that no misfortune delays our journey.

I have already spoken with Dux Pol: Pentacoste's father has said he will not oppose my taking her, for he does not think she would be committing adultery since her husband has forsaken her for the White Christ. I have thought on this for some time, and I have decided that if she is content to remain the wife of a man who has set himself apart from her, then I will not compel her to accept me. But if she is discontented or if she has been made to suffer, then I will remain with her or bring her out of Saxony, whichever is the wiser course.

You have told me I am mad, and it may be true that I am. It is a mania, to be so determined to have one woman above another when the families are satisfied with a different choice. I have no complaint against Delice, and her bride-price is a fair one, especially since it would include her younger sister. But Pentacoste has lodged in my soul like a barbed arrow and I cannot be rid of her, try as I may. I have confessed my obsession and I have begged the White Christ to break the hold she has placed on me, but I remain as I am. Be grateful, my father, that I do not wish for a woman who despises me, or whose family would make any union but rape impossible. It may be that Pentacoste and I will yet have years together, and children to show how greatly our lives are bound.

I am shamed by how I have behaved in regard to your orders. You are my father and you have authority over my life. But my soul is the pledge of Pentacoste's, and not even the White Christ can change that, or He would have kindled fires in me when I saw Delice. I care nothing for what is said of her father, I care nothing for the whispers about her sisters. I care only for Pentacoste herself. She is the star on which my destiny is fixed, and I will not turn from her.

May you come to forgive me, if you can. If you order my death, I will go with all the blood I can spill to wash me out to sea, and will count my dying a worthy death. Yet I warn you now, if you seek to do any ill to Pentacoste or to Dux Pol, I will require Pentacoste's husband to arm the men he once commanded to strike back at you for anything you may do to her. If I must strike from the grave, I will avenge Pentacoste and her honor though it send my soul to perdition and end our Family with my brothers and me. Thus it must be, from your son Berengar.

By the hand of Brother Audvarht

6

Twice a day, at dawn and sunset, the slaves collected the slops and dung from the fortress and disposed of them down the midden-slope on the south-west side of the wall. The villagers below brought the same, as well as the chaff from the field and the sawdust from their lumber. Heat from the midden kept it the one piece of clear ground when the rest of the area, save the frozen, rutted road, was calf-deep in snow. The roofs of the timber houses sagged with it, and the cut logs were buried in white blankets.

"At least we will have good tath for the fields in spring," said Ranegonda as she looked down from the parapet toward the dark, steaming, pungent swath below.

"Because of the extra wood? The bark and the shavings are added with the rest, aren't they?" asked Saint-Germanius, who had taken to accompanying her on her daily rounds.

"That, yes, and so far the stock is healthy, so the dung is good." She moved further along, to the angle where the fortress kennels were. "Tomorrow there will be one more hunt, for boar, I think, unless the ground is so frozen that it is not safe to chase over it." She glanced toward the coops that faced the long row of stalls. There were fewer geese, ducks, and chickens than had been there a week ago. "I have set a few of the men to trapping geese for us. I am afraid the outlaws are getting them all."

"They are probably getting some," Saint-Germanius said as they continued to walk on the uneven stones. "They want food, as all men do."

Now the Baltic was coming into view, rolling in from the north, all green-and-slate, the breakers appearing like shifting fissures in rock. Its sound was muted compared to what it had been the day before, and Ranegonda studied the surface uneasily. "I don't like it, so still and dark. They say that in winter it is often like this before the storms begin afresh."

"So I have heard," said Saint-Germanius, and continued with faint self-mockery, "But I fear that although I have traveled by ship, I am a bad sailor, and I have no advice to offer you. For me, all seas are equally distressing, even on the calmest of days."

She looked over at him, trying to discover if he was trying to amuse her. "What do you mean?" she asked him at last.

"I mean that I am a poor sailor. Surely you have heard of those who cannot ride on the sea without becoming sick?" His quick smile was sardonic, and hid his deeper anxiety: that she would discern his nature and despise him, or worse. "I am one such. When I am far from the protection of earth, I am often miserable."

"Yet you are a merchant," she said.

"Yes, though I was not born to it," he agreed. "And whenever it is possible, I travel over land." For the three thousand years since he left his tomb, he had never learned how to fortify himself against the misery he felt crossing water. His soles, lined with his native earth, alleviated his distress somewhat, but with so much water and the ties of earth so tenuous . . . He shuddered as he recalled the two days he had clung to the wreckage of the *Midnight Sun* and how ardently he had longed for the true death then.

"What is it?" Ranegonda asked him sharply.

He realized that something of his memories had shown on his face, and he made a quick, dismissing gesture. "It is only my thought of the sea."

She made no attempt to pursue the matter. Instead, she pointed down at the roof of the stables as they walked above them. "They will not stand much more weight. After the next snowfall, the slaves will have to shovel them or they could collapse on the horses. We can't lose any of them."

Saint-Germanius pointed to the smithy. "There is greater danger there, because there is more ice. The heat from the forge melts the snow during the day, and in the night it freezes again. You need the forge as much as you need your horses, or more."

She saw the long icicles around the entrance to the smithy and she made an abrupt sign of agreement. "The kitchens and bake-house, too, must have their roofs swept clear. And we need an ax at each of the cisterns, to break the ice in the morning."

"Yes, you do," Saint-Germanius said. "That, at least, I can supply you." His athanor was more than half-complete, and so far, in spite of the cold, the seal between the stones was holding. "It will take another week at most, but I should be ready then to set about making arrowheads for you."

"Radulph has complained to me," Ranegonda said, turning to Saint-Germanius. "It troubles me. I told him you would be able to melt down the pots and form them for arrowheads, and he said that you . . . you were using devils to do your work, and the metal would be cursed."

"The metal is iron," said Saint-Germanius, dismissing the matter. "Devils cannot touch it, and well he knows." He smiled at her. "I won't interfere with his work: tell him that."

She scowled. "He has already told a few of the men, including Duart, that you cannot be trusted, and the things you make bear ill omens." Her face clouded. "He says you have bewitched me, as Pentacoste bewitches men."

Saint-Germanius watched her face. "And what do you think?" he asked quietly.

"I believe that you have . . . have done something to me." She caught her lower lip in her teeth. "Whether you bring an omen, or are a messenger, or . . . or something beyond either, I do not know."

"You accepted my pledge of fealty," he said. He reached out and took her hand, raising it to press her knuckles to his forehead to reinforce his oath. "If this is an error, or you are affronted, you have only to tell me."

"No, I'm not affronted," she said, and continued along the ramparts, passing Ulfrid as he kept his watch. She glanced at the man-at-arms, then said impulsively, "Everything that can be done is being done, Ulfrid."

He swung around gracelessly, his heavy spear already angled across his chest for combat, his eyes sunken and bloodshot. "I . . ." He turned the spearpoint upward and put his hand to his forehead. "Your pardon, Gerefa. I didn't intend . . . My thoughts were elsewhere."

"With Flogelind," said Ranegonda, aware of the long hours he had spent at her side with Culfre's wife and Brother Erchboge. "It is a credit to you. Many another man would leave her to the care of the women."

"She is failing," he said, hating the words he spoke. "Today she is weaker than yesterday and her thoughts wander. She cannot eat."

"I fear for her, as you do," said Ranegonda, and Signed herself. "But pray for her, and hope." She studied his worn features. "Have Aedelar relieve you. I think you cannot keep watch when you are so tired."

"I know my duty," he declared, standing straighter.

"You do," she agreed. "And you know that you cannot discharge it when you are falling asleep as you stand," she went on. "Assign your post to one who can guard the fortress. Aedelar is in the armory, with Alefonz. Go tell him to take your place. Saint-Germanius and I will wait here until he comes."

Ulfrid tried to protest, but the words would not come. He leaned his long spear against the battlement. "I will find Aedelar," he said at last.

As he watched Ulfrid descend the narrow stairs between the saddlery and the seaward tower, Saint-Germanius said, "They are not going to be able to save her. He knows it."

"The White Christ will save her, but in Paradise." She shook her head in regret. "And the children will have no mother. They will have to be put with one of the women." As she continued, she spoke as much to herself as to Saint-Germanius. "Rupoerht's wife has four and cannot deal with more; Faxon's wife will deliver in another month or so, and she cannot have these three other children as well when she has an infant of her own to care for; Njorberhta is too sick with the child she carries to be burdened with more; Sigrad will probably end up tending them, for her children are grown, and with Captain Meyrih growing more blind, she will want something to do to save them from charity."

"Who will replace Meyrih as Captain?" asked Saint-Germanius.

"Probably Amalric; he would be my choice, if it were mine to make," she answered. "I will have to speak to my brother before any decision is reached." She went nearer to the crenellated battlements and peered over them, looking down the foot of the seaward tower and the cliff below.

"Do you think your brother will agree?" asked Saint-Germanius, aware that she was bothered. "Or is there some difficulty?"

"Amalric has not always been willing . . ." She would not face him. "He is one who respects the old gods as much as he respects the White Christ, and my brother knows this. He may not want such a man leading the soldiers of this fortress, for fear that the White Christ may desert them in battle."

"And does this worry you?" asked Saint-Germanius.

"What worries me more is that there should be a Captain here who prays better than he leads men in battle," she said with asperity, and at last turned back to face him. "But there is nothing I can do until the snows melt enough to let us ride to the Monastery of the Holy Cross." She began to pace, in part out of restlessness, in part to keep warm, for the keen wind sliced through her mantel and bliaut and chanise as if it were Damascus steel.

"And in the meantime?" Saint-Germanius prompted.

"In the meantime, I will have Amalric act as Captain, but give him no title and privilege," she said. "He will accept it until my brother can be consulted, but after that he will demand a resolution, which is his right." She was shivering now but continued to pace, moving faster and clapping her hands against her arms. "Giselberht will favor Ulfrid, I suppose, for Ulfrid has served him and bowed to the White Christ. But Ulfrid will bury his wife before another week is out, and the men will not want to follow him into battle, for fear his grief should bring them all to bad ends."

At the base of the stairs Aedelar appeared at a run, calling up to Ranegonda. "Gerefa! The village headman is here, at the gate. He wants a word with you."

"The headman? Ormanrih?" she shouted back.

"Yes!" Aedelar was already coming up the stairs by twos, and as he reached the parapet, he touched his forehead. "He says it's urgent."

"Did he say why?" she asked.

"No. It is for your ears alone," answered Aedelar, catching his breath.

She nodded and made a signal to Saint-Germanius to follow her. "I will tend to him at once. See that you keep good watch, though it will be longer today."

"So long as there is hot mead waiting for me at the end, it is a small matter," said Aedelar as he picked up the spear.

Making her way down the narrow flight of stairs was too hazardous for Ranegonda to do more than concentrate on her weak ankle. It was only when they reached the courtyard that she spoke to Saint-Germanius again. "This fellow Ormanrih is a good headman. He is prudent and sensible."

"Excellent qualities," said Saint-Germanius, anticipating what was to come. "But he is wary of foreigners, and you are concerned that he might not want to speak to you in my presence."

She made a gesture of resignation. "He might take you to be a bad omen if he is coming to tell me of something ill."

"I will await you in my workroom," he said, indicating the seaward tower behind them. "And you may tell the headman as little or as much as you wish about the foreigner you are holding for ransom." His irony was gentle, but Ranegonda brought her head up sharply.

She flushed. "Yes, there is the ransom. He will understand that." She turned away from him and hurried off between the bake-house and the quarters given to the cooks and the smith.

One side of the double gate had been opened, and waiting in the gap, with Reginhart and Culfre to watch him, stood Ormanrih, his grizzled countenance set in harsh lines, his big, hard hands twisting on his woven belt. He went down on his knees as Ranegonda came up to him. "God protect you, sister-of-our-Gerefa," he mumbled as he dutifully Signed himself.

"And you," said Ranegonda, Signing herself in response. "Rise and tell me why you need to speak with me."

"These men will listen?" he inquired anxiously as he got to his feet.

"If it is what you want," said Ranegonda. "Otherwise I will dismiss them and you may say what you wish privately."

Ormanrih gestured to the men-at-arms. "Remain with us. I will want someone who understands to hear me out." He coughed once out of nervousness and once because he was near winter illness, and then said, "Last night there were men at the edge of the village, near where the first part of the stockade is up. They were searching for animals to steal. They are probably outlaws, and we in the village are certain that these were the scouts for a larger band. We were able to frighten them off, but if they come in greater numbers and we cannot flee to the fortress, or they burn us out of our homes, as they have done to many another village, we will be killed or made into slaves, and you will be at their mercy the next time they come." It was clearly a rehearsed speech, and when he had finished it, he folded his arms and stared directly at Ranegonda.

"How many men were there last night?" she asked him, making her voice level to show that she was not put into despair by this news.

"There were four," said Ormanrih. "Or four that we counted. More could have been waiting in the woods. They got away with a young sheep and a nanny-goat. The nanny is the greater loss; she produced much milk."

"I see." Ranegonda considered this report. "What makes you believe that these were scouts and not just desperate men trying to find enough to stay alive?"

"They were not gaunt," said Ormanrih. "There are villagers leaner than they were. And their weapons were very good."

Ranegonda nodded, aware that she would have come to the same conclusion herself with such men. "Four of them?"

"That we saw," answered Ormanrih. "We are willing to set up guards through the night, but . . . we have our axes and our saws and our hoes, but they do not make good weapons against spears and bows and swords."

"No, they do not," said Ranegonda, and for the first time looked at Reginhart. "Well? How does it seem to you? Do you think Ormanrih has reason to fear for the village? And that we must protect them?"

"If the stockade were complete there would be no question," said Reginhart. "I know that the Margerefa expects the woodcutting to continue. If the outlaws burn the village, that won't be possible, and the fortress will be blamed for it." He stared hard at Ormanrih. "You would not be spinning tales, would you?"

"Not with a sheep and a goat gone," he said, and spat for emphasis.

"No, I suppose not," said Ranegonda, and glanced at Culfre. "What do you make of it?"

Culfre shrugged. "I don't want to spend the winter fighting off outlaw raids," he said. "And I don't want any of mine to be slaves to the

Danes. Stopping the outlaws now is easier than waiting for worse to happen, then facing enemies with fewer men and supplies. And we would have the advantage of them this first time."

"Yes," said Ranegonda, satisfied that one of her men-at-arms had explained their predicament as she saw it, for that would have greater credibility with Ormanrih than if she gave her opinion first. "It appears we had better make preparations to mount a guard tonight." She motioned for Ormanrih to come inside the gates as she addressed Reginhart. "I want you to summon all our men but the ones on duty to the Common Hall at once."

"The foreigner as well?" asked Reginhart as he prepared to climb to the parapet and sound the wooden horn.

As much as Ranegonda wanted to say yes, she told him, "No; I will discuss as much of our plans as I decide is prudent with him later, in case he has anything that will help us win the battle. He will remain in his quarters."

Ormanrih, who had become suspicious at the mention of the foreigner, gave Ranegonda a grudging gesture of approval. "No telling what a foreigner might do. This is not his land. He has no reason to protect it."

"He is being held here," said Ranegonda. "To the extent that his fate is tied to ours, he must have some regard for the fortress." She had started to walk away from the gates toward the Common Hall, Culfre at her side, Ormanrih a respectful two steps behind her. "I will deal with that later. In the meantime I must arrange for you to drive your stock inside these walls for the night, and place my men-at-arms with you in the houses."

"What about our families?" demanded Ormanrih as he strode along in her wake.

"Something will be arranged," said Ranegonda, who had not yet decided how best to handle the villagers. She listened to the sound of the wooden horn—two long notes followed by a short one—signaling the men of the fortress to gather in the Common Hall.

Ulfrid was already inside and seated at the head of one of the long plank tables when Ranegonda stepped through the door, his worn face in his hands. He glanced at the new arrivals and nodded to them. "Sigrad is with Flogelind," he said distantly. "She will sit with her."

"Very good," said Ranegonda, aware that such a sentiment was foolish. She made a sign to the slave who kept the hearth to bring more wood, then gave her attention to Ulfrid once again. "How are your children?"

"Frightened," he said bluntly. "As well they might be, poor mice. They know their mother will die soon." He looked directly at Ormanrih. "There is trouble in the village, too?"

"Unfortunately," said Reginhart. He sat opposite Ulfrid as the other men began to arrive, three of them clearly newly risen from sleep and annoyed at having their rest interrupted.

The slave returned dragging a sledge with half a dozen logs piled on it. This he dragged to the fireplace and waited for Ranegonda to order him to build up the fire.

Ranegonda stepped to the head of the Common Hall, next to the hearth. It was quite warm there and she made a point of casting off her mantel before ordering that the slave put on more logs. "Just two for now," she said. "If we need more, you have them there."

The slave ducked his head and put his hand to his forehead before he set about his task.

Duart was almost the last to arrive; he was about to close the doors when Brother Erchboge came in, his face blank and his steps uncertain.

"Brother? Are you ill?" asked the monitor as he pulled the doors closed.

"No . . ." said Brother Erchboge vaguely. "I was praying. I have . . . prayed for almost . . . two days without stopping."

"You'd better sit down," recommended Duart, and only in part because it was proper. "I'll send word to the kitchens to—"

"No," whispered Brother Erchboge, his voice cracking from enervation. "I do not want to break my fast yet. I am getting close, very close."

The general hum of low and speculative conversations ceased as Ranegonda held up her right hand. "There is trouble in the village, and we must attend to it," she began, and proceeded to recount what Ormanrih had told her. "It is our duty to protect the village, and those who live in it, man and beast."

There was a grudging sound of assent.

"Listen to me," said Ranegonda before the men could become caught up in their own opinions. "We have sworn to the King that we will hold this region for him, and so we shall. Leosan Fortress will prove its loyalty." She had her hand resting on the hilt of the dagger she carried in her belt. "We will bring the women and children and livestock within our gates; we will have to leave the poultry and dogs because we have no room for them, and because we will want them to warn us. We will send our men-at-arms to take their places in the houses and barns, so that no building will offer a hiding place for any outlaw or raider, be it house or barn or sawing shed." There was nothing remarkable about this plan, but the men welcomed it with hoots of approval.

Ormanrih glowered at the floor. "What if they attack the fortress directly?"

"Then they are fools," said Ranegonda. "Danish raiders might try an attack from the sea, but for outlaws to come from the forest, no, they must first secure the village if they are to have any hope of reaching these walls. And we will be at pains to keep them from doing it."

This time the answering growl was one of enthusiasm, and Ranegonda felt less apprehension as she began to outline her plan, taking heart from the way her men-at-arms heard her out without cavil.

By sundown the women and children from the village, along with two woodmen who had lost an arm each to their work, were inside Leosan Fortress, their stock milling in hastily constructed pens which took up most of the Marshaling Court. The cooks had accepted the half-dozen geese and two goats the villagers brought to augment the food for their increased numbers, but they balked at serving two meals instead of one; Duart had to persuade them to take on the extra task by promising the villagers would not be inside the fortress for more than a day, so that the crowding would not become oppressive to all of them.

But the outlaws did not come the first night, nor the second, and by the third the men-at-arms were getting restive and had started to complain that their precautions were useless, claiming that Ormanrih had been mistaken in his report and that what he had taken for outlaws were only a family of outcasts scavenging their way through the forest; a few of the villagers agreed, determined to get back to their houses and their work before they fell so far behind that they could not catch up before spring came and the demands of the new planting claimed most of their waking hours.

"I tell you there is no reason to keep up the patrol at the stockade," complained Berahtram as he rubbed his gloved hands together. "We can do a good enough watch from the houses. And this shed is colder than the tomb."

"Still," Amalric told him as they peered out into the night, "we have to do it until the Gerefa says otherwise."

"What does she know of fighting?" asked Berahtram. "She knows women's things, and to do as her brother instructs her. But he cannot be reached, and she is floundering, afraid of shadows."

"She is Gerefa here," said Amalric, "and therefore she is our master."

"Better she should be our mistress," said Berahtram, and sniggered.
Amalric gave him a hard look that was not lost on Berahtram even
in the darkness. "If you repeat that, you may find yourself in the cold,
comrade-at-arms."

Berahtram shrugged. "Surely it makes no sense to let an unmarried
woman have charge of fighting men. How will she do when she sees
battle?"

"She is Gerefa, that is all I can say of her. It is all any of us need to
know her. If she brings us to grief, I might ask for Margerefa Oelrih to
find us another, or require her brother to appoint another. But until she
does that, I have my vow to uphold." He hunkered down in the door
of the rough shed where the logs were stripped of branches and cut in
half lengthwise. "Rupoerht and Frey are keeping guard over the stockade until midnight. Geraint and Maugde will relieve them. Remember
to watch for their signal."

"Forty-three men-at-arms at this fortress and we have to be the ones
sitting in this freezing shed!" whispered Berahtram. "Where is the sense
in that?"

"It is the task we have been given," said Amalric.

"All very fine for you; you're going to be Captain next. But why
should it fall to me to be here?" He picked up a palm-sized chip of wood
and flipped it into the air.

"Stop that," said Amalric. "If we're being watched that could be
noticed."

"So could our talking," said Berahtram. "If anyone was out there.
But it is all phantoms. Not that they are not bad enough, but there is
nothing we can do to stop them, and mounting a guard is senseless."

"Phantoms don't steal sheep or goats," said Amalric, and shifted his
position to keep his legs from falling asleep.

"You want to know what I reckon about that?" volunteered Berahtram.

"No," said Amalric.

"I reckon that they killed them for themselves, and didn't want the
Gerefa to know." He wagged a finger at Amalric. "You wait and see.
It will turn out to be just that. I know it will. Farmers are always trying
to find ways to cheat the fortress. In the meantime, we're getting slow
and stupid, waiting for something that will not happen." He had just
started to rise in order to stretch his legs when a quarrel caught him
high in the shoulder near the neck.

There was blood everywhere, gouting from Berahtram's jagged
wound; he staggered and fell, hoarse, low bellows coming from him
with each breath as he writhed in pain. More than breath the blood

steamed in the frozen winter air, filling the shed with the scent of hot metal.

Two more bolts crashed into the cutting shed, one of them narrowly missing Amalric. He flung himself across the dirt floor to Berahtram, landing almost atop the other man, pinning him to the ground. "Lie still. Lie still," he whispered, and when Berahtram ceased to struggle, he crawled toward the door, peering out into the dark.

At the edge of the houses there was movement. At least a dozen men were sidling through the shadows. Amalric could see the dull gleam of a sword blade on the other side of the rutted road. Very carefully he inched backward, pausing to be certain that Berahtram was still breathing before he made it out the rear of the cutting shed. He got to his feet and sprinted toward the nearest house, keeping low in case the sound of his footfalls should alert the armed men.

Faxon opened the door to Amalric's signal, and stared in horror as he saw in the feeble light from the oil-lamp the blood smeared on Amalric's face and clothing. "What . . . ?"

Speaking just loudly enough to be heard, Amalric shoved his way through the door. "The outlaws are here. They've got Berahtram. He's badly wounded. They are on the other side of the village, maybe twelve of them, maybe more." He Signed himself and reached for his battle-ax. "Get ready. And warn the rest. As quietly as you can."

Faxon nodded dumbly, touched his hand to his forehead, and hurried past Amalric into the night.

"You say Berahtram is wounded," whispered Walderih.

"Base of the neck. He's bleeding worse than a pig." Amalric kept his voice low, too, and added, "Be careful for fire. They may try to burn the houses."

"I will," said Walderih, drawing his sword.

"Good." Amalric opened the door a little way, trying to make out any movement on the other side of the road. "Wait for my signal and then attack."

"A whistle like a kite makes," said Walderih.

"That's it," said Amalric, and again slipped into the night, this time hurrying toward the approach to the fortress where Ewarht was waiting. "They're here. Tell the Gerefa."

"At once," said Ewarht, and moved away swiftly up the slope toward the gates.

Amalric did not linger; he ducked and ran for the next house, rapping out the recognition code as he slipped around the corner to the door. He did not bother to enter the door but whispered his orders, then slunk toward the next house, the lure of battle starting to sing in his veins.

He felt more than saw the sword cleave downward, and swerved away from its deadly descent just as he brought his battle-ax around in an arc. The blade struck and bit deep, and a high, wailing cry rent the night. At once Amalric gave his kite's-cry signal and straightened up, jerking his ax free, prepared to battle anything coming against him.

Behind him was the drumming of hooves as ten mounted men-at-arms careened down the road from the fortress, all of them with long-swords drawn, each with a torch in his hand with his reins.

From the other side of the road angry shouts arose, and suddenly the deep shadows were alive with men. They plunged forward, swords and spears at the ready as the doors of the village houses burst open.

Amalric swore by the White Christ and the old gods by turn as he rushed toward the outlaws, slipping and stumbling through the frozen ruts. Once he nearly fell; his out-flung arm steadied him but sent a jolt of pain through his shoulder. He longed for even the sliver of a moon to light the battle, but there were scudding clouds overhead. With a loud shout he rushed toward the men he could barely see on the far side of the road.

The mounted men slammed into the outlaws at almost the same moment, their horses pawing and whinnying, the torches showing little but the occasional face or shoulder of one of the outlaws, or the shine from their weapons.

It was a chaotic, blundering encounter, and it ended almost as quickly as it had begun. At one instant the outlaws were grappling with the men-at-arms from the fortress, in the next they were fleeing back through the snow-bright fields to the shelter of the forest. A few of the mounted men took off after them, whooping and harrying the outlaws, but most were willing to remain at the houses and to hand their torches to the soldiers on foot the better to assess the damage that had been done in that brief, deadly encounter.

"There are two of our men dead, and three of the outlaws that we can find," Amalric reported to Ranegonda shortly after first light. He was at once exhausted and exhilarated, and he spoke quickly, pacing as he talked. "One of the horses was badly cut in the cannon bone and we will have to kill him. The cooks can use the meat afterward and the hide goes to the saddler, unless you have other orders. We have five wounded men, one seriously, the others less so. We captured four of the outlaws, each one of them is hurt somehow. They are in the village still. One of the houses was damaged but it can be repaired."

"Who died?" asked Ranegonda. "Of our men? And what was lost with them?" She was at the writing table in the muniment room, and her face was grave, more for Amalric's news than for the steady ache from her ankle. "Did we lose weapons as well as men?"

"One spear was lost. Berahtram and Frey are dead. Neither of them could have been saved." He Signed himself. "Reginhart is wounded, and so are Maugde, Aedelar, Culfre, and Ferrir." He stopped still. "Reginhart is badly hurt."

"I am sorry to hear of it," said Ranegonda steadily as she wrote this down on the scraped sheet of parchment where the earlier writing had not been entirely eradicated. "When you say Reginhart is badly hurt, how badly?"

"He has a wound deep in his arm and the bone is broken." His face grew more somber. "It would be best to take the arm off; that might save him."

"And it could kill him, too," said Ranegonda, setting her quill aside. "I will speak with Culfre's wife, to see what she advises." She knew she would also ask Saint-Germanius to advise her, though she would not admit it to her men. "The outlaws have exacted a high price from us for their defeat."

"It is not what we hoped for," said Amalric, and continued his report. "The men have taken the wounded to the Common Hall, for Brother Erchboge to bless them and pardon their sins in case their wounds rot."

"Brother Erchboge is not . . . not himself," said Ranegonda, who had found the monk on the parapet leaning on the landward tower with arms outstretched, muttering about the power of God in stones. He was shaking with cold but his hands and forehead were hot, and now he lay in his quarters, a slave minding his fire, speaking to things only he could see.

"That's bad," said Amalric, Signing himself again, and adding, "Who is to bless them, if they die?"

"I don't know," said Ranegonda. "We will all have to pray for them and hope that it is enough." She looked up from the parchment. "Is there anything else?"

This last was difficult for Amalric to get out. "Geraint claims . . . he told me he saw . . . he saw Karagern among the outlaws." Now that the words were out he looked away from her as if to disown this identification. "I did not see him, nor have any of the others said anything of it. But Geraint is convinced."

Ranegonda sighed. "Tell him I want to speak with him later."

"All right," said Amalric. "And the wounded?"

"I will visit them shortly," she promised. "Go and heat the bathhouse. If Brother Erchboge upbraids us for it later, we will endure it.

You do not bathe for vanity, but to be rid of blood. For now, it is fitting that you should wash away that blood, yours and others', as well."

"Thank you, Gerefa," said Amalric, then added with an odd expression, "The foreigner is waiting to talk to you. He has already been with the wounded."

"Has he?" She discovered this did not surprise her.

"He claims he can help some of them." He studied her. "I don't know if the men will want him near them."

"If he can help them, they will have to accept his presence," said Ranegonda firmly, hoping she could find a way to persuade them. "Tell him to come in." She was glad she had a reason to send for him; for most of the evening she had wished she might have him with her.

"If you want," said Amalric, and started toward the door of the muniment room. "I will see those men myself before I sleep."

"Do that before you set the watch for the morning. Then have your bath and get some rest. You are worn to the bone by the look of you." She had risen and as she came around the end of the writing table she raised her skirt to just above her ankles as a sign of her respect for what he had done.

Amalric looked at her in surprise, then touched his forehead. "You are very kind to a soldier, Gerefa."

"You deserve kindness, Captain Amalric," she answered, now determined to convince her brother that Amalric must be given the promotion he had temporarily assumed. "I will speak to you after the mid-day meal. I will need your assistance in getting the villagers back to their houses before sunset."

"Very well," he said, "I will obey you, Gerefa." He touched his forehead and then withdrew from the muniment room, his step prouder than it had been when he arrived. He paused at the entrance to the landward tower, looking out into the pens of the Marshaling Court. "Foreigner," he called.

Saint-Germanius stepped toward him, his dark mantel so wrapped around him that the wan first light revealed nothing of his face. "Yes?"

"The Gerefa will speak with you." He did not move aside. "Is there really anything you can do for the wounded?"

"I trust there is," said Saint-Germanius. "Not as much as I would like, but I can give them some relief, and perhaps help them recover."

Amalric considered this response. "Then I pray you will do all you can. We haven't enough men as it is; with five wounded, we are in great danger."

"I am aware of that," said Saint-Germanius, and went toward the muniment room as Amalric stepped out of his way.

Ranegonda had opened one of the three massive books that held the records of the fortress, and she did not look toward Saint-Germanius as he entered the room. "Wait a moment," she said distantly as she frowned at the page. "I'm almost finished with this."

Saint-Germanius closed the door and stood quietly while she read, his compassionate dark eyes on her. Only when she closed the book did he move toward her. "Gerefa."

"What can you do for the wounded men?" she asked abruptly. "You told Amalric you might be able to help them."

"Yes." The firm line of his mouth softened. "I have some knowledge of sickness and injuries," he said, thinking back to the seven hundred years he had served in the Temple of Imhotep tending the sick and the dying in long-vanished Thebes, and the many times since then he had seen war and plague and famine and wished there were more he could do. "And while I do not have every medicament I would like to have, there are a few things I can do to treat your soldiers. If you will permit me." He was saddened that his athanor was not quite complete, for there were certain substances that could only be created within it, substances of great power against disease and rot.

"I will speak to the men; it will have to be their decision. If they do not refuse, I will not, and you will have my gratitude," she told him, and leaned back in her wooden chair, regarding him with a certain speculation. "It is a pity we are holding you for ransom, or I might have asked you to ride with my soldiers. We are short-handed enough that it may yet be necessary." She chuckled at the absurdity of the idea, and was surprised when he did not laugh with her.

"If your soldiers would have accepted me, I would have done it," he said, and came another step closer to the table. "You may ask it of me at any time."

"To what purpose?" she inquired, too downcast to enjoy matching wits with him.

"To defend you," said Saint-Germanius simply.

She shook her head and looked away from him, aware that she wanted to hear him say this, and knowing that she could not trust herself where he was concerned. "Because you have told me you would? What other oaths have you made that must be honored before yours to me? And you say you will not fight your way out of my troops and our enemies, to be free?" she asked, realizing how near he stood.

His smile was quick and ironic. "If all that held me here were stone walls and armed men, I would have been gone more than a month since," he said.

"Oh?" She wanted to sound unconvinced and hard, but she could hear the hope in her voice and chided herself for a wayward dreamer.

"It isn't the prospect of being ransomed that binds me. What holds me here, Ranegonda, is you." His eyes were so fascinating that she could not look away from them.

"Because you swore to me," she said, appalled at how eager she sounded.

"Yes." He put his hands on the table and leaned forward. "I am bound to you until the true death. Believe this."

Because she wanted so much to be convinced, she shook her head in disdain. "You are trying to mislead me, to confuse me. I will not be confused by you. I will accept your help because it is needed, not because I have faith in your vow, or because I find you engrossing company. You offer me your help to lessen the debt you have to ransom. It is not your word to me; it cannot be that. No man willingly remains a captive."

Her attempts to goad him into a sharp retort or a betrayal of his oath failed; his enigmatic, knowing eyes were warm with comprehension. He reached out and ran one finger along the line of her jaw. "Then perhaps," he said gently, "I am not a captive."

Text of a letter from the factor Bientuet of Quentovic in Francia to Hrotiger in Rome. Carried by merchants' messenger to Auxerre, transferred to a company of monks and taken to Fraxinetum, where it was placed aboard a ship bound for Ostia, and received by Saint-Germanius's factor there and personally delivered in Rome on April 6, 938.

To the most honorable Hrotiger, bondsman of the Excellent Comites Saint-Germanius, my greeting on this 9th day of February in God's Year 938.

It is my regretted duty to report to you that there has been no word from Hedaby on the fate of the Golden Eye *or the* Midnight Sun. *I have spoken with three Captains whose ships have come through the worst of the storms to land here with the first goods of the new year, and the tales they tell do not leave me much reason to hope for your master.*

From what has been learned at Hedaby, more than eight ships went down in that first early storm of the winter, and there has not yet been any notice of the wreckage of the ships at any place near Hedaby. The magistrate at Slieswic has also sent information regarding these missing ships. No record has been made revealing the fate of those two ships, their crews, or your master; not even a demand for ransom has been received there.

I will do as you wish, of course, and I will speak to each Captain I can to discover if there is any news. If there is, I will send it to you as quickly as may be, so that whatever you learn, you will be able to act swiftly.

Do not give up hope, I pray you, for these are only the first ships of the spring, and they have come from nearby harbors. Surely when ships arrive from greater distances there will be someone who will know what has become of the two ships, and from that you will be able to learn the fate of the Excellent Comites.

When the other ships reach Quentovic I will be at pains to find the most profitable market for the goods they carry, and I will require that the Captains report to me everything they can remember in regard to their voyages. This, too, I vow to send to you by the fastest means. These men may give you the greatest aid, for they were the last to see the missing ships.

In the certainty that the White Christ answers all prayers, I commend the Excellent Comites to the care of Him, and I beseech you to do the same.

By the hand of Lazurin,
scribe of the factor Bientuet of Quentovic

7

A soft spring rain was turning the remaining snow to dirty slush; the fields, newly plowed, offered bare rows to the women who donned pluvials and set about the planting in spite of the weather. At the edge of the forest, the men continued to raise the stockade they had been ordered to build; by now a third of the log wall was up and the holes for the next ten logs were being dug.

The sound of the wooden horn announced the arrival of the first visitor to the fortress since the previous autumn, and summoned most of the residents of the fortress to the Marshaling Court.

Ranegonda, who had been at prayers with Brother Erchboge, looked up as she heard the sound. "What on earth?"

"If it is on earth it has no place in your prayers," said Brother Erchboge sternly. He was still not entirely recovered from the fever that had seized him more than a month ago, and the glassy shine of his eyes warned that he was about to suffer another bout of the debilitating illness.

"Then I had best leave this chapel," said Ranegonda, grateful for the excuse to rise from the dank stones. She dragged on her pluvial and limped out toward the Common Hall, glancing up at the landward tower as she went.

"Two riders!" shouted Aedelar from the parapet. "On good horses." Ranegonda shouted back, "Open the gates!"

Her order was relayed through the men on guard, and three of them rushed to draw back the massive bolt. As one side moved ponderously open, Ranegonda reached the gate.

"Is it the Margerefa?" she asked Chlodwic as he struggled with the gate.

"No, I don't think so," he answered, breathing hard. "He'd have more men with him, wouldn't he?"

"I would have thought so," said Ranegonda quietly, aware that if the visit were not official Margerefa Oelrih would want as few men with him as possible. She stood to the side of the opening, waiting to see who was coming.

A short while later, Berengar and his servant came to a halt at the open gate. "Leosan Fortress!" the young nobleman called out. "The son of Pranz Balduin seeks to enter."

"The gate is open," said Ranegonda, stepping forward so that she could be seen. "As Gerefa here, I make you welcome." She raised her skirts above her knees in deference to his rank.

Berengar rode through the gate and halted, his servant behind him. "I am Berengar," he announced, and swung off his horse as one of the stable slaves came running to take the reins from him. "My servant's mount as well," he reminded the slave, then turned to Ranegonda. He was wrapped in a pluvial of fine boiled wool, the hood ornamented with an embroidered edge. His brown hair was longer than most soldiers wore theirs; his face was open and handsome. "Allow me to present you ten gold pieces and a bag of grain for planting." He had pulled a large bag from behind his saddle, and this he offered to Ranegonda, then reached for the wallet hanging from his belt and opened it, drawing out ten gold pieces and handing them to her with a flourish. "It is my intention to remain here at least a month. This will render my accommodation no burden."

"At least a month," Ranegonda repeated, her eyes narrowing. "For what reason do you come here at all?"

He waved his hands as if he had taken a whim. "I have long been curious about these remote fortresses. I thought I would learn if I wanted to seek one for my own. And," he added, "as an old friend of mine is here, I decided this would be the best place to come."

Ranegonda felt her spine go cold. "An old friend, you say? Which of these men has been your friend?"

"Oh, not the men here," he said with a charming smile as if the rain meant nothing to him. "The wife of Gerefa Giselberht, Pentacoste. I have known her for some time."

For a dozen heartbeats Ranegonda could find nothing to say to this new arrival, for she was in no position to remind the son of a Pranz that he was behaving incorrectly to come here without the invitation of her brother. Surely, she told herself, he must know this. And that he is here means that he does not care. She cocked her head to the side. "I fear you will find our hospitality poor, not at all what you are used to. We live very simply here, as you see, and we have no entertainments to offer you beyond stag-hunting. For a man from the court of Pranz Balduin, you may find our ways limited."

The servant had dismounted and was now busying himself unfastening various containers and bags from his saddle; he set them on the ground with an expression of distaste.

"I supposed I might," said Berengar. "But I have brought my kithre with me, to fill any empty hours. Perhaps some of your families here would find it enjoyable to hear." He beamed at her, his square, regular features so open that she realized she could not object.

"I will have to tell my brother of this when I visit him at his monastery in three days." It was the best response she could make, she decided.

"Excellent. Excellent." He looked around the courtyard. "Where do you intend that my servant and I should stay?"

It was tempting to say that she did not intend them to stay anywhere within the walls, but that was beyond the bounds of vassalage and courtesy. She considered the problem briefly, knowing that to delay the answer would be offensive to her unwanted guest. There were two rooms she might give him without offering him insult: one on the level between the cloth room and the light room in the seaward tower, one immediately above Pentacoste's suite in the landward tower. She pointed north, toward the sea. "There is a chamber on the fourth level that is empty now," she said, glad that Saint-Germanius was housed on the second level of the seaward tower, and that there was always a guard awake to tend the flame on the fifth level. "You may go there. Your servant will have to sleep there, too. We haven't any room to spare for servants."

A number of the men-at-arms not on duty found an excuse to wander out into the Marshaling Court to have a look at this unexpected arrival, and in the alleys between the soldiers' quarters several of the wives peeked out, with their younger children gathered around their skirts to stare. One of the cooks had left the kitchen and was standing in front of the bake-house, openly staring. A few of the slaves dared to watch the encounter at the gate.

"That is most satisfactory," said Berengar, his face again showing his pleasure. "Have your monitor show my servant the way."

Ranegonda looked around the gate-court, and signaled Theobald, the eleven-year-old son of Radulph, the smith, who had been idling near the Common Hall watching the new arrivals. "Come here, boy," she shouted to him, and went on more moderately as he approached, "I want you to take this servant to the fourth level of the seaward tower."

Theobald put his hand to his forehead and regarded the servant with undisguised curiosity. "The fourth level," he repeated. "Follow me, well-born fellow," he said.

Berengar laughed again. "He's not any more well-born than you, whelp," he said to the smith's boy. "He's just better dressed."

The servant gave his master a sour look but said nothing as he picked up two of the cases and strode after the youngster.

"A good man in his way, is Ingvalt," Berengar said with sunny approval. "He has been with me for three years now, and aside from his constant disgust with the world, I have no complaint of him."

"Many worthy men have disgust with the world," said Ranegonda, with her brother in mind.

"True, but someone has to live in it, and attend to it, and people it, or Creation is in vain." His smile was more determined than ever.

Belatedly two more slaves from the stable came running, their heads lowered in shame, to take the horses. Both of them were sniffling from the wet clothing they wore. One of them muttered an excuse for their tardiness while the other tried to get a look at the Pranz's son from over the rump of his horse.

"Rub them down and clean the mud from their legs. Bring the saddles to my quarters. And see to it that they have grain, and some honey," said Berengar as the slaves started to lead the horses away.

Ranegonda signaled them to stop. "I fear we have neither to spare. Your horses will have the same feed as ours."

Berengar considered this and shrugged. "In a place like this, I suppose it is the sensible thing to do."

"If you want to purchase extra grain, talk to the villagers. They may have some extra, but I doubt it." Ranegonda was not willing to extend more than minimal privileges to this newcomer, not when she suspected his errand might well serve to dishonor her brother and the fortress.

There was a sudden cry of recognition, and Pentacoste emerged from the seaward tower, where she had been in the cloth room. "My dear friend," she exclaimed as she hurried toward Berengar with unseemly pleasure. She stopped a short distance from him and raised her skirt to the middle of her thighs. "I never imagined you would come to a place like this."

"I might say the same of you," Berengar countered, and while he did not so far forget himself as to go on one knee to her, he bent over her hands as deeply as if she were a Dux like her father.

"How good to see you," Pentacoste went on, her beautiful mouth curved in a smile. "I cannot tell you how happy you make me."

Around the Marshaling Court the men-at-arms pretended to be at tasks while they continued to listen.

Berengar looked her full in the face. "It was worth the bad roads and the terrible weather to be here with you."

Ranegonda was filled with despair as she watched, and she strove to put an end to this disastrous meeting. "Pentacoste," she said as firmly as she could, "I want you to escort this son of Pranz Balduin to the Common Hall, where you may speak with him. I will arrange for bread and hot mead to be brought." The cooks would object, she knew, but it was better than permitting this display to continue.

Pentacoste's lovely eyes were glittering as she turned to regard her sister-in-law. "How good you are," she said, an edge in her voice.

"And then," Ranegonda went on, speaking more loudly, "the rest of us can return to our work."

There was a general shift of attention in the Marshaling Court, and those children who had crept to the edges of the gate-court vanished.

Berengar bent down and retrieved one of the cases still waiting to be taken to the fourth-level room in the seaward tower. "My kithre. I would not like it to get wet, not after coming so far."

"Oh," said Pentacoste with a sigh of delight. "It has been forever since I heard someone play."

"I am better now than when you heard me last," said Berengar as he fell into step beside her.

Ranegonda watched them go with foreboding. "What possessed him to come here?" she asked the air quietly, and cringed at the answers she heard in her mind, fears that increased the next day as Pentacoste flaunted her way around the parapet with Berengar, taking care that everyone saw her with the handsome nobleman, making certain that his attentions were observed and his every courtesy noticed.

"Is that the reason you asked for my escort? You wish to make a

point to Pentacoste and her Pranz's son?" Saint-Germanius inquired as
he rode out of the gates with Ranegonda the following morning. It was
the first time he had been on a horse in five months; he longed for his
Persian saddle in place of this high-pommeled, high-canteled thing. The
raw-boned chestnut mare had a jaw-breaking trot and a hard mouth.

"And to the others," she said after a silence. "I thought . . . they
would be less conspicuous if you came with me." She held her dun to
a mincing trot as they made their way to the gap in the incomplete
stockade wall that would become a gate by the end of summer.

He accepted this, but added, "What of you? Will my presence be
regarded with disfavor by your brother?" He nudged his horse to take
the lead as his escort duty stipulated.

The edge of the forest was just ahead, and the horses had to be
slowed to a walk as they entered the trees, for the road was narrow here
and the branches low. Many an unwary rider had been unhorsed by
striking a limb, or by a horse tripping on a knot of root. They reached
the place where the road divided, the better track turning off to the
south-west to join with the road from Slieswic to Hamburh, the nar-
rower one turning east toward the Monastery of the Holy Cross; they
left the main track for the lesser one.

Ranegonda did not answer his question. "I've decided that we must
send a few groups of men into the forest to find hives. The cooks have
almost no honey left, and they have asked repeatedly that more be
supplied."

Saint-Germanius said nothing about her change of subject. "Why
not build hives in the village? It would not be difficult to do. Surely that
is safer and more reliable than having to search the forest for hives?"
When she did not answer, he looked back over his shoulder and went
on, "I can show you how." He had first learned the skill nearly two
thousand years before, in his homeland far to the south. There the
farmers had built hives in their vineyards and reaped a double bounty.

"Yes," she said suddenly. "Yes, do that. The villagers would like
that, as well as the cooks. And tell the Brothers how to, as well, while
we are at the monastery. I know my brother would be appreciative of
such a gift, and the other Brothers as well. It will lessen—" She broke
off.

"Your brother will be less upset by me if I can present him something
of use," said Saint-Germanius, long-familiar with that particular
bargain.

Her face darkened. "Yes."

As the words abruptly ceased between them, Saint-Germanius became aware of something more immediately troubling than her apprehension at facing her brother. He drew in, one hand raised, then shifted his weight forward and pulled his sword from the saddle-scabbard.

Ranegonda looked at him in surprise, then unsheathed her short sword. "What is it?" she demanded in a voice not much louder than the clop of their horses' hooves.

"It's too quiet," he answered her just as softly. He tightened his calves and the horse moved on, lifting her knees higher in response to the pressure. "Soon," he warned Ranegonda.

She made a sound to indicate she heard him.

Not far ahead the track swung around the massive trunk of a long-fallen oak. There was a stream beyond it that had to be jumped, Saint-Germanius remembered from the description he had been given the evening before. It was an ideal place for an ambush. Saint-Germanius wished now that he knew the mare he rode better. He drew the reins in hard and at the same time drove his spurred heels into her. As he hoped, she reared.

Two men in old-fashioned leather armor vaulted over the fallen tree, one with a sword, one with a maul. They took up a position on the road ahead, crouched and ready to fight, but they kept their distance for fear of the chestnut mare's hooves, which lashed out as she came down.

Saint-Germanius forced the mare forward and then pulled her up again; at the height of her rear, he leaned down and struck the man with the maul on the side of his head with the flat of his sword. There was a loud crack and the man collapsed soundlessly, blood running from his ear.

The second man was already starting forward, but Saint-Germanius dragged the mare's head around as she descended, and her iron-shod feet once again drove the outlaw back, swiping ineffectively at her legs with his weapon. Saint-Germanius tossed his sword into his left hand and slammed the outlaw's sword aside with his own blade before hacking into his ribs, pulling the mare back as the man staggered, bleeding, making a last try to hurt him.

"Forward!" Ranegonda shouted. "There are more behind us!"

Saint-Germanius gave the mare her head and clapped his heels to her, swaying as she bounded ahead, leaping the stream and racing some distance as he clung to her neck, hearing the frantic hoofbeats of Ranegonda's dun behind him.

Only when they were more than a safe distance away from the ambush did Saint-Germanius signal Ranegonda to slow her horse even as he pulled the chestnut mare to a trot, and then a walk. Both horses were flecked with foam and their coats dark with sweat; they gulped air and carried their heads low as they went on.

"How many were there, could you tell?" Saint-Germanius asked when they were further on. Although he was breathing quickly, no sweat was on his face.

"I counted five," she said, wanting to conceal her fear.

"Dangerous odds," said Saint-Germanius, looking back at her, he read her set expression, and told her kindly. "Do not castigate yourself; there is no shame in being frightened, Ranegonda. Only fools and madmen have no fear. The shame is in allowing the fear to keep you from acting."

"We ran," she said, her voice as pinched as her face.

"Be grateful that we could," he said. "What use would it have been to remain and risk dying?"

"We're mounted, they're not," she said defiantly, her chin coming up. "There were only five more."

"That you could see," Saint-Germanius reminded her. "If the trees concealed a dozen more, what then?" He gave his attention to the road ahead. "And they may well be waiting for us on our return. Is there another way we could come?"

She shrugged. "If we had to we could ride the shore, I suppose. The tide will be low in the afternoon." She hesitated. "We would have to go quickly."

"Because of the tide?" he asked.

"Among other things," she replied.

"Outlaws?" He wiped the blade of his sword at last and returned it to the scabbard hung on his saddle.

"Sometimes." She faltered. "And the old gods. There are two coves where the old gods are honored."

"And we would not be welcomed," he guessed aloud.

"No." She indicated a hollowed tree not far ahead of them. "Look. In the tree. There are favors tied to the branches. The carved ox and the little stone man? you see them? and the others? Those are offerings for the old gods. To get the things the White Christ does not give."

Saint-Germanius noticed a number of small objects, most of them looking like toys, each secured to the tree with red yarn; some of it was badly faded. He pulled his mare to a stop and looked at the little images, some of them readily understandable, some obscure. "Is the color so important?"

"Yes," said Ranegonda, and continued reluctantly as she brought her dun to a halt. "And the tree, as well. It is hollow so that an old god will live in it."

"And the coves along the shore also provide a place for old gods to live? Offer them a haven of sorts?" asked Saint-Germanius, wry amusement in his face, and an old sadness. "Those who come here—they must be very devoted or very desperate to venture so far into the forest to leave these tokens."

"No one would dare to stop anyone coming here. Not even the outlaws. They have to live in the forest, where the old gods are still strong. The White Christ rules in Heaven, not this forest." Ranegonda Signed herself.

"The same is true of the shore," guessed Saint-Germanius.

"Yes." Ranegonda stared at the tree a little longer, then shook off the odd fascination of the place. "Come. We must not stay here."

This time he held back so that she could lead the rest of the way to the edge of the forest. As they emerged from the trees they could see the high wooden walls of the monastery, and Ranegonda motioned to Saint-Germanius to ride beside her.

"Will your brother mind that you have only one man to guard you?" he asked as they set their horses at the trot again. It was nearing mid-day and the bright sunlight made the open and marshy land where the monastery's flock of goats grazed seem preternaturally green.

"He may, or he may not," she said doubtfully. "He and I have not spoken since the autumn, and I do not know . . . I do not know how heavily his sins weigh on him."

Saint-Germanius could feel her increasing misgivings as they approached the stockaded settlement, and he did his best to find a way to provide her a mainstay against them. "Whatever the state of his soul, remember that you are the one he has chosen to represent him in the world; he must have a good opinion of your judgment or he would not have put you in his place." He let her have a little time to consider this, then added, "Leosan Fortress could not have a better Gerefa."

She glanced over at him. "Do you think so?" she asked wistfully. "And what do you know of it?"

His dark eyes held distant pain but his answer was direct. "Because my father was a King, until his enemies over-ran his country. I was at his side until I was thirty-two. I know capable rule when I see it."

There was the sound of chanting on the wind now, the monks of the Matins Choir praising the White Christ and the Angel of the Resurrection in strophic cadences.

"And you are now a merchant," she said, baffled by such a change in fortune. "How could you accept such a change?"

"I am more alchemist than merchant; I've told you that," he reminded her as they drew up at the gate of the Monastery of the Holy Cross. "You know change, transformation, is the work of alchemists."

"Yes." She glanced over at him nervously, as if his remarks had been intended to rebuke her. "I should have thanked you before now. For saving those men. And for trying to save Njorberhta and her infant. My brother . . . will be grateful."

"You hope," he added for her, and got out of the saddle, holding the mare's reins in one hand. "Is there a place to stable the horses while you speak with your brother?"

"No. You will have to remain with them." She realized how harsh this seemed. "You can lead them to the grass and let them eat."

"All right," he said, taking the reins of her dun gelding as she started to dismount. Before she put her weak ankle down, he stepped up behind her and held her while she steadied herself, saying nothing. The horses pressed them close.

Then she shoved her dun away and turned to face him. "You . . . it wasn't necessary."

"I was pleased to do it," he said quietly.

She looked directly at him, staring with bafflement into his eyes. "Why do you bother? What in your oath demands this of you?"

Swiftly, lightly, he kissed the corner of her mouth, then stepped back from her, pushing the mare over as he did. "Nothing demands it." He nodded once in the direction of the door. "Go on. See your brother."

She turned quickly and started away from him as if lost. She made herself stop and put her mind on her errand here and the report her brother was expecting.

Brother Ehren was warder for the day, and he squinted at Ranegonda as if she were in a disguise and he determined to penetrate it. "May God and the White Christ bless you," he said.

Ranegonda Signed herself. "Praise Them," she said dutifully before adding, "I am Ranegonda, sister of Brother Giselberht, Gerefa of Leosan Fortress."

"Brother Giselberht is at personal prayers," said Brother Ehren.

"I humbly ask you to inform him I have come." She knew the monk would be disgusted by her insistence, and she did what she could to lessen the offense she had given. "I am here to do my duty to my brother and my fortress as my vow demands. I bring him information he must have; it was his stated order that I should do so when he left the world for your monastery. I pray you will permit me to uphold my vow as you uphold yours."

"So," said Brother Ehren. "I will speak to him, and to Brother

Haganrih, who will decide if you are to be permitted to deliver your message."

She knew better than to sigh or show any sign of exasperation, for the monk would only see this as a lack of respect for the monastery; she bowed her head, Signed herself, and said, "Glory to the White Christ. I will be with my escort, who is tending our horses." She pointed toward the edge of the grass where Saint-Germanius stood with the chestnut and dun.

"If you are to be admitted, someone will come to fetch you," said Brother Ehren with an air of condescension.

Ranegonda did not trust herself to speak again; she backed away from the warder's post, then turned and walked toward Saint-Germanius, proud that she did not limp.

"Is everything well?" asked Saint-Germanius as Ranegonda approached, taking care to speak clearly in case they were being overheard.

"Just the ordinary delays, I suppose," she answered, shading her eyes to look at the walls of the monastery. "The Rule here is very strict."

"So it would appear," said Saint-Germanius as he watched the two horses crop grass. "Will you have to wait long?"

"I don't know," she said, and bent to pick one of the new wildflowers growing in the long spring grass. "There's water on the far side of the walls. The horses will want some."

"Yes; I'll take care of it." His gaze flicked toward the gate of the monastery, then back to the horses. He accepted the silence that fell without question.

"What you said—that you are a King's son. Is that true?" She asked it in a burst, as if she was afraid to stop even for a breath.

"It is true," he answered, looking steadily at her.

"And you were thirty-two when the Kingdom was conquered?" She was not so hasty this time but still the words were rapid.

"Yes."

"You were thirty-two and your father still alive," she persisted.

"Those of my blood are long-lived," he said, although his father had not been of his blood, which was the blood of their god.

She took a long preparatory breath before she asked, "Then how old are you now? You cannot be much more than that, not with your hair dark and having all your teeth."

"I am older than thirty-two," he said quietly, not adding that his years could be measured in many centuries.

She shut her mouth, pressing her lips together; her grey eyes were somber. "I had no intention of—"

He shook his head. "You have no reason to apologize, Ranegonda." He reached out and brushed a tendril of wheat-colored hair back from her face. "If I told you my age, I fear you would not believe me." More than that, he reminded himself inwardly, he was apprehensive about what she might do if she did believe him.

Something in the way he spoke silenced her and she wandered away from him along the monastery wall, then came back, tossing the flower away as she did. "Why did you ask the cooks for moldy bread?"

This was safer ground for both of them, and he said, "It is part of the remedy I made in the athanor."

"Moldy bread? What good is that?" She was relieved to be incredulous over so minor a thing.

"It has virtues. If you are pleased that your men recovered, it is in part due to that moldy bread." This time he could not look away from her, though he dreaded the possibility of her disgust or wrath. "Does that cause you—"

"If it made them well again, then I have nothing against it." She looked toward the gate again, her nervousness returning. "When I come here, it is always the same. I hate it when they delay me seeing Giselberht. I fear that it means he has finally put the world completely behind him. It is a failing in me to be so impatient, but I hate it."

"It is also a failing in him, that he requires you to wait," said Saint-Germanius, his voice soft so that anyone listening from beyond the walls could not hear.

She looked at him narrowly. "You are bewildering."

"Why?" Saint-Germanius asked her in genuine puzzlement.

"Because you are . . . you are . . ." She could not find the words; she paced a short distance down the wall, then came back to him once more. "I am going to the gate."

Saint-Germanius's dark eyes lingered on her. "As you wish." He walked a few steps further into the grass to allow the horses to extend their grazing.

Before she went, she stood for an instant longer, watching him, searching for something she could not name. More than his foreignness he was an enigma to her, which made him as enthralling as he was strange to her; it was hard to look away, or to put him from her mind. But she made herself do both, thinking of the purpose of her visit and the duty she owed her brother and the people of Leosan Fortress. With a single shake of her head, she hurried toward the entrance to the monastery, trying to ignore her limp.

Brother Giselberht stood in the open gate, his hands tucked into the sleeves of his habit. He averted his gaze as she stopped to raise her skirt to her knees. "It is not fitting that you should do that now."

"Because you are a monk?" she said. "You are my brother, as well, and you are still my Gerefa." She came nearer, wanting to see how he had come through the winter. He seemed too pale to her, and she told herself it was from fasting and long hours of praying, but could not entirely believe it. "How are you, Brother Giselberht?"

"I am gaining strength," he answered as he retreated into the monastery, going as far as the line of white stones that marked the limit to where the worldly could come. "God tested me in the winter, during the long snows, by permitting me to take a fever." He Signed himself, and watched critically as she did the same. "I was in its grips for many days when only the prayers of my Brothers and the White Christ sustained me."

Although she knew it was improper, she reached out a hand to him in comfort. "Giselberht," she said. "But you are well now?"

"I am improved, thanks be to God," he said. "I have suffered, which is fitting for my sins, and I have been given the triumph of the White Christ." His grey eyes burned as if the fever still possessed him. "I saw the omens of fever and I did not heed them in time. For this my suffering was longer."

"Was there much sickness at the monastery?" She asked with reserve, for it was possible that Brother Haganrih had forbade his monks to speak of such things.

"Nine Brothers were ill. Many were weakened by the early cold." He made an impatient gesture. "We are in the hands of the White Christ. It is not right to question Him and His Wisdom." With an air of great resignation, he asked, "What did winter bring to Leosan Fortress?"

She stood straight to answer him, giving her report in the same manner that Amalric had given his to her. "I am saddened to have to tell you that we have lost six men, three women, three children, two horses, a goat, and a sheep. The goat and the sheep were stolen by outlaws who attacked the fortress and its village; we lost men in the defense. We had several wounded to care for, and we were fortunate that the stranger we found on the beach last autumn has some skill in treating the wounded. Without his help I fear we would have lost more."

"We will pray for the souls of those who died," said Brother Giselberht, Signing himself before clasping his hands.

She sensed that he was more concerned with the dead than the living, but she persevered. "Our stores are very low, and although spring planting is under way, there are not as many lambs or kids in the fields, which bodes ill for the summer. The harvest will need to be bountiful and the ewes will have to drop thriving lambs if next winter is not to be hungry. Or the King will have to requisition us more supplies." She coughed delicately. "We are building the stockade the King has ordered, but the men have no time to till, for they are forever cutting trees. We are to have more men transferred to the fortress before the end of summer, though they would be of more use now. The women are working the fields now, tending to the planting, and the wives of the soldiers in the fortress have had to increase their spinning and weaving."

"It is well that all work, for that is part of service to the White Christ," said Brother Giselberht. He paused. "My wife: does she set an example?"

"Yes, she does," said Ranegonda, more sharply than she had intended. "Not a very laudable one." Again she paused, and went on with as much tact as she could. "Oh, she is industrious at her spinning, and her cloth is good. But she has set herself to the ways of courtesy. Two days since the son of Pranz Balduin, a young man named Berengar, came to the fortress. He intends to stay for a month a least, and brought coins to buy his welcome."

Brother Giselberht scowled. "Do you say he came to see my wife?"

"He claims they are old friends. I have put him in the seaward tower, just below the light room. Saint-Germanius still quarters in that tower as well, and so there are two guards on Berengar." She showed him up-turned palms. "What else can I do? He is the son of a Pranz, and his father . . ."

After a short, inconclusive silence, Brother Giselberht said, "As vassal to King Otto, the son of Pranz Balduin must be accorded a courteous welcome. To do otherwise would bring disgrace to the fortress and our family." He glared at Ranegonda. "What else have you done?"

"Nothing. I have made certain they are not private together, Berengar and Pentacoste. But what more can I do?" She stared at him, finding his remote anger made him more unfamiliar than the foreigner who held her horse outside the walls.

"You are not to permit her to compromise herself. I have had to drown one wife; I will not drown another." His voice had risen and his face looked more like a mask for a priest of the old gods than a human countenance. "Give what courtesy you must, but let there be no whisper of sin."

"How?" she asked. "I have done as much as I can without open offense. What more do you expect me to do? Giselberht! There are things you must know of, things you must act upon."

He gave her no answer, striding across the line of white stones, away from her toward the ambulatory. He stopped once and called back to her, "Tell me in a month what has transpired. Until then, leave me to pray. You have torn me from my contemplation of the White Christ, and I must be given time to restore my devotion before I can speak with you again. If you come before a month, the warder-Brother will deny me to you."

"But Giselberht, there are other matters we must discuss," she cried out, resisting the urge to go after him, for only those sworn to the monastery were permitted to cross the line of white stones separating the monks from the worldly.

"Manage as you must. You are Gerefa. I will not have the world intrude on this place." He increased his stride and disappeared around the corner of the first log building.

Ranegonda stared after him. He had not inquired about who had been injured or killed. She had not been able to discuss Captain Mey-rih's replacement. He had given her no orders regarding planting in the village or cutting in the forest or additional defenses to use against the outlaw bands. There had been no chance to tell him of Saint-Ger-manius's offer to establish hives in the village, or to ask her brother to meet the foreigner. She stood for a short while, waiting for her brother to reappear. All she saw were monks making their way along the ambulatory. She sighed once, Signed herself, and went out of the Monastery of the Holy Cross.

Saint-Germanius had moved a little farther into the grass, no frown of impatience to darken his brow. As Ranegonda approached he looked up. "The horses have been watered, Gerefa," he said in a voice intended to be overheard.

"Tighten their girths," she said curtly, reaching out for the dun's reins.

"We are leaving?" he asked in some surprise as he swung her iron stirrup back to reach the buckle of the girth.

"Yes. My brother has obligations to the White Christ he must fulfill." She grabbed the high pommel and pulled herself into the saddle as soon as Saint-Germanius stepped back.

"Ah," said Saint-Germanius, tightening the girth on the chestnut's saddle before mounting. "Do we ride along the beach, then?"

"We might as well," she answered, pulling the dun around toward the path leading toward the shore. "There is no reason to fight the outlaws twice in one day."

"No, there is not," he agreed, and urged the chestnut ahead of her dun to give her proper escort.

They turned to the west once they reached the beach, letting the horses trot side-by-side in the wet sand. Ranegonda sat erect in her saddle, her eyes directed ahead, her hands clenched on the reins; Saint-Germanius was content to put some distance between them and the monastery before he risked speaking to her.

"You and your brother disagreed?" he asked as they drew abreast of a lttle cove where painted pieces of driftwood marked a place where the old gods were honored.

"We hardly had time to do that." Her words were sharp.

Saint-Germanius knew better than to offer her any soft phrases of consolation. "That was ill-done of him; he ought to permit you to discharge your duty whether it suits his Hours or not."

She looked at him, her cheeks red, her lips white; for an instant she prepared to defend her brother against her very complaint of him. Then she smiled ruefully. "You have the right of it. I am vexed with him and disgusted with myself because I am vexed with him."

They went on further in silence. Then he said, "If he gave you no instruction, then you must discharge your office as best you can according to your judgment."

"I suppose so," she answered, her manner less irate than before. "I know my duty, at least."

Saint-Germanius noticed another of the little beach hollows, and the tokens left there for the gods. He frowned. "Tell me, Ranegonda," he said as if he were talking about the color of his chanise, "the cove where you found me, was that an old god's cove?"

Color mounted in her face for no reason she could recognize. "Yes," she said at last.

"There were no tokens there," he said uncertainly, for his memory of the place was dim.

"No," she said before she urged her dun into the canter. "They washed away when you came."

Text of a letter from Atta Olivia Clemens in Avlona to Hrotiger in Rome, carried by messenger, in passage for thirty-four days.

To my old friend who serves my greatest friend, my greetings at the Vernal Equinox.

No, I assure you he is not dead, Rogerian. I would have known it if it had happened, as I have known when those of my blood who were of my making died the true death. He has been in some distress, of that much I am certain, but no more than that, at least not recently. He is not entirely recovered; I sense that his strength is less than it can be, and he is not able to seek what he most ardently needs, so he cannot be wholly restored. It is saddening to me that were I with him, that is the one thing I could not offer him. But it saddens me, too, that I could not have it of him, either. Such is the fate of those of our blood.

Do not be offended that I keep to the old Roman ways and call you Rogerian, as I always have. These new versions of old names make my jaws ache. Hrotiger is no sort of name for a man of your age to have. My bondsman Niklos Aulirios has fared better than most for his name has not been maimed by fashion, at least not so far.

I have purchased a pleasant villa here on the Dalmatian coast, and I would be overjoyed if Sanct' Germain would join me here for a year or two. He would be able to recover his strength once he found a willing companion, and I would have the pleasure of his company, and yours as well. I have always been delighted to share my house with Sanct' Germain, for although certain fulfillment has been lost to us, his steadfast friendship is a satisfaction I will always welcome.

The rumors are that more barbarians are coming to ravage poor old Rome again. I thought it prudent to get out of their path for a time. And to be candid, it pains me to see Rome assaulted. It has happened more than enough times already. So, when the invaders are gone I will come again and see what damage they have done to my villa this time. Should you decide that it might be best to remove from the city, you need only cross the Adriatic and I will accommodate you for your own sake as well as Sanct' Germain's.

I know I need not say this, but when you do eventually locate him, tell him that I am thoroughly annoyed with him for causing us such worry on his behalf. And tell him that I send him my devoted love.

With my fond remembrances, and the reassurance that wherever Sanct' Germain may be, he is there as alive as he ever was, I tender you my gratitude as well as these various invitations.

Olivia

8

Berengar set his kithre aside and beamed at Pentacoste as the rest of those in the Common Hall drummed their tankards on the table to show their appreciation. "Mine is no great skill, truly, only a modest gift," he said with a satisfaction that belied this denial. He was wearing a wine-colored bliaut with embroidery at the neck over a yellow chanise, and his chausses were a deep shade of rust. On his right hand he wore two rings and on his left, three. He was the most richly dressed man the people of the fortress had ever seen within their walls, and the most courtly.

"It was a beautiful song," said Pentacoste with a languishing look that she made no effort to conceal or alter, though to show such an approval was beyond anything proper for a married woman to offer a man not her husband. "I liked the part about how Roland gave his pledge to Carl-le-Magne to achieve victory or die. 'I must always hold my duty sacred; / My obligation is my highest purpose, / And my life cheap in the balance: / Death is welcome if it vindicates my vow.' "

"It is very stirring, yes, and those lines in particular," Berengar agreed. "These tales of great heros are always reminders of what has been done by valiant men, and what we must strive to do ourselves."

"Imagine what a fine thing it must be, having someone die for you," said Pentacoste with unaccustomed eagerness. "To know that someone has died and rotted to keep you alive!"

There was an awkward silence in the Common Hall.

Then Maugde held up his maimed hand, the result of the fight with the outlaws, and said, "It makes this bearable, to know that others have had honorable wounds. It is heartening to hear these tales." He lifted his tankard. "To a fine singer."

Again there was the drumming of tankards, this time with a few additional hoots to give emphasis to their approval. The women slapped the table-tops with their hands in a strong, regular rhythm.

Near the half-open door, Ranegonda watched with dismay. She had spoken to Pentacoste that morning, asking her to conduct herself more correctly; at that time Pentacoste had blithely assured her she would do nothing to bring disgrace upon the fortress or her husband and now she flaunted Berengar's infatuation, all but announced her approval of the man's unstated rivalry with her absent husband, her behavior more fitting for a common trull than a Gerefa's wife.

"One more song, for me," Pentacoste pleaded prettily, her lovely eyes turned toward Berengar in what looked very like adoration.

"It is hardly fitting to take so much time for songs when the Hour for prayers approaches," said Berengar, pleased and flattered in spite of his proper response.

"I will pray for another song, then, and I will listen with devotion. Surely that would be acceptable?" Pentacoste looked around the room, as if seeking others to support her petition.

Ranegonda turned to Saint-Germanius, who stood beside her.

"Look at her. What am I to do about—" Her gesture finished her thought.

He regarded her with sympathy. "Anything you do will draw attention to her actions, not diminish their significance," he said quietly. "And Berengar may claim that taking a stance against Pentacoste offends him or impugns his honor. That would be more disruptive still."

"Yes," she said as she glanced out into the last of the afternoon sun. "But he is right. It is almost time for evening prayers. That's something." She had half-expected Brother Erchboge to arrive while Berengar was singing; she was grateful this had not occurred, for Brother Erchboge was not inclined to look tolerantly on such displays as the one Berengar made with his kithre.

"If you want to lessen the damage Pentacoste is causing, praise Berengar for his songs," Saint-Germanius suggested suddenly. "It will make Pentacoste's attentions less obvious."

She glanced at him with a slight frown, then smiled as she realized what Saint-Germanius was suggesting. "Very subtle," she approved, and went to the center of the Common Hall. "We are all grateful to you, Berengar, son of Pranz Balduin, for giving us so much delight. We here at Leosan Fortress have rarely been provided an opportunity to hear music as fine as yours. If your songs are any standard for judgment, life at the great courts must be very pleasant indeed." She raised her skirts to her calves to show respect for his singing.

"How kind you are to your guest," said Berengar, doing his utmost to be as courteous as he could in this rough setting.

Pentacoste gave Ranegonda a swift, condemning glare, then favored Berengar with a melting smile. "Why should she not be kind? We are the ones who are honored by your presence. You are in company beneath your place." She rose from the bench in a single, graceful motion. "You show your excellence in many ways, and this is not the least of them, that you will sing of valor and devotion to these rough soldiers in this remote fortress."

Observing from the door, Saint-Germanius had to admit Pentacoste's ploy was neatly executed. He watched as Berengar reached for the hook hanging from the beam above and secured his kithre to it, a tacit promise that he would sing again the next day as well as a continuing challenge to Ranegonda. He noticed that Duart had stationed himself a few steps away, and remarked to him, "I must take it that music is rare at the fortress."

"Except when the soldiers are drunk," said Duart stiffly, "or Faxon plays his pipes for us."

"That is not the same kind of music, is it?" Saint-Germanius asked, refusing to be daunted by the monitor's uncompromising stance.

"Possibly not," Duart allowed, before bowing and starting to move away as the bustle in the Common Hall increased. His right hand was held at the small of his back, the fingers fixed in the sign to ward off the Evil Eye.

"Monitor," Saint-Germanius called after him, deliberately keeping his voice low, "I do not know why you distrust me, but I tell you that there is no reason for it."

Duart stopped and stood with his back very straight. Then, quite deliberately, he rounded on Saint-Germanius. "Isn't there? I have seen the omens, and I know what I know."

Saint-Germanius did not want to argue with Duart, least of all here where most of the people of the fortress would witness it. "The omens," he said carefully, "may not pertain to me."

"You are a stranger here," said Duart, and moved further away from him as if to avoid the possibility of contamination.

With Pentacoste beside him, Berengar was making his way toward the door, smiling broadly and accepting the adulation of his audience as his due. He paused long enough to address Saint-Germanius. "Foreigner that you are, I'd wager you've heard some interesting songs in your travels; I certainly have." He intended to show his worldliness by this, and gestured as if to indicate that he, too, had been to distant places. "Wouldn't you say that the world has many beautiful songs in it?"

"Yes," said Saint-Germanius, and added with deliberate cordiality, "if you will let me use your kithre sometime, I will be pleased to sing a few of them, and teach them to you if they are acceptable to you."

This was not the response Berengar had anticipated, and he was disgruntled by it. "Of course," he said lamely, trying to recover his position of preeminence without being drawn into a contest with the dark-clad foreigner. "It is always worthwhile to learn new songs. There are many who would not be willing to share what they know with a stranger, as I must be to you, since you are foreign."

Saint-Germanius bowed with just enough deference to show respect for Berengar's rank. "I will be at your service whenever you like."

"How good of you to . . ." He moved by without finishing, making sure that Pentacoste was near enough to demand his attention.

When they were out of the Common Hall, Saint-Germanius drew Ranegonda aside. "Tell me, why are you so apprehensive? This fancy Pranz's son is not the true reason for your distress: what is it?" He had been sensing her restiveness since Berengar arrived, and over the last few days there had been a marked increase in her anxiety.

Ordinarily she would not have answered his question, or claimed that he was mistaken, but there was something in his dark eyes that compelled her to answer. "Margerefa Oelrih is supposed to arrive here very soon. I expect him to arrive any day; I have tried to prepare for his coming for more than a week. He is bringing supplies we need, and more men to reinforce us. He will inspect the fortress and give his report to King Otto."

The air smelled of the sea and fresh sawdust and the green of growing things; now that the sun was low it was cool enough to make several of the people in the Marshaling Court wish for a mantel or the lighter casula to ward off the chill of coming night. In the Marshaling Court a few of the younger soldiers had just finished practicing fighting with blunted spears; Captain Meyrih shouted instructions to them although they were now nothing more than moving shadows to him.

"You have no reason to be distressed about that," Saint-Germanius told her with conviction. "Everyone knows that you have managed Leosan Fortress as well or better than your brother could."

Color mounted in her face but her frown did not fade. "There is more to it than I've— You recall I told you that Margerefa Oelrih arranged the match between Giselberht and Pentacoste?" When he nodded, she went on. "He wanted her for himself but his father would not approve the match because of the reputation of Pentacoste's father. Dux Pol is debauched, you see, and for some this makes his children—" She broke off, gave herself a quick shake, and continued. "But it was a good alliance, and Margerefa Oelrih chose my brother because we would benefit from the marriage."

"And Margerefa Oelrih never supposed that there would be another man pursuing Pentacoste, not out here," said Saint-Germanius, thinking of the many times he had seen arranged marriages come to grief.

"He has not said so. He rarely says anything about Pentacoste; it wouldn't be fitting." Ranegonda glanced in the direction of the landward tower, where Pentacoste had taken her ladies, leaving Berengar to fend for himself among the men-at-arms. "But I have suspected that was the case. So did my brother before he retired from the world."

The wooden horn sounded for the change of guards on the parapet; in the Marshaling Court there was a flurry of activity as those about to go on duty gathered their weapons and hurried up the narrow stairs. Reginhart stood at the top, waiting to be relieved, four men behind him.

"You're anticipating trouble between the Margerefa and the Pranz's son, is that it?" Saint-Germanius asked, then saw that Brother Erchboge was making his way toward the front of the chapel, prepared to begin evening prayers, signaling to all to follow him.

Ranegonda watched the monk, and regretfully moved away from Saint-Germanius; as Gerefa it was her duty to be present before the prayers could begin. "Perhaps later?" she said over her shoulder.

"I am at your service, Gerefa," said Saint-Germanius, watching her walk away from him. When most of the people of the fortress had reached the chapel, he went to his workroom in the seaward tower.

There were ten oil lamps hanging from the massive beams in the low ceiling, and Saint-Germanius lit each of them in turn, using flint-and-steel for a spark. The chamber was almost to his satisfaction now, given where he was and the state of his supplies. He longed for the fine laboratory at Villa Ragoczy in Rome, and thought with a mixture of nostalgia and revulsion of the house he had built in the city of Toledo not quite two centuries ago. At least, he thought as he examined the athanor, the fortress had a good supply of moldy bread to give him; that was a start. There would be other compounds he could make later, when he had gathered more materials. He gave a short sigh; at times like this he could not shake off his melancholy for the world that had flourished a millennium before and was now relegated to tales of magic, peopled by figures made unrecognizable by legend as the people Saint-Germanius had known.

Some considerable time later he left the chamber, walking out into the Marshaling Court; overhead the moon glowed in the sky and limned the darkness below, not yet quite full. On the ramparts ahead of him, Saint-Germanius could see Faxon and Osbern standing together above the slaves' quarters, watching the village and the forest beyond. He walked toward the stairs and paused at the foot, calling up, "Men-at-arms."

Faxon looked down, one hand hefting his spear. "Saint-Germanius. What do you want?"

"I'd like to have a walk along the battlements, if you would not mind," said Saint-Germanius as genially as he could. "I will try not to get in your way."

"It is very late," said Faxon, with a glance toward Osbern. "You choose a strange hour for your walk."

"Regrettably, I do not often sleep the night through," said Saint-Germanius, starting up the stairs. "I hoped that a view of the sea and some little exercise might tire me. My meditations have not helped, and it is not the hour to continue with my studies." Only part of this was true, but he consoled himself with the knowledge that this was not outright prevarication; those of his blood rarely needed more than a short nap except when removed from their native earth or when famished.

Faxon moved his spear aside. "Come ahead," he said, mildly suspicious. "But remember, these are guarded ramparts. You will have to identify yourself to each of the men on watch."

"I will be pleased to do it," said Saint-Germanius, his thoughts ranging back to the days when he had first left Egypt and the Temple of Imhotep for his home, and had found himself among strangers on his native earth. Then it had caused him anguish to have to move among them as an interloper. But that was more than two thousand years ago and over the centuries he had become accustomed to abiding by the restraints placed on foreigners.

"Next along is Culfre, and then Kynr. Call out your name as you near them," said Faxon, unbending a little. "They will not harm you if you speak to them first." He stepped aside so that there was room on the narrow parapet for Saint-Germanius to pass him. "If you use these stairs to descend, I will escort you down. If you use the seaward stairs, then it must be Ewarht."

"Fine," said Saint-Germanius, and strolled away to the western end of the walls, whistling softly as he went. He identified himself to Culfre, and stopped not far away from him to watch the night. To his right the Baltic sighed its waves onto the sands, to his left the small village huddled at the foot of the promontory, the thatch-roofed log houses closed and silent. Straight ahead he could see the line of the forest and the expanse of sand almost as pale as snow in the moonlight, leading to the sea. It was comforting to stare at the place where the trees gave way to the beach.

A short while later, he became aware of a movement at the edge of the trees, and then, as he watched with suddenly keen interest, a solitary figure moved onto the sands, moving furtively toward one of the small coves a short distance to the west of the fortress. Saint-Germanius leaned forward, his dark, intent eyes piercing the darkness. Someone from the village, he thought, slipping through the unfinished stockade to leave an offering for the old gods. He wished the mantel-shrouded person would turn so that he might recognize who it was.

"What is it?" Culfre asked as he came up beside Saint-Germanius, having noticed his sudden attentiveness. "Is anything wrong?"

Saint-Germanius glanced at the man-at-arms. "I thought I saw movement by the trees," he answered.

"An animal?" asked Culfre.

"I do not think so," said Saint-Germanius, masking his certainty with a frown as if he could not see any better than Culfre could. "How can you tell? The woods are a long way from here and . . ." His words trailed off as he moved his hand to indicate the night.

"I noticed some . . . something." He paused, pointing to the place he had first seen the unknown person leave the cover of the trees. "It was just there. I was afraid it might be another band of outlaws seeking to attack the village again, or perhaps Danes coming to take prisoners."

Culfre Signed himself. "Surely that won't happen," he said, sounding very uncertain. He peered into the darkness again. "I can't see anything out there."

Saint-Germanius's night vision was much better than most, but he made no boast of it now. "I may have been mistaken."

"Well," Culfre said, willing to make a few allowances for the foreigner, "it is better that you make mention of it and have it be nothing than that you overlook something that could mean danger to all of us."

"Yes, I suppose so," said Saint-Germanius, once again staring out toward the line of the trees. "There would appear to be no hazard just now."

"If you see anything you believe is important, you tell me. I won't laugh at you and I won't ignore you." He made an encouraging gesture to Saint-Germanius. "I'll even tell the Gerefa that you've been a help to us."

"You are very kind," said Saint-Germanius, meaning it; few of the men-at-arms treated him with more than minimal respect and avoided him when possible.

"It would be a good thing if more of those within these walls cared for what transpires around us as you do. Captain Amalric himself has remarked on how careful you are," said Culfre with some heat. "It is admirable, especially in a foreigner. Too many of our own people suppose that we are safe because our walls are stone."

"But you do not think so," said Saint-Germanius, interested in what Culfre was saying, for it was untypical of most of those living at Leosan Fortress. "Is it the outlaws you fear? Danes? Or is it something Captain Amalric has taught you?"

"Every one of those things are part of my thoughts, for the omens are dangerous, very dangerous," said Culfre with a portentous glare. "And it is more than omens. This place is getting larger, and that means that it will be noticed. Whether it is pirates at sea or outlaws on land, or the Danes, looking for plunder, the larger this fortress and its village become, the more others will wish to take what we have, because they know we have it." He looked out in the same direction Saint-Germanius had. "And that's why I don't laugh when you tell me you've seen something."

"You're a very sensible man, Culfre; that surprises me," said Saint-Germanius, thinking that this youth displayed the kind of judgment he would have expected a soldier to possess hundreds of years ago. It was rare to find such prudence in these times, or in such a place as Leosan Fortress.

"Captain Amalric has been teaching me, as you say. He says he wants a lieutenant and he has said I am the best of the lot. I want to be worthy of the honor he has given me, taking me as his student." His naive pride increased. "I look forward to aiding him. I wish to be prepared to act."

"It would appear Captain Amalric shows good judgment in his choice of pupil," said Saint-Germanius.

"It is my hope that it will be so," said Culfre, and added, "It is useful that my wife is skilled with herbs. Between us, we can be of value to everyone here."

"Your wife is fortunate in your esteem," said Saint-Germanius, thinking of the number of women who were little more than conveniences to their men.

"So I think," said Culfre with naïveté, and continued in a conscientious manner, "Captain Amalric has also said that he will train Geraint, but after he has trained me." He stood straighter. "I pray to be worthy of the task."

"And the Gerefa, does she know of these plans?" asked Saint-Germanius, wondering why Ranegonda had not mentioned the matter to him. "Does she approve them, do you—"

"I don't know," said Culfre. "Captain Amalric has not told me." He hefted his spear. "I have to be about my watch." His patrol was from the western cistern to the seaward stairs, not a great distance, but he held himself as if he expected to have to walk all the way to Laboeric.

"God and the White Christ be with you," said Saint-Germanius, unwilling to leave his place on the parapet. "I will depart in a while."

"Let me know if you see anything again," said Culfre with a slight wave as he started back along his station.

Saint-Germanius lingered, his attention fixed on the stretch of beach; whoever had gone to the cove would have to come back along the same track or risk greater dangers in the forest. Sometime before dawn, before the villagers rose to their first chores, before the watch changed on the ramparts, the person would return, and he would try once more to see who it was.

As he waited, he found his thoughts again turning to Ranegonda and his strengthening link with her. It was not only his esurient need that caused it, for his native earth and occasional animals kept his hunger in check; it was his longing for the completion of unity that first taste of her blood began. He had considered visiting her in her sleep, but could not bring himself to do it; she might not know him for what he was, but his bond with her deserved more than a pleasant dream and the delight of ethereal indulgence. If he had not tasted her blood, it might be otherwise, but now there could be little satisfaction for either of them in the vision he could evoke. If he approached her directly, however, he risked not only her detestation but exile as well, or perhaps more punitive measures. While being cast out from Leosan Fortress would not be pleasant, he had survived much worse over the centuries; the worst of it would be the loss of Ranegonda without ever attaining her fulfillment. That rankled like the sting of nettles.

Finally he saw a figure emerge from behind the curve of the beach, the same manteled figure he had watched before. He leaned forward, his concentration on the distant person, trying to make out features or some distinctive piece of clothing.

A sudden gust of wind blew the hood of the mantel back, and for an instant the canescent moonlight revealed the features which had been so successfully concealed. Then the hood was pulled back into place.

"Pentacoste," whispered Saint-Germanius, taken aback that he was surprised. He straightened up, telling himself he should have anticipated something like this, for it was apparent that Pentacoste's defiance went deep, and her hatred of all that her husband had done to her certainly included a loathing of the White Christ as well as a disgust of everything in the fortress that came from Giselberht. He watched while she made her way carefully to the trees, then disappeared.

She would have to come through one of the breaks in the stockade, thought Saint-Germanius. And she would have to be able to get into the fortress without attracting notice. This last perplexed him more than the rest, for the gate was twice-barred and the men on watch were forbidden to open it without first sounding the wooden horn to rouse the inhabitants. Which meant, he decided, that there was another way into the fortress, or she had suborned one of the men-at-arms. Perhaps, he added grimly to himself, both. He made his way along the ramparts back to the place where Faxon and Osbern kept guard, taking care to speak first.

Faxon indicated the moon, now sinking into the west. "It's been some time; the watch is almost over."

"Yes, it has been a considerable time," said Saint-Germanius.

"Are you prepared to sleep yet?" He cocked his head, watching Saint-Germanius as if the answer would be significant.

"I am prepared to try," said Saint-Germanius calmly, and shifted the subject. "Osbern has the next station, is that right?"

"Osbern and then Gottarht, if he isn't drunk again," said Faxon with disgust. "The day will come when Captain Amalric will refuse to post him." He hitched his shoulder in the direction of the moon. "It won't be long now, and we will give our stations over to the morning watch. Severic will have the watch of the seaward tower where Aedelar is now. Geraint will replace me, and Chlodwic will have duty in the light room."

"Who replaces Osbern and Gottarht?" asked Saint-Germanius, as if his interest was only in passing.

"Rupoerht and Maugde," said Faxon. "Culfre will give over to Ulfrid."

"And they watch until mid-day," said Saint-Germanius, who had long since become familiar with the four divisions of day and night. "When do you resume your duty on the walls?"

"I do not keep watch again until sunset," said Faxon, "and then it is in the light room." He patted his chest. "Not so much wind up there."

While they were talking, Saint-Germanius kept a part of his attention on the gate below. No one approached it. He caught Faxon watching him narrowly. In order not to reveal the reason for his observation of the gates, he said, "Tell me, how many men does it take to pull both sides of the gates open?" He was aware that Faxon was still suspicious, so he went on, "I have never seen both sides opened at once. I am curious about—"

"Six," said Faxon. "Three on each side."

Saint-Germanius nodded. "If I could provide the means to open it using only two men, do you think it would be acceptable to you men-at-arms?" It would not be difficult to make the simple gears and counter-weights that would accomplish this; now that he considered it, he decided that it would be worthwhile.

"If it is not ill-omened and Brother Erchboge does not forbid it, I would think we would all be glad of it," said Faxon with more enthusiasm than Saint-Germanius had ever heard him express. "The gates are the very heart of damnation to move. If it were easier, we would all be grateful."

"Then I will show your Gerefa how it might be done, and hope that she will permit me to build this for you." He bowed slightly, once again glancing toward the gate; nothing had changed.

"You want to reduce your ransom, is that it?" asked Faxon with a wicked grin. "I can't say I blame you for that. Waiting for a chance to reach your people must be wearing on you."

"Occasionally, yes, it is wearing," said Saint-Germanius with little emotion.

"Margerefa Oelrih ought to be the one to give permission," said Faxon. "If Giselberht were still here, it would be a simple matter. But with Giselberht gone, our Gerefa will have to persuade the Margerefa." He shook his head once, showing his reservations about the possibility of her success. "He will not give much credence to a woman. What man in his position does?"

"A wise one, if the woman is Gerefa Ranegonda," said Saint-Germanius with asperity. "She is sensible and she keeps herself above the squabbles in the fortress." All but one, he added to himself, thinking again of Pentacoste.

"It is the counsel of her brother that makes her so," said Faxon, tossing his head. "But she is willing to consult him and to listen to him, unlike many women."

Saint-Germanius knew better than to argue this point; he said, "Until the Margerefa arrives there is little any of us can do." It was a compromise, and for that reason it bothered him.

"You will have time to explain it to the Gerefa, so that she will know what she is to say when Margerefa Oelrih arrives," said Faxon. "And if it is decided that what you propose will be permitted, then we will lift a cup to make it welcome. All of us who have guarded the gates will." He indicated the stairs to the Marshaling Court. "Can you see your way down?"

Saint-Germanius recognized the dismissal for what it was. "Yes."

"Remember the third stair from the bottom is a trip stair. Don't fall." Faxon waved him on, and Saint-Germanius left him on the ramparts.

As he started across the Marshaling Court he encountered Brother Erchboge. He paused, lowering his head to the monk. "You rise early," he said, and hoped that Brother Erchboge would not encounter Pentacoste in the village.

"There was a death yesterday in the village, and the corpse has lain at the door of his house through the night with a torch to guard it. Nothing has come to disturb it, and therefore it can be buried inside the stockade walls, as fits the blessed. I must attend to the Hour of the Dead," he responded, then added, "It will be washed once the Hours have been said. The body will be buried at sundown if the White Christ does not bring life back into it."

"And do you think He will?" asked Saint-Germanius, trying to keep his manner as respectful as he could, for Brother Erchboge was very touchy about his place in the order of the fortress.

"It has happened before, and not only for Lazarus." He directed his hot stare at Saint-Germanius. "There are many who appear to be lost to death who are returned to life by the White Christ. You are a foreigner, so you may not believe it to be possible, but I swear by the Hosts of Heaven that those who trust in Him eat His flesh and drink His blood so that they will live again."

At this Saint-Germanius concealed an ironic smile. "There you are mistaken, good Brother. I most certainly believe that men rise from the dead." It had been so long ago when it had happened to him, he thought.

Brother Erchboge gave him a hard scrutiny, as if trying to determine how candid Saint-Germanius was. Then he Signed himself and motioned toward the gate. "It will be dawn soon, and I must begin the Hour by that time. To do otherwise dishonors the White Christ."

"Then be about your calling, good Brother," said Saint-Germanius, Signing himself in the Greek manner. He stepped back from the monk and watched as he strode to the gates, signaling the warder to draw back the massive bolts. There was a single, short blast on the wooden horn, warning everyone that the gate was being opened. While the warder and two slaves struggled to pull one side of the gate ajar for Brother Erchboge, Saint-Germanius thought again about Pentacoste. Somehow she had left the fortress without drawing any attention to herself: she might have persuaded the warder to let her out, but she would never bother with the slaves. Pentacoste, he realized, knew she could come and go with impunity; that could only mean that there was another way into the fortress.

Returning to his quarters, he looked around at the few items in the chamber. It would not be difficult to put the bed and the small wooden chest where he put his clothing down to his workroom on the floor below. He decided he would suggest that arrangement to Ranegonda in the morning, for if the fortress was to have the Margerefa and his escort within the walls, space would be at a premium. What he would tell her about Pentacoste was less certain. If he told her of the incident, it would trouble her; if he failed to tell her, it could expose her to risk. It was possible that in time Pentacoste would betray herself. But if she did, the consequences to her and the fortress would be severe, if his understanding of the law was accurate. Sighing, he stretched out on his bed, feeling the sustaining force of his native earth through the straw stuffing of the mattress. For a short while he dozed, letting his thoughts drift over the centuries.

Text of a letter from Dux Pol in Lorraria to his daughter Pentacoste at Leosan Fortress. Brought by Margerefa Oelrih from Hamburh where it was received by the factor Braudelir on May 6, 938.

To my dearest daughter Pentacoste at Leosan Fortress, greetings from your father on this seventeenth day of March, 938, from his castle of Durance near Luitich.

It has been long since you sent me word of how you fare in that distant place. I have been at pains to learn of your current position now that your husband has left you for the White Christ, but there is little to be learned of fortresses like Leosan. You have not informed me of any changes in your life beyond the departure of your husband, and for that reason I seek to know more.

When you left my court, you told me then that whatever befell you was my fault. You did not wish to go to the distant shores of the sea to be lost at the edge of the forest with the sea at your back and no one for leagues in any direction. If that is the case, then you must tell me what has become of you that I may more fully understand the consequences of my decisions.

You claim that you could have married better than the Gerefa Giselberht. I have said to you from the time you were a child that such marriages are not for those in my household, not only because of my reputation, which has been made extreme by the envy of others, but because of the ambitions I have had in my youth and which I still foster when I can. This is known by many and King Otto is wary of me, and not without cause. It is not to be expected that I would be allowed to marry my daughters well, and my two surviving sons are beyond my power to control. That your brother Ancelot has made a marriage with a noblewoman in Hungary is no longer important to me. Your brother Perzeval has taken himself to King Otto for the purpose of finding his fortune in royal favor. In time he plans to claim my title and my lands for himself, and thus strengthen his position in the world. Your sisters have finally gone to Comites Charlot, Dorlisse as his wife, Odile for his concubine. They have been accepted by the Comites because of the men I can put in the field, not because he has not heard the tales told of me.

You have not yet given a child to your husband, and now that he has taken to the White Christ, you may never do so. A woman who has given her husband no children is hardly a wife at all. That you were barren before your husband left is doubly a fault: this is not to my liking and was not part of the bargain made at your marriage. Therefore I wish you to know that I no longer consider your marriage valid. You might as well be a widow, and as a widow, I will do my good office as your father and find you another suitable husband. It is not fitting that a young woman like you be left to wither away in a remote fortress at the edge of the world.

Let me warn you, however, my daughter, that you were the one I left untouched so that there would always be a bargain I could strike. If you compromise your chastity, I will be shut of you forever. Have any courtiers you like—such indulgence is in our blood—but do not bring shame upon yourself. I have no authority to stop the law from being rid of you, and if you were to disgrace the family I would not attempt to save you from the consequences of your cupidity. Let it be known that any man other than your husband has touched you and you will be cast out of my love unto the last day. Do not suppose that I will welcome you back into my holdings, for I will not. Either you will conduct yourself in a way to bring esteem to me, or I will forget that you were ever mine.

I will expect you to send word to me before the autumn comes, telling me what has become of you. If I have no message from you by the time of spring planting next year, I will declare that you are dead to me, either as my daughter or to the world, whichever is correct in the eyes of the King. Nothing of mine will come to you, not land nor titles nor favors nor gold. I will tolerate no deception on your part, and I will not permit you to seek aid from another before you ask it of me. Let me never hear that you have taken protection with one of those demented suitors who fawn over you. For such disloyalty I will act against you and the man who has dared to defy me. I will not hesitate to arm myself against such a treasonous act. Do not doubt that I vow to see you dead before I will permit you to go free in the world to claim that I have not acted to stop your disgrace.

There is a monk at that fortress, or there was when you last sent word to me. Tell him to write down everything I must know, and have him fix his name to it as proof that he believes his dispatch to be the truth. If he refuses to do this, then speak to the sister of your husband—you have said she can read and write—and tell her to inform me of your good conduct, and of your misbehavior. When I am made fully aware of your circumstances, I will authorize your husband's sister to act in my stead in whatever manner I deem the most appropriate. You are to submit to her as you would to me.

Let me learn nothing to your discredit, my beloved daughter, and remember that if I withdraw my favor from you, you are no better than any common trollop selling her body on market day.

Dux Pol
of Luitich
by the hand of Brother Luprician

9

By mid-morning the Common Hall had become so hot and stuffy that Margerefa Oelrih had ordered all the tables to be carried out into the Marshaling Court and set up there. The slaves had hurried to execute his orders and the men-at-arms stationed themselves at regular intervals around the court so that no miscreant could take advantage of the greater freedom the place afforded.

Ormanrih faced the Margerefa across the plank table, his face ruddy from contained temper. "But it would be sensible to permit us to build boats for fishing," he protested as reasonably as he could. "We would not need to have extra food requisitioned from the King's stores, and our men who cannot work in the forest any longer would be able to do more than herd the goats and sheep, or tend the fields with the children and the women. As they are unable to cut trees, they often claim that they cannot remain in the village; they declare they must take their families and go away from here. But where? If they cannot cut wood here, they cannot cut it elsewhere, and if they leave, they risk becoming slaves or being taken captive by outlaws. I believe it is better that they remain here, and their families with them, and that they be put to more than simple tasks, for they are not children. It is fitting that they should have such work as fishing to do, for everyone in the fortress as well as the rest of the village." For Ormanrih, this was a long and eloquent appeal.

"There are lakes in the forest where you can fish," said Margerefa Oelrih. He was a squat, powerful man with massive forearms and a neck like the trunk of an oak. His ruddy hair was short, his beard was closely trimmed, and he wore a fillet on his brow to show his rank. His bliaut was of good-quality wool but without the touches of embroidery that marked Berengar as a rich and nobly born courtier. This was the third day of receiving petitions, and he had worked his way through the inhabitants of the fortress and was now hearing from the villagers; he had already given permission for the villagers to build salt-pans for harvesting salt from the sea, and had upheld Brother Erchboge's insistence that the dead be buried inside the stockade instead of outside. This was the third decision he had to make. "If you must eat like monks, then take your nets there."

"There are outlaws in the forest, Margerefa, and Danes as well. If we are to fish in safety, it must be in the sea, not the lakes, unless we go with armed men." Ormanrih put his hands on his hips though his eyes were frightened.

"But you would need timber for the boats, and that cannot be spared," said Margerefa Oelrih as if Ormanrih were a foolish child. "King Otto has required that the village be enclosed in the stockade—which will be completed before harvest, you tell me—and that more logs be delivered to him. If you are to do what the King demands of you, you cannot give men over to making boats and fishing in the sea, you must have all that can cut in the forest, and the rest should devote themselves to making the carts needed to haul the logs to Hamburh, where the King's minister will receive them. If you cannot do this, we cannot allocate men and supplies here, for they will be needed elsewhere." He gestured to his Captain, a scarred veteran in leather-and-scale armor standing behind him. "Jouarre here, he will tell you if you ask him, how difficult it is when there are men who put their wishes ahead of those of the King. The King is made to suffer because his people put their pettiness ahead of his needs, which is for all of Germania."

"It is true," said Jouarre in a voice made harsh by years of shouting orders. "Either you are for the King or you are his enemy. If you are his enemy, then you will have to battle with his army."

"We are not against the King," said Ormanrih, lowering his head and touching his forehead to show respectful submission. "But there are men we could use better if we could fish the sea."

Ranegonda, who was seated at the far end of the plank table, suddenly spoke up. "Margerefa, let me suggest something." She was deferential, but she could see that she had annoyed the Margerefa by speaking at all. "There are trees that cannot be used for the stockade and cannot be sent to the King. You yourself have seen these trunks. They are misshapen and they do not fall true. Some of them have breaks or knots or burls that make them useless to most purposes. Yet they must be cut so that the true trees may be felled without damage. Why not permit the men who are no longer able to work at cutting to have those trees, and to do with them what they may? If they can make boats from them, well and good. If not, at worst there will be timber for repairing the houses in the village, for finishing the new ones we have been required to provide, and for making tables and stools and bed frames. And we will have wood to burn in the winter." She saw that her recommendation was not well-received. "If they learn that they cannot make boats of this wood, perhaps they can make ax-handles and saw-rockers for those who cut, as well as stools and tables."

Ormanrih nodded several times, his square, rough face as close to

pleased as it ever got. "The men can make carts, too. They can fit
shelves to the walls and make chests for keeping goods safe. They can
fence the fields, as well, and the pens for the animals; they need new
fences. Some can make the salt-pans, and mind them."

"Then they need not make boats at all." The Margerefa looked over
to the monk on his left. "What do you think, Brother Andoche? Does
any of this seem wise to you?"

The monk pulled at his beard and looked down at the sheet of
parchment lying in front of him as if he expected words to appear on
it by magic. "It is not good that men should be idle, even those who
have suffered injuries. In that the headman is right. But you are right
in demanding that the wishes of the King be placed above all others but
Heaven's." He tapped his stylus on the table, his long fingers like dried
twigs. "Put it before the White Christ, Margerefa, and in the morning
tell these people what you have decided to do."

Margerefa Oelrih pressed his lips together, his face set as he considers
this suggestion. "Very well," he says at last. "Tonight I will call upon
the White Christ to advise me." He Signed himself, and looked directly
at Ormanrih, his hazel eyes more brown than green in the brightness.
"Before mid-day tomorrow, I will tell you what it is to be. Do not seek
to sway me. And do not cavil with whatever answer I give, for it will
be that of the White Christ as well as the King's."

Ormanrih put his hand to his forehead again, bowing so that his hair
brushed the edge of the plank table. "I will be satisfied with your
answer, Margerefa. God and the White Christ bring you wisdom."

"And so say all good Christians," said Margerefa Oelrih, waving
Ormanrih away from the table.

The next villager was Nisse, the swineherd. He tugged his hair as he
touched his forehead, and bowed as far as his thick-muscled back
would allow. At twenty, he had four living children and a wife who was
known to be distracted in her mind, given to fits of melancholy and
occasional outbursts of temper or laughter that were equally incompre-
hensible. "Margerefa, I wish to make a request." It was difficult for him
to speak without stammering, so his words came out slowly.

"Of course you do," said Margerefa Oelrih with asperity. "It is why
you are here. Tell me your request." He slapped his fingers on the table
to emphasize the need for speed and brevity.

Nisse looked over at Ranegonda, and now spoke so quickly that he
was not easily understood. "It is about the pigs. The pigs I herd here.
I have not been permitted to take my pigs to market at Oeldenburh,
though it would mean better food for us, and a place where we could
make the most of our crops. I could take more than pigs. I could carry,

oh, all sorts of things: sheep, goats, apples, pears, and onions. I would like to be able to bring them to market there." He faltered, then hurried on. "It would take a day to reach the town, and a day to get back. I would need four armed men with me to keep the outlaws away. But there are many things I could trade for there on market day. If you are willing to let me—"

"Oeldenburh is not in our hands. Oeldenburh has not yet wholly submitted to King Otto, and as such it is not considered safe for Otto's vassals and subjects," Margerefa Oelrih needlessly reminded Nisse, his head held at an arrogant tilt. "The town is full of Obodrites and Wagrians who do not honor the White Christ and who treat with the Danes and the wild men of Pomerania."

"It is the only town we can reach without taking several days and running great risks," Nisse objected, and did what he could to defend his request. "We cannot safely take stock to Hamburh, for it is too far and the outlaws prey on those traveling the Hamburh road; could we travel there in safety, it is still too far for market; the piglets and the lambs and the kids would have to be carried or die during the journey because it is too hard. But we go often to the Monastery of the Holy Cross, and Oeldenburh is not much farther on from there. We could take our tithe to the Brothers and continue to market." His eyes were desperate and there was an edge in his voice. "We could do it, if you would grant us—"

"I will not permit any of King Otto's people to go among his enemies. How can you be certain that the people of Oeldenburh would not rob you the way the outlaws of the forest would? You would not be safe there. The ones who worship the old gods would make you prisoners or slaves to shame the White Christ and those who oppose King Otto would demand that you be ransomed. No." Margerefa Oelrih's face had darkened and now he spoke with low determination. "Let me hear no more of this."

"But the monks go there, from the monastery," said Nisse, at once bewildered and aggravated. "If the monks go there, why should we not?"

"They are holy men bound on the task set them by the White Christ," said Margerefa Oelrih. "They do not go to sit in the market-place and wrangle for a sack of dried peas."

"I do not want to dispute prices, either," said Nisse. "I think of what we have endured here for the last winter and I want to give the village more food, so that with the new families you have brought here we will not all face true famine next winter, which we may do if we do not have more food. All of our effort has gone to cutting trees, and we have left the fields to the children and women. What we have planted now is not enough, and the stores you have given us will not—"

"You will not go to Oeldenburh," said Margerefa Oelrih in a tone that would allow for no argument.

Nisse's voice was higher and he twisted the hem of his knee-length bliaut in agitation. "What if we made arrangements with the monks at Holy Cross to take our stock when they go there? They could take our pigs and goats and sell them. We could increase the tithe we pay, and still we would benefit from the market without putting ourselves or King Otto at—"

Margerefa Oelrih's face darkened. "If I learn that you have done it, the supplies we are supposed to bring at the end of summer will be given to villages and fortresses more worthy than this one."

Nisse's brows drew together and he lowered his head still further, belatedly bringing his hand to his forehead. "It is wrong for you to do this, Margerefa. I fear that the men-at-arms and the woodcutters you have brought here will suffer for it in days to come."

"Then slaughter more of your pigs and put them in salt," the Margerefa recommended in a brusque manner. "Who is next?"

There were two men whose wives wished to keep bees. Jennes, who was one of the three leaders of woodcutting teams, spoke for them both. "We have industrious wives, both of us. And they desire to use the secrets imparted by the foreigner who came here last autumn in the storms; they could make hives and keep bees, if they do what he has shown them. Or so the foreigner claims." This last was a bit defiant, making it clear that if the bees did not come it would be the foreigner's fault, and any ill fortune because of it would be his.

Margerefa Oelrih scowled. "Make hives." He stared at the table. "I have seen it done, but that was in the south, in Franconia, near the border with Lorraria." He directed his gaze toward Pentacoste, who was standing somewhat apart from the other women of the fortress, not far from Berengar. She was dressed in a bliaut of linen and her chanise beneath was as fine as cobwebs. "What do you say, Hohdama Pentacoste? Have you seen such hives in your father's—"

Pentacoste did what others would not dream of doing: she interrupted Margerefa Oelrih. "I never learned what was done in the field. I was taught to weave and to sew and to make dyes, not the tending of beasts or other creatures."

"But there were hives," Margerefa Oelrih persisted.

"We certainly had honey, so there must have been." She managed a brilliant smile and then glanced at Berengar. "Ask Pranz Balduin's son. He may know more than I."

Both Margerefa Oelrih and Berengar regarded each other with marked distaste. Finally Berengar said, "I know little of bees."

"Then I will speak to the foreigner," said Margerefa Oelrih, his attitude condemning. He signaled to another one of his men-at-arms. "Gallaen, bring him out to me. I want to have word with him."

The bearded young soldier gave a Roman salute, then hurried to obey the order, passing behind the plank table so as not to offer any insult to the proceedings as he moved toward the seaward tower.

"It would be useful to have bees, if keeping them does not offend the White Christ and if it does not take time from the work your women do now," said Margerefa Oelrih with a nod of approval. "There are many women who seek to lessen their labors by pretending to have more of them. If your wives are such slatterns, they must be beaten for their sloth. Women are not to be coddled, for that brings weak children." He slapped his hand on the table again. "What are the omens regarding the bees? Have any been noted?"

Captain Amalric answered the question. "If you will allow me to answer, Margerefa," he said, making a covert signal to Ranegonda for her to be silent. "I have twice found hives in trees that had grown up along the edge of the main wall of the fortress. On the outside, naturally. It would appear that the bees themselves have made their wishes known. I cannot think that the hives would be in that place if it were wrong for villagers to make hives of their own."

Margerefa Oelrih pondered this. "Has anyone else seen omens in this regard?"

"In one of the old trees, where the unwise leave tokens to the old gods," said Ranegonda very clearly, "I have found a hive where the bees were most ferocious. They stung me and my brother when he first went to enter the Monastery of the Holy Cross. I do not know what the White Christ wishes, but I think it would serve His purpose to bring God's creatures to the care of men."

"A hive in a hollow tree!" said Margerefa Oelrih, Signing himself. "It is the work of the old gods, luring the bees to those places." He turned to Brother Andoche. "What does that impart to you, Brother?"

The monk stroked his beard. "It is an important omen, and I believe that is possible the Gerefa is right, that the White Christ is tasking these people with bringing the bees away from the old gods."

There was a flurry of muttered remarks among those watching, and the two men shifted uneasily, disliking the attention their simple request was attracting.

A moment later Gallaen shoved his way through the crowd, the black-clad Saint-Germanius directly behind him. This was made more difficult as many of the youngsters pressed forward to touch the young soldier, his presence exciting; it was good fortune to touch a fortunate man. He stopped at the end of the table and said, "Here is the foreigner," before he offered the Margerefa another Roman salute. Then he stepped back to the place he had stood before, leaving Saint-Germanius to face the Margerefa on his own.

"Margerefa Oelrih," said Saint-Germanius pleasantly as he touched his left shoulder with his right hand, nodding his head slightly as he did. "What may I do to be of assistance to you?"

It had been a difficult morning for the Margerefa and he would have liked nothing more than the chance to take this foreigner to task for some slight or other offense, but he could find nothing in Saint-Germanius's demeanor that gave him the excuse. He glowered. "These men say that you know how to establish hives for bees, the way they do it in Lorraria."

Saint-Germanius's smile was swift and apologetic. "Well, no," he said deferentially, "not in the manner of Lorraria, but as the Romans and the Byzantines make them. Their methods are somewhat different than those used in Lorraria."

"In what way?" demanded the Margerefa.

"The Romans find a hive in the wild and transfer it to the one they have built, keeping it near the original hive at first, and then move it to the site they wish and so establish the bees in that way. The hives are made like bread ovens, with many entrances for the bees to use, and sliding panels to permit the keeper to remove the honey without causing the bees too much distress. There is wood enough here to make several hives." He looked over at Jennes. "This man's wife has gone into the forest for honey, and knows the nature of bees. But it is no longer safe for her to go there without escort, and most of the men are needed to fell trees."

"True enough," said Margerefa Oelrih grudgingly. He looked at the two men once more. "Your wives spin and weave?"

"Yes," the two said at once.

"And they do not let their children run wild?" asked the Margerefa, hoping to find some flaw in the idea. "They attend to their tasks and make themselves worthy of their families?"

"I have no children; my wife has—" said Jennes, while Leutpald answered, "We have three living, and they are obedient."

"No children?" Margerefa Oelrih demanded, seizing on this information with zeal. "Has your wife sinned, or is she cursed by envious rivals? Or is there some evil in her heart?"

Jennes shook his head. "The monks tell us that the fever she had when she tried to have our first has settled in her womb. They tell her to pray to the Mädchen Mairia who bore the White Christ, but she has not yet had another."

"In Byzantium they say that women who tend bees get many children," said Saint-Germanius, repeating what he knew to be an old fable.

From the expression he wore, Margerefa Oelrih was not pleased to hear this. He regarded Saint-Germanius critically. "And those who say this, do they worship the White Christ?"

"Yes," said Saint-Germanius. "The Byzantines are renowned for their devotion to the White Christ, and the Church in Rome would not permit anyone to invoke the old gods so near to the place where the first Pope was martyred." He appeared unperturbed as he spoke, and his dark eyes glinted with amusement.

This time it was Brother Andoche who Signed himself, and touched his hands together afterward, to reveal that he was praying. As he opened his eyes, he asked Saint-Germanius, "How is it that you know these ways, Comites?" The use of the title was unflattering. "You are a foreigner here, and you claim to have come from Christian lands. Are you Byzantine or Roman?"

"Neither," said Saint-Germanius. "But I have lived in both places, and hold them in high esteem."

"And you learned the keeping of bees?" asked the monk with open incredulity.

"Good Brother," said Saint-Germanius, undaunted by the accusation in the monk's craggy visage, "when one is a stranger, a foreigner, there are many things it is wise to learn, for the place of foreigners is always changing. In my time I have learned many skills for that reason. It was why I first began the Egyptian study." It was a truthful answer, but a limited one.

Margerefa Oelrih made a gesture that was part exasperation, part resignation. "Very well. If it does not dishonor your name, help the women to make hives for bees. It is not work I would set a man to do, but . . ." He turned the palms of his hands up.

"But you like honey, do you not? And mead?" asked Saint-Germanius lightly. "This way there will be more of each for you the next time you come here."

Rather than answer the question, Margerefa Oelrih shrugged. "If the work can be done without compromising what King Otto requires of the people of this village and the fortress, it is acceptable."

Jennes bowed deeply, and Leutpald followed his example, both of them saying quickly that they were grateful to the Margerefa for his wisdom.

Ranegonda watched Saint-Germanius as he started to step back. She was about to motion to him to remain when she realized that this could lead to the sort of confrontation with the Margerefa she did not want to have. She changed the gesture to one of approval, and she kept her place in silence.

Margerefa Oelrih rose from his place. "It is time that we ate," he announced, clapping his hands together in anticipation. "The cooks have two goats and a dozen geese turning on spits, and the cauldron is at the boil."

This should have been the announcement that Ranegonda made, but she said nothing, for Margerefa Oelrih did not like to be reminded that a woman was in charge of this fortress. She rose, lifted her skirts to above her knees, and then signaled to the leader of the slaves to fetch the food, and felt her ankle threaten to give way as she stood aside. She knew that Margerefa Oelrih had seen her weakness, and she cursed herself inwardly for permitting it to happen. Shame filled her and she sought for escape from the confusion and noise that accompanied the coming of food. Without stopping to assess her situation, she moved toward the kitchens, and then toward the wall, as if having no goal in mind but putting distance between herself and the Marshaling Court.

As the tables were moved and all those in the Marshaling Court brought out their tankards and knives, Saint-Germanius went back to the seaward tower, and was surprised to find that Ranegonda had followed him. He stopped in the door of what was now both his workroom and living quarters. "Do you want something, Gerefa?"

She seemed startled by his question. "An answer," she said, standing just out of the light. Now that she saw him, she realized that she had been seeking him; she found this troubling and comforting at once, which only increased her confusion.

"If I am able," he said, and waited while she strove to frame her question.

"You will not eat with us?" she said at last. The odor of grilled meat was heavy on the air, and the people in the Marshaling Court were cheering for the slaves bringing out the big spits with their luxurious cargo; some of the men-at-arms were stamping their feet.

"It would not be . . . appropriate," he said quietly.

"But no one will—" She faltered. "You have been here long enough that it isn't required that you keep apart."

Saint-Germanius's eyes softened as he sensed her emotions. "You are very kind to me, Gerefa Ranegonda, and I thank you for it. But I think that the Margerefa and the Pranz's son would not share your sentiments." He disliked having to disappoint her, or to leave her feeling as isolated as she did, and so he added, "I would not like to give them a reason to question your right to your position; it would be poor gratitude indeed to bring suspicions on you."

"No," she said after a short pause.

"And I fear that is what I would do if I flaunted your customs. It would not be seemly. You would be held accountable for my misbehavior." He held out his hand to her. "You deserve better than the Margerefa has given you."

Without thinking she put her hand in his, surprised at how small it was, and how strong. "So much is left to me to decide. If my brother would tell me what he wishes me to do, it would be better."

"Would it?" Saint-Germanius asked gently, drawing her a step closer to him. "Do you think your brother could deal with this fortress and the village better than you have? I doubt it. You know I think you have done his work better than he would have done; my opinion has not changed, nor has your brother. He has left the world, Ranegonda, and does not want to be recalled to it."

A shout went up in the Marshaling yard Court, and a burst of oaths and laughter followed.

"Do you mean what you say? You are always so willing to listen, and you tell me things that comfort me, but do you mean them?" She would not let him answer. "When I come to speak with you, when there is only you to hear, I believe each word. But when I am away from you, when I hear the men speaking and see the way the women look at me, I think you are mistaken, that it is your foreignness that makes you misunderstand and hold me in better opinion than I deserve."

He looked down at her hand in his. "Ranegonda, I do not lie to you."

"But you have not learned our ways, and you do not understand how it is with us when—" She stopped, and started again slowly. "You treat me as if I were Gerefa truly born, but that is not so: I have been put in my brother's place, I have not become Gerefa except in his stead."

"A difficult position to maintain," said Saint-Germanius, thinking of how untenable her appointment was. "Especially now when your brother has ceased to instruct you."

"He was sworn to this place," she said in a small, adamant voice.

"And now he is sworn to the White Christ," said Saint-Germanius. "He has traded one master for another; you have not."

"He is a worthy man," she insisted. "He has taken a great burden on him, the sins of all mankind, for love of the White Christ." How many times she had heard Giselberht say that to her in the months before he went to the monastery. And now how odd it sounded to her.

"That does not make you any the less worthy," said Saint-Germanius. "You have upheld his place with honor and good sense."

"But he—" She stopped, and said in a different tone, "You have been getting thinner."

"Yes," Saint-Germanius agreed, needing no mirror to tell him it was so; in the past whenever he had to live on the blood of animals he lost flesh.

"Let me tell them to bring you something to eat," she said, suddenly pulling her hand away. There was confusion in her grey eyes, and beyond that, a need she could not bring herself to name.

"Not another shoat, not with the Margerefa here, and not while Nisse can complain," he protested, regarding her steadily. "I will fend for myself, later."

"And what will you do?" She turned abruptly and closed his door, cutting them off from the shouts and babble from the Marshaling Court.

He shook his head. "Ah, that would cause you distress to know. Rest assured it will touch nothing of this fortress or the village." For the last two nights he had found deer feeding not far from the stockade, and for a while they would provide his basic need.

"But you . . ." She came back to him, and put one hand on his shoulder. "There must be some way to restore you. It is summer, and this is the time to grow fat, so that winter will not bring starvation."

There was such loneliness in her grey eyes, and so much courage that Saint-Germanius took her face in his hands. "You restore me, Ranegonda. Your presence nourishes me." His kiss was soft, hardly more than the brush of his lips on her mouth; then he moved back from her, his eyes never leaving hers. "I cannot apologize for that." He hooked his thumbs in his hip-slung belt to show her he would not demand more of her than she was prepared to give.

She stood very still, watching him with astonishment. "Why did you do it?"

"Because I am bound to you," he answered, leaning back against the wall next to the narrow window. "Because I admire you. Because I love you."

Her laughter was short and high, a nervous whinny. "Foreigners like lame women with scarred faces?"

"I do, if the woman is you," said Saint-Germanius tranquilly.

A number of rejoinders jumbled in her mind, but she could bring herself to speak none of them. She knew what the Great Pox had done to her; its seal was everywhere on her skin. Her face and neck flushed and she knotted her hands together, looking away from him so that she would not have to see the warmth in his compelling eyes. "You should not tell me such things."

"I know that," he said, not moving from his place. "As a foreigner I realize I should say nothing to you that I would not say to your brother. I know that is what I am expected to do. But that is not possible for me, Ranegonda."

Fascinated in spite of herself, Ranegonda asked, "Why?"

His single laugh was quiet and sad. "That is another thing I should not tell you." He had never been able to bring himself to visit her at night; now he could not admit the desire which would not let him take that advantage of her.

"It is part of your foreignness," she said with certainty.

"Yes." He did not move from his place by the window.

"You have rituals you must observe—everyone does." Her brows flicked into a frown. "Is it the same sort of reason that you kill your food yourself? Is there a ritual of your people that you must keep secret?" So many things were secret, she thought, and wondered again who had been leaving tokens on the hollow oak trees.

"Not so much secret as private." His answer was gently sardonic. "But it is something of that sort, yes."

She made a gesture of acceptance and sighed. "I will not press you if it would dishonor you to speak of those things."

"It would not dishonor me," said Saint-Germanius. "Except, perhaps, in your eyes." And that, he added to himself, would be more of a burden than he wished to bear.

Her smile faded quickly. "It would have to be a heinous rite to do such a thing."

He could think of nothing to say that would reassure her; he remained where he was as she began to pace, his thoughts caught up with memories of Nineveh and Thebes and Rome and Thessaly and Burma and the road from Baghdad. How many times his true nature had brought about panic for those around him and despair for himself. Only when he became aware that her silence masked more pressing concerns did he speak again. "What else is worrying you, Gerefa?"

She halted. "I fear that list is a long one." She brushed her hand across her forehead to wipe the tendrils of hair away.

"Should you return to the Marshaling Court?" he asked, not wanting to draw attention to their absence. "I am honored by your company, but are you—"

"It is not necessary for me to eat with the rest. Margerefa Oelrih will seat Pentacoste beside him and no one will be surprised that I am not there. They will eat, and the Margerefa will go to inspect the stockade and the logs ready to be carted to King Otto, and then they will come back for Mass. I will not be missed until then." Her sudden resentment faded as quickly as it arose. "It is better here with you."

"My thanks, Gerefa." He paused. "Then, what is the matter?"

"Why did you kiss me that way?" The words were out before she knew she intended to speak them.

"I've told you why," said Saint-Germanius.

"That was courtesy," she said.

"That was the truth," he said.

Again her face grew rosy. "It isn't possible." Her denial, intended to be brusque, was a plea.

"What isn't possible: that I love you?" At last he came away from the wall. "That is the most possible of all, Ranegonda."

They were more than an arm's length apart, yet she dared not close the space between them. "You want me to forgive the ransom," she challenged.

"You may have double whatever amount you demand," he answered, and seeing doubt in her eyes, he continued, "And that is not an idle offer. In Rome I am very rich."

"You seek to gain power here through me," she accused him.

"Then I had better speak with your brother," he said calmly. "If his decisions are the ones that matter here, it would be foolish for me to seek for authority in you." He shook his head once, anticipating her protests. "I do not seek advancement, I do not want to coerce you in any way. I am not attempting to compromise your family or this fortress. I have no allies who seek to exploit this place. I do not want to bring outlaws or Danes or the old gods down on you. And I am not trying to cause you to become indebted to me, or to owe me obligation. It is I who am indebted to you, and the obligation is mine."

"And you wish your debt discharged," she said a little wildly. "You want to be free of this place."

He smiled, and this time it was not tinged with any irony or sorrow. "Do you know, Ranegonda, I do not wish that at all. If anything, I want to compound my debt to you."

Her eyes were perplexed, though she tried to set her features against him. "A man would be worse than a fool to do such a thing."

He held out his hands to her again. "I will not be provoked to anger, my life; you may try as you like, but I will not speak against you."

Ranegonda turned to walk away, and then, as if drawn by power beyond her ability to resist, she swung back toward him, persistent as a magnet. "Why should I believe anything you say?"

For a moment Saint-Germanius could think of no response, and then he came to her. "I do not know your omens well enough to answer."

She had braced herself to refute any arguments he presented; now that he offered none, she was disarmed. "I . . ." When nothing else occurred to her, she put her hands to her cheeks.

"If scars offend you," Saint-Germanius said with tenderness, "then it is I who should fear you." He put one hand to his waist. "When you saved me, you saw my scars."

"There are many of them," she whispered. "Across you."

"Yes," he said softly. "Are they repellent to you?"

"No." She looked at him curiously. "Why should they be?"

His answer was sympathetic and kindly. "You expect me to be repelled by yours."

"It is not . . . yours are . . . I could not . . ." She gave up trying to sort out her feelings; she could not hold herself away from him. As she came to him, she started to raise her skirts to show her submission to him.

"Let me do that; but later," said Saint-Germanius quietly, gathering her close to him, his arms around her, feeling her need of him turn from orectic to erotic. He kissed her again, very slowly and passionately, answering at last the ardor he had felt the first time her blood touched his mouth.

Ranegonda clung to him, shivering with the intensity of her carnality, and horrified by the unchaste eagerness that coursed through her. She pushed against him, trying to break away and at the same time press more of her body to his. Her senses were in tumult. She managed to say one thing. "I am virgin."

"And so you will remain." Saint-Germanius felt her stiffen in his embrace, and he hastened to soothe her. "I will bring no disgrace on you, Gerefa." He moved his hands over her, feeling her flesh beneath the wool and linen. "But I will give you pleasure, if you will have it from me, now or anytime."

She wanted him so relentlessly that she was queasy. She pulled him to her, seeking his kisses with her own. "Yes, I will have it," she murmured breathlessly. There had been no omens for this, she decided; it was wholly new.

Her recklessness was more astonishing to Ranegonda than it was to Saint-Germanius; he had discovered it in her blood. But he eased her, his caresses steadying her before he took one step away from her and led her toward his bed.

Impulsively she unbuckled her belt and flung it away. Her bliaut hung loosely around her, softening the taut lines of her. To her amazement, Saint-Germanius lifted the garment off her, laying it over one of his chests. As she faced him in her chanise, she said in sudden nervousness, "I have never heard any of the other women say their men would be their servants."

"My foreign ways," whispered Saint-Germanius, and drew her chanise off, putting it with the bliaut. He wanted to tell her how beautiful she was, but knew she would not believe him. So his hands spoke for him, gently, reverently, as they traveled the whole of her.

She gasped when he teased her nipples erect, and stifled a moan when, some time later, he eased his hands between her legs; she held his shoulders to keep from falling and an instant later he lifted her easily and carried her the last few steps to his bed, then knelt next to her while he lavished kisses on her breasts and flanks. Every touch and pressing and stroke increased her pleasure. She recalled the stories she had heard in the cloth room and the women's quarters. Nothing had prepared her for the immensity of what she felt, not even the most extreme of Pentacoste's tales. She was drawn down beside him, and as she trembled with the joy he had summoned from the depth of her soul, she felt her frenzy become his as well, carrying them timelessly through the long afternoon.

Text of a letter from Franzin Ragoczy, Comites Saint-Germanius to his bondsman Hrotiger in Rome, dated June 19, 938. Carried by the Margerefa Oelrih and destroyed in a battle with raiding Danes.

To my loyal friend Hrotiger,

Let me assure you that I am well. No doubt you know the fate of my ships in the storms of last autumn; suffice it to say that I was fortunate enough to be found by a company from Leosan Fortress on the Baltic coast, the better part of a day's ride from Oeldenburh.

The Gerefa here has taken me in. There was enough gold remaining in my belt to make me seem worth ransoming, and I have since then been able to be of use to her. I do not know what she wants for me, but whatever sum is given, be sure to send twice as much. No, I do not expect her to change her mind as many of these regional rulers do; I wish her to know that I am beholden to her.

Once the debt is paid, I will want to go to Hamburh and from there make my way to Ghent. These roads are far from safe, and so I ask that you provide escort, both for the gold and for my return. You know which men to entrust with this task, and I rely on you to choose those with integrity. I do not wish to be held for ransom again; I doubt I would be as fortunate in my captors a second time.

Whatever cargo was salvaged from my ships, I ask you to make arrangements for its disposal if you have not done so already. When I return to Rome I will want to review the extent of the losses suffered in that storm. Doubtless we have seen worse privation before now, and will experience it again. Still, I will need to know how much is required so that appropriate measures may be taken.

This is being carried by the company of the Margerefa Oelrih, who has read it and has said he is willing to pass it on in Hamburh to merchants traveling south. I reckon it will take two to three months to reach you, which may mean that you cannot get the ransom here before winter. I would prefer you wait until next spring rather than risk losing men to cold, and I leave the decision in your hands.

With my thanks for all I know you have done in my absence, and with the promise that I will return,

Franzin Ragoczy
Comites Saint-Germanius
(his sigil, the eclipse)

10

Pentacoste stood at the concealed door, her whole being alert to any noises in the women's quarters. At this late hour only the parapet guards and the man in the light room should be awake, she thought, but still she hesitated, fearing that she might be discovered. Worst of all, she decided, would be if that puppy Berengar had not yet gone to sleep, for he had been tagging after her for the last three days, ever since Margerefa Oelrih had left. She fondled the small wooden figure she held, and once again inspected the red yarn wound around it. The knots were in the right place and she had prepared it correctly; this time the old gods would have to take note of her desires.

She eased the long woven hanging aside and pulled the two slightly projecting stone blocks downward, using most of her weight. She had few reasons to be grateful to Giselberht, but this was one: he had shown this to her shortly after he brought her to the fortress, a gesture to amuse the lovely creature who had besotted him since their wedding. He had sworn to her then that Ranegonda knew nothing about this tunnel, that his father had made him swear to tell only his sons. "And you will be their mother, so you might as well know about this as well, in case of a misfortune which will take me from you early," Giselberht had said with pride. "You will honor my trust in you, and use it to protect this place and our children." There was a low, grinding sound like a millstone, and a portion of the wall swung downward, leaving a low doorway in the wall and forming a bridge over a wide gap in the stones of the landward tower.

The corridor revealed was cramped, not much higher than Pentacoste herself and so narrow that a stout man would have trouble walking down it. She took her oil lamp and held it up, sniffing with disdain at the musty, loamy odor. It was demeaning for her to have to use this coward's way, but with Giselberht no longer at the fortress, she was forced to accommodate Ranegonda's rules, a state of affairs that galled her, and never more so than now, when she sought to be free again. It was bad enough that her husband had forsaken her for the White Christ, but to be ruled by his sister instead was so great an insult that it made her pulse pound in her neck to think of it.

Beyond the midden slope, near the kennels inside the walls, the corridor took a sharp dip, and where the wall turned toward the ocean, there was another concealed entrance, this one blocked by two large bushes that successfully concealed the irregularity in the wall. Pentacoste clutched her offering to the old gods and stepped out into the warm summer night.

She was still inside the stockade, with the cutting shed just beneath her. She slipped behind the rough walls of the shed, and then to the place where the stockade met the rise of the fortress. Here the ground was uneven and the tall logs set in place side-by-side were not quite as close as they were on the rest of the perimeter. Pentacoste found the widest gap and deliberately squeezed through, taking care not to rip her clothes on the bark; she had no intention of having to explain how her garments came to be damaged, for that might lead to suppositions she did not want to have to counter. There were rumors enough about her already, and to give rise to more would be foolish when there was important work at hand.

The woodcutters had been busy, and where a stand of trees had been a month ago there was now little more than a field of stumps. This annoyed Pentacoste, for she did not want to take the time to stay within the shadow of the trees, but neither did she intend to expose herself to view. Reluctantly she followed the clumps of brush that stood near the trees, wincing at the crackle her steps made as she trod on wood chips left by the cutters. She went as quickly as she could without making too much noise, her casula drawn around her face, making her a bit too warm. As she reached the hillock north-west of the fortress, she gratefully abandoned the noisy footing for the rough sand.

Now she moved more quickly, her skirts held up to keep them from tripping her as she sank to the tops of her heuse. She knew her destination as surely as she knew the texture of the wool she wove during the day. There was magic in the fabric, in the knots she put in the fabric, but there was greater magic in this; offerings to the old gods always brought the might of storms and mountains with them. The night was her ally, full of the presence of the old gods. She wanted to draw them to her, to surround herself with their power so that they would do her will. In their holy place she would bind them to her with the knots she had made.

The cove was deep, a hollow in the low cliff shaped by rocks and the roots of trees from the forest just above; occasionally the lowest part was wet, but not tonight. Pentacoste was delighted at the firm, damp sand, and as she stepped inside the ring of carved wooden offerings, she did a little dance, humming to herself. In the old days, before the White Christ came, women often danced for the old gods: according to what was whispered in the village, they still did on feast days in Oeldenburh. Her own offering was held tightly in her hand, and she raised this over her head so that the old gods could see it clearly before she tied it to the massive, broken roots projecting from the wall of the cove. She spun and swayed and tossed her head, sweat holding her linen bliaut to her skin. It was a pity, she thought, that the old gods could see her, for they would long to share her dancing. She opened her arms as if to embrace the sky, and turned in a circle until she was dizzy and panting.

Pentacoste selected the part of the root that looked most like scrawny fingers. Then she pulled five strands of her hair and tied them to what she decided was the middle finger of the root: it would be the most powerful omen. Then she took the little carved figure and licked it, her tongue lingering on the rough cross in the center of the figure's chest. Before she tied it onto the root, she blew on its face and said, "This is your breath, Giselberht, my monk-husband, and it is leaving you. I do not want to remain here, with less freedom than your widow and none of the pleasures of your wife, and no children to value me. I will be shut of you at last, of this marriage that is less than widowhood. If you will not be husband to me, I will be your widow. The breath is going out of you, and you will die of it. Every breeze will steal from you." She blew again. "The old gods will take your breath from your lungs. And I will be released from you at last." The third time she blew she also kissed the figure. "Farewell, Giselberht." As she fixed the little figure in place, she seemed to hear Giselberht's voice, as soft and distant as the night breeze, speak her name in regret.

She wrapped her casula around her shoulders and stood in the center of the offerings set up in the cove. She basked in the gathering she sensed. There were old gods all around this place, making the night thrum with their presence. She was smiling as she made her way back along the beach toward the brush.

"We can take her," whispered one of the two men who had watched her.

"Why?" asked the other, his voice no louder than the first's.

"Ransom," said the first, a battle-scarred, bearded man whose long, fair hair was clubbed at the back of his neck. "They'd pay a lot to get her back." He glowered. "We should have captured more of the others than we did. We could make it up with her."

"Her husband is a monk now," said the other. "I doubt he'd give anything for her, or let the fortress ransom her once he learned what she was doing out here. He would probably thank us for ridding him of her, since she is leaving poppets for the old gods." Karagern was rangier than when he was dismissed from the fortress, and he had grown a little; he kept his beard and hair short, in imitation of the men-at-arms at Leosan Fortress.

"Take her for ourselves. We're short on women," said Valdic.

"You don't want that one," said Karagern with great certainty.

Valdic was disgusted. "Then why did you want to watch for her? What good does it do?"

Karagern smiled unpleasantly, and motioned for Valdic to follow him. "If she came to this place," he said as he started cautiously after Pentacoste, "it means that she has some way in and out of the fortress that does not require anyone to open the gates, not at the fortress and not at the stockade. Such knowledge is useful."

"How do you—" Valdic broke off. "Yes. Of course you are right."

"Come on, then," Karagern urged.

Of the two of them Valdic was the more experienced tracker, and the better at moving through the trees without making much sound. After a short distance he took the lead, making sure that Karagern was never more than two steps behind him.

They kept to the shelter of the trees as they watched Pentacoste press through the gap in the stockade wall, Valdic muttering, "You couldn't do that. Only a boy could fit through that space."

"There are boys with Helgi," said Karagern. "Two of them could do the work for us." He slipped up to the stockade and made his way to the place where Pentacoste had gone. He peered through, and to his surprise could not see her anywhere. There was no noise from the animal pens, and no alarms shouted from the parapet. He narrowed his eyes, remembering his own long hours on watch. Somewhere along this part of the wall, there was a way in. He knew it as he knew the sound of his own heartbeat. Slowly he moved back to where Valdic waited for him.

"Did you find your door?" asked the older man in an undervoice.

"Not exactly, but I have found where it must be," he answered. "She'll be back in a few more nights. We will watch the stockade, not the cove, and we will discover the place, now that we know where to look for it." He rubbed his eyes, then pointed up to the parapet. "Make sure the guards cannot see you. They will raise the alarm if they do."

"Let them," said Valdic.

Karagern was not so sanguine. "If they think someone is watching their walls, they might investigate more closely. That would not serve our purpose."

Valdic shrugged. "There will be another way if this one fails."

Since he had no wish to be drawn into a dispute with the older man, Karagern changed the subject. "How long will it be until we have money for the men we caught?"

"If the messenger can find a King's man at Hamburh, perhaps a month. If he must go to Bremen, it will take longer." Valdic slapped his hand on the padded leather tunic he wore. "We can always sell them to the Danes if the King will not give ransom. We need not fear we will profit. In these times anyone taking to the road must know that there is always a chance of capture."

"What about the families of the men?" Karagern could not help asking; it was a question that had troubled him when he was a soldier.

"What family has more than twenty gold coins in a lifetime? They will be able to ransom only one. It must be the King or the White Christ that saves them." said Valdic as he started into the forest, tugging at the horn-sewn sleeve of Karagern's broigne.

Karagern could not dispute that. "And the monks will not pay ransoms." He shook his head at the foolishness of it, and fell into step behind Valdic.

"A poor thing, being wife to a monk," said Valdic, keeping to a path he knew with his bones rather than his eyes.

"Worse for her than most," said Karagern, with the comprehensive cynicism of his youth, and the lingering desire Pentacoste stirred in him.

As she shoved the two stones to reset the hidden door, Pentacoste could not help but smile. She had made the yarn perfectly, and the figure she had carved, although small, was clearly a monk. She had given it her husband's name and said the spell correctly. There had been whispers in the wind as she danced; the old gods were pleased with her offering. They would do her bidding because she had pleased them. How long would it take? she wondered. When could she expect the monks of Holy Cross to send word that Giselberht was dead at last? She Signed herself out of habit, and started toward her quarters, going up the narrow stairs with care, for she would have to pass Ranegonda's chamber before she came to her own.

She reached her chamber without discovery, smiling a little at Daga, who was in the grip of sleep brought on by mead mixed with pansy and wolfsbane. No one could say anything against her, for her waiting-woman had been in her chamber all night. There could be no suspicions about her that did not compromise her women as well. Smiling, Pentacoste removed her bliaut and her chanise, and climbed naked into her bed. It was disappointing to have Margerefa Oelrih gone, she thought, for now she was constantly besieged by Berengar, who thought that he now had the advantage. With a contemptuous smile, Pentacoste laid her head on the pillow Giselberht had given her as one of his wedding presents.

Shortly before dawn the village and Leosan Fortress were awakened by shouts and cries coming from the newly installed gate of the stockade. Early-rising villagers broke off their labors as the din increased.

"Let us in! It is Margerefa Oelrih!" shouted one of those on the far side of the gate as a dozen woodcutters rushed to draw back the bolt.

From the parapets of the fortress, Rupoerht saw the mounted men pressing against the doors. He reached for the wooden horn and sounded it three times, paused, and blew it three times more, putting the fortress on alert.

"What is it?" demanded Ulfrid as he came along the narrow walkway. "Why did you—" He pointed to the horn.

"Out there. Beyond the stockade. It is the Margerefa returning." He peered into the watery pre-dawn light, trying to see more clearly.

"The Margerefa?" said Ulfrid. "Why would he return?"

"I don't know," said Rupoerht, who disliked each of the ideas he had on the matter. "But there must be a reason he has come back. He said when he left that he would not be here again until autumn."

"Is there danger?" asked Ulfrid, and glanced at Maugde, who had been standing his watch at the north-eastern quadrant of the walls. "Where are the men-at-arms?"

"There is nothing out to sea," he said, to account for his coming to them.

"We need more men up here, ready," said Rupoerht. "If we are going to have to fight, we must prepare."

Below the slaves were struggling with the gate, six of them working to pull it open. Near them, unfinished, was Saint-Germanius's counter-weight device that in a week or two would do the task with two men instead of six.

"The stockade gate is open," said Maugde, pointing to the gate. "Look."

The Margerefa was the first through, riding directly for the fortress; he had lost his heaum and there was a large, purple bruise on his forehead, visible even in the early gloom of morning. His men tagged after him, two of them tied into their saddles, one man riding pillion.

"What happened?" asked Rupoerht of the air.

"We'll know soon enough," said Ulfrid, and leaned down to yell at the slaves to move faster.

"They must have been in a fight," said Maugde. "A few of them are wounded. Look at Jouarre."

"And where is his wife?" asked Ulfrid with an inward shudder as he thought of Flogelind. He Signed himself for protection.

In the Marshaling Court a half-dozen men had already gathered, most of them still tugging on their leather broignes and coiffes, preparing to fight. Walderih had already gone to the armory and was pulling out spears and swords and bucklers, handing them to the men who approached him.

At last the gates were open enough to admit the Margerefa and his men; Rupoerht sounded the horn to signal that the first of them had arrived.

Ranegonda rushed, limping, out of the landward tower, arriving at the gates in time to lift her skirts to Margerefa Oelrih. Her long braids were still wrapped together down her back, and her bliaut was not belted. "Give you welcome," she said automatically as she watched the Margerefa struggle off his horse. In the half-light the blood on his broigne and forehead looked nearly black.

"And thankful," said Margerefa Oelrih. He leaned against his big roan mare, holding himself upright by clinging to his saddle. "There were Danes, a large party of them. We fought them." He coughed twice, spat, and looked down at himself. "They fought hard."

"Yes," said Ranegonda, signaling to Kynr. "Get the women up. Tell them to bring their herbs and dressings." She was about to wave him away, but added, "Fetch Saint-Germanius. Tell him there are wounded men."

The man-at-arms swung around and jogged toward the seaward tower.

"They captured a few of my men. And two women. We fought hard. We killed three of them," said Margerefa Oelrih with a strangled sob. "They will make slaves of them, brand them, sell them."

"How many?" asked Ranegonda as the remaining men pressed their mounts through the gates.

"Four men," he muttered.

In the increasing light Ranegonda could see the blood on his shoulder and the pallor of his features. "Hold on, Margerefa. I will get help for you." She heard the horn, and knew that they were all inside. "Close the east gate, and set guards," she ordered. "And Aedelar," she added to the nearest man-at-arms, "fetch Ormanrih. I must see him at once."

"Yes, Gerefa," he said, rushing to obey her.

Margerefa Oelrih groaned and his horse shied. The Margerefa sank to his knees, one hand grasping the stirrup. "We fought. Hard."

"Where is Winolda?" asked Ranegonda of Chlodwic as he rushed toward the gates to help close them. "Culfre is watching the fire in the light room. I want his wife, and her herbs. Get them." She motioned to Ewarht, who had started toward the ramparts. "Wake Captain Meyrih and his wife. Put them to work tending these men. And rouse the rest of the slaves."

Ewarht made a gesture of assent. "It is done, Gerefa."

She was about to summon Duart when she saw Saint-Germanius coming toward her, a small case in his hands. He was in his black bliaut, as neat as if he had been given hours to prepare for this meeting; his movements were swift and unhurried at once. As he reached her, he offered her a Roman salute. "I brought my instruments and medicaments."

"Thank you," she said, profoundly relieved that he had anticipated her need. She felt something else as well, a comfort as welcome as shade on a hot day. "The Margerefa is hurt."

"I see," said Saint-Germanius, reaching for the reins of the Margerefa's horse before he bent down to give a superficial inspection to the wounds. "This is a bad injury, and I cannot treat it properly without cleaning it; there is leather and cloth embedded in his flesh. He will need attentive care, not just a rag tied over the hurt. I know Brother Erchboge will not approve, but will you authorize me to fire the bathhouse?" he asked, his voice steady.

"Why?" She had already started away from him, but this request brought her back. "Would it help?"

"It is easier to treat wounds if they are clean, and if the men bathe, it will enable me to see how extensively they are injured. If they do not bathe, injuries could be overlooked. And some of them may need to wash their blood off," said Saint-Germanius in the same unhurried way; he missed those long-vanished centuries when bathing was not feared as the sins of vanity and pride.

Ranegonda nodded. "Very well. Duart will tend to it." She regarded the chaos in the Marshaling Court with a growing sense of despair. "How are we to care for all these men? We haven't supplies enough, and if the Danes are making raids, how can we get more?"

"It will be done," said Saint-Germanius gently as he knelt beside the Margerefa. "Where are you cut?"

"Shoulder," said the Margerefa in a faint voice. "And thigh."

Saint-Germanius gave a swift, appraising glance. "I'll take care of you," he promised, and rose to his feet with the larger man in his arms; he saw the astonishment in Ranegonda's eyes; he raised his brows. "Those of my blood are known for their strength," he said.

"He is no light burden," said Ranegonda, too caught up in this emergency to be surprised by Saint-Germanius's feat; she hurried toward Duart, giving him instructions to have the bathhouses fired up before she went to check on the other men.

"Head. Hurts." There was sweat on Margerefa Oelrih's face and a white line around his mouth when Saint-Germanius set him down in the bathhouse. "There were. Too many of them."

"Sit still and let me see how extensive your wounds are," said Saint-Germanius with the composure he had learned more than two thousand years before at the Temple of Imhotep. He propped the Margerefa on a bench with the stone wall at his back. "Try not to move."

The Margerefa yelled as Saint-Germanius tugged off his broigne; his double-layered chanise was dark with blood. "One of their axes," he said, panting with pain.

"A bad wound," Saint-Germanius said without apparent distress; he had thought it would be worse. "I will need bandages to keep it from opening. And you will have to rest in order to recover." As he spoke he considered his predicament: in this place where every scrap of cloth was precious, obtaining bandages was not easily done. He would have to convince Ranegonda they were necessary. "Hold still if you can, Margerefa." Carefully he probed the shoulder wound with two fingers.

Behind him the door opened and Duart stepped into the bathhouse. "The Gerefa said you want the bath heated."

"Yes," he said without taking his attention away from Margerefa Oelrih. "And I will want a pot of water set on the boil."

Duart was shocked. "A pot of water? For what reason?"

"The Romans of old boiled their tools, and I have learned their ways," he answered. "It is not your practice here, I know, but I am a foreigner and my ways are foreign."

The monitor was filled with disapproval. "Brother Erchboge has said that the Romans of old turned against the followers of the White Christ."

"They may have," answered Saint-Germanius in deliberate evasion. "It is not their religion that interests me, only their healing arts."

"That is found in prayer," said Duart.

"Then let us pray, by all means," said Saint-Germanius; he could see the white of Margerefa Oelrih's collarbone at the lower edge of the wound. "Tell the swineherd, Nisse, that I will need to buy pigs' guts from him. I will want short lengths." He had the needles to sew the wound closed, and with the intestines could have the strong material he required for the task. A new idea occurred to him. "And bring me all the selvage from the looms." That would do for bandages until he could get proper strips of cloth.

"It will be done," said Duart grudgingly. He made a gesture to show he washed his hands of anything Saint-Germanius might do. "The Gerefa has said I am to follow your orders." As he started out of the bathhouse, Amalric appeared in the door, half-dragging, half-carrying Gallaen.

"Where?" he asked breathlessly.

"Bring him over here," said Saint-Germanius, indicating another of the benches. He paid no heed to the shock in Duart's face, but put his attention on the young man-at-arms. "Careful with him."

Amalric gave heed to this admonition. He handled Gallaen as if the man were made of crockery. "Now what?" he asked when he had settled Gallaen on the bench.

"Would you mind staying here to assist me?" Saint-Germanius asked Amalric, noticing that Duart was lingering in the doorway. "I will need help if I am to care for these wounded."

There was a fleeting hesitation, then Amalric nodded. "Very well," he said.

"Good," said Saint-Germanius. It would be less difficult to get the cooperation of the rest of the residents of the fortress if one of their number worked with him and could vouch for him. "Get his clothes off, and as soon as the water is heated, wash him."

"All over?" asked Amalric, doing his best not to appear too shocked.

"All over," Saint-Germanius confirmed. "And take care to keep his wounds from bleeding again. These men have already lost too much blood."

"They are pale," said Amalric, knowing that some response was expected of him. He started to take the broigne off Gallaen, and then stopped. "He is bleeding still. From the side."

"Then undress him and put your hand against the wound and press it," said Saint-Germanius, who had most of the clothes off Margerefa Oelrih; the wound on his thigh was superficial, although it looked dreadful, swollen and chafed. He directed his attention to the swollen bruise on Oelrih's brow. "How badly does your head hurt, Margerefa?"

"It is . . . there are rats in my skull," he said, and gulped for air.

Saint-Germanius had the answer he expected. "You will need constant watching for a day and a night," he said. "If you worsen during that time, it will be a bad sign for you."

It was an effort for Margerefa Oelrih to Sign himself, but he managed it. "May the White Christ guard me."

"We will be certain that one of the women does, as well," said Saint-Germanius, and went on soothingly. "You will feel better once I have stitched your shoulder closed."

Margerefa Oelrih gave a ragged cry. "It is a bad omen."

Amalric echoed this sentiment. "They say that those whose wounds are closed seal infection inside them."

Knowing that he should have anticipated such a reaction, Saint-Germanius said, "Possibly that would be the case, but I have something here that will drive the infection out." He tapped a small vial, one of the few to survive his shipwreck. "It is a sovereign remedy for such injuries, taught to Christians by the Apostle Luke, who was a physician and had inspired knowledge." He had used that facile explanation more than once in the last six hundred years; generally it sufficed.

"It is said that those who are of the company of the White Christ were given the power to cure all ills and cast out all demons," said Amalric, his eyes widening as he stared at the case open at Saint-Germanius's feet. "How do you come by such knowledge?"

Again Saint-Germanius used the answer that he had offered many times before. "It is knowledge given to those who study at the feet of great priests," he replied, though the great priests he meant had been the servants of Imhotep and not the White Christ.

"Then Brother Erchboge cannot object," said Amalric with undisguised relief, and gingerly resumed the task of undressing Gallaen.

A short while later two unconscious men-at-arms were brought to the bathhouse—Wipertic and Leodegar. The men carrying them left them on the floor, hurrying off before either Saint-Germanius or Amalric could ask them any questions.

Saint-Germanius left Margerefa Oelrih for a moment to give a quick examination of the two men: Wipertic was breathing high and fast and his face was the color of chalk; his pulse was racing but without power. Saint-Germanius shook his head and for the benefit of Amalric Signed himself. "This one is beyond saving," he said quietly. Leodegar's shoulder was out of joint and he had a nasty cut on his forearm, but otherwise there was nothing more seriously wrong. "I think this one will live."

"How can you be certain?" asked Amalric, who had finally got Gallaen's clothes off him.

"I cannot be, not absolutely," said Saint-Germanius as he reached for his case. He wished he had syrup of poppies to give Wipertic to lessen his suffering, but at least he had recently made an anodyne tincture of certain roots and flowers. He opened the vial and dropped a little onto Wipertic's mouth.

"Why do you do that, if the man will not live?" asked Amalric as Saint-Germanius rubbed Wipertic's throat to make him swallow.

He answered without thinking. "The man is in agony. I want to spare him any more suffering."

"Brother Erchboge will not permit you to do that," warned Amalric. "The White Christ demands suffering, because He suffered. It is worthy for Christians to share in the anguish of the White Christ. You endanger the soul of the dying if you seek to lessen the pain." He Signed himself.

Saint-Germanius raised his head and stared at Amalric, his dark eyes unreadable. "Do you truly believe that?" he asked at last.

"I believe it," said Amalric, but he could not face Saint-Germanius's penetrating gaze.

After he smeared more of the thick liquid across Wipertic's mouth, Saint-Germanius turned back to Leodegar. He stood, assessing the amount of strength he would need to put the shoulder-joint to rights again; it was best done quickly, he knew, but with no more stretching or twisting than absolutely necessary. Then he reached down and began the process, working as efficiently as he could; it was not long before he had restored the joint and placed Leodegar against a bench to protect that side of his body.

"You do that handily," said Amalric, trying to make amends for what he had said. He placed Gallaen's chanise over his body for modesty.

"I have some experience in this work," said Saint-Germanius. "He will have to guard this arm, and it will be weak for some time, but eventually it will be strong again if he does not demand too much of it before it has healed." He met Amalric's eyes. "I am almost certain of it."

"But not entirely," said Amalric.

"There is always the will of God and the White Christ," said Saint-Germanius. "No man can oppose that."

"No," said Amalric, and looked less troubled than he had been.

The bathhouse was starting to heat up as the fire lit in the oven on the other side of the wall from the large stone tub began to blaze. Over the tub the first wraiths of steam appeared.

Saint-Germanius went back to the Margerefa and said, speaking with great care, "I want you to get into the water, Margerefa, and I want you to wash your wounds."

Weakly Margerefa Oelrih Signed himself. "It is not fitting. We have been told. To wash invites the Devil."

"If you wish to recover, you will do this," said Saint-Germanius, and went on, hoping that he had chosen the best way to persuade the Margerefa that the cleaning was necessary. "They say the White Christ bathed his followers in the river to wash away the evil in their souls. You must wash away the evil of the Danes that was on their axes."

"There is evil. In their axes," said the Margerefa.

"Then ask the White Christ to cleanse you," said Saint-Germanius, and bent to lift the Margerefa again.

The door of the bathhouse banged open and Brother Erchboge strode in. His gaunt face was alight with emotion and zeal. He strode forward, holding out his hand to stop the wrongs he saw before him. "It is what I feared."

Amalric stepped back, away from the monk's outrage, but Saint-Germanius continued his task of lowering the Margerefa into the water. "What is there to fear here, good Brother?" he asked quietly.

"You are seeking to bring these men to the ways of the flesh," he declared, his anger growing sharper. "You have tainted them."

"Not I," said Saint-Germanius, rising now that the Margerefa was secure. "I have sought to rid them of taint." He addressed Brother Erchboge directly. "These men have fought the Danes, who worship the old gods. You have said yourself that there is contamination in this worship. Therefore it must be necessary to wash away all traces of the old gods before the White Christ may work to save these injured men."

Amalric regarded Saint-Germanius with increased respect. "Yes," he said, "the Danes dedicate their weapons to the old gods."

Brother Erchboge halted and stood silent for a moment. "The water here has not been blessed," he said with a gesture of condemnation.

"Then you are come in good time to correct that," said Saint-Germanius, and stepped aside to give the monk access to the large stone tub. "Neither Captain Amalric nor I have the right to do such a thing, but you are dedicated to the White Christ and may invoke His aid."

Faxon appeared in the door behind the monk, carrying the front end of a litter where another of Margerefa Oelrih's men lay, groaning steadily from the pain of a broken leg. "This is the last of the ones who are badly hurt," he announced.

As if he had been shoved or kicked, Brother Erchboge lurched forward and put his hands into the tub. "In the Name of the White Christ, and for His glory, let this water be consecrated to His work." He spoke quickly, in a low mutter that seemed more a curse than a blessing.

The Margerefa Signed himself. "The White Christ. Protect you."

"And all good Christians," said Brother Erchboge as he bolted for the door. He looked back over his shoulder once, staring at Saint-Germanius with such detestation that his features appeared to be a carved mask rather than a human face. "I will pray for these men, that they will not suffer because of you."

As Amalric watched the monk go, he said to Saint-Germanius, "He will not forget you made him do this, foreigner."

"No," said Saint-Germanius thoughtfully. "I don't suppose he will."

Text of a letter from Brother Andoche at Leosan Fortress to Brother Haganrih at the Monastery of the Holy Cross. Carried by Geraint in the company of Ranegonda, Aedelar, and Culfre.

In the Name of the White Christ and those who have died in His Name, the kiss of peace on this first Lord's Day in August, 938.

You have been told already of the men who have died protecting Margerefa Oelrih. Sadly we must add the man-at-arms Gallaen to their numbers. He had been recovering with the rest, but then he worsened, and in a short while he was lost in a delirious fever from which he never awakened. We pray that the White Christ raises him up to be with Him in Paradise.

The Margerefa has said that he will remain here at Leosan Fortress for another week while his own wounds knit. He is much better now, and he has been able to ride for half a day without becoming too weak to stay in the saddle. For this we thank the Mercy of God, and give glory to the White Christ.

We have not yet received any word of ransom being demanded for the four men who were taken by the Danes, or for the women. The King has said that he does not want one copper coin going to the cause of his enemies, but he does permit the ransoming of his vassals. If the men cannot be returned because of death or because they have been carried beyond the Danish territories and sold to others, King Otto has said that he will not be satisfied until the price of these men is given to their families. Yet it is not possible to demand the wergeld from these savages, or to obtain any word from them as to the fate of these men, and so the Margerefa has given me the task of pleading with you to go to Oeldenburh for the purpose of asking those who still trade with the Danes to carry word to them, offering to pay for the return of those good Saxons who are their captives.

It is the wish of the Margerefa Oelrih that the fate of the women be discovered, as well. If they have been killed, their husbands must be told so that they may marry again. If they have been made whores or concubines then there can be no question of their return. If they have been branded as slaves it is also impossible to accept them as chaste, and only if they wish to serve a Prioress of unblemished reputation may they come again into Germania. The Margerefa has said that it is not fitting that we should suffer the insult of disgraced women, and if such shame is given to any of his vassals the Danes will be made to answer for it.

For your charity to the men of the Margerefa, his prayers to your good and his thanks, for in serving him you serve also the cause of King Otto, which is always the cause of the White Christ. The four sacks of early grain are much welcomed and will be tasted first at Mass. Though there is grain ripening in the village fields at this hour, it is not yet ready for harvest, and the headman of the village has said that some of the ears are not thriving as he would wish. It is said that the sultriness of the weather is the cause of this, but some fear it is the fault of those who still pray to the old gods, and bring misfortune to the village. The other villagers tell the same story of poor yield, and although it might be thought that they do this to keep grain for themselves, the woman serving as Gerefa has said that the fields are truly not as bountiful as she had hoped they would be. Your grains appear to be in better heart, which is certainly a sign that the White Christ favors all you do. Let us pray that the misguided and erring villagers who leave tokens for the old gods will learn from their harvest that the White Christ is not mocked, nor is He betrayed without exacting His just retribution.

The men who have died are buried in the village and their names are enrolled in the records of the muniment room of the fortress. At the order of the Margerefa I will add them to the list I have kept for him, to be presented to King Otto when we once again bow to him.

If it is your decision to go to Oeldenburh and do as the Margerefa requests you will be rewarded by King Otto when the Margerefa reports all you have done. If you cannot do this, then no blame shall be held, for those who devote themselves to the White Christ cannot be said to be blameful. Rest assured that your piety protects you as surely as a regiment of mounted soldiers would, and that if you choose to protect yourselves from the dangers of those who are far from salvation no fault will attach to that choice.

All this at the behest of Margerefa Oelrih, and with the prayers of all his men.

Brother Andoche

11

"You are very beautiful," Saint-Germanius whispered as he reached out to draw Ranegonda, naked, into his arms.

She went rigid. "How can you say that?"

"Because it is true," he said softly, then went on candidly. "All right. Since you will have it: you are not pretty. But you are beautiful, and that is the rarer quality."

"And in the dark you do not have to see my scars," she said, still holding back from him; though the night was warm she shivered, crossing her arms over her chest. "You can tell me that and pretend—"

Deliberately, tenderly, he touched her face. "I see them," he told her. "The dark makes no difference."

She pressed her lips together and pulled away from him, going to the narrow window and staring out at the distant line of spent waves glistening in the moonlight. "You cannot believe that."

"But I do," he said, and went toward her, his sleeveless black chanise very like the tunica he had worn a thousand years before. He stood behind her, not quite touching her except to brush her hands with the back of his. "Tell me, Ranegonda," he said, his voice low, "why will you not believe that I find you beautiful? What must I do to convince you?"

"Pentacoste is beautiful," said Ranegonda in a small, hard voice.

"She is certainly lovely," said Saint-Germanius in an even tone. "She is like a large, brilliant blossom with a heavy scent and poison at its heart. But she is not beautiful. You are." He laid his hand on her neck; her braids rested against his wrist. "I know you, Ranegonda. I know you are beautiful."

She refused to hear him because she yearned too much to accept his avowal; she put her hands to her face, shaking her head. "Look at me, see what I am. There were five of us once. Three died of the Great Pox. Giselberht was not taken by it at all. I lived. I am the token."

"The Great Pox is a terrible disease," said Saint-Germanius quietly, and thought of the thousands upon thousands he had seen struck down by it over the centuries. At first it had seemed to him an implacable enemy, one that struck with merciless hatred; in time he realized that it was not attacking humanity, but that humanity was susceptible to it, and when it was present, people died.

"Yes. It is terrible. Doesn't it frighten you, to be so near to it?" She turned abruptly toward him, facing him; his hand dropped from her neck. "What of the danger you are in? The miasma might still linger."

"No, it doesn't frighten me. I am in no danger," he said truthfully and compassionately, his dark eyes filled with an echo of her pain. "And it need never frighten you again."

She Signed herself. "It is the master of Kings. Nothing, no one has power against it."

"Yes. But those who have survived it will not be its vassals again, for it may strike but once," he said carefully, and when she stared at him incredulously, he went on. "You are beyond its reach. I give you my word. If another outbreak should come, it will not take you. Those scars you regard with such horror are your badge of honor, and seals to protect you, a pledge of your delivery." Again he touched her face, this time lingeringly, then lowered his hands slowly, his fingers brushing her arms, her breasts, her hands. "There is nothing you—"

"They do not let those who have had the Great Pox marry, because of the miasma they carry," she said, challenging him.

"And they are in error," he responded, refusing to be provoked into an argument. His hands closed on hers.

"The Bishop himself said that women who have had the Great Pox could carry it to their husbands and their children. None of us is safe." She looked at him directly, refusing his comfort. "My scars are the omen; I would bear death, not life."

Taking a chance, Saint-Germanius said, "Your Bishop is a fool." His hands tightened, then relaxed. "But even if there were a miasma it would make no difference to me, none at all. Those of my blood are beyond infection. And if I were not, I am still bound to you more stringently than the grip of fever. I will not forsake you, no matter what any Bishop or Pope or King might say. It is not in my nature to do that."

Her expression did not change, but tears welled in her grey eyes.

His throat ached as he watched her, and he wished that he could weep with her; he had lost that capacity when he left his grave. "There is no reason for you to turn away from me unless it is what you, in your soul, want to do." Again he touched her face, his fingers tracing where the tears had been. His voice was deep. "In your soul, Ranegonda."

"You . . ." Her eyes beseeched him to spare her even as she moved into his arms. Her face was turned away from him though she held his shoulders fiercely. "You bewilder me, Saint-Germanius. Your kindness and your gentle ways, I do not know what they mean. Your care frightens me, sometimes. You treat me as if I—I—mattered. Why do you want me."

"Because of who you are," he said, turning her head and kissing the line of her brow softly. He felt her body through the thin linen of his sleeveless chanise. "Because it is as I have said: I am bound to you; I have been since you restored me to life. You do matter to me." He drew back just enough to be able to look deeply into her eyes. "From the moment I tasted your blood, I was bound to you."

"Yes; yes, you have said this to me," she murmured, caught now in the power of his eyes and the splendor of the moonlight. A frisson passed over her and she felt the strength of him as if he were the might of the tides, as constant and as inexorable. "From the first."

"And I knew you, as if you were flesh of my flesh." His voice had dropped to a deep, clear purr. "From that moment you have been precious to me."

Her arms went around his neck, her taut, lean body pressed against his. She wanted his caresses as she longed for salvation but she could not speak the words aloud, and she could not make herself kiss him, afraid that he would draw from her or find some excuse to make light of her desire. Or perhaps he would make a claim on her, demanding her utter capitulation to him, in her will and her station as well as her flesh. She had no words to tell him of her longings, or of her fears, and her unschooled body was awkward in its awakened need of him. She wanted to flee as much as she wanted to lock herself to his side, and her ambivalence shook her to the limits of her being.

He sensed all this, and his answer was a kiss, one that was long and thorough, his passion increasing with her arousal as he held her, his arms moving down her back to bring them still closer together. A second, more abandoned kiss followed, and a third.

"To my bed," he whispered as they broke apart.

Her eyes were dazed, wild. "Yes," she said urgently.

He led her unerringly through his equipment, his eyes less hampered by the dark than hers. As he reached his bed, he stood aside so that she could choose where she wished to lie. "Do whatever you wish," he said as he indicated the fur coverlet. "Tell me what you want of me, Ranegonda."

She laughed a little, nervously; her hands clasped and unclasped. "I don't know how to answer you," she admitted. "What gives you pleasure, do it." She sat on the edge of the bed, staring at him. "Take your pleasure of me."

His dark eyes were filled with a sad and ironic light though he spoke without hesitation or evident discomfort. "That I can only obtain from the pleasure you feel; I am bound to you in that, as well," he reminded her quietly, watching her stretch out on the bed. A gentle smile curved his mouth. "Your pleasure *is* my pleasure. There can be no other for me. I will be fulfilled as you are, Ranegonda. You are the source of my Epiphany." He reached out and ran his hand lightly over the arch of her ribs; swiftly he bent to follow the same line with his lips, so very softly. He trailed his fingers across her shoulders.

She gasped, and reached out to him, her hands eager for the solace of his body. As he moved next to her, she caught her fingers in the loose, dark curls of his hair and pulled his head down to hers. Her lips opened to his, and their tongues met, their breath quickening.

Her breasts, small and high, fit his hands, the nipples swelling at his touch as their kiss went on; he stroked her taut belly and hip, each motion drawing her closer to him. She drew her breath sharply through her teeth as her skin grew more sensitive to his touch. Then he bent his head to her breasts, nuzzling and tweaking until she sighed and her tension was replaced with vibrant receptivity. She whispered his name, her body now malleable to his hands and mouth. In a life of little luxury she sought the opulence of his passion with her own.

In joyous slowness he parted her legs and reached the secret depths between them. He lingered over the treasure he discovered there, letting her attain the highest pitch of pleasure in her own time.

Ranegonda had never felt such bone-melting rapture as Saint-Germanius gave her then. The exultation that filled her was so vast and immediate that it could never be truly remembered, only glimpsed as something ineffable made invisible by its lucidity. As she trembled, her head back, her body quivering like the strings of a kithre, there was something more than her joy that enveloped her; his desire matched her own, and as his reverent touch and supplicant lips worked their wizardry on her, their need joined as well, and carried them both on the crest of its sweet, delirious current.

Some time later she turned toward him, her eyes shining. She brushed his hair back from his forehead. "What is it you do? What do you do to me?"

"Only what is in you to do," he answered softly, and traced the line of her mouth with his finger. "I can create nothing in you, only discover what has always been there."

She shook her head. "This was never mine. There was never an omen or sign to warn me."

"It was always yours," he said, his voice dropping. "It is in your blood: blood cannot lie."

"Is that why—?" She broke off, her hand moving to cover the two little cuts he had made.

"Yes," he whispered. "Because it is the core of you, as your elation is. To have one with the other sustains me."

"I'm glad," she said dreamily. "If you can give this to me, it is well that you share it." Her eyes were half-closed and she curled against him, prepared to go to sleep.

"Ranegonda," he said, so softly that she could hardly hear him.

Her eyes opened slowly, then the heavy lids sank again. "There is no vision better than what you have shown me."

"I gave you no vision, except what a mirror might give." His sardonic smile was quickly gone.

She said nothing for a short while, and then murmured, "If this damns me, I will walk singing in Hell."

He cradled her against his side as she slept, and only nudged her to wakefulness a short time before dawn. He kissed her lightly, then moved away from her to fetch her clothes.

"I had a strange dream," she said as she pulled on her chanise.

"Which was?" he prompted her.

She frowned as she reached for her bliaut. "I dreamed that the crops were taken with a pox of their own, and that it spread through the land, so that there was no bread. The pox brought madness and death to all it touched. Everywhere there were people with the bodies of skeletons, and the dead were so many that there were not enough left to bury them." Her frown deepened. "And then there were people everywhere, all as blighted as the grain, and every one of them so desperate that the outlaws in the forest feared them. They tore through the forest and every village in Saxony, eating them like locusts, as Brother Erchboge has preached." She belted her garments, rubbing her eyes before looking toward the window. "You woke early."

"I didn't sleep," he told her. "I rarely do."

She Signed herself. "Those who do not sleep are unhallowed, if they are not in prayer or meditation."

Saint-Germanius gave a tiny shake of his head. "No. That is Brother Erchboge talking, not you."

"I don't understand these things," she said, making it an apology. "I don't understand your foreignness, for all I want you and find comfort in your presence."

It took him a long moment to answer. "You humble me, Ranegonda."

She came nearer to him, reaching out to take his hand. "Why?"

He looked past her, to a distant place that existed only in his memories. His voice was distant, hushed with remembered pain. "A long time ago, when I was much younger than I am now, I fed on terror for it was all I had, and it filled me with fear and anger, the more so, I think, because what I did was the denial of what I sought. Blood does not lie, and I refused to know the truth of it; it hurt me too deeply to know it. So I thrust it away from me and told myself that only dread was possible." He looked at her, his dark eyes enigmatic. "Then I learned to accept the gift that was given to me, to take the risk of touching, and from that time I changed. It had been hard to endure the loneliness, but I accepted it only when I was willing to know the truth in the core of blood. Now I rejoice in the bonds recognition forges and I seek them for their strength. I know the price of intimacy." He lifted her hand and kissed the palm of it. "But you are willing to receive me without understanding; you were willing from the beginning. You have never required an explanation of me, or sought to alter our bond."

"You are a foreigner, and the omens—" She stopped as he shook his head.

"This isn't a question of omens, it is a question of knowledge." He came to her, his arms going around her. "You will have to decide soon if you are still willing to have me as your lover, because your risk is growing."

"The others don't suspect us. No one has said anything," she assured him.

"Perhaps," he said.

"If they do suspect, they will say it in Confession and Brother Erchboge will denounce us both. If we are declared guilty—" She looked around the stone room, noticing that it was growing lighter. "I mustn't stay much longer."

"No, you mustn't," he agreed, releasing her. He went to the door and opened it, saying loudly enough to be heard by anyone who might be awake near the entrance to the tower, "God give you good morning, Gerefa. You are here early."

Ranegonda had come to his side. When she spoke her tone was remote. "I need to have word with you today in regard to the quarrels you have offered to make. It is necessary that we have them soon. The Margerefa will want to number them when he makes his autumn inspection, and that will mean that you do not have long to produce them."

"I fear that Radulph has not been able to spare the iron I need for the task." It was accurate enough as far as it went, and it was something that had concerned him, for the smith of Leosan Fortress made no secret of his distrust of the foreign alchemist. "I have certain ways to increase the mettle of the quarrels, but I can do that only if the iron is good."

"I will speak to him. We need more quarrels. King Otto commands we have them," said Ranegonda, and pausing only long enough to kiss the corner of his mouth, left him alone.

Saint-Germanius stood in the center of his chamber, lost in thought. In a basket by the athanor a dozen moldy rolls waited; by the following morning they would be transformed into a sovereign remedy against infection. Now he gave the bread nothing more than a single, disinterested glance; he was concerned for Ranegonda's safety, not only from the gossip of the people of the fortress and the village, but for the place itself. Though there were more men-at-arms now than there had been when he came, the outlaws and Danes were growing bolder. The time might well come when a fight could not be avoided. Then Ranegonda would be especially vulnerable, for she would be expected to defend the village and the fortress as if she were truly Gerefa and not her brother's deputy. That would be dangerous. The soldiers would dislike following a woman in combat and were not likely to defend her. It was ironic: she had less risk from her lover, he thought, than from the hazards of battle.

There was a sound on the stairs outside as the women went to the cloth room to begin the day's spinning and weaving.

"Berengar has said he will remain here all the winter if you do not send him away," said Sigrad with a rich laugh.

"He seeks to claim you for himself," said Genovefe.

Pentacoste laughed merrily. "If his father will permit it, I will not tell him to leave. Pranz Balduin is above my Dux father. So I will bow my head to whatever Pranz Balduin says, and pray that my father does not want to go to war over a daughter."

"It is only a matter of rank," one of the other women said sarcastically.

"Do not say to me that *you* would act against so powerful a lord as Pranz Balduin?" said Pentacoste in mock outrage. "My father is a reckless man, but not one who would undertake a war over me. Or any of my sisters."

The women all laughed, the sound echoing and blending as they climbed, their words lost as the echoes increased.

Saint-Germanius heard this with misgivings. He went to the door and opened it cautiously, peering out into the half-light of the morning. The sounds of the women's voices drifted down, no longer distinct, mixed to a continuous susurrus like the murmur of a slack tide.

"They do more gossiping than weaving," remarked Captain Amalric as he descended from the light room; he was at the end of his watch and he looked tired. "The other morning they were telling tales of their husbands again, and the unmarried ones laughed the loudest."

"Did they?" Saint-Germanius nodded to the Captain and was about to step back into his quarters when he realized that Amalric had something on his mind. "Do not be offended, Captain, but would you like to join me for a short while? After a long watch, you might enjoy the opportunity to sit over a slice of cheese?" Ranegonda had arranged for him to be allocated cheeses so that the people of the fortress would not remark too much on his avoidance of their communal meals. He was glad of the chance to put the cheese to some use.

"I must arrange for Geraint to take my place, but yes, then it would please me to spend a while in your company." His somber expression did not alter and this made Saint-Germanius apprehensive; whatever was troubling Captain Amalric he did not want to trust to Brother Erchboge.

"It is an honor to me," Saint-Germanius said. He stepped back and bowed to the Captain, then pulled the door closed. As he went to cut the cheese, he heard the muffled sound of women's laughter.

Captain Amalric arrived a short time later. He had removed his heaum and broigne and was adjusting his belt over his bliaut. "I'm grateful you're willing to give me your time, Comites."

Since his title was rarely used at Leosan Fortress, Saint-Germanius was instantly on the alert. "You are Captain here," he said smoothly, "and it is fitting that your visit offers me distinguishment."

Captain Amalric shrugged. "In a great city, it might be, but here . . . Let us say that it is a necessary precaution."

"Necessary in what way?" Saint-Germanius asked.

"Necessary in that I am in need of counsel that will not cause embarrassment to this place." He lowered his eyes as he sat on one of the earth-filled chests. "You are a foreigner and you will not turn what I say against the Gerefa."

"No, I will not," said Saint-Germanius with quiet conviction.

"And another would," said Captain Amalric bluntly, cocking his chin toward the ceiling to indicate the cloth room two levels above. "She would be made to answer for what happens here, and her brother could not protect her."

"Do you think he would try to?" asked Saint-Germanius as he held out two wedges of light-yellow cheese.

Captain Amalric took one of them, avoiding an answer to Saint-Germanius's question. "First quality, this is." He sniffed at it, tasted it, his eyes half-closed the better to judge the savor of the cheese. "You had it from Jennes's wife. She has the best goats and sheep."

"Yes," said Saint-Germanius, offering the second wedge to the Captain. "It is my understanding that she is regarded as the best cheesemaker in the village."

"Don't you want this?" Captain Amalric asked, hesitating to take it.

"I've fed today already. Take it with my thanks." Saint-Germanius could see the satisfaction in Captain Amalric's eyes. He watched while the Captain ate, unwilling to hurry him.

"It is good of you to permit me to speak with you," said Captain Amalric at last as he sucked his fingers. "I have been filled with distress and there has been no one who would be willing to listen to what I have learned. Ranegonda herself has forbid me to talk to her about it."

"About what?" asked Saint-Germanius. He let Captain Amalric take whatever time he needed to answer.

Captain Amalric lowered his head. "About Pentacoste, of course."

"Ah," said Saint-Germanius.

"It is more than her shameful flouting of her marriage that troubles me," he went on, still distressed at having to speak.

"What is it?" Saint-Germanius asked.

This time it was more difficult than ever for Captain Amalric to speak. "I have seen her leave this fortress by the hidden gate, always at night. I have not followed her where she goes, but I have gone to the cove sacred to the old gods, and I have seen what she has left there." He said it increasingly quickly, his nervousness becoming breathlessness as he went on. "She has been giving offerings to them, and they have sought death for many, and things for herself that no married woman should wish for. If Brother Erchboge learned of it, he would cast her out into the world. Ranegonda could not save her, and Brother Giselberht would not."

Saint-Germanius listened without any change of expression. "She does something with her spinning and her weaving, doesn't she? Those knots are not slubs; they have meaning, haven't they?" he asked when Captain Amalric fell silent.

This was also a difficult thing for Captain Amalric to answer. "Yes. All the women know it and all of them say nothing, because they are afraid of her. They say that she is powerful with the old gods, and that if they oppose her, she will bring evil upon them and their husbands and children." He Signed himself. "Everyone in the fortress and the village has seen the tokens she has left. All of them know that she would not hesitate to use her might on them."

"Does that include Ranegonda?" Saint-Germanius felt a cold certainty claim him as he spoke.

"Ranegonda must not notice anything, or she would have to tell all to Brother Erchboge and Brother Giselberht. That would be a mistake. And she would have to drown Pentacoste, or do worse than drown her. Margerefa Oelrih would not permit that to take place, and the monks would insist on it." He lifted his hands in helplessness. "What can our Gerefa do, but close her eyes to it?"

"She is leaving herself terribly exposed," said Saint-Germanius softly.

"But what else is possible?" asked Captain Amalric. "I tried to ask her about it once, and she would not allow me to say anything, then or ever. I cannot take my suspicions to Brother Erchboge, because he would then pursue Pentacoste for the White Christ, and there would be dreadful things done."

"To say nothing of what Pentacoste's father might demand if anything happened to his daughter?" Saint-Germanius ventured. He cut another wedge of cheese and handed it to Captain Amalric. "If there is so much appreciation of Pentacoste's strength, it would imply that she is not the only one leaving tokens for the old gods."

Captain Amalric stared at the far wall. "The White Christ is the Lord of King Otto," he said stiffly.

"But Leosan Fortress is a long way from King Otto," said Saint-Germanius.

"You understand, then," said Captain Amalric. "It is why we are not permitted to go to Oeldenburh, and it is unwise to speak of it often, in case it would give power to their ways. The people here are not all

Saxons, or truly Germans, and their old gods do not welcome interlopers. It is wise to placate them, and to show them respect, or face the wrath they can visit on us. The White Christ has His servants to war for him, but we are not so fortunate. The omens have always favored the old gods in this place."

"The omens," said Saint-Germanius. "Tell me more about them."

"There are many omens," said Captain Amalric evasively. "A wise man could spend his life and not learn the whole of them."

"Very possibly," agreed Saint-Germanius.

"We are on our own in this place. The King and all his men could not reach us in time to aid us, even if we possessed some way to inform him of our need. So we must rely on everything we can learn. The omens aid us."

"I understand that," said Saint-Germanius with an emotion between sympathy and exasperation.

"Ever since Gerefa Giselberht went to the White Christ, there have been more omens from the old gods. They are displeased that the Gerefa should forsake them for another. The ravens have been flying more often than the cranes have this summer," said Captain Amalric in a steady manner, although his voice was tinged with fright. "We have all seen it, and we have recognized the portent, but we say nothing, because Brother Erchboge denounces us if we remark upon it."

"The ravens are the birds of one of the old gods," said Saint-Germanius with certainty.

"They are. The cranes have been said to be the heralds of Mädchen Mairia by the monks, but there are those who still say they belong to . . . to another." Captain Amalric was once again embarrassed.

"To the old goddess of spring and planting, perhaps?" guessed Saint-Germanius, knowing that such confusion existed elsewhere. "The monks will tell you that they are not the same, but they have so much in common."

"Yes, they are alike." Captain Amalric ducked his head. "There are those who claim that they are the same, but the monks deny it." He glanced at Saint-Germanius. "The omen is still not a good one, whosever they are."

Saint-Germanius nodded. "Why is that?"

"They herald death, the ravens; the cranes bring the fruits of love; in spring there should be more cranes than ravens," said Captain Amalric as if the omen must be obvious to any sensible person over the age of six.

"And when there are not, everyone is afraid," said Saint-Germanius.

"Not if Brother Erchboge is near," said Captain Amalric dryly.

"Though I have seen him watch the sky, too. He says it is in the hope of glimpsing Heaven."

"You aren't convinced that is the case?" said Saint-Germanius. "Why?"

"Because he Signs himself when the ravens are in the air. He has said that they are the souls of the dead being sent to Hell, but I believe that he is as wary of them as we are, and for the same reason." Captain Amalric hitched his shoulder, indicating the small window with the partial view of the beach. "He has not gone down to the shore for months and months. He says it is because there is danger. I suspect his danger comes from the cove where the old gods are given tokens."

"It seems likely," said Saint-Germanius, trying to keep his voice level. He could sense the Captain's apprehension in the air like a strong odor. "He may have already decided on what course he must take to deal with those who are not faithful to the White Christ. Perhaps he does not wish to give himself away, or to put those who still worship the old gods on alert by taking notice of what they do."

Captain Amalric stared at Saint-Germanius. "The Gerefa says you are a clever one, and I have never reckoned she was in error. But I doubted her trust of you. Foreigners are often at a loss in a strange place. They do not know what to make of the people and their ways. So they see things without understanding and they mistake what they do understand." He rose from the chest. "But you are not cut of that cloth, are you?"

"I am a foreigner, as you say," Saint-Germanius responded cautiously.

"Careful and watchful," said Captain Amalric. "When I spoke of Pentacoste, you were not surprised. Would that mean that you knew something of what she has been doing?"

Saint-Germanius gave a half-smile and answered with an ease he did not feel, "It does not surprise me that a woman as defiant as Pentacoste would find a way to increase her defiance. You might have said that you had seen her enter Berengar's chamber and that would not astonish me either." It was a portion of the truth and he salved his conscience with the reminder that he had no authority to act in this place, no matter what he might know.

"I fear she does more than bow to the old gods," said Captain Amalric suddenly. "She wants to be shut of this place, and I worry she will do something unwise in her haste to be gone." He directed his gaze at the window again. "There are outlaws in the forest, not so far from this village, and most of them bow to the old gods, too. If they could be persuaded to attack us, Pentacoste would have the excuse she seeks

to be returned to her father and released from her obligations here."
Now that he had admitted his apprehension, he went on with a suggestion of relief. "She would never treat with the Danes. They would seize
her and take her as a slave, or hold her for ransom. But the outlaws
might be willing to reward her if she gave them access to the fortress."

"And there is such a way," said Saint-Germanius. "Pentacoste
knows it."

"I am afraid it's true," said Captain Amalric. "And I doubt she
would hesitate to use it if it gained her the release she seeks." He looked
directly at Saint-Germanius. "How does it seem to you?"

"I wish I could say I think your fears are groundless," he answered
slowly. "For Ranegonda's sake I wish I could say that. But there is
reason to suppose that you have at least some of the puzzle."

"You are worried, then?" asked Captain Amalric.

"Yes," admitted Saint-Germanius.

The Captain nodded twice, and then added, "It isn't only the outlaws
who trouble me."

"You are concerned that Brother Erchboge may discover what Pentacoste is doing," Saint-Germanius said, following Captain Amalric's
thought.

"Yes. Then Brother Giselberht will be sure to learn of it, and then it
will be impossible for anyone to prevent more death here." He indicated the upper levels of the seaward tower. "I know how Gerefa
Giselberht was when Pentacoste first came here. He sought to forget
Iselda and tried to lose himself in this Lorrarian beauty, but he could
not do it. He did all in his power to bind her to him, but the more he
tried, the more she laughed at him. Only when he went to the White
Christ did she cease to laugh. Brother Giselberht would have no reason
to defend her if any claim could be laid against her. Let any whisper of
treason be made and she will have to pay the price of it."

Saint-Germanius considered this for a short while. "And what would
that mean to this fortress and the village? for I assume that is what
causes you anguish."

"The King would be expected to avenge the daughter of Dux Pol, if
he hopes to retain his Lorrarian allies. At least, that is what Margerefa
Oelrih implied before he left. And he would be the one to carry out the
order of King Otto." Captain Amalric paced the stone chamber. "I
cannot raise my sword against an officer of the King. None of the men
here can. The Gerefa would have to answer the death of Pentacoste
herself, and Dux Pol would not be satisfied with less than her broken
corpse."

"If Pentacoste were guilty would it make any difference?" asked Saint-Germanius, anticipating the answer.

'She is the daughter of Dux Pol, a powerful man. No matter that she deserved death or that to permit her to live would bring dishonor to this place; Dux Pol is of greater station than any Gerefa, and for that the Gerefa must answer." Captain Amalric stood quite still. "She is almost a man, Gerefa Ranegonda. She has done all that her brother could ever require of her. It would be a pity to see her have to answer for a foreign harlot because the harlot has a noble father."

"Yes, it would be a pity," said Saint-Germanius as the stairwell began to resound with the spinning songs the women in the cloth room sang as they worked.

Captain Amalric gestured to indicate the sound. "The women are as much in her spell as the men. They would defend her if they could. Is it any wonder Pentacoste believes she is unassailable."

"From what you have described, she is," said Saint-Germanius grimly.

Text of a dispatch from Karal of Bremen, merchants' factor, to King Otto, carried by armed messenger from Luneburh to Goslar.

To my most puissant lord and King, Otto, son of Haganrih, my hurried report of what has befallen my family and those with us since the Devil's Magyars devastated our city.

It is the twentieth day of August in God's Year 938. We have reached a village half a day's walk from Luneburh and have discovered that there is no room for us here, either. They tell us that they have already taken in more than two hundred of those who fled Bremen and there is no room for more, or food to spare. Over four thousand escaped from Bremen before the Magyars sacked it—you would suppose that villagers and townsmen would open their doors to us in gratitude for their deliverance from the predations of the foe. Yet such is not the case. Everywhere we are as distrusted as the barbarians who pillaged our city. Any man of Bremen must think himself a leper for the welcome he is given. There are so few of us in this party you would imagine that we could not be refused some sign of charity, but it means nothing to the people of the town. It was the same in the smaller towns, and we were told that to the south it is worse. We have been warned that if any more of us attempt to come inside the walls, we will be repelled as if we were an invading army. This, in the wake of Brother Capravic's treachery, has been enough to reduce many of us to near madness, and the hunger that has dogged us from the time we left Bremen in flames has grown from an annoyance to a disaster nearly as great as the ruin of our homes.

If it is possible, let your Margerefas look for this Brother Capravic and treat him as the vile thing that he is. To have come to us as he did not a fortnight ago, offering what he claimed was the charity of his monastery to us, leading us away from the road and into the forest where his lawless band attacked us, taking what little we had been able to salvage from the fury of the Magyars! They were merciless as wolves, and Brother Capravic was the most pernicious of them all. He himself raped more than a dozen women and I myself saw him cut the throat of one who did not please him, and then complained that his habit was fouled with blood. No female of our company, not even Old Klothilde, who is past forty, came away unravished. All that was of value he and his men took from us: food, clothing, coins, rings, chastity; and then they pointed the way back to the road and drove us off with clubs and swords, except for the five young boys whom they kept to sell to the Danes as slaves.

Now that we have reached Luneburh, we are truly desperate. We have nothing. Already three of our number have died from hunger, and another will not be able to last much longer. The villagers here have put guards around their byres and sties as well as their houses. They have set out a sack of new cheese and some hard bread, which is all they are willing to part with. And since the gates of Luneburh are closed against us, we all face starvation if nothing can be done. I pray you, as King and as the soul of all the Germans, succor us. The roads from Bremen are already filled with bodies; do not allow their numbers to increase. Surely there is some place in this land where we can go without being pelted with rocks and filth, where we can trade honest labor for food and a place to lie safe at night. The villagers here have vouchsafed me the use of a stylus and this old parchment to write to you, which is more than the others have been willing to do. They have promised to hand this to one of your couriers, for those men regularly ride this part of the road. Because they have sworn this on your crown, I am moved to believe them and to entrust them with this report, in the hope that it will reach you before we are beyond all aid.

We have been told that there is a monastery to the north of here, the walk of a day or two in this hot weather. We have decided to go to that place and beg the monks to take us in, at least those who are weakest, and the children. There are two girls and one infant boy who are yet living, and if they can be given shelter I will thank all those who serve the White Christ. If they are not willing to do that, then I have no thought but to find the swiftest and kindest death for my family and those with us. Already my father, who has been blind for many years, has said he wishes to be *left behind, so that he will not deprive those younger and stronger than he of life. I am ashamed that I must hear him out, and more ashamed that I am tempted to do as he requests.*

In the past I have given you regular reports on the merchants in Bremen, and the trade between the Danes that continues. You have been good enough to say that this was a useful service to you. If that is truly the case, then do something to end the suffering of my family and those with us. There are now twenty-nine of us remaining. If nothing is done to save us, we will shortly be skeletons without graves to lie in. Let your answer be swift, good King, and let your mercy be bountiful. In this hour of great need, it is you we seek to uphold us, for all else has failed.

When the Magyars are driven from Germania, I vow that then I and my family, if we are yet living, will do all in our power to restore the city to its glory, and that we will labor in your good cause to make it better than it was. It is wholly fitting for us to dedicate our lives to our city and your cause, King Otto. To that end we will pray until the White Christ seals our breath forever.

> *Karal of Bremen*
> *one-time merchants' factor*
> *on the road north of Luneburh*

12

Reciting the blessing in a strong voice, Brother Erchboge lifted the basket of new bread over his head, showing it to all those gathered in the Common Hall. He had been fasting for the last two days and the bread looked more beautiful than gold. The people were on their knees in reverence and he felt as if he could ascend to Heaven if only he knew how to summon the angels to carry him. The cask of wine stood open, ready to be offered to the followers of the White Christ. It was warm and the stone room smelled of old sweat and garments in need of washing. It had rained the day before, leaving the summer air moist and clinging.

Sigrad was directly in front of Father Erchboge, her lined, sweat-spangled face bowed and her grey hair discreetly veiled. Beside her, Captain Meyrih waited for her help; he was now so blind that he rarely saw more than shadows. He had come to depend on his wife the same way Ulfrid's children did.

"When you eat this, the flesh of the White Christ will nourish you," Brother Erchboge announced, abandoning the Latin of the text in order to teach the lesson to these worshipers more effectively. "When you drink the wine, the soul of the White Christ will fill you."

"May the White Christ have mercy on us," said the people on their knees.

"Let each of you come with a humble heart," said Brother Erchboge, his eloquence increasing as he set the basket down on the altar next to the cask of wine. "Let you kneel before the Great King Who triumphed over death and harrowed Hell so that you could be saved." He selected one of the small loaves and broke it in half, raising them above his head. "We lift this to Heaven as we lift our hearts up."

"May the White Christ have mercy on us," the people chanted.

"It is fitting that you come to this place having fasted through the night and the morning, for this celestial food should not be eaten while the food of the world lingers. Only when the White Christ is uncontaminated can He work His miracles." Brother Erchboge indicated the bread again. "This is the wealth of the spirit, not the food of the flesh, free from the burdens of the world, and for that reason it satisfies after hunger as no mortal food can. It is the purity of the White Christ as we mortals can know it while bound to this sinful place. It is nourishment beyond life, fulfillment beyond the body's need."

Saint-Germanius stood just beyond the open doors, listening to the ritual with its promise, a faint, ironic smile at the corners of his mouth. He had not intended to watch the Mass, but when Ranegonda had been delayed in the village over a dispute about soured milk, he had indulged his curiosity and taken up this position just outside the Common Hall door where he would not be regarded as an intruder. When she returned, he thought, they would have a short while to themselves; not long enough to make love, but at least enough time to enjoy their privacy. He was about to turn away when he saw Berengar hurrying toward the Common Hall, his servant Ingvalt coming quickly after him.

"Move aside," Berengar said without apology as he thrust out his arm to shove Saint-Germanius aside. He was in his green linen bliaut, and in spite of the heat wore the yellow casula Pentacoste had woven for him. He had perfumed his beard with oil of cloves, and that combined with the odor of his body resulted in a nearly overwhelming presence.

"Certainly," said Saint-Germanius, stepping back so that the young nobleman could pass. "They are about to give the bread."

Berengar Signed himself. "For eternal life."

"That is the blood, I think," said Saint-Germanius seriously.

But Berengar was already beyond the door and was giving his attention to Brother Erchboge. Ingvalt hesitated before going through the large doors. He regarded Saint-Germanius narrowly, his large eyes seeming to accuse the foreigner of undreamt-of villainy. "You are not kneeling with us."

"I am not of your religion," said Saint-Germanius quietly. "It would offend the White Christ if I took His gifts. And it would offend all of you."

Ingvalt's hard look did not change. "It is wrong for you to be here at all, if that is the case. You should not look on our worship if you do not count yourself one of the followers of the White Christ."

"That's likely," said Saint-Germanius, about to step away.

"Why do you watch us at all?" asked Ingvalt suspiciously.

"I am curious to know how the White Christ is worshiped," said Saint-Germanius. "According to what I am told, there is great beauty and power in the adoration of the White Christ." Over the centuries the rituals had become more complex and more remote from their origins, and the process fascinated and troubled him.

"You could have other reasons to watch," said Ingvalt.

"I could, but I do not," said Saint-Germanius. "I only wanted to see this celebration for myself."

"It is not fitting that you should," said Ingvalt. "You are foreign and your presence is an insult to this fortress."

Saint-Germanius shook his head. "I am here because I have not yet been ransomed, as I am certain you know. In this place, it is wise for me to—"

"I will watch you, so that my master will come to no harm from your foreign ways," Ingvalt warned him abruptly, cutting him off. "Never forget I am watching you."

"Your master has nothing to fear from me," said Saint-Germanius.

"Not as long as I am with him," Ingvalt stated in a manner intended to be derogatory. "You think that if you pay compliments to the Gerefa's sister that others will be as gullible as she, but you are wrong. I see the omens."

"You study them?" asked Saint-Germanius.

Ingvalt Signed himself. "You seek to deceive me with foreign mischief. I am not so foolish. Study is for those who want to go mad. It addles the mind to put too much in it, and brings unrest to the soul. If one learns too many things, one can no longer see the omens, and you will have to go about the world without warning but what study can give you. If you study, you are made blind."

"Blind," Saint-Germanius repeated. "Are you certain?"

"As certain as I am of your evil intent," said the servant, then went abruptly into the Common Hall where Brother Erchboge was passing out the small loaves of new bread.

Saint-Germanius moved back a few more steps toward the soldiers' family quarters. The enmity of the servant did not surprise him, only that Ingvalt had dared to express it so openly. He waited a short while, listening as Brother Erchboge again admonished each recipient of the White Christ to share in the purity of the Savior. Next they would have the wine, a full cup for each person. No doubt, he thought, some of them would have visions.

In the Marshaling Court Genovefe and Winolda tended the children of the fortress, urging them to play games in a circle so that they would not easily go astray. Genovefe was an unhealthy shade of red, the sun and heat taking their toll on her. She was not paying close attention to her charges and as Saint-Germanius watched, one of the little boys swung his fist at another and the two of them went down in thrashing limbs.

Winolda shouted to the other children to remain still, for it was apparent that it would take little to turn the whole gathering into a melee; Genovefe reached out to separate the two boys and was struck in the face for her trouble.

Saint-Germanius came forward, moving quickly but without menace. He took one of the fighting boys by the shoulder and lifted the other off of the ground, the motion appearing effortless. "That will do," he said gently as one of the two boys began sobbing.

Genovefe had her hand to her face, and when she lowered it, her fingers were smeared with blood. "It is my nose," she whispered. "I'm bleeding."

"Gods of the trees! Not again! It's the weather," said Winolda, exasperated and distressed at once. "Oh, Genovefe."

Saint-Germanius bent down, keeping himself between the two boys, and while not threatening them in any way made more fighting impossible. "You've had your chance to fight, and now that chance is over," he said evenly. "No more of it now."

"No," said the one who was not crying.

"Good. You will stand there with Winolda." He gave the child a gentle push to get him moving in the direction of Culfre's wife. "And you," he said the to other, "you will dry your tears because they frighten the others. You're tired. It is time you rested, so that the heat will not rob any more of your strength."

The boy nodded as Saint-Germanius spoke, then did his best to kick the foreigner in the shins before he ran off toward his parents' quarters.

As Saint-Germanius straightened up, he looked directly at Genovefe. "Has this happened before?" he asked.

She was staring at the blood that continued to run, her cupped hand filling with it. "Yes," she whispered in fright, her eyes huge in her ruddy face. "Not often, no, not often. But occasionally. Yes. When the weather is like this, I have bled if I became too hot, and the miasma reaches me. Certain afflictions rise on hot air. It is never a good thing, bleeding from the nose. It is the omen of coming death."

"Why do you say that?" Saint-Germanius asked. "It may be true that someone of this fortress or the village may die soon, but not for your nosebleed. There have been many others afflicted like you."

"It is death because the blood comes from the head," said Genovefe softly. "It is a warning to someone living here, perhaps to me." She stared at her hand and then at him. "How can you not know that? There is always a reason for blood, and only the prideful ignore it." She looked around apprehensively. "Someone at this fortress will die by violence before the moon is full."

Saint-Germanius knew better than to dispute this. "Then perhaps we should stop the blood as quickly as possible."

Winolda regarded her anxiously. "I have used stringent herbs to stop it in the past," she said to Saint-Germanius. "Prayers are not enough. My herbs are in my quarters. I'll fetch them." Her apprehension was increasing. "The blood is a bad sign. Truly, it is."

"You have the children to watch," said Saint-Germanius. "Let me look after Genovefe. I will work no foreign harm on her, I give you my word: I have a preparation that may help her. If it does not stop her bleeding, then I will watch the children for you while you attend to her."

Genovefe's eyes grew large with anxiety. "There is nothing . . . I must stay here."

"On the contrary," said Saint-Germanius sensibly, "you must not remain here where the sight of your blood could cause the children to take fright." He looked at Winolda. "Tell her it is best that she come with me."

She nodded several times. "It is best," she said without any emotion at all.

"Good," said Saint-Germanius as if he had not noticed how she sounded. "Come, Genovefe. Winolda will mind the children for you. Let me help you out of my duty to your Gerefa." He was prepared to carry her, but she would not allow him to touch her; she staggered after him toward the seaward tower, her hands clapped over her face, blood leaking through her fingers.

Once inside his chamber he gave her a tincture to drink with water, and then held out a length of selvage. "Use it to clean your face and soak up the blood," he recommended. "Otherwise you'll stain your clothes."

Genovefe wadded up the selvage and thrust it under her nose. "It is wrong blood, this blood. You will have to destroy this," she said, holding up the matted selvage. "This can bring much evil if it is not . . . It must be got rid of."

"You must do what you think best; take the selvage with you," said Saint-Germanius, unwilling to be drawn into any dispute with her. He waited a short while, then asked in a disinterested way, "This bleeding from the nose—how often has this happened to you?"

"This is the first time this summer," she said. "Last year it did not happen, but the year before it happened twice."

"I see," said Saint-Germanius, thinking that it probably had happened oftener and she had been able to conceal it. "It has happened in the summer, then? And have you noticed that your head aches more before the blood comes, or that your eyes are sore during harvest?"

"It would be a very bad omen," she told him. "With the harvest under way, blood could harm it."

"For you, most assuredly the blood could be harmful if the condition remains untreated. I notice that you are very flushed; I suppose that has been the case before when you have bled from the nose," he said affably so that his observations would not frighten her. "But if you suffer in that way, you can alleviate it with tinctures." He wished he had a proper array of medicaments to work with, but even with what little he had he could spare her the worst of her reaction.

"The bleeding is a sign, an omen. It is the omen that makes my face redden and my head hurt. Tinctures will not alter it." She held her head at a defiant angle.

"But you said this has happened before in the summer, when the weather was hot," he reminded her.

"That is when the omen comes with this blood," she said firmly.

He was fairly certain that the weather and the harvest season combined to bring her nose-bleeds and not a cryptic imposition from the old gods, but he decided it was useless to pursue the matter now, while she was caught up with her fears of death. "Then the time of year is coincidental? The heat does not make you feel ill?"

"Sometimes, when the air is close, I sicken from heat," she allowed reluctantly, and Signed herself, moving the selvage to her left hand before she did. "But the harvest is not part of it. The old gods no longer touch the harvest, and therefore no harm comes from it. Besides, this year the rye has been harder than usual, so that if there was anything it might do, the miasma would be lesser, not greater. The rye has been like little beans."

Saint-Germanius glanced at her, alarm coursing through him. Of all she had said, this worried him the most. "The rye has been hard? How do you mean?" he asked, hoping that his sudden assumption was wrong.

"Only that. The peasants' wives have been saying that they have had quite a task grinding it for flour, and the monks at Holy Cross have made the same complaint. I haven't seen the grain myself, of course, but the first flour is in the bread for the Mass, to guard the crop. The villagers will not have any until tonight, unless they steal some." She smiled at him, confident now. "This blood is not caused by the harvest; the crops have been protected."

Saint-Germanius knew it was useless to press her about the harvest, although what she had told him was worrying, for blighted grain could lead to hunger in the winter; he decided there was no point in challenging her. "I have something I think may help you for the next month or so, while the heat persists," he said carefully. "I would like to give you a little of it, if you would allow it."

"What is it?" she asked suspiciously.

He did his best to explain in terms she would understand. "Another tincture, this one for those who have antipathies to the humors of the air. You say this does not happen to you, and that is a fortunate thing, but it would be sensible to take reasonable precautions against them. You cannot be certain that you are completely safe from such; no one can. I have seen too often how a wound attracts miasmic vapors as well as maggots, all for the lack of a tincture or balsam. Because of the bleeding you want to be certain that it cannot leave you open to the working of the miasmas on the body's humors." He thought that this argument might be acceptable to her, and he decided to give her one more reason to accept his offer. "It is said that Mädchen Mairia used such a tincture to stanch the wounds of the White Christ when He was bleeding from the Crown of Thorns." To him it sounded blatantly false, but he realized that she was not so critical.

"Is that true?" Her eyes were huge.

"Certainly," Saint-Germanius said mendaciously.

"It would have protection in it, then," she said, measuring him with her eyes. "It would bring holiness, wouldn't it?"

"It brings healing, Mädchen, and that is what you need," he corrected her kindly.

"But the holiness is the greatest healing," she said, convincing herself.

For an instant Saint-Germanius felt a stab of despair; this terribly young woman's assumption that magic alone could bring her relief filled him with dejection. Reluctantly he gave her a truthful response. "There are times this is so."

"Where did you learn such a thing?" she accused, unwilling to be too easily persuaded. "You are foreign."

"In Egypt," he answered truthfully.

"They say that the White Christ was taken there when He was a boy, to protect Him," said Genovefe.

"Yes, that is what they say. He went to Alexandria, which is a city facing the sea." He took a small vial and held it out to her. "Mix it in mead or water, just two drops, and drink it in the morning. If you become troubled by the heat, have another single drop in water after midday, but not before. Take too much and you will become faint."

"It is poison!" she protested, trying to give the vial back to him.

"No, no." He held up his small hands palms outward to show his benign intent. "But it is strong, and its virtue potent, and too much of it can imbalance the humors." It was an accurate enough description, he decided.

"All right," she said, her tone dubious.

Saint-Germanius saw her doubts and added, "It is what they do in Egypt, where the sun is much hotter than it is here, and men go about in garments like tents to keep the heat from hurting them."

"Is that what you saw there?" she asked, becoming awed.

"Yes. It is dry there, parched. There are cliffs so hot that nothing but lizards and snakes and scorpions can live on them. They say that tombs of unimaginable riches are hidden in those cliffs, protected by the asps and the desert. Except where the Nile flows the land is barren, but where the Nile runs, there are farms and fields so green and fine that it seems impossible that such richness and such desolation can exist side by side." He smiled at her, his expression mild. "The Temple where I was taught to heal was in a city amid the fields."

"You are an Egyptian, then," she said, satisfied to have some name to put to him other than foreigner.

"No," he said slowly. "But I lived there for many years, and their greatest teachers taught me." The years, he added inwardly, were reckoned in centuries, and his teachers were the priests of Imhotep.

"Oh." She looked at the vial, her blood-caked fingers closing around it. "I will try this, and if it keeps my nose from bleeding I will ask you for more." She said it generously, to let him know she trusted him.

"It will be my privilege to supply you with the tincture," he said. "For your sake and the sake of Gerefa Ranegonda."

This mollified her still more. "In her name I accept," she said, and at last pulled the wad of selvage away from her face. "It's stopped."

"For the time being," said Saint-Germanius. "But your color is still high and the day is hot. You would do well to lie down for a while so that the blood can quieten." He knew this was not enough to convince her, and went on, "And so that you can pray in peace and without other demands making your prayers incomplete."

She Signed herself, holding the vial tightly as she did. "Yes. It would be prudent to do that, and to consider the omens. I must not take the bread of the White Christ until I do." With that, she backed away from him for several steps as if uncertain of her chance to escape, then turned and hastened out the door, leaving it open as she went out.

Saint-Germanius kept the door open, for the chamber was stifling and would worsen as the day wore on. He set about putting his few belongings in order; so much had been lost at sea. But there had been other losses as devastating before and he had survived them, he reminded himself, survived them and prospered. When he had come to Egypt, he had been a slave who was thought to be a demon and yet he had eventually come to be regarded as Imhotep himself. Five hundred years past he had been fortunate to escape the wrath of the Huns, and had only done that by lying naked with the dead victims in the snow. And in Tunis two centuries ago he had been stripped of everything, yet he had emerged from degradation and slavery to triumph over his captors. He thought of his villa in Rome and hoped that it was still standing. So many of his former homes were not.

Suddenly there was a shout from inside the Common Hall, and a figure staggered out, one arm slashing at the vacant air. "Armies! Devils!" the man bellowed, and fell forward, screaming as he fell.

Saint-Germanius moved at once, going directly toward the man, who was now gathered into a tight ball and hooting with terror; he could not make out who it was until he was quite near. "Chlodwic," he said as he reached him.

Inside the Common Hall someone was shouting while others cried out or wept.

Chlodwic shrieked and averted his face, so consumed with fear that he urinated, trembling with dread and shame.

"It is the end of the world!" Brother Erchboge announced over the din in a voice of thunderous fear. "See where the monsters of the end are coming! Look! Hell is opening! There! *There!*"

A long, keening wail greeted this, and another man crawled from the Common Hall, beating at the paving stones as if battling them for his life.

Saint-Germanius straightened up and made his way toward the door of the Common Hall, steeling himself, knowing what he would find; the rye was hard, or so Genovefe had said: hard rye carried madness and death in it.

Half of the people gathered inside were doubled over like Chlodwic, their faces fixed in grimaces so appalling that it was painful to look at them. Brother Erchboge was at his altar, splayed across it as if pinned to it; there was foam on his lips and his eyes were turned toward the ceiling with a look of unmitigated horror. Osbern was sitting near the far wall, steadily banging his forehead against it. Daga lay near him, her face vacant, her whole body passively limp. Woland the saddler had taken refuge in a far corner of the Common Hall, his head between his knees, his keening high and almost constant. Gottharht was reeling about in a small circle, both arms raised to protect his head from persistent blows only he perceived. Pentacoste had her arms tightly around Berengar as she pressed against him with a lust that approached fury; he had already torn his clothes in a fervid effort to get them off so that he could possess her. Duart brushed at his arms and legs as if striving to rid himself of vermin. The noise was continuous and so unhuman that it seemed impossible that these stricken throats could make such sounds.

"Damnation claims us!" Brother Erchboge cried.

Saint-Germanius hurried away from the Common Hall, motioning to the men-at-arms coming down from the parapets to stay back. "No nearer!" he shouted, and heard an answering moan from the Common Hall.

Two of the men-at-arms hesitated.

"They have been taken in madness," said Saint-Germanius. "And you must stay away, so that it does not touch you!" He knew that if these three men once got into the Common Hall they would be too shocked to be useful.

Now all three of the men halted.

"Ulfrid!" Saint-Germanius shouted to him. "Go to the village and fetch the Gerefa. At once! Captain Amalric is with her. Tell them it is urgent. And tell her that no one in the village should eat anything! The miasma has touched the food."

The men-at-arms Signed themselves, and only Ulfrid moved forward. "What is that sound?"

"The distress of your companions," said Saint-Germanius bluntly. "They must have your help. The Gerefa and Captain Amalric must return!"

Faxon looked stubborn. "Why are they shouting? We have to go to—"

"No!" Saint-Germanius ordered. "Bring the Gerefa. And have Winolda take the children to the village. Then secure the slaves. At once!"

"Saint-Germanius—" Ulfrid began.

"Now!" Saint-Germanius would brook no opposition. "Hurry! or the madness may spread! and you will be answerable for it." This, he hoped, would spur them to activity. He turned and went back toward the Common Hall, trusting that the men-at-arms would do as they were told.

The men did not move at once, and then Ulfrid hefted his spear. "The children first," he said to Faxon. "And you"—this to Severic—"do as the foreigner says. Bring the Gerefa."

As he entered the Common Hall once more, Saint-Germanius went first to take the basket where a few small loaves of bread remained. This he put to one side, and then began the difficult task of treating the sufferers. He started with Sigrad, because he knew he needed her help.

"No, no," she whispered as he approached her; she cringed, hunkering down into a crouch as if to save herself from destruction.

Whatever it was that her mind had conjured, he realized he could not combat it with words, and so he made no attempt. Hallucinations, he knew from long, long years of treating the sick, were infinitely persuasive and impossible to deny to those experiencing them. For the people of this fortress, their hold was doubly strong because of their belief in omens. He came up to Sigrad and put his hand firmly on her shoulder. "Feel this, Sigrad," he said firmly, and tightened his fingers twice. "This is not a dream or a vision."

She started to shake so badly that she could not Sign herself for protection; this increased her fear. With a moan of distress she pulled further away from him. "Never," she said. "Never never never never."

If only he had more time, Saint-Germanius thought, and Hrotiger with him; his steadfast reliability was sorely needed now. He put his bondsman from his thoughts and made a second attempt at gaining Sigrad's notice in spite of the lunacy that had seized her. Again he put his hand on her shoulder, and this time her eyes flicked in his direction before fixing on a place near the center of the room. "What is it?" he asked quietly. "What do you see?"

"There is a monster," she said, barely audibly. "He is searching, searching. He will devour us all."

"If the monster is seeking you," said Saint-Germanius in a low, steady tone, "you have the weapon you need to strike him down. In your hand you have a mace blessed by monks and made by a magician. It always strikes true and it always kills its enemy." He could not be sure that she would be led by him, but it was the only way he could bring her out of the illusion that had been pressed upon her.

"He is going to ruin this hall," she whispered. "He will find us and eat us."

"You will strike him down. It is in your power to do it," said Saint-Germanius. "In your hand, you can feel the mace. Lift it, and you will feel how mighty it is."

Very slowly Sigrad swung her arm, moving as if she held something heavy in her hand. "It is a good weapon."

Saint-Germanius was more relieved than he could express. "It will strike down the monster. Use it. Before the monster can find you, act first."

Sigrad was shaking, but she lurched to her feet and began to swing about, using her arms in large arcs. Her breath hissed through her clenched teeth.

Pentacoste was half-naked now, and she began to laugh derisively as Berengar pawed at her breasts. When he struck her across the face she laughed harder and with greater anger.

Brother Erchboge writhed on the altar, too lost in his vision to be coherent, gobbling, guttural sounds coming from deep inside him.

At last Sigrad stopped moving, then looked toward Saint-Germanius, blinking as if dazzled. "Foreigner. Why are you battling monsters?"

"I am battling them for the sake of your Gerefa," he answered. He did not want to challenge whatever she saw.

"It is a terrible thing," she said. Her manner shifted subtly. "I have not seen the world this way before."

Captain Meyrih, hearing her voice, reached out for her, his voice ragged with pain. "I am lost, Sigrad. I am *lost.*"

"You are brave," said Saint-Germanius to him steadily. "You know what it is to hold on in battle. You must hold on now."

Captain Meyrih wailed, and although she was still disoriented, Sigrad reached out for his hand. "You are not dead," her husband marveled.

"Not yet," said Sigrad without a trace of her usual good humor. "There are monsters, however."

"Monsters," Captain Meyrih agreed, his voice hushed with dread and awe.

Woland was vomiting, the furious spasms producing little, for the saddler, like the rest of the inhabitants of the fortress, had eaten nothing but the bread and wine of the Mass since the previous afternoon. He coughed and moaned; it was the first encouraging thing Saint-Germanius had seen since this began.

Sigrad Signed herself. "There is a monster on your brow, foreigner," she said to Saint-Germanius and began to move away from him, apprehension increasing again.

"It is the shadow of a forgotten god," said Saint-Germanius gently. "It cannot harm you."

This explanation seemed reasonable to Sigrad, and she moved closer to him once again. "This is a bad omen. That so many monsters would come here, it is a dire sign."

For once Saint-Germanius had to agree. "Yes," he said as he looked around at the chaos of the Common Hall. "Yes."

Text of a letter from Bientuet, merchants' factor in Quentovic, Francia, to Hrotiger in Rome. Carried overland to Mende by Hieronomite monks, then transferred to a party of carpenters bound for Luna in Italia, and from there carried by a company of men-at-arms to Rome, delivered there on September 23, 938.

To the honorable bondsman of the Comites Saint-Germanius, my greetings on this twenty-first day of August in White Christ's Year 938.

It is my sad duty to inform you that there is no word yet. I have been at pains to speak to all merchants coming from the east, and those who have dealt with Danes and the other northern peoples, but I can learn nothing. If the man has been taken captive, we can learn nothing of it. I am afraid that he might have been made a slave by now, or been carried into the lands of the Russians, at Kiev or Novgorod. There is also the possibility that the Magyars have captured him, or killed him, for their raids have been appalling. The city of Bremen has been sacked and there are now thousands of men from that city wandering the country, many of them starving. If the Comites Saint-Germanius has fallen in with any of these, it may be many months before we learn of his fate.

We have done all that we could to discover if anyone has seen him, and we have made several attempts to learn if anyone has heard any reliable tales of him, or of his missing cargo. I wish to state that I have been as diligent as a man in my position may be, and that no rumor that could possibly lead to your master has been overlooked. The tales we have heard would be enough to make the most credulous man doubt his wits.

Do not be despondent at this news, I pray you, for we have found nothing that could be thought to be a good omen. Had your master been killed, I think we might have heard of it by now. It is true that the death of some men takes many years to discover, but those men are not of the rank or wealth of your master. Anyone who had enriched themselves through his death must surely have made it known by now. Even the outlaws who live in bands in the forests are not beyond boasting of their greatest triumphs. Many of them have found that they cannot keep from telling how they came to have many gold coins. Since your master always travels with fifty gold coins in his belt, he would be a rare prize indeed for any robber.

The ships will be ready to put to sea in the spring. I have had word that the repairs are nearing completion, and that with the end of winter storms it should be possible to fit them out again. What is it you would wish me to do? I can hold the ships at Hedaby or any other port you specify as long as the fees are paid, which can easily be done from the profits of the last voyage.

If another voyage were to be undertaken it could serve a double purpose: adding to the wealth of your master as well as locating him. It seems to me that the best course would be to put two or three of the ships to sea; I have certain goods left in the stores I have held for your master, and they would do nicely. I know of three reliable captains who are looking for ships to command, and who would be diligent in carrying out any orders you may give in regard to your master. If you will send authorization, I will put the plans to work.

When you send your answer, let me advise you to have it carried through Francia, not through Germania, for not only are the Magyars fighting there, it has been said that many of the people have been struck by a plague of madness, and that in many places all the men and women have been possessed by demons. The priests and monks are helpless against it, and it is said that even the old gods can be of no help against this affliction. Many are dead from these visitations, and others are left with crippled and barren bodies.

I pray that the White Christ will yet bring back the Comites Saint-Germanius to us, and that you will see him whole and prosperous again.

If there is anything that I have not done that you wish me to do, let me know of it. I will do whatever is in my power to aid your search, and I will rejoice with you upon the Comites Saint-Germanius's return.

Bientuet of Quentovic
merchants' factor
by the hand of the scribe Lazurin

PART II

FRANZIN RAGOCZY,
COMITES
SAINT-GERMANIUS

*T*ext of a dispatch from the village leader of Oeldenburh to the Margerefa Oelrih; carried by courier with armed escort.

To the puissant Margerefa Oelrih, the heartfelt prayers that our need will be answered and speedily, for our peril is great and without assistance we will perish. It is true that in the past we of Oeldenburh have not kept to the rule of King Otto, and have turned from the White Christ, but that must change now, and you must hear our pleas and deliver us from ruin.

A double catastrophe has overtaken us, and either is sufficient to bring this village to destruction. Since the city of Bremen was laid waste by the barbarians, we have been visited by many wretched people of that place who have no home and who now wander the roads in search of food and somewhere to live. Now that autumn is coming, they are more desperate than they were, and some of them have armed themselves in order to demand what they are not given. I am certain that many of them have joined with the outlaws in the forest, and that others have fallen into the hands of the Danes and will end their lives as slaves. While we could we admitted those who came to us, but now the town is full and we cannot have more within our walls without putting all of us in danger of starvation this winter. Our grain supplies are low for the harvest has been poor, and we cannot give them the bread they seek without taking from the mouths of our own people, and that would condemn us more certainly than refusing to take in more of those who have escaped the force of the Magyars. All those who leave tribute for the old gods have not been answered with favor, and their service goes unacknowledged.

This trouble alone would be reason enough to ask for your help, but there is worse, and some say it is sent to us as punishment because we have turned the people of Bremen away, but others say it was brought to us by them as a curse, and had we taken them in it would be more disastrous than it is already. *Those who speak in this way are not just the followers of the old gods, but those devoted to the White Christ as well. Everyone has seen the omens and everyone knows that we face obliteration.*

A madness has come among us, a madness so great that we are powerless against it, and our prayers, to the old gods and White Christ alike, go unanswered. Women with children in their wombs have miscarried, and all the babes have died. Men are also stricken: some have developed rottenness in the feet and the guts, and some have been so overwhelmed by their visions and their possession that they have leaped and spun and danced until their flesh could no longer support them and they collapsed from it, falling into a profound stupor and then into lethargy so great that no subsequent action has been possible; some have lain abed ever since the madness came over them, and are without strength or will. Those who have been in these transports continue to have visions and their sleep is constantly haunted by the spectres of madness. Visions are the least of the torments the madness brings. Many of those who have taken the miasma have died, as well, and we dare not let them lie in consecrated ground for fear that evil will befall us for such sacrilege.

We cannot say if the poor men from Bremen have suffered this madness, but we fear it may be so, for the miasma is wide. There are many who have come to this town for market and all tell of the madness. Many more have refused to enter the gates at all for fear of being struck with it. Those who have braved their way here have been filled with fear by what they have seen. We have told those who have brought their goods to market here to wait until spring before undertaking to come here again. We have word that this madness has touched the monks at the Monastery of the Holy Cross and the village at Leosan Fortress. There can be no succor for us in either place.

Therefore we beseech you and the King to send us what relief you can, whether it is monks to pray for us and bury us or armed men to keep those fleeing Bremen from storming our walls in this time when we cannot defend ourselves. We know that the miasma may reach any you send here, but we beg your help for fear of our deaths.

This on the twentieth day of September.

Thomaz
Elder of Oeldenburh

1

From the parapets Ranegonda could watch the villagers guarding the stockade gates. Her exhaustion showed in her face, in the darkness around her eyes and the deepening of the lines by her mouth. In the fading afternoon sun the scars on her skin stood out clearly. She regarded Saint-Germanius beside her for some little time before she said, "It is out of the question."

"Gerefa," he said more urgently, wanting to protect her and knowing she would prevent it if she could, "believe this: the madness comes from the rye. The rye is blighted, and that brings the madness."

"The madness is from the old gods, or the White Christ," said Ranegonda with conviction. She stared away toward the stockade again, refusing to look at him. "Since the monks at Holy Cross have been taken with it, perhaps it is the Devil who has brought it. Brother Erchboge says so."

"It is the grain," Saint-Germanius insisted. "The grain has been contaminated; the hard, enlarged kernels are the sign of it. I have seen it before, and I tell you that you must destroy the crop, and all the flour that has been ground. As long as anyone can eat of that rye, the madness will linger."

She folded her arms. "There are those who might do so desperate a thing in the hope that the old gods or the White Christ would honor their sacrifice, but I will not be so profligate."

"Then more will madden and more will die," said Saint-Germanius very quietly. "You have lost nine men already, four women, and six children. You can't afford to lose more. Burn the fields, Ranegonda, I beg you."

Ranegonda had no answer to give to that. She leaned on the battlement and watched as the last of the woodcutting parties came back through the stockade gate. "At least we are protected. If we had not built the wall, we would be all but defenseless with so much madness."

"Ranegonda," he said, making another attempt to persuade her, "If I can show you that the grain carries the madness, will you destroy it? Let me have one of the pigs and—"

"For blood?" she asked, deliberately trying to turn him away from her.

He would not be distracted. "To show you that it, too, will become mad if given the grain."

"Devils enter pigs all the time," said Ranegonda. "Everyone knows that."

Saint-Germanius frowned. "Then tell me what it would take to convince you. What will you believe?"

"You could use one of the slaves, I suppose, give the slave the good bread and see if the madness comes as you tell me it will," she said.

"No," said Saint-Germanius softly and with such conviction that she stared at him. "I will not mistreat a slave, not even to show you your error. I know what it is to be a slave. I was one after my father was defeated by his enemies." It had been the first time he had worn a collar but not the last, and each time he had loathed it.

Ranegonda Signed herself. "That is an evil thing."

"Yes," he said with feeling. "It is."

She realized that she had trespassed in some way she did not understand; she attempted to rectify that error. "If we can capture an outlaw, you can show me with him; it will be his punishment, if he becomes mad and dies."

Saint-Germanius liked that little better than he liked the notion of using slaves, but he was aware of what the gesture meant to her. "If you capture one, he may already have the madness, if he has eaten blighted grain."

"We will not know until we have caught one," she said, ending the matter by reiterating, "You can show how the grain brings madness to the outlaw."

"Very well," he said, aware that he would not receive better from her.

"They need to rethatch the roofs of most of the houses in the village," she said, deliberately changing the subject. "Once the rain comes, it will not be possible until the spring, and if the roofs are not repaired they will leak and rot in the wet."

"The villagers are short-handed, and they are frightened as well," Saint-Germanius remarked, and did not add that it was because so many of them had been taken with the madness.

"We are all short-handed, and the children are suffering." She looked over at him as she began to walk along the narrow ledge, taking care not to limp, for here she could not risk compromising her balance. "You said that you could work the forge? With Radulph and Alefonz both dead, I will need you to do it."

"Of course," he said, his irritation with her fading as he spoke; she had too much required of her already, and he had been adding to her burdens in his attempt to alleviate them: it was a small thing to undertake the work of the armorer and the smith. "And anything else you may need, tell me."

She said nothing more for a while as they continued their walk. "I fear the winter is going to be hard. They say the signs are for storms." It was a bit later, and she had just paused to look down at the counter-weight device Saint-Germanius had installed on the gates. "We will be glad of that many times before spring comes; having need for no more than two men is useful. If the slaves become ill along with the rest of us, we will be without any recourse at all, and who knows what will befall us? We could be overrun by the outlaws if there are no men to defend the fortress and the village. But you give me courage. With you here, I hope we will get through the worst of it." Then she stopped and regarded him with a trace of worry. "Unless you are ransomed."

Saint-Germanius met her eyes steadily, and he spoke with persuasive strength. "Ranegonda, I give you my word on it: I will not leave you when you face such trouble."

After a moment she nodded, but doubt remained, and the vertical line between her pale brows deepened. "But you . . . It would dishonor this fortress to keep you here once the money has been paid."

"It is not a question of money, or ransom, or honor; none of that matters," he said, speaking very quietly so that only she could hear. "It is a matter of blood, Ranegonda, and its bond."

"Yes," she said, but without inflection.

He was aware that she did not yet understand the extent of his tie to her just as she could not be persuaded that the madness came from the rye in the fields, for such thoughts were alien to her sense of the world. He said at last, "No matter why you gave me back my life, you gave it, and I owe it to you. And I know you because of it, and that is the strongest bond of all."

She shrugged, pulling her casula around her shoulders at the same time. "Margerefa Oelrih is expected to return shortly. He will have more men for us, and he will bring orders from the King."

"For more cut trees?" Saint-Germanius guessed. "With the village and the fortress so hard-hit by the madness, how can you give what he may want of you?"

"It is for us to find the way," she said as she reached the stairway by the landward tower. "It is our duty to him. We would not have more men-at-arms coming, and more villagers, if the King did not know we would deliver the trees he requires of us. And it is a good thing to grow as the King wishes. There are supposed to be more men coming with the Margerefa, men with families. Most will live in the village, but a few will live here, inside the walls." She looked back and up at him, the sunlight striking one eye and angling across her cheek. "There are empty quarters for some of them."

"And more orphans," said Saint-Germanius.

Ranegonda nodded. "When plagues come, there are always orphans, if the White Christ favors us. Otherwise all the children die along with their mothers, and the line is extinguished."

It was tempting to bring up the grain again, but Saint-Germanius knew it was futile. "Sigrad will be put to care for them?"

"With her husband dead, she will want something to do; we cannot let her sit idle, and Pentacoste will not let her assume more of the weaving tasks, for she wants no one learning what she is doing with her spinning and her weaving. Sigrad is not like Winolda and her herbs; she cannot be left to herself. She is happiest when there are others with her, in the cloth room or the women's quarters, or among the children. The children know her and she is old enough that they will obey her, and so will their mothers." She had reached the foot of the stairs, now fully in shadow. "Captain Meyrih was blind, and he died well, fighting the visions that tormented him. We will remember his name without saying he had lasted too long in the world."

Such ruthless practicality did not strike Saint-Germanius as mistaken, not in this part of the world. "He fought well for this fortress."

"As long as he could, yes he did. And he was not a burden afterward." She gestured toward the Marshaling Court. "But Amalric is Captain now, and at least he was not taken severely with the madness." She waited a moment, then added, "Brother Erchboge has made tomorrow another fast day. He has ordered all the people in the village to fast with us, including the woodcutters."

"For everyone?" Saint-Germanius asked. "He has been declaring many fast days since the madness came." It was one of the few decisions of Brother Erchboge's he could applaud, for while the people of the fortress did not eat the madness was not renewed. What troubled Saint-Germanius the most about the monk was that he continued to administer the Sacraments, and that occasionally meant the Host, and here the Host was made of tainted flour.

"For all but the very young and the ill," said Ranegonda. "And he is spending all night on his knees, singing the Psalms, for our protection and salvation." She paused, and when she looked at him again there was more in her voice than a simple request; her vulnerability was painful to admit. "I will have to ride to Holy Cross tomorrow. I would like you to come with me."

"Of course," he said, wondering how the monks had come through their first brush with madness. "I will be ready shortly after sunrise."

"Good," she said with relief. She lowered her voice to add, "We are supposed to take them salted meat, but there is not much left, and I dare not take more than a little of it. Brother Haganrih will be displeased, and Brother Giselberht will probably be angry, for he made a vow to the monastery to keep it supplied when he entered it." Again she fell silent for a moment. "Should I tell him what happened to Pentacoste with Berengar? It is my duty, but—"

Saint-Germanius had a vivid impression of the two locked in a frenzied embrace, coupling in the midst of the first outbreak; and he remembered the smile on Pentacoste's lovely mouth, one that was at once satiated and disdainful. "But they were compelled by the madness," he said. "Neither of them knew what they were doing, not as the Church demands that they know. It was not sin."

"Perhaps not. But if my brother should learn of what happened, and that I said nothing, he will despise me," she said.

"If he learns of it, then tell him it was their madness, the presence of the miasma that made such a thing happen. Tell him of what the others did, of how they were as strange as animals. He will believe it then, and will not blame you for it." He came to her side. "It would be different if they had been lovers before that day, or since, wouldn't it?"

"Yes," she said, going on softly as if speaking were physically painful. "And I pray each morning that they are not lovers, that Pentacoste has not decided that since she has sinned once in madness she may continue to sin in knowledge. It would bring great disgrace on this fortress to have such a thing happen, and her guilt would have to be known."

"And do you think it has happened?" asked Saint-Germanius, walking beside her across the Marshaling Court toward the smithy.

"I pray it has not, morning and night; I say nothing in Confession, and yet I fear that it might have happened, and that the disgrace has come and I do not know it," she said with determination. "I have tried to speak with her, to tell her how many here could regard how she behaves, how the Margerefa Oelrih might see it. But Pentacoste . . . she wishes men to serve her, to bow to her and do all but worship her. And then she shows them contempt for their weakness, but she will not release them." Her hands pressed against her mouth, and she whispered, "You will say nothing of this, will you? I will not have anyone adding to the rumors."

"Who would listen to me, assuming I said something?" Saint-Germanius inquired with a faint smile. "Surely a word from you would—"

"Give me your oath that you will say nothing," she demanded suddenly.

He bowed slightly. "You have it already; I thought you knew that."

"Tell me," she insisted.

"Very well." He stood still, facing her; when he spoke his voice was low but it carried to her as if to wrap around her. "By all the forgotten gods, Ranegonda, I swear I will say nothing of what you tell me in regard to your sister-in-law, now or ever." He could read her relief mixed with distress in her eyes. "What is it: will you tell me?"

She started away from him, and then came back to him, speaking very softly. "What makes you do this, Saint-Germanius? Why is there a bond? Why has my blood done this to you?"

His arresting, irregular features shifted, and for an instant the immensity of his age was visible; then he took her hand, and his dark, compelling eyes were deep and tranquil. "Because that is how we are when we change, when death has touched us and passed on. To have the life you offer, those of my blood must know everything or nothing of you. I can raven and be worse than a maddened wolf and spare myself the pain of valuing you, or I can know you completely, and cherish you, and accept the pain of losing you. I choose to know everything."

"You obtain your life from mine," she said, her voice so soft he had to lean closer to hear her at all. "Because you know me. You know me from my blood." She stared at him. "I cannot grasp it."

"It is the nature of those of my blood," he said, his voice deep and quiet. "Ask as many times as you wish and my answer will always be the same. I cannot deny the bond of blood any more than I can painlessly cross running water without my earth-lined shoes."

"And because of this bond you do not dishonor me," she whispered.

"Because of this I *cannot* dishonor you, nor would I if I could," he corrected her, and finally released her hand. "I will be in the smithy, should you—"

She reached out, putting her fingers to his lips. "I will come there later. After prayers, when the slaves have been confined and the cooks have left the kitchen. After the dead have been put out of doors, and Brother Erchboge has sealed their lips with holy water. I will come then. There will be fewer men-at-arms on watch and they will not be looking here, but toward the forest."

"I will be in the smithy," he said again, adding "all night," before he made himself walk away from her, for he could see that two of the men on guard were watching them closely and he did not want it to appear they were remaining together improperly, though he could feel her need of him pull at him as relentlessly as the stoutest chain.

Radulph's son Theobald was in the smithy, his rough linen bliaut covered with soot. He looked up sharply as Saint-Germanius came through the door, and he folded his arms, trying to look contemptuous instead of grief-stricken as he was. "What are you doing here?"

"I am going to fire the forge," said Saint-Germanius steadily. "The Gerefa has asked it of me."

Theobald stared in outrage. "My father is not yet cold in the ground, and you cross this threshold? How can you dare to do this?" His voice was high, but it cracked once during this outburst, which served only to fluster him.

"The Gerefa has asked it," Saint-Germanius said again. He indicated the forge and the pile of ash beside it. "It is sad that your father died. You have every right to mourn him. But this fortress must have the forge ready."

"It . . ." Theobald faltered. "My father was teaching me. If the village smith will help me, I will have it fired."

"And the smith in the village will take you as apprentice," said Saint-Germanius, "if you do not want to be trained as a man-at-arms. But the forge must be readied. The fortress cannot wait for you to learn the craft. There is necessary work to do." He had come no further than two steps beyond the door, and now kept his place there, neither retreating nor advancing. "It will not injure the memory of your father if I work this forge."

"It is not likely that could happen," said Theobald emphatically, shaking his head to show his protest more clearly.

Saint-Germanius said nothing, but inclined his head slightly, waiting.

In a sudden gesture Theobald moved away from the forge. "Your clothes will get dirty."

"Then I will wash them," said Saint-Germanius, standing aside so that the youth could leave.

"No smith is fussy about soot and charring, as a miller cannot mind the dust of the mill, or the fisherman the smell of his catch." His face was defiant.

"True enough," Saint-Germanius agreed.

"This place will be mine when you are ransomed," Theobald offered as a final warning. "And I will forget you."

Saint-Germanius watched Theobald go, and remembered his own searing grief when his father had been killed, three millennia ago. That Theobald should resent him was not surprising, he knew; he had felt that he had been betrayed when his father died—which, in fact, turned out to be true. Even now the memories evoked a twinge deep within him. He could still distantly recall the hideous vengeance he had wrought on the family who had gone over to their enemy and exposed them to conquest; as always the impressions were bloody, and little as he wanted to recognize it, he could feel an echo in himself for the appalling satisfaction he had known when he had felt his second cousin's spine break under his hands. At the time he had known exultation, but that had vanished more than two thousand years before. A grief welled up in him, fueled by the shame he had learned. He hoped that he would never again experience such horrendous rage as he had then. He noticed his small hands were shaking and he banished the memories for the time being, clenching his fists as he did, feeling the shaking fade. Then he set about cleaning the forge and setting it for refiring.

Three oil lamps and the shine of the forge gave the smithy a false gilding. Night had fallen sometime before, but Saint-Germanius continued at his task with the tools Radulph had used. The forge was hot now, and he was working with iron, making horseshoes against the time they would be needed, shaping the metal on a stone anvil with an iron hammer. He had removed his bliaut and chanise and hung them near the door; now he was dressed only in black linen braies, belted with a wide band of leather that did not entirely conceal the tremendous swath of scars that crossed his torso from the base of his sternum to his pubis. His short-cropped loose curls were in disorder and there was a smear of soot on his cheek.

Ranegonda stood in the doorway, staring at him, her eyes wide. She took a step toward him. "You are a strong man."

"Yes," Saint-Germanius said, continuing to hammer out another horseshoe, working the metal with steady, ringing blows.

"Your chest is deep," she informed him, as if she had never noticed it before.

"Yes," he agreed, concentrating on the glowing metal.

She watched him a short while in silence. "You don't sweat."

"No, I don't." He plunged the iron horseshoe into a bucket of seawater. "And I cannot weep, either."

"And the rest of your blood?" she asked.

"No; no vampire can weep." He pulled the horseshoe from the bucket and set it to heat again.

She winced at the word, but continued to stare at him. "You are pleasant to look at."

"So are you," he said, putting the horseshoe aside and approaching her. "I wish you could believe that. I know you, and I know you are made of beauty, yet you will not recognize it. In this world you see so little beauty; I wish you could see what is there and treasure it."

"Why?" she asked, coming to him and putting her arm around his waist; her weak ankle was aching after her long, arduous day.

"Because we need beauty, Ranegonda, and knowing, as we need food and sleep and shelter from the cold. We need it as parched ground needs rain." He brushed the wisps of blonde hair back from her brow. "Where we find beauty we flourish and where we deny it we wither."

"Those of your blood?" She cocked her head to the side.

"Everyone," he answered with great sadness in his voice. "Every human walking this earth." He kissed her gently. "This is beauty."

"It is very pleasant," she said.

"It is beautiful," he said, and kissed her again, this time with passion and yearning. He moved his hands over her, seeking to increase her ardor, to reach the part of herself that she hid from the world and her own eyes. "There is beauty in you, and fire, and you have never let yourself know either. But I know them in you, for they are in your blood, and I want to help you know them for yourself."

"It isn't fitting," she said, and sighed, but kept within the protection of his arms.

"Oh, Ranegonda, no." There was regret and despair in his voice now, and his words were rough. "It isn't fitting to speak falsely or to leave unwanted children in the forest. It isn't fitting to withhold food from a starving man or succor to a wounded one, or shelter to a lone woman." He took her face in his hands, his compelling eyes on hers; there was warmth in his voice and desire in his touch. "But to deny yourself knowledge of yourself? because it isn't fitting? That is an error, my love."

"It is a sin. Brother Erchboge has said so, and my brother." She could not move away from him; she could not make herself want to. "To bear such sins is the fate of women, for Eve."

"And I say it is a sin to keep you from that knowledge of yourself," he said, and kissed her deeply, seeking her release. He opened her chanise with one small hand and his fingers sought the swell of her breasts. "There is glory in you. I say that anyone who demands you be less than you are is damned beyond all redemption. It matters not that the person is Brother Erchboge or the Pope or King Otto. No one has the right to do that."

She felt dizzy without any sense of movement; he was caressing her so gently, and yet his fingers left a sensation of enjoyable heat where they touched her. No matter how wrong she knew it to be, she wanted him to continue, in spite of the wildness she felt stir within her. She wanted to be rid of her clothes and yet she dreaded what might happen to her without them. "Tell me again," she said, shocked that she could speak the words aloud.

"You are radiant. You are beautiful." This time his kiss was long and slow and deep.

She staggered, and her ankle was a small factor in it. "How can you say that?" she asked, and held him.

"Because it is what I know of you." Now one hand stroked her side and her flat belly. Then he withdrew it and drew her against him.

"But beauty?" She could not mask the hope in her grey eyes.

"It is yours, Ranegonda," he whispered to her as he lifted her easily, holding her above him as if she were little more than a lamb. "Take it."

"I have my duty to my family," she said with a trace of stubbornness, repeating the lesson she had been rigorously taught since she was a child. "Since I cannot marry, I must—"

"Your duty is first to yourself," he said to her in an undervoice. "I know that makes me a heretic, and a blasphemer and a dissenter; and so be it." He held her closer, lowering her a little to embrace her more fully. "You are true and strong, like the swords made by masters. You are upright and honorable. Surely your family should be gratified with such a woman as you are." His lips opened hers, and he sought her tongue with his own, pleased that she was beginning to respond to him with more than her loneliness. Gradually he lowered her to the earthen floor but kept her pressed close against him.

"It is wrong," she said. "To do this is wrong." But she kissed him again, on the mouth and then on his neck and shoulders, reveling in his strength and the joy he wakened in her. "The White Christ forbids—"

"The White Christ knows nothing about this," Saint-Germanius assured her, feeling the rough texture of her clothing on his bare chest. "This is between us, intimate, private. No god has any part of what we have now together. It is ours alone, love, ours alone."

"But—" She stopped herself. "How can the commands of the White Christ be wrong? My brother has given up everything for the glory of the White Christ." She found Saint-Germanius's nearness disturbing and reassuring at once, and she struggled to make herself impervious to his overwhelming presence. "How can anything the White Christ teaches be wrong?" Even as she asked she recalled the lengths of yarn she had tied to the limbs of hollow oak trees when she was younger. That had been wrong, too.

"The man died," said Saint-Germanius bluntly. "He died and His followers have added to His work, made changes in it, tried to explain it, and now it is no longer what He said, but what hundreds have assumed He said, or said themselves and put the words in His mouth."

He drew her close to him again, and kissed her throat and the arch of her collar-bone. "His words have been distorted long ago."

This was the worst of anything Saint-Germanius had said to her, and she stiffened in his arms, only to feel him loosen his hold on her at once. As if she feared falling she clung to him. "No. Don't let me go."

"I will not force anything on you," he said, not yet holding her again. "There is no purpose in forcing you. If you want what I have to give you, then it is yours. If you do not, then you have nothing to fear from me."

"What do you sense?" she asked softly, more to herself than to him. "What is it you know that others do not?"

"I sense the whole of you," he murmured, and continued to work his private magic on her. "I sense your soul."

"Why do you want this of me?" she whispered as they moved far enough apart for her to loosen her clothes.

"I want it for you, not of you," he said, and outlined her brow and the curve of her lip with kisses.

It would be easy, she decided, to allow him to decide how they would proceed. It would be pleasant and satisfactory and she would enjoy everything he did to her. She tried very hard not to reflect on what she would find in herself, for that was too disturbing, too potent and profound to be thought of. Better, she told herself, to let this be an enjoyment between them, a carnal entertainment, more amusing than watching the young men-at-arms at their clumsy mock-battles, and more satisfying than hearing Berengar play the kithre. Assuring herself that she was protected from the ravages of his kindness, that his compassion would not reach her as his body could, she ran her hands along his arms and for the first time realized how much power was contained in his compact body. As she caught his hands in hers, she felt an echo of his strength as his fingers closed. She leaned against him. "You make me want impossible things." It was too much to admit, and she turned her face away so that her expression would not give her away to him. "Let us take our delight and be happy for it."

"No, no, love," he said, and moved back just far enough to look directly into her somber grey eyes with greater promise in his. "Nothing you want is impossible."

"Except children," she said at once, hating herself for speaking of it, yet wanting it to be a barrier between them. "You told me that—"

"All right," he responded without heat, his eyes steady and his voice low. "I cannot give you children. Nor would you want them, since you cannot marry, and I will not. That is my burden, not yours. Were I the same as other men, I would still not permit you to risk having a child, since that is punishable by drowning, and that would be . . . intolerable." He traced the line of her cheek, her jaw, her neck with two fingers. "I have told you before: those of my blood have no progeny. But I can offer you yourself instead of children." Very gently he reached to lift her bliaut over her head. "Is my love so terrible?" He read the answer in her eyes. "Let me give you everything I can, Ranegonda. Let me show you how I know you." He indicated the far side of the low-ceilinged room, away from the forge and the soot, as he hung her bliaut on the nail beside his own. "I have put down cloths for us. We will not be disturbed, or noticed."

She started to break away from him, and then made a gesture of futility. She began to Sign herself and then stopped. "There is madness in the air. I can feel it."

"There is no madness, not here," he said, his dark eyes serious. "There is only the beauty and wildness of your soul. There is love." He touched her chanise lightly. "Only these things, Ranegonda."

Her eyes fixed on his, and she had the oddest sensation of falling into great depths. She put out one hand to steady herself; she felt him support her and for a moment she was motionless with panic. And then the fall claimed her, languorous and pleasant, guarded by his arms. "Saint-Germanius," she whispered as his fingers brushed her nipples through the thin fabric of her chanise, and a wave of pleasure went over her, and something feral and rapturous trembled deep within her that for once did not fill her with revulsion but promised fulfillment instead, "I am lost."

"No, love," he said tenderly as he took off her chanise. "You are found."

Text of a dispatch from King Otto sent to all his Margerefas, given to couriers on October 3, 938; dispatches received by Margerefas from October 9 until October 26.

To my steadfast vassals, the greetings and orders of your King.

Be it known that we have pursued the Magyars back toward their borders and now can claim that they have been routed from the north of Germania and no longer pose a danger to any Germanian subject living north of Fulda or west of Werla.

Any Germanian subject who has taken a Magyar prisoner is expected to kill the prisoner. There is to be no ransoming of captives. These Magyars put no value on gold, and for that they shall have none. It is my wish that when it is possible, the deaths given be exemplary, so that in future the Magyars will know that Germanians are as prepared to slaugh-

ter them as they are to slaughter us. In any village or town where more than ten Magyar are prisoners, they are to be hacked into pieces and the heads put above the gates. Where fewer are held, it is left to the village elders to decide what death would be most demeaning. Any Germanians who refuse to kill captive Magyars in the hope of selling them to the Russians or the Poles or the Danes for slaves will be killed themselves for treachery. We make no bargains with this enemy, and so it will be.

To those who have been taken with the madness that is currently possessing the people in the northern part of the Kingdom, we order you to turn travelers away until such time as the madness has passed and the priests have declared that the area is without the miasma. This madness must not be allowed to reach more than it already has. Anyone who has entered the area of the miasma must not leave it until the miasma itself is gone. Those who attempt to leave the areas are to be killed at once, and their bodies left to rot where they fall. No effort is to be spared to put down this madness. Every monk and priest and prioress is hereby ordered to double the prayers recited to the White Christ. Any who leave their devotions for any reason but the possession of madness are to be immured. If any monk, priest, or nun disregards this, take them to the seacoast and sell the miscreant to Danes, to be slaves the rest of their days.

Yet there is the work of the Kingdom to continue, and I order that all mandates be honored. No slacking can be permitted in these difficult times. Now, when we are most beset we must be the most prepared. Where work has been ordered, it is to continue no matter what misfortune overtakes those who have been given the task. Only death will be regarded as good reason to fail at completing the work that has been assigned.

These are my instructions to you. See that they are carried out at once. Any Margerefa who fails to act upon these orders is to be stripped of rank and sent eastward into exile. I accept nothing less than your fealty, and the fealty of your vassals and my subjects.

Otto of Germania
King
by the hand of Father Broge

2

Pentacoste was dancing, her arms spread, her chanise billowing around her in the wan moonlight, limning her like a frost. She held her head to the side, humming to herself in accompaniment to her slow, sinuous turns. The old gods would have to be delighted, she assured herself, to have such tribute as her dancing; they could not refuse her anything she asked once they saw how splendidly she danced for them. The sand underfoot was gritty and uneven, and occasionally she had to dip lower or spin longer because of its shifting. Still, there was no fault in her movements, and she felt proud of what she did; she would gladly have done the same for King Otto or any friend of her father's. The cool night wind held the promise of coming autumn and it reached through the soft linen of her chanise to raise gooseflesh on her skin. A short way from the cove where she performed the Baltic Sea lapped placidly at the beach, adding its rhythm to her dance. She could feel the old gods gather to watch her, and she set herself to finer movements, more elegant and sweeping, like the dances great ladies performed, not the romping of peasants.

At last she dropped gracefully to the foot of the massive projection of roots that protruded from the wall of the cove. "It was for you, all for you," she said breathlessly. "It was for you. All you are given my tribute, and my submission. I offer it to you to show my dedication to you. I have not forgot you; I will not forget you, who give me the gifts I seek and who have favored me since I was born. I rejoice in the privilege you give me, and the power you possess. I know that you alone are mighty and that the White Christ is nothing but a ghost story." She raised her head and reached up to take one of the roots in her hand. "And for this, and the many things I have done for you, you will bring me that foreigner as my lover. He has tried to provoke me by his attentions to Ranegonda, but I know that it is me he seeks. And it is time he turned to me. He is to be my servant, my devoted suitor. Perhaps, if he is as wealthy as it is rumored he may be, he will take me with him when he is ransomed. That would be best, to be the wife of such a man, with wealth and position, in some place far away from—" She stopped and looked around in distress. "I do not want to be away from you, old gods, but from this fortress and that eunuch who is still my husband, locked behind monastery walls."

She got to her feet and moved nearer to the tangle of roots so that they pressed her skin through her chanise. "I am yours, devoted and faithful to you, and you will reward my loyalty. It is the delight of my life to serve you. I am yours, always yours, and you will raise me to the height of your esteem. Everything I have done is to bring greater respect and veneration to you. And to show your power, you will grant my request, providing me with the things I want most, so that I will continue to show you the regard you deserve. You will make the foreigner my willing and besotted servant, you will bring death to my monk-husband, you will guard me against all evil and the demands of Brother Erchboge. You have already shown your strength to those whose faith has faltered, giving madness to those who bow to the White Christ. I saw the men of the fortress made into sniveling infants and worse than that at the end of the Mass, and I knew it was your answer to those who have turned from you to follow the White Christ. You have taken my companion Daga for her disrespectful wrongs and her interminable spying on me. It was good to have her die, because it revealed your strength in the face of the White Christ. You punished her lack of propriety and her misbehavior with madness. You sent her to death for worshiping the White Christ. Now I ask you to send me another woman, one who knows your ways and who will help me to achieve all that you can give me."

She raised her chanise and took from around her waist a narrow, woven length of wool in which she had worked a number of knots. She ran it through her fingers twice and pulled out one long, pale strand which she knotted around her waist again, leaving the woven red strands in her hands. This she wrapped around the largest protruding root, taking care to form the knot in the sacred way. "Saint-Germanius is mine. Ranegonda will not have him, she will not. I want him and I want him to surrender to me so that all the world knows of it. Give him to me. Let me command him as the King commands his vassals, as the master commands the slave." She raised the hem of her chanise as high as her neck, exposing most of her body. "Everything I possess is given to you. Give me now what I desire."

There was a sound in the forest, the breaking of branches as something unknown made its way through the undergrowth.

Pentacoste lowered her chanise. "I am grateful to you for everything," she said to the old gods. "You are my protections against all the misfortunes which have claimed others. You will deliver to me the things I ask and you will take away the things I do not want. You will make me your chosen one, honored above all others." She stepped back from the knotted roots. "It would suit me if Berengar and Margerefa Oelrih were to be gone once I have secured the foreigner; gone from this place and gone from the world. They are useful now but once I have

Saint-Germanius they will no longer be necessary, and their jealousy would be difficult. They would be unwilling to permit him to take me away from here, and they might try to claim me for themselves. I never want that to happen. If they killed each other I would leave you the offering of my gold ring." It was the most valuable thing she owned, the gift given her by her father when she married. To part with it was unthinkable. "I will tie it here, with red wool, and the red will be from blood."

Satisfied that her offer was as handsome as any of the old gods could wish, she moved back, reverencing the carved tokens flanking the roots. She rubbed her face to brush off the sand, and tossed her head so that her two long braids once again fell down her back. "I want a sign from you, a sign that Saint-Germanius will surrender. I want him to kiss me, not the kiss of peace, or the kiss of allegiance, but the kiss of lovers. I want that now. I want it before the sun sets tomorrow." She backed out of the cove, all but stumbling in the sand.

As she ran along the edge of the trees she cursed the villagers for all they had cut down, for they had eliminated the cover she had used for so long in going from the fortress to the cove and her return. She hurried across the open stretch of cleared land, crying out once as she stepped on an abrasive low stump. She paused long enough to look at her foot and to curse the cut she saw. It would have to be bandaged, and that would require an explanation as to how she got it. She scowled as she started moving, favoring her injured foot. Now she was ungainly and slow, and that infuriated her. At least it was past midnight and no one would see her as she made her way toward the fortress. She glared at the stockade as she neared it, panting from exertion and pain. As she searched for the gap in the logs she cursed, for her foot was beginning to swell and it hurt more acutely.

She tore her chanise as she squeezed through the narrow space, and when she tumbled into the concealed entrance to the fortress, she had to collapse against the wall for a short while, sobbing with effort and frustration as well as pain. Finally she made herself stand. Her foot ached but she was able to make her way up the cramped corridor to the concealed door in the women's quarters. She pulled on the lever to swing the door down, and all but screamed in vexation as she realized she needed more strength. For a short while she stood in the darkness, whispering words to the old gods and asking them to aid her. When she was certain that they had heard her, she reached for the lever again, this time pressing on it with all her might, her breath hissing between her teeth.

Finally the door swung downward, becoming a bridge over the gap between the corridor and the hidden entrance. Pentacoste staggered across it, one arm held out in case she lost her footing, and flung herself against the wall of the women's quarters. She braced herself there, her eyes closed and her concentration on calming her inner distress. This was not the time to succumb to fear, or to be weak. She had just left a token of great power, one that could not help but succeed. "It is under way," she whispered to the darkness. Then she forced herself to struggle with the protruding stone in order to close the door once again; she could not make a mistake now, when she was at last reaching the goal she longed for.

Now that she was back in the fortress she shuddered. It was impossible for her not to hate the place. Her father had promised her a position in the world and he had permitted her to come here, to this dreadful place. And he had left her here when her husband had become a monk, in spite of her entreaties to be permitted to marry again. She made her way to the stairs leading to her quarters, putting as little weight on her foot as possible. As she started to climb the stairs she bit her lip, her teeth pressing the sensitive skin. She must be silent. She must not waken Ranegonda, not now, with her clothing torn and her foot cut.

She reached her level without incident, and noticed with satisfaction that Genovefe was sleeping deeply in the antechamber adjoining her own. If there was ever any question of her conduct, Genovefe would answer for it, saying that she had slept in the antechamber and she had not seen Pentacoste leave the fortress; it would be Genovefe's honor that would suffer, not hers. The idea pleased Pentacoste, who decided to leave a small token on Genovefe's behalf the next time she danced for the old gods. With that to soothe her, she went into her own chamber. Once the door was closed, she leaned back against it, her eyes half-closed. She would have to be rid of the chanise and account for its loss somehow. In her father's castle she would accuse one of the slaves of theft, but here that was not possible; she would have to account for it in some other manner. She made her way to her bed, pulling her torn chanise over her head and wadding it up. It might be possible to save the fabric, she thought, and make poppets with it, to leave for the old gods.

Her head was nearly as sore as her foot as she lay in the darkness. It was a warm night for this time of year but her chamber was chilly in spite of the long, sunny afternoon. She drew one of the bear-skin rugs around her shoulders and contemplated the darkness. At last she decided she would ask for the women's bath-house to be heated in the morning, and she would insist that all the women of the fortress join her. She would think of some excuse that Brother Erchboge could not object to, and then she would order the other women to bathe with her. That would end any criticism of her. Yes, she decided, that would succeed. She would make sure that all the women washed together, and her culpability would be less because of it, no matter what the monk said. She could receive a dressing for her foot from Winolda and no one would think anything of it; it would be nothing more than part of the bath. Afterward she would prevail upon Berengar to play his kithre for them all, and she would watch Hrosia, Enolda, and Juste long for him in vain with their eyes. While she considered this, sleep came over her.

Not far from the landward tower where Pentacoste at last slept, Captain Amalric was standing night watch, his spear held firmly as he struggled to stay awake. It was nearing the end of the night and even the forest was still.

"Would you mind some company, Captain?" asked a familiar foreign voice from the gate-court below.

"Saint-Germanius. Come up, and welcome." He peered down into the darkness but even his night-accustomed eyes could not penetrate the deep shadows. "Watch yourself," he recommended.

"I was working in the smithy," he said as he climbed the narrow stairs. He had heard the distant sound of the concealed door closing, and although he had not located the door itself, he realized its meaning: that Pentacoste had made offerings to the old gods again.

"You have been busy there, this last month," said Captain Amalric, making room for Saint-Germanius beside him on the parapet. "I have noticed how long you have worked at the forge."

"It is a skill I learned many years ago," said Saint-Germanius, dismissing the implied compliment. "With both the smith and the armorer dead, it was the least I could do for the fortress. It is nearly autumn and there are things that must be done before winter arrives."

"Yes. With the miasma here, no one is strong enough to complete the tasks, not if we are to cut enough trees for the King," said Captain Amalric with a twist of his hand that implied it was beyond him.

"Then it's as well I was here to help; the people in the fortress and the village need more hands than they possess." Saint-Germanius looked toward the dark mass of the forest. "And the trees themselves besiege us."

"Yes," said Captain Amalric. "Which I pray will not suggest to the outlaws that they come here now we are weak."

"When I have finished the iron gate for the fortress and the iron braces for the stockade, we will be much less weak," said Saint-Germanius. "I think there is enough iron to complete both of them."

Captain Amalric rubbed his chin. "For a stranger waiting ransom, you have been very accommodating to this place, Saint-Germanius."

Saint-Germanius shook his head. "What good would it do to be ransomed from a fortress that had been conquered by outlaws or Danes?"

"And the Gerefa?" said Captain Amalric, his remark pointed. "What have you done for her? Are you seeking to place her in obligation to you? Or do you want to win her favor for more than your liberty? Is it the fortress or the Gerefa who commands your skills?" He waited for the foreigner's response.

"Especially the Gerefa," said Saint-Germanius in his unruffled way, pleased that he had not been the one to bring up Ranegonda.

This startled Captain Amalric, who turned and tried to make out Saint-Germanius's features. "Then you admit you single her out from all others?"

"Yes. As she has singled me from the first. She is an admirable woman," said Saint-Germanius with a swift smile. "This place is fortunate to have her. With her brother gone to the monastery, she has done more than anyone has asked of her, and done it well."

Captain Amalric nodded heavily. "Yes, that is surely so." He looked out over the village, his face set in harsh lines. "There were two more deaths today, down there. The rot took them. Brother Erchboge has sealed their mouths to protect them through the night."

Saint-Germanius stared down thoughtfully, his vision largely unhampered by the night; he noticed two of the long mats used for the dead laid across the entrances to village houses. "How is it," he inquired, "that the dead are left outside the door until dawn? Isn't that a risk to the village and the people in the houses? If dogs or pigs reach them—"

"It would be a dire omen," said Captain Amalric, Signing himself. "It has happened only once before, and the Danes were on us before the next full moon."

"Then why take the risk." Saint-Germanius indicated the mats. "Leaving them this way is courting disaster, or desecration of the dead."

"They may yet rise, those dead," said Captain Amalric with a trace of surprise. "If they are inside the house, and they rise because of demons, who knows what evil they might do. But if they are left outside, with their mouths sealed, they may rise if the White Christ wills it." He Signed himself as an afterthought.

"I see." Saint-Germanius considered what he had been told. A short while later he asked, "And what would happen if one of the dead did actually rise? What would become of that risen one."

Captain Amalric turned to him, his attention caught. "If one of the dead . . . But that has never happened."

"But if it did?" Saint-Germanius persisted.

It took Captain Amalric a short while to answer. "I suppose Brother Erchboge would have to decide if . . . if the rising was in the Name of the White Christ. They say that He can do that: raise the dead. Because He rose from the dead."

"So He did," said Saint-Germanius with a faint, elusive smile.

There was another short silence between them, then Captain Amalric gestured to the walkway. "I must keep at my rounds."

"Do you object to my company as you walk?" Saint-Germanius asked, prepared to descend to the gate court.

"No; I'm glad of it, to say truth." He went ahead of Saint-Germanius, watching the darkness. "These last weeks, with our people dying and maddened, I am grateful for good company. It keeps me from too much reflection. At times likes these, it is not wise to dwell on misfortunes, for it hides the omens."

"Then it pleases me to be here," said Saint-Germanius.

When Captain Amalric stopped again he rounded on Saint-Germanius, speaking with emphasis, as if he had been developing his ideas for some little time. "Since you are a foreigner, you may not know that the Gerefa cannot be permitted to marry. The Bishop himself has forbidden it; because of the miasma of the Pox."

"So I understand," said Saint-Germanius with unruffled calm, and did not add that he had learned of it from Ranegonda herself.

"We punish erring women with drowning, as the law requires," Captain Amalric went on, his voice a little louder as if more sound would be persuasive. "Not her brother nor her position could save her if she were to get with child. She would be beaten by Brother Erchboge if she appeared to be your woman, to make an example of her defiance." He paused, letting Saint-Germanius have the opportunity to respond, then added, "She is the more carefully watched because of who she is, and she will be the more strictly punished if she transgresses. King Otto does not permit his Gerefas to flout the laws or the White Christ."

"And do you think she is transgressing?" asked Saint-Germanius softly. "With me?"

"She is much in your company. You are private together. She smiles at you." He coughed. "And you smile at her, foreigner."

"She will not get any child of me, if that is your meaning," said Saint-Germanius quietly. "Believe this, Captain Amalric: she has done me a great kindness and I would be beneath contempt if I disgraced her for it."

This seemed to reassure Captain Amalric a bit. He nodded several times as he thought over the answers he had been given. "Yet you say you favor her."

"Of course," said Saint-Germanius in the same steady voice. "Why should this surprise you? I am her servant to command." The phrase was old-fashioned, more Roman than Germanian, and spoken with formality.

"This fortress cannot be compromised more than it has been already," Captain Amalric warned Saint-Germanius. "We could be ruined, cut off from all aid, or condemned as traitors, if it is learned that the Gerefa has given herself to you, or to any man. There are few secrets possible inside these walls. If I have any sign that you have done this to her, I will act for the fortress and for the protection of the Gerefa. I like you, foreigner, and I approve what you have done while you have been here, but I will not overlook anything that would redound to our discredit."

"Well enough," said Saint-Germanius. "But I tell you now that you will not have reason. I do not plan to disgrace Ranegonda."

"I pray this is so," said Captain Amalric, and continued to walk his post.

This time Saint-Germanius waited for him, leaning against the battlement, the village behind him. As Captain Amalric came back even with him, he said, "Your worry for the honor of the fortress: does that include Pentacoste?"

"I suppose it should," said Saint-Germanius thoughtfully. "She is the more apt to bring such notice as concerns you here."

Captain Amalric lowered his head. "In the village they are saying that she leaves tokens for the old gods. They say that she has cursed her husband and Ranegonda. They have found the tokens she left to grant her—" He waved his hand. "They are peasant women, and they do not like Pentacoste; she is unlike them and they do not want their men to look at her."

"There are women of the fortress who feel much the same," Saint-Germanius pointed out. "And with more cause."

"Then you believe that she is capable of bringing disgrace on us," said Captain Amalric as he set his spear down and joined Saint-Germanius. "I can speak of this to no one, for the men-at-arms will not heed it, and Brother Erchboge has already said that he wants to flog Pentacoste for her laxness. If her father were not a Dux, he would have done it before now."

"Does Brother Erchboge have that right?" asked Saint-Germanius with some dismay.

"He is the servant of the White Christ for this fortress. He is permitted to do what the White Christ requires of him, the King has said so, and that would include the wife of the Gerefa, if Giselberht were not a monk," answered Captain Amalric. "He is required to chastise those who go against the laws of the White Christ."

"Would he like to flog Berengar as well, I wonder?" Saint-Germanius asked, anticipating the answer.

"For what reason? Where is the sin? And consider who he is. Flog the son of Pranz Balduin? Certainly not. It is Pentacoste who has driven him to this obsession. He is her victim, caught in her toils. Brother Erchboge has told us all that women are a snare and a trap and they wait for men to desire them in order to bring them to damnation."

"Is Ranegonda such a doorway to perdition, too?" asked Saint-Germanius with deceptive innocence. "Or your wife?" He did not wait for an answer, but straightened up and stretched. "Look. Dawn is coming soon." He pointed eastward, along the expanse of ocean and beach toward the horizon.

Captain Amalric noticed no difference in the light. "How can you tell?"

Saint-Germanius cocked his head and glanced upward. "The stars." It was not entirely the truth, for those of his blood could feel the coming of the sun more accurately than a lodestone could feel the north.

This response took Captain Amalric aback, for he had been expecting a more foreign answer. "Do you know the stars, as well?"

"When you have watched as many nights as I have, Captain," said Saint-Germanius in an ironic tone, "the stars become your familiar talismans."

"There was a rain of stars in the sky, many years ago," said Captain Amalric with a look of apprehension. "It was at the time that old King Haganrih conquered Brennabor, and we all feared that it would bring destruction to us, not to those he warred against. We kept two lights blazing in the light room, and lit fires on the beaches as well, so that ships would not mistake the rain of stars for beacons."

"How many nights did the rain last?" asked Saint-Germanius, who had seen the same thing from the deck of his ship.

"Four nights, and then it was over," said Captain Amalric, his remembered relief evident in his voice. "It was a wondrous thing, and

Brother Erchboge told us that we had to pray for salvation or the White Christ would bring His fire to earth and we would be consumed in it. He had not been here long then, and there were fewer people in the village. Most of them fell into error and left tokens for the old gods, but Brother Erchboge whipped anyone whom he discovered with tokens. One man died of it, and the villagers all forswore the old gods, or so they vowed, so they would not be whipped." He cleared his throat. "He might still whip them."

"And does Pentacoste know this?" asked Saint-Germanius in a neutral voice. "Or does she suppose she can control him, as she seeks to control other men?"

"I don't know," said Captain Amalric, and walked away from Saint-Germanius again, keeping to his rounds.

"Captain," Saint-Germanius called after him, raising his voice only a little so as not to disturb those asleep. "Who is keeping the light tonight?"

"Ewarht's son Delwin. He is just old enough." He stopped and looked back. "Why do you ask?"

"You are short-handed, and I am often awake at night. You have allowed me to keep the light before; you may do so again." He was able to give his expression a look of interest.

Captain Amalric regarded him steadily. "I might," he answered, and continued along the ramparts once again. Below in the village there were the first sounds of movement from the penned and cooped animals as they felt the morning coming; Captain Amalric paused and looked down, then glanced back at Saint-Germanius, a dark place in the night. He was about to ask him another question, then decided it would keep, and kept walking.

It was shortly after dawn that the wooden horn sounded three times, announcing new arrivals at the entrance to the stockade. In his quarters Saint-Germanius heard this with mingled surprise and apprehension; he reached for his linen bliaut and dragged it over his head as he started toward the door.

The stockade gates were opened by the woodcutters from the village who were just setting out for a day in the forest. They stood aside as the large party of men and wagons swept through the gates, their armed escort bringing up the rear.

"Who is it?" Saint-Germanius asked Duart as he crossed the Marshaling Court.

"They say it is Margerefa Oelrih returned, with the men and supplies he vowed he would provide," said the monitor. He moved unsteadily and there was a glaze to his eyes which had not left him since he had been seized with visions from the Host. He gave Saint-Germanius a look of disapproval. "He may bring your ransom."

"That he may," said Saint-Germanius steadily, though he knew it would not for Margerefa Oelrih himself told him his message to Hrotiger had been destroyed.

"And then you will be gone before the snows come," said Duart with satisfaction. "We will be proof against misfortune once you have gone."

"If that is what the White Christ wishes, then surely I will go," said Saint-Germanius in a tone calculated to keep Duart from protesting more vehemently.

Duart glared at him. "True, foreigner." He indicated the gate that was already swinging open and said with grudging respect, "It is a worthy device, the one you have made for the gates. Two slaves at the cranks instead of six for the doors, it is better for us." That was all he was prepared to say in Saint-Germanius's favor, and he turned away from him, going into the landward tower.

Margerefa Oelrih was the first through the gates, his big red-roan gelding showing signs of going lame. As he swung out of the saddle, he thrust the reins into the hands of one of the slaves who had come hurrying up a moment before. "Where is the Gerefa?" he demanded without ceremony.

"She will be here directly," said Geraint, who was the first man down from the parapet. "You have come early in the morning."

Saint-Germanius paused beside the Common Hall, the bath-houses directly behind him. In the pink-colored light he studied the newcomers, noticing that the horses showed signs of harder riding than usual, and that all the men wore broignes and heaumes as if expecting to fight.

"We spent the night in the fields at Holy Cross Monastery," said Margerefa Oelrih. "We should not be here at all, judging from what the monks told us." He signaled to his Captain, who had just come through the gates, a woman riding pillion behind him. "Jouarre, get down."

The Captain climbed out of the saddle at once. There was a fresh scar on his forehead, a jagged red line that puckered at the end, pulling up the eyebrow beneath. He kept the reins in his hand, and drew his horse forward to permit those behind them to enter the fortress. "The carts will stay down in the village," he said, repeating what they already had agreed upon.

"Yes. Dispatch Brother Andoche to tend to the arrangements once we're settled here." He rubbed his gloved hand across his face. "That monastery . . . they are in a bad way."

"If Brother Haganrih had not died," said Jouarre distantly.

"And of rot. His feet were filled with the miasma," said Margerefa Oelrih with a motion of distaste. "The Bishop will not like to hear of this."

"Nor will the King," said Ranegonda as she approached the two men and raised her skirts to above her knees in respect. "I've hoped that you would come, though I did not expect you, Margerefa. There has been great travail here." It was apparent that she had wakened only a short while ago; her braids were still wrapped together and her face bore the softened look of sleep. "We are to break our fasts in a short while, if you want to eat with us."

Margerefa Oelrih Signed himself. "Most certainly," he declared. "It is what we hoped." He made a conciliatory gesture. "With the superior of the monastery not yet in his grave, we could not eat there. The monks are fasting, and—" He held out his hand to show that he could not order the monks to feed him and his men.

Ranegonda sighed. "Certainly. My cooks must be warned," she said. "And it will mean that the meal will be delayed a short while." She looked at the party of riders who were now within the fortress gates. "How many?"

"There are sixty-three of us altogether," said Margerefa Oelrih, and hurried on as he read dismay in her eyes. "Of that, twenty-seven are to remain here. They are the men you were promised, to help guard the village and increase the number of logs you can cut. Eleven of the men are married, and their wives are with them. There are even a few children."

"Thanks to the White Christ and the King," said Ranegonda, Signing herself. "They are welcome. With the miasma here, we have need of strong bodies and capable hands." She looked at Jouarre. "What of weapons? Will we be provided more?"

"We have few to spare, but we'll do what we can," said Captain Jouarre, and glanced again at the woman on his horse. "We ransomed my wife," he explained. "But she is not faring well."

"She has been hard-used," said the Margerefa. "In fact, Brother Andoche advised Jouarre not to take her back because of what had happened, but he was adamant." He shrugged. "She will need gentle care, or so the women have said. I have not seen that coddling does any good, but Jouarre permits it."

"I will set women to the task," said Ranegonda, and then looked over the new arrivals again, making up her mind as she considered what she saw. "I will order the baths heated at once. You will want to bathe to be rid of the dust of the road." As she glanced in the direction of the bath-houses she saw Saint-Germanius, and felt reassured. "With all the hours you have been on the road for the last several days, doubtless it would be good to wash away the dust."

Margerefa Oelrih started to shake his head. "It would be seen as vanity, and after spending the night at the monastery, to have it said we are vain would—"

At that Saint-Germanius spoke up. "It might also wash away the lingering trace of the miasma as well as the dust of the road, if you have been touched by it. If Brother Erchboge will bless the water for you, it may save you."

Apparently Margerefa Oelrih was much struck by this suggestion. He regarded Saint-Germanius for a short while, his expression of surprise unchanging. Then he nodded. "It is well. If Brother Erchboge will bless the water, then it is piety and not vanity that works upon us."

"And there will be less notice paid to Jouarre's wife," Saint-Germanius added.

"I will have to give new orders," said Ranegonda, and lifted her skirts to Margerefa Oelrih again. "I will be about it. You are welcome to Leosan Fortress, Margerefa, for your sake and for the sake of the King." With that she turned on her heel and strode off toward the kitchens.

There was confusion in the gate court, and it was spilling over into the larger Marshaling Court. Men and horses were milling in the area; a few of the men had already removed their heaums and were becoming restless about food.

"It's a bad thing," said Margerefa Oelrih, shaking his head and turning his gaze in the general direction of Milo. "Not one woman in a thousand is worth such an effort. And see what she is like now; branded on the forehead and back, and listless as a sick puppy. I fear he has made a bad bargain in her ransom."

"Would you think so if it were . . . oh, let us say Pentacoste?" Saint-Germanius suggested in a low voice.

Margerefa Oelrih swung his head back and fixed Saint-Germanius with a penetrating stare. "By what right—" he began in hushed fury.

Saint-Germanius's smile was inoffensive to the point of blandness. "She is the daughter of a high-ranking father, and if anything so . . . unlucky were to happen to her, surely you would be obliged to ransom her, for the honor of King Otto if not for her own sake?"

"If the King so ordered, I would," said Margerefa Oelrih suspiciously, his brow darkening. "But foreigners should not speak slightingly of such a lady as Pentacoste is." He paused. "There are those who would be offended."

"That was not my intention," said Saint-Germanius.

"But it could offend. You have not been here long enough to realize how stringent we are in such matters." The warning was clear; Margerefa Oelrih rested his hand on the hilt of his dagger.

"It is not quite a year since I washed ashore here," said Saint-Germanius seriously. "This place and its people are strange to me, but they have preserved me when many another would not, and for that I am grateful. I would not want to offend them. That would be poor payment for so great a service."

"Unless it could bring you freedom," said Margerefa Oelrih with unapologetic cynicism.

"Surely not," said Saint-Germanius in feigned astonishment. "You carried a message from me which was taken in your fight with outlaws. There has been no other chance for me to send a letter on its way to Rome. And I would be more of a fool than I am to try to strike out alone, with outlaws and Danes—"

"And the people of Bremen," added Margerefa Oelrih. "They, too, are abroad since Magyars sacked their city."

"We have heard little of that," said Saint-Germanius, thinking of the fragmented report Ranegonda had been given by her brother.

"And there are those held for ransom, as Milo was," said Margerefa Oelrih. "There will be more of it in future. That much is certain. No matter how little you think of women." This last was added with a look of derision. "What foreigner knows the worth of women?"

"But what have I said that suggests that? To say that a woman holds value, how can that be a slight?" Saint-Germanius regarded the Margerefa for a moment. "You are to uphold the word of the King. Wouldn't that include ransoming a woman like Pentacoste? Or Ranegonda?"

"It is possible," Margerefa Oelrih allowed, but with such reservation that Saint-Germanius had to suppress a smile. "Where is that monk? I will have to arrange with him to bless the baths."

"He was in the chapel before first light," said Saint-Germanius, who had caught sight of the monk as he returned to his quarters after walking on the parapet with Captain Amalric. "He prays there most of the day."

Margerefa Oelrih nodded, and then added, as if it meant nothing to him, "That whelp of Pranz Balduin's? Is he still here? Or has he come to his senses and left for his father's lands?"

"Yes, Margerefa, he is still here," said Saint-Germanius in a very neutral tone.

There was a brief pause as Margerefa Oelrih considered this; then he nodded. "I will have to speak to him."

"He will rise shortly. It is his practice to hunt in the mornings," said Saint-Germanius.

The Margerefa looked mildly startled, and managed to ask smoothly, "You mean that he actually goes into the forest with weapons? That he can be useful? That pretty fellow?"

"He brings back game twice a week, and he has helped skin everything he has provided. There are traders in Hedaby who will welcome good furs." Saint-Germanius was briefly silent. "I noticed your horse needs attention. With our smith and our armorer dead, I have been carrying out their duties. If you will bring your horse to the stable, I'll do what I can for him."

"He needs shoes, in any case," said Margerefa Oelrih. "After I have bathed, I'll do it." He looked around the Marshaling Court, this time with a degree of confidence. "Some of the others will need the same."

"If there is iron enough, I will tend to all of them," said Saint-Germanius.

"Be careful of the bay mare, the one Baldric is riding. She has been having colic for two days, and sweating. Tell me if she can go on." He glanced toward the landward tower, looked away and then back again. Without taking his eyes from what he saw through the jumbled activity, he said, "If she won't survive, tell me."

Saint-Germanius's dark eyes were sardonically bright. "I will," he said, uncertain that Margerefa Oelrih had heard him as he hurried through the confusion toward the place where Pentacoste was standing, Berengar at her side.

Text of a letter from the Priory of Most Holy Grace to Bishop Gerht in Hamburh, carried by a dozen armed men, delivered thirteen days after being written.

To the great Bishop Gerht at the Cathedral of the Nativity in Hamburh, my submissive greetings and prayers in the Name of the White Christ on this sixteenth day of October in the Year of Grace 938.

It is not fitting that I should address you directly, Excellency, but the circumstances are such that I can no longer do those things you have instructed me to do without assistance in this terrible time.

You have given it as your will and the will of the White Christ that we nuns succor those who suffer. When they were fewer in number it was a joyous task to do it. But now, with so very many in need, we no longer have the room or the stores to aid them. Of greatest concern are the countless children we find every day. They have been abandoned by their parents and are without any means in the world. If we refuse to take them in, they will surely starve or become the slaves of Danes. We fear most for those children who fall into the hands of the brothel-keepers, who treat them more brutally than the Danes do.

In the last months we have taken in over a hundred such children, and we have done all that we could to care for them in the way the White Christ demands we do. But it is becoming impossible to feed them all, let alone find a place and work for the new ones who arrive almost daily. We have tried to learn where the families are who left these children, but it is a fruitless hope that they will come for their children, not if they have been abandoned.

For every boy we have four girls here, and that increases our problems, for not only can we not feed them now, we are in no position to fix them with a dowry or bride-price. Even should every one of them be touched by Grace and seek to enter the service of the White Christ, our priory is inadequate to the task of housing them. We must have more room, more places to put them, more employment for them, or we must consign those who live to the lives of servants and concubines. It troubles me that we who seek to live in the way the White Christ taught should have to do these things.

You must know of some other priory or religious house where some of these children may be taken. I ask you to give authorization to us, so that these children may be protected and cared for as they expected to be when they came to this priory. I have hope that you will want to guard these children because those who prey upon them become hourly more numerous. There is a man from Bremen called Mang who has already taken more than a dozen of the children, promising them advancement and favor, who then sells them to Captains of ships bound for distant ports. What becomes of the children then is unknown.

Some of the children also tell of another man from Bremen, called Hadelin, who is said to lure children to his camp where he then kills them for food. It does not give me much satisfaction to realize that this must surely have happened at least once. They say there are places in the forest where there are heaps of children's bones. Those nameless graves will be the fate of many more than have fallen already if you cannot find a refuge for them.

All the omens point to a wet winter, and the longer the children have to live wild, the greater the chance that wild beasts or a malign miasma will find them, and they will die alone and unguarded, their souls left to wander for eternity, neither saved nor damned.

We have already decided that we must care first for the children and only then for the adults who come here, and for that reason we have failed, we are aware, to do all that the White Christ requires of us. But it is not *possible for us to take in all, and there are other places where the parents are more welcome than their children. We have told those who have come that we care for the children. Only when the adult is clearly in the throes of illness do we offer them our charity. For this we ask your understanding.*

Those who are transfixed with visions or who are made ill with dancing we have not permitted to enter. While we will have to answer for this in Hell, we have seen how great this sickness is and we are powerless against it. We cannot let the miasma come here, and nothing we can do can arrest it. Therefore we will not open our doors to it, for the sake of those we have promised to protect. Our decision was made after days of fasting and prayer, and we trust that you will not condemn us for what we have done.

I pray that the White Christ will guide you in your prayers and that you will find some way that will allow us to preserve these unfortunates. There is so little time, and the children have already suffered so much. My Sisters here and I are at our wits' ends. Your aid will set us all on the right course again.

May the White Christ and you forgive me for writing this to you, but I believe it is what I must do in order to save these children. I do not write for my own benefit nor to ask for benefits to me, but for your help on behalf of the abandoned children, who are forever in my prayers and in the prayers of the Sisters here.

Sister Mourna
Prioress, Priory of the Most Holy Grace
by my own hand

3

That afternoon the hunting party brought back three hares, a boar, two deer, and seven geese. They rode through the stockade gates while the sun was still high enough to make the day seem full of promise, and entered through the fortress gates after leaving their kills at the slaughterhouse in the village.

"We could have got another boar, if we'd stayed out longer," Berengar protested as he and Margerefa Oelrih entered the Common Hall together. "It's going to rain tomorrow, and we won't get out again for three or four days, and by then most of the roads will be bogs, and there won't be any good footing in the whole forest." He looked up at the corner of the sky he could see through the door. "Then the ground will freeze and that will be worse."

Margerefa Oelrih shook his head; he found the young man's petulance amusing and wearing at once. "The horses are tired, we have a good kill, and there is no reason we should have to devote all our time to the hunt." He indicated where Berengar's kithre was hung. "You could sing for us, that would be—"

"I am not a poor traveler who has to entertain in order to eat!" Berengar burst out, the irritation of several days' goading finally becoming intolerable.

"No," Margerefa Oelrih agreed with a trace of anger. "You're not a poor traveler; that no one is permitted to assume." He looked around the Common Hall, and noticed that two of the slaves were busy building up the fire in the yawning fireplace. "Good. Very good. It is chilly at night, now that the days are short."

One of the slaves looked over at him; the other paid no attention as they continued their labors.

"How soon will you be away from here?" asked Berengar. "Given that the winter is coming and you have said you do not wish to remain here through it all? Surely you cannot stay much longer without risking such a predicament."

"The new houses in the village will be finished in another ten days. If all is well, that is when my men and I will depart," said the Margerefa Oelrih in a disinterested tone, unwilling to be dragged into yet another dispute with the young nobleman that was not of his making. "None of the soldiers want to winter here."

"And if the houses are not finished, what then?" demanded Berengar. "Do you extend your stay, and—"

"We will have to decide that in ten days," said Margerefa Oelrih, deliberately provoking Berengar now, hoping to settle the matter for the time being. "I regret that I cannot tell you when it will be possible for you to have this fortress to yourself again."

"Hardly to myself," muttered Berengar, and flung himself down on one of the two backed chairs in the Common Hall, the chair usually reserved for Brother Erchboge's use.

"Then to your use," said the Margerefa, making no attempt to speak cordially. "You have determined to present yourself to Pentacoste so that when she is permitted to marry again, you will be the one she decides upon, before anything can be arranged with her father." He paused. "If her father does not recognize the marriage, it will be nothing but concubinage, and your father will not tolerate that, not if you have to take one of her debauched sisters to wife in order to have

Pentacoste." This time his pause was a bit longer. "They say that the father whores his own daughters."

"Her father will recognize it; he will not risk offending my father." Berengar grinned in triumph, ignoring the Margerefa's last remark.

"Assuming your father recognizes the marriage. He might not, given what is said about Dux Pol," the Margerefa pointed out. "And if he does not, you will be answerable for what becomes of Pentacoste. If she were accused of harlotry, you could not deny it, not if you had lain with her. There would be nothing you could do to save her, not without armed troops. I hope you have considered that while making your plans."

"I haven't any fixed plans," said Berengar negligently. "The omens favor me, Margerefa, and I will put my trust in the omens."

"Omens are not enough to hold Pentacoste, not she," Margerefa Oelrih said sharply. "You do not know her if you believe that."

"I know her better than you do," Berengar countered, coming out of the chair. "I have been here with her. I have not careered all over the countryside, anticipating she would welcome my return. You are here for a short while and then you are gone."

"That's the crux of it." The Margerefa laughed unpleasantly. "You want me away because you fear the interest Pentacoste has for me. You want her to be fascinated by you, and you can only be assured of that when I am not by."

"She prefers my company; we spend time together every day, because it pleases her to be with me," declared Berengar, stung by Margerefa Oelrih's canny observation. "You see how she sends for me, to tell her tales and to sing to her. She gives you no such distinction."

"Not often," said Margerefa Oelrih with false modesty. "I sing poorly. But I do other things very well, as she has reason to know."

Berengar flushed. "You say you have dishonored her?"

"No more than you have," Margerefa Oelrih countered, his eyes growing hard.

The two men regarded one another with implacable hostility, both of them breathing faster than necessary. Finally Berengar stepped back. "Not here, not within the walls of the fortress. We are guests here and neither of us can demand anything of the other without the grant of the Gerefa. And you are a magistrate for King Otto. It would not be permissible for me to question you further without the authorization of the King, not while you are about your duties."

"See you remember that," Margerefa Oelrih advised. "As I remember who your father is." This barb struck true and deep; the Margerefa had the satisfaction of watching Berengar flinch. "I have heard that your father has tried to arrange a suitable marriage for you. He has taken time to consider many well-born women who would honor your House. How sad that you are here and cannot accept the bride your father has found for you at last. They say she brings wealth and honor and power, if you will have her." The speculative tone of his voice served only to annoy Berengar.

"She is ten years my senior; she writes poetry about martyrs and sacrifice, and I am told she has a stammer," said Berengar. "What wife is that for me?"

"One that your father finds satisfactory," said the Margerefa in daunting tones. "And you as his son are bound to respect his wishes and his wisdom."

Berengar lifted his chin. "You haven't married, though you are well past the age for it," he reminded his tormentor.

"I am an officer of the King," said Margerefa Oelrih, as if that explained everything. "My family is secure in the line: I have three brothers who are wed and have children."

"And that leaves you to yearn for another man's wife," said Berengar.

"As you are doing," the Margerefa challenged, facing Berengar squarely. "I, at least, have my duty to bring me here. What do you have, but your desire and the despair of your family?"

What Berengar might have answered was forestalled by Brother Erchboge, who came into the Common Hall, his sunken eyes alight with indignation. "Who saw fit to bring that woman inside these walls?" he demanded of the Margerefa. "I saw her just now with two of the women as they went into the landward tower. How does she come to be here?"

Margerefa Oelrih stood a little straighter. "You are not spending the day in prayer, good Brother?" he asked.

"My week of fasting is over," said Brother Erchboge with an emotion that in anyone but a pious monk might seem to be pride. "I have my duties to the people of the fortress. I am the one they turn to for the solace of the White Christ. They have had my prayers and now they need my ministration." His face darkened. "If that woman has been here while I fasted and prayed—"

Berengar concealed an impatient sigh. "Is there something the matter, Brother?"

"What woman is that?" asked Margerefa Oelrih, for there were a dozen women in his company, and another dozen in the village below;

he hoped that perhaps the monk had not actually seen Captain Jouarre's wife, who had been living in the women's quarters since they arrived.

"The one with the brands!" exclaimed the monk, his hands flung out with the intensity of his feeling. "On her forehead and cheek! You know the signs!"

"That is the wife of my Captain Jouarre," said the Margerefa, speaking slowly and carefully as if Brother Erchboge were a bit deaf.

"Wife? She is no wife, not with such brands," said Brother Erchboge, condemning her absolutely. "If she has been a wife, so much the worse, for she has chosen harlotry over virtue." He Signed himself and directed his gaze at the Margerefa.

"She was captured," said Margerefa Oelrih. "She has been ransomed. While she was a captive of the Danes she was branded."

Berengar had retreated to a corner of the Common Hall, pausing only to take down his kithre so that he could make a pretense of practicing.

"It was a sinful thing to do, to pay for that woman. There is no honor in such ransom. She is an adulteress. She must face the penalty for adultery." He cocked his head, regarding Margerefa Oelrih with intensity. "You know your duty. Any woman who is married and permits a man other than her husband to use her carnally is an adulteress, and for that crime she must die, and because it is sin, she must drown, so that the sin will be washed away in her death. How could you have forgot it, when the law is in your hands? You must enforce the law, Margerefa. It states that any adulteress cannot live."

There was a brief silence, then Margerefa Oelrih said, "She was taken by our enemies. Surely that is not adultery."

"Her brands show she was a whore for them. Enemies or not, she has committed adultery. She has been used by a man—probably many men—who are not her husband. What else is adultery, if not that?" Again he locked his hot gaze on Margerefa Oelrih. "The superior at Holy Cross must be notified."

"The superior at Holy Cross is dead," Margerefa Oelrih countered. "His feet and legs rotted. They have not found his successor yet."

"The monks must be informed, then. They will supervise the drowning and attend to her burial," said Brother Erchboge. "Do not delay carrying out the law; it will only serve to make other women become wanton, believing that they will not have to suffer the consequences of their lusts." He put his hand to his gaunt cheeks. "The White Christ will not forgive your laxness, Margerefa, and neither will the King."

Margerefa Oelrih cleared his throat. "She was taken prisoner. They took her during a battle, as they seize horses and goods, as a prize. She has been ransomed. There is no adultery in that."

"If she was not branded to show she has been a whore, possibly not," said Brother Erchboge more confidently. "If they had made her a slave, she would be disgraced but without sin. But you know the meaning of those brands as well as any man, and you know that she did not remain chaste. Therefore she is an adulteress. She must pay the penalty for it."

"The Danes did that to her when they made her their prisoner," Margerefa Oelrih insisted. "It was the fault of her Godless captors, she said so in her Confession to Brother Andoche. She did not want them, or seek them, or trade her favors for their favor. She has been listless and frightened as a sick child since we brought her back. She is—"

"She is an adulteress," said Brother Erchboge uncompromisingly, "and all the world knows it, because the brands show it clearly. She has dishonored her husband and the White Christ."

Margerefa Oelrih sighed. "Brother Andoche said that she had not erred, and it was he who heard her Confession. He questioned her very closely, for more than two hours. When he heard all that she said he informed me that there was no deliberate sin, only the need for penitence, not the sin of adultery. He said that those who defiled her were not Christians and therefore she was not an adulteress. He said that the brands meant nothing."

"He is wrong," said Brother Erchboge. "And he must surely know it. The woman was fouled and now she must answer for it."

"Captain Jouarre will not like it," he predicted. "He has paid gold for her return."

"He should have spent the money more wisely," said Brother Erchboge, refusing to be persuaded. "To give gold for a woman who is disgraced and sinful is the act of a foolish man." He held out both hands as if grappling with an unseen figure. "It would be wrong if she were a concubine, but if she is his wife, her betrayal of him is twice as damning."

From his place in the corner, Berengar watched with apprehension and avidity. He had seen a woman drowned only once, and it had disturbed him for some time afterward. Now, it seemed, he would have the chance to see it again. He worked the tuning pegs of his kithre, plucking them very lightly so that they would not be heard.

"My Captain will not accept this," said Margerefa Oelrih with regret. "He cannot fight you, but he will not permit you to take her from him, not after what he has done to get her once again."

"You are sworn to uphold the law of the King and the White Christ. You are the one who must rule on this case, and determine what she will answer for." He Signed himself. "May we be protected from sin and from sinners, who are as great a miasma as the terrible diseases that have been visited upon us. If we are to be spared more deaths, we must be vigilant in removing the sin. Sin and disease are one in the same, and to eradicate one is to eradicate the other."

"You have no reason to condemn this woman. Captain Jouarre is satisfied that his wife is blameless for whatever has happened to her, and Brother Andoche has agreed that her husband has that right. She has agreed that if she has a child in the next year she will leave it in the forest." Margerefa Oelrih folded his arms. "The White Christ surely does not have greater rights than a husband in regard to his wife."

"Certainly He does," said Brother Erchboge. "He has rule of all mankind, and His Kingdom is eternal." There was spittle clinging to his skimpy beard and his eyes were fixed. "That woman must be drowned, and it must be soon if the White Christ is not to visit us with greater misfortune for our lack of obedience to His will."

Margerefa Oelrih Signed himself, as much because it was expected as because he felt the monk's assertions were correct. "It is not fitting that the woman should die. She has suffered already. Her husband has reclaimed her. If he wants to beat her for what she has done, that is his right. But you may not claim her."

Brother Erchboge took a long, noisy breath. "If you defy me, you defy the White Christ. For that alone your King Otto would condemn you. If you will not turn the woman over for the judgment of the monks of Holy Cross, then I must address my complaint to the Bishop. I will have to ask him to request that soldiers be withdrawn from this part of the country until the people here show themselves accepting of the rule of the White Christ."

"The Bishop isn't so foolish," said Margerefa Oelrih, but not as confidently as he would have liked.

"The Bishop is the servant of the White Christ, and he will do whatever the White Christ demands of him, though it bring suffering to many who are innocent, for they will be welcomed in Heaven. How could he tolerate the insolence of the men of this place? It is more than a brazen affront to the laws established by the King, it is the audacity of men who do not bow to the reign of the White Christ. The Bishop has a double obligation, and he would compromise himself in this world and the next if he permitted this refusal to go unanswered. He would grieve for all that might have been spared had the White Christ been defended instead of a sin-ridden woman." Brother Erchboge sensed his advantage, and pressed it. "That the stubbornness of one man to defend an adulteress wife should lead to the ruin of this place.

Without the men of the King, the outlaws and the Danes would soon make short work of Leosan Fortress, wouldn't they?" His eyes were crafty now, and there was a satisfaction in his half-smile that made Margerefa Oelrih shudder as facing armed men in battle could not.

Margerefa Oelrih squared his stance. "She is not going to be turned over to you. Brother Andoche has already decided that she is not responsible for what happened to her, and Captain Jouarre has—"

"I have seen angels of God dancing," said Brother Erchboge with an abrupt sweep of his arm. "I have watched them and longed for their purity and the serene delights they know in Heaven. It is given to me to witness the perfection of souls who are the true servants of the White Christ. When I fast I see them clearly, and I know that the flesh and its rule are vile. We are common clay and dung. How can I be content with this earth when I have seen the splendor of perfect Grace? And how can I permit this woman to live when she embodies all that the White Christ abhors?" He Signed himself. "The White Christ gives such visions as those I have seen to those who live according to His will. And I know that it is my task to be sure that sin is extirpated wherever it thrusts itself into the world. That woman is the very fabric of sin. It is in the despair of her eyes and the brands on her flesh. She reeks of the lust that she inspires, like a bitch in heat. Lust is one of the Great Sins, and the stench of it surrounds her, and nothing she touches can remain pure. Sin is in the pall she casts by her presence, the very cerements of Hell enshroud her. She is the rottenness of the world, and it is necessary that she be destroyed."

The Margerefa rested one hand on the hilt of his sword, and he said very firmly, "I say that you have no rights in this case. I say that the matter is settled. I say that Brother Andoche has declared that there has been no adultery. I say that the King will say the same, and so will the Bishop. I say that you should keep to your prayers, and your fasting."

Berengar raised his head sharply; killing monks was always a bad business, and he wanted no part of an enforced pilgrimage to Rome, not when he was so close to winning Pentacoste. "Have a care, Margerefa."

Brother Erchboge nodded emphatically. "Yes, you must have a care. If you stand against me, you stand against the laws of the White Christ Himself. You are risking eternal damnation for a woman who is less than a wound rotten with pus."

"Then I will have to answer to the White Christ when I come before him," said Margerefa Oelrih. "I will gladly bow to His judgment, but I will not accept yours when Brother Andoche has already spoken."

"He is more your hound than a servant of the White Christ," said

Brother Erchboge with vehemence as he turned on his heel and rushed out of the Common Hall.

"Better my hound than a cur," said Margerefa Oelrih to the monk's back, his hand closing on his sword hilt. He stood silently, prepared to fight, for a short while, then rounded on Berengar. "What a fine man you are, to strum those strings instead of maintaining the right."

Berengar shook his head. "I am not an officer of the King, it is not my Captain's wife who is accused, and I have no authority in this place; I am only a guest of the former Gerefa's wife," he said, excusing himself with what he hoped was grace. "If I were to say anything, no matter what it was or to whom, I would be committing some fault. As it is, I thought it best to remain silent."

Margerefa Oelrih was not convinced. "Would you have said the same thing if he had been questioning Pentacoste's chastity? Or do you suppose that Brother Erchboge would not ask such questions of her?"

For an instant Berengar said nothing as his face suffused with color. "He would not dare to do such a thing."

"Wouldn't he?" Margerefa Oelrih challenged. "Are you certain of that? Do you suppose that her father's rank impresses the monk so much?" He came across the room, his stride long and swinging. "If you ever again take refuge in so craven a way, I will settle it with you in the forest."

Berengar held his kithre more tightly; his voice was higher than usual when he spoke. "You are not the son of a man of my father's rank. You would not dare to do such a thing. It wouldn't be worth it, killing me. You would be broken on the wheel for it."

"If it were ever known, I suppose I would be," said Margerefa Oelrih. "But I doubt my men would mention it, and who would come here for King Otto but myself? You would be one of those who vanish in the forest, the victim of outlaws or Danes, or those poor wretches on the road from Bremen. Think of that when we hunt again tomorrow." Before Berengar could summon a response, Margerefa Oelrih left the Common Hall, shouting for Captain Jouarre as he went.

But the next day it rained, as Berengar had predicted, and the next, so that only the last desperate scramble to thatch roofs was undertaken at the fortress and the village below; no hunting parties ventured on the muddy roads into the forest, but everyone was kept busy. With the new arrivals in the village, houses emptied by madness and death were once again filled and the space for three new houses cleared.

The Margerefa Oelrih sought Ranegonda out in the muniment room shortly after breakfast on the third day. He had spent the last evening pondering how best to broach the matter of Brother Erchboge's demands to her, and in the end had decided that the best way was to speak directly to her, without apology. He made up his mind to approach her privately, when she would not have to answer to Brother Erchboge. Still, as he crossed the threshold of the muniment room, he had a moment of intense doubt, and it made his approach more tentative than he had planned. As he tried to decide how best to approach the matter, Ranegonda became aware of him.

"Yes?" said Ranegonda, looking up from the sheets of parchment spread across the trestle table where she worked, perched on a stool. "What is it?"

Caught off-guard by her acuteness, the Margerefa asked without any preparation, "Have you spoken to Brother Erchboge in the last few days?"

She blinked at him. "Brother Erchboge? No." She turned toward him, her brow marked with a vertical crease. "What is the matter? Has something happened?"

"It is . . . it is Captain Jouarre's wife. There has been a dispute. Brother Erchboge wants her drowned because he thinks she is an adulteress." He said it more bluntly than he had intended. "He claims that he has the power to require it."

Ranegonda faltered. "Is this the woman who was ransomed?" she asked, recalling the terrible things the woman had told them in the women's quarters. "Is she the one he—"

"Yes," said Margerefa Oelrih impatiently. "Captain Jouarre will not let anything happen to her, not after the money he paid for her. If Brother Erchboge attempts to act against her, he will fight him."

"No," whispered Ranegonda, Signing herself. "It is bad enough that we have had the miasma here, and madness, and dying. And the omens are all for greater misfortune. But this—" She rose from the stool. "No. I have not spoken to Brother Erchboge for nearly four days. He has said nothing to me about this woman, or anyone. I have assumed he was at prayers again, and fasting."

"I expected he would come to you," said Margerefa Oelrih, wondering if he had embarrassed himself for no reason. "He was determined to have his way."

She laughed uneasily. "Brother Erchboge would not speak with me, then, if that was his desire. He disapproved of my brother leaving me in his stead, and he does not expect me to have the strength to understand him. He is like most monks, believing that women damage the chastity of men; without women men could be sacred again. He has often told me, too, that it is not for women to supplant men. Women are weak, and are persuaded by their bodies." She regarded him a moment. "You say that he was adamant?"

"He did not want to accept the decision of Brother Andoche in regard to Captain Jouarre's wife. He said that her brands meant that she committed adultery and that she must be punished for it." Margerefa Oelrih glanced over his shoulder toward the gate-court. "When you did not send for me, I . . ." He shrugged.

"I wasn't aware that anything had happened." But even as she spoke the words, she realized she should have been more cognizant that something was not right; there had been silences that ought to have alerted her.

"He was angry," said the Margerefa. "He was determined."

"About Captain Jouarre's wife?" said Ranegonda. She started toward the door. "Come." She went past the Margerefa.

"Where?" asked Margerefa Oelrih, following her out of the landward tower.

"To the chapel. To find out what has become of Brother Erchboge." As she increased her stride she limped.

"And what then?" asked Margerefa Oelrih, growing apprehensive.

"That will depend on what Brother Erchboge has to say," Ranegonda told him as they reached the door to the chapel. She looked toward Margerefa Oelrih and then slapped the stout wooden door with the flat of her hand. The sound was very loud; in a moment she did it again, and then she reached for the wooden bolt, sliding it back before tugging the door open.

The triangular room was dark and it stank of burnt oil and stale sweat. A single lamp burned at the narrow altar, making the little room seem darker in contrast to the little scrap of flame. The chapel was empty.

"Is he in the village?" asked the Margerefa after a brief moment. He paced around the confines once.

"Not that I—" She broke off, biting her lower lip with anxiety. "But he isn't here. I'll ask the slave on duty at the gates. If Brother Erchboge left the fortress, the slaves will know."

The Margerefa had to contain his own apprehension. "He will be in the village. With the new sites being cleared, he will want to bless the stones laid at the corners, so that no one can dedicate them to the old gods."

Ranegonda nodded, her manner still distracted. "They will know at the gates." She frowned. "It is not like him to behave in this fashion."

"Perhaps he fears . . . the followers of the old gods?" He let the question hang between them.

"There are those who still keep to the old ways," said Ranegonda as she started toward the gates, hurrying. "Brother Erchboge has criticized them and he has said that they will burn for eternity, but—"

One of the slaves was slumped at the foot of the stairs leading to the parapet walkway. He was grey with fatigue and there was a yeasty smell to his body. He tugged his hair and bowed his head as he saw Ranegonda approaching.

"How long have you been set to watch?" Ranegonda demanded as she neared the man.

"Since last night," the slave answered, his Danish accent very strong.

"Then when you have answered my questions, get some rest. A slave asleep on his feet is no use to me." She stopped several steps away from him. "Have you seen Brother Erchboge?"

"He left yesterday, after the mid-day meal," said the slave at once. "We talked about it yesterday evening, in our quarters."

"Yesterday?" Ranegonda said in surprise. She recalled Brother Erchboge saying he was going to pray from dawn to sunset for six days. "Where did he go?"

"To Holy Cross, or so he told Jennes in the village when he took his mule," said the slave.

"Ah," Ranegonda said, and remarked to Margerefa Oelrih, "It is always thus: the slaves know everything."

"In the King's court, as well," said the Margerefa, and addressed the Dane. "Tell the other slaves they are not to mention this to the others here at the fortress or in the village."

The slave bowed deeply, sliding his hair aside so that the nape of his neck was exposed, where the collar lay; it was the submission Margerefa Oelrih was entitled to receive. "We do not speak of what we know, Margerefa, except among ourselves. We know what is expected of us."

"Just as well you do," said Margerefa Oelrih. "Or you'll lose your tongue. Slaves who speak out of turn do not speak at all."

"You say he went to Holy Cross," Ranegonda said to the slave. "Did he say for what purpose?"

"I did not hear him speak of it, and Jennes said nothing of it, not where I could hear it." He paused. "Brother Erchboge was very angry, according to what Jennes said to his wife. The monk upbraided Jennes and Ormanrih for the seedlings planted in the new roof thatch."

"Ravens and Wolves!" exclaimed Ranegonda, and then remembered to Sign herself. "Who has been daring enough to do that?"

"Five of the houses have them," said the slave. "Brother Erchboge noticed three of them. He was outraged that anyone in this village would be so blatant in asking protection of demons—he says all the old gods are demons."

"That could be why he went to Holy Cross," said Margerefa Oelrih, trying to make the best of the situation. He motioned Ranegonda to move away from the gates, where the slave could not easily overhear them.

"He will complain of it," said Ranegonda with certainty as she moved along beside him. "But he was determined to go before then, for he had already left the fortress to borrow the mule; he had his task decided upon, and I suppose Milo was the cause."

"He told me the White Christ demands her death. He wants her to be drowned." He shook his head. "It was settled before we came here. Her husband paid her ransom and he is satisfied that she was not an adulteress, that as a captive she was the tool of the Danes. Brother Andoche said that she was not an adulteress when he heard her Confession."

"Brother Erchboge would not accept her Confession as true, not if he thought she was afraid for her life," said Ranegonda.

"But Brother Andoche heard her Confession, and he said she spoke the truth and accepted her penance with humility and true repentance. He said she wanted to be free of the sins she had been forced to commit." The Margerefa looked vexed. "What sort of monk is this Brother Erchboge, that he disputes other monks?"

"He is zealous, and he is righteous," said Ranegonda, trying to make it sound as if she admired these qualities. "He says that the White Christ sees all and is a stern judge. He did not believe Iselda when she swore that she did not strangle her baby in the womb. The baby was dead and the cause was plain to see. Brother Erchboge castigated her for lying in the face of her guilt. He will make the same claim for Captain Jouarre's wife." She glanced up and noticed that Geraint was looking down from the parapet above.

"Captain Jouarre will not surrender her willingly," Margerefa Oelrih warned. "He has an attachment to the woman and he has paid a great deal for her return. It would disgrace him to have her taken as an adulteress now that he has her again."

"It would be a bad thing to fight with monks," said Ranegonda. "It would surely bring more misfortune to the fortress."

"Captain Jouarre will not give her up only to satisfy monks. He is like many soldiers, and considers those who live in monasteries to be less than men. He will not allow them to separate him from his wife." The Margerefa hunched his big shoulders. "And I would stand with him. He is my vassal."

"All this for the woman?" Ranegonda marveled. "Is she well-born? The daughter of a favored concubine, perhaps?"

"I know nothing of her family, and I doubt that Captain Jouarre does, either," said Margerefa Oelrih. "He took her from a conquered town before any of the soldiers could do anything to harm her. He has kept her with him ever since."

"There was no reason for him to marry her, then?" Ranegonda asked.

"No. At the time his brother did not approve, but Captain Jouarre said it would be that woman or no woman, and so his brother relented, though by then Captain Jouarre and Milo were married already." He cocked his head at the strangeness of it. "Ordinarily Jouarre is an obedient brother, but not where she is concerned."

"Does she have any children?" asked Ranegonda.

"Not alive. She has borne three that I know of; there may be more, but—" He coughed. "When a woman cannot bring children into the world and keep them alive, it goes badly for her. There are always fears that she is giving them to the old gods, or to slavers. The monk may claim that she is not worthy of mercy."

"Do you mean they were abandoned?" Ranegonda looked up at Geraint again, wondering if he could hear what she and the Margerefa were saying to each other.

"I know that one was. The rest, who can tell? A soldier's life is hard on wives, and children. They may have died. They may have been sent to his family, but Captain Jouarre has never spoken of it." He Signed himself. "She has been a good wife to him. He does not have to beat her often."

"She is weak now, and cannot defend herself," said Ranegonda, her face somber. "And she is ill. She suffers. I have asked Saint-Germanius to help her, if he can."

Margerefa Oelrih's face darkened. "That foreigner."

"He is skilled with medicaments," said Ranegonda, and squared her jaw. "He gave his word he will tend her."

"For your sake?" the Margerefa guessed shrewdly.

"He did not say so," Ranegonda told him quickly; it was true enough, though she suspected that Saint-Germanius had remained silent on that point to protect her from any suspicion that might fall on her. "He will tell me what he thinks of her condition when he has seen her and talked with her."

"Captain Jouarre will not like it," said the Margerefa.

"Possibly not, but he must see that his wife is afflicted. She is filled with lassitude, without strength. Surely Captain Jouarre does not wish her to continue in this way, for such lethargy can lead to a wasting." Ranegonda saw that she had nearly persuaded Margerefa Oelrih to endorse her request.

"Well, if Brother Erchboge is going to demand a trial, Captain Jouarre's wife will need to be stronger. Let that foreigner do what he can for her." He stood straighter. "Do you suppose the monks will agree with Brother Erchboge?"

"I don't know," she said, her eyes troubled. "A year ago, two, I might have been able to guess what my brother would want, but no more." She stared down at the uneven paving stones. "He is more monk now than my brother, and I no longer know him."

This admission caused Margerefa Oelrih great discomfort. He glowered at her. "He is your brother and you are his deputy."

"Yes," she agreed. "That is all true. But I don't know him anymore."

Text of a letter from Franzin Ragoczy, Comites Saint-Germanius, to his bondsman Hrotiger. Entrusted to Brothers Desidir and Thorbjorn and carried by them to Hamburh, then given over to a company of merchants bound for Ghent, where it was delivered to the factor Huon, who placed it aboard a merchant ship bound for the Mediterranean. Delivered to Hrotiger in Rome on January 11, 939.

To my most loyal bondsman Hrotiger, greetings from the Baltic coast of Saxony.

My first attempt to reach you did not succeed: perhaps this will.

I am still at the fortress where I was brought after my ships were lost. It is an isolated place, not easily reached either by land or sea. The Gerefa here is asking a ransom for my release, but it is more a gesture of honor at this point. Nevertheless, I ask you to give her twice whatever amount she demands for me. She has received me with kindness from the first; kindness is beyond price.

When you send the ransom, I ask you to send also my red chest, and all the medicines and tinctures and salves it contains. This place is rife with disease and although I can provide some relief, there are many times when I can do nothing but watch the life wrenched out of the body. Most disturbing is the madness and rot that come from tainted grain, because

I am unable to convince the Gerefa or the monks that the grain is responsible and that it must be destroyed if the illness is not to recur.

To reach this place, you must come to Breisach or Toul, then cross to Pohide in Thuringia. From there you will be able to travel to Hamburh with merchants. At Hamburh, hire men-at-arms for an escort, and turn east and north. There is a peninsula on the east coast of Saxony, and this fortress is on the north side. It is called Leosan Fortress. There is forest behind it, and there are bands of robbers who live in the forest, as well as raiding parties of Danes who seize goods and slaves when they have the chance.

Let me ask you to send word to Comites Pacal at Hedaby, to pay any debts that my ships and salvaged cargoes may owe there, and to ready them for another voyage, if you have not done so already. The Comites will require a gift for his work, so select one of the alabaster urns. It will suit his sense of importance to have such a treasure, and that will speed the ships on their way.

I am grateful to you for the care I know you have given to my lands and holdings; more than that I thank you for your loyalty which is as enduring as the snows in the mountains of Asia.

Franzin Ragoczy
Comites Saint-Germanius
by my own hand
(his sigil, the eclipse)

4

Inside the walls of the monastery there were eleven new graves, each marked with a tall stone, a cross carved into it and the name of the monk beneath it painted on. Outside the walls there were two more graves, much larger and unmarked, for those unfortunates who had sought help at the monastery and had found only death.

Brother Giselberht stood in the open gateway at the head of the monks now, newly made their superior. Only the None Choir was absent, and its singing could be heard from the chapel. Some of his old demeanor of authority had returned; he stood straighter than the rest, and he wore his habit with an air that the other monks could not achieve. He glared at his sister and the company with her. "Brother Erchboge brought me word of this situation. It should have come from you." He had already chastised her in private for failing to do her duty, but now he required that she accept his attack in public as well.

"I told you before, I was satisfied that the Margerefa's scribe and Confessor was willing to say that the woman was not an adulteress; those more wise than I am have decided," she answered, less willing to permit this indignity than she had been a year ago. "It is not for me to question the decisions of Margerefa Oelrih, nor those of Brother Andoche."

Brother Giselberht refused to be stymied. "While that is true, you, of all people, should have understood that in this they erred." He signaled to the monks. "Bring the table and then the benches. We will decide this today."

Half a dozen of the monks hastened to do his bidding; Brother Giselberht indicated the area directly in front of the monastery gates. "The trial must be outside the walls. We will sit here"—he pointed to a section of the wall—"where the sin of the woman cannot reach our sanctuary."

It was a cold day, the wind whipping out of a brittle sky so clear that it seemed the gusts must have come all the way from Heaven, driven by angels in pursuit of the minions of Satan. The field grasses where the monastery's sheep had not been sent to graze bent and bowed as the air rushed over them, and behind them the forest thrashed in the heavy gusts. The sea was foam-flecked from the beach to the limits of sight, the waves loud enough to drown the monks' singing as they kept up their relentless assault on the land.

The group from Leosan Fortress numbered sixteen in addition to the accused woman; there were now forty-eight monks at the Monastery of the Holy Cross, and all of them were gathered near the gates to watch; this was a great occasion, and everyone knew it.

"I will sit next to you," said Margerefa Oelrih firmly, facing Brother Giselberht. "And I will have Brother Andoche record all that is said here, so that it is not left to memory alone. I want to present it to King Otto when I return to his court."

"Brother Desidir and Brother Thorbjorn have already vowed to carry a report of this incident to the Bishop, along with my own account of what transpires here," said Brother Giselberht. "They will leave as soon as we conclude this trial." He indicated two of the monks. "It is their vow to let the truth of this be known beyond this place. They have made it a point of duty to serve the White Christ in this way."

"All the more reason for Brother Andoche to have his account, then, so that any questions about what is decided may be answered by those above us," said the Margerefa. He folded his arms over his broigne and mantel. "That way neither of us will be able to avoid answering for any mistake we make."

"Where the White Christ is, there can be no mistake," said Brother Giselberht, directing his attention to his sister once again. "And you who are in the world are always in the realm of the flesh and the senses."

Ranegonda flushed. "Since the woman in question is said to have erred in the flesh and the senses, it is as well we are by," she answered curtly, and indicated their horses before anything more inflammatory could be said. "Before we start there are other matters to attend to, Brother Giselberht. We have brought feed for our animals, so that we need not impose on your charity." She raised her voice sufficiently for those accompanying her to hear what she said. "They will need rest while we are at our labors here. We require a place to tether them, or a field where they may be turned out."

"Better they should be tethered," said the Margerefa at once. "We must be prepared to leave hurriedly and if they are turned out we will have to catch and saddle and bridle them before we travel. We will arrange for them to be watered while they wait for our departure, watered and fed. I will appoint men-at-arms for the task." He shot an angry look toward Brother Giselberht, and another at Brother Erchboge, who stood beside the new superior. At most monasteries the task of looking after their horses would be given to novice monks, for their humility and their prayers.

"There is a place that will suit," said Brother Giselberht, resigning himself to accommodating the Margerefa to that degree. "Brother Dionnys will show you." He signaled one of the young monks. "In the name of the White Christ, take the Margerefa's man to the western stands."

The youth lowered his head and pulled his maniple higher up his neck to show the proper spirit of service. "In the name of the White Christ," he murmured as he came up to the bay the Margerefa rode.

"Geraint," said Ranegonda without turning, selecting one of her men who was still in the saddle, "go with him. And stay with the horses."

"Yes, Gerefa," said Geraint as he nudged his horse away from their place in the loose formation they had taken up.

Three monks appeared in the gateway, struggling with a massive, rough-hewn table. One of them addressed Brother Giselberht, panting a little. "Where should it be?"

"Outside the gates," said Brother Giselberht at once. "To the left; that is the world's side."

From his place with the other mounted men, Saint-Germanius watched this complex game of countermoves with curiosity and dismay. Brother Giselberht was making it as inhospitable as possible, using all his authority as the superior to put his sister in a posture of shame: there was to be no concession granted to the Margerefa or his Captain's wife. It was an unpromising beginning. He felt the letter he had written the night before press against his chest, the fur of his sleeveless pelicon making the stiff parchment more noticeable. He had hoped that the monks would carry it for him; watching the maneuvering now, he had doubts. He glanced at Ewarht astride his bay beside him, and thought how lucky the man-at-arms had been to escape death when he had been overwhelmed by the blighted rye.

Ewarht turned his head suddenly, looking at Saint-Germanius with sharp intent. "What is it?" he asked in an undervoice as the monks struggled to place the table to Brother Giselberht's satisfaction. "What is it you see, foreigner? What is the omen?"

He had an answer to offer. "It saddens me that Brother Giselberht has so little regard for our Gerefa."

"*Our* Gerefa?" Ewarht repeated with incredulity, then added softly so they would not be overheard, "But I suppose you are right. It does not bode well for this trial."

"No; nor for Captain Jouarre's wife," said Saint-Germanius. He lowered his head, his dark eyes filled with anguish. In this place where life was already hard, there was going to be needless suffering as well, because Brother Erchboge demanded it to keep the worst of his fears at bay.

Ewarht nodded slightly. "It's a bad business when monks dispute. No one is safe from their wrath."

"Yes," said Saint-Germanius.

"But it is wrong for the monks to question the Margerefa. They will next question the Duces and Pranzes, and then the King himself," whispered Ewarht in growing indignation.

"Yes," Saint-Germanius agreed, thinking of the many times in the past he had seen just such minor confrontations as this one escalate into insurrection and rebellion, the servants of religion locked in fatal argument with the servants of the state. He shielded his eyes and stared beyond the monastery to the rolling grey-green mass of the sea.

The table was now in a location that Brother Giselberht approved, and he permitted the other monks to bring chairs; they were little more than stools, backless and with only the suggestion of arms.

"There will be one set for me, as superior of this monastery," said Brother Giselberht, pointing to a place near the center of the table, "and one for Margerefa Oelrih, as the magistrate of the King. The rest will have benches. The accused woman must stand. Away from us."

"He insults Ranegonda," muttered Ewarht.

"Yes," said Saint-Germanius. "He intends to."

"A bad business," Ewart said again. "He makes no place for her." Brother Giselberht stared at Brother Andoche. "You will want to sit at the table?"

Brother Andoche inclined his head and stepped forward. "It is my judgment in question. It is fitting that I sit with you."

"You will have a stool, then," said Brother Giselberht, and signaled to another of the monks. "Bring a stool for Brother Andoche, and then make ready to take your places. As soon as the benches are in place, we will begin. We are to be strict in our observance, so that there is no question of our probity. The company with the Margerefa will sit on that side, and the monks will sit on this side of the benches," he informed everyone, pointing to the west and then the east.

"I want to stand with my wife," said Captain Jouarre, his voice strong. "It is my right to be with her."

"It is not certain that she is worthy to be your wife," said Brother Giselberht with finality. "And until her guilt is established or she is vindicated, you will sit with the rest."

There was a muttered susurrus among the men-at-arms, and Captain Jouarre put his hand to the hilt of his sword. "She is my wife, and I will defend her, or you will answer for it."

The Margerefa intervened. "He has the right. I have already said that Captain Jouarre may hold to his wife, and so it will be."

Brother Giselberht hesitated for the first time, and finally he shrugged. "If he wishes to share her disgrace, it is his decision. But he must be aware that he will not be able to disown her if we find against her, not if he stands with her now." He Signed himself to show that he wanted no part of the woman, then took his seat as Brother Aranolht placed the chair for him and stood behind it as if he were a Marshal and not a monk.

Captain Jouarre visibly relaxed; his wife, riding pillion, showed no interest in anything going on around her. When he turned to speak to her, she lifted one shoulder and stared at the horizon.

"Take your woman to the place she must stand," said Brother Giselberht, adding reluctantly, "and remain with her if that is what you wish, though it is a poor example you set your men in doing so."

A few monks emerged from the monastery carrying benches. They forced the mounted party from Leosan Fortress to move back as they put their burdens down in the places Brother Giselberht indicated.

Behind them more of their Brothers were coming, bearing more benches.

"The rest of you had better dismount," said Ranegonda, signaling to those still in the saddle. "Turn your horses over to Brother—" She broke off and turned to her brother. "You will have to decide, Giselberht. Which of these Brothers will deal with our horses?"

"Brother Gailharht and Brother Njorvald," said Brother Giselberht. "Tend to the horses. Give them water and the feed provided by the Gerefa."

Two monks, one with a noticeable hunch to his back, hurried to do his bidding.

"It was an ill thing, telling Captain Jouarre to forsake his wife," said Ewarht, swinging his leg over the high cantel of his saddle. "The monks are told to hold marriage in high esteem."

"They want her abandoned, so that they need fear no opposition to her condemnation." As Saint-Germanius got out of the tall saddle, he said to Ewarht with the deliberate intention of changing to a less dangerous subject, "There are Danes at this monastery. Njorvald is a Danish name, isn't it? and Thorbjorn?" He nodded in the direction of the monks closest to Brother Giselberht, the ones he had said would carry a record of the trial to the Bishop.

"Yes," said Ewarht. "They come here when they decide to forsake the old gods and follow the White Christ."

"Does this happen often?" asked Saint-Germanius, his curiosity piqued, for he had been told that Danes were no longer welcome in this part of Saxony.

Ewarht considered the question before he answered. "I have been told that over the years there have been perhaps a dozen Danes who have come here." He held out his reins to the hunch-backed monk. "They say that there are more at monasteries on the west coast."

Saint-Germanius nodded. "The land there is less disputed, I understand."

"And therefore the monasteries are safer," said Ewarht, making a show of Signing himself. He rocked back on his heels. "It is easier to follow the White Christ when you are not running from your enemies, or your brothers."

"Truly," said Saint-Germanius, with a faint, ironic smile as he gave his reins to the other monk assigned to care for the horses.

Brother Andoche had taken his seat now, and Brother Erchboge as well as the two scribe-monks. Brother Giselberht rose to his feet as the company from Leosan Fortress took their places on the benches, being careful to keep a little distance from the monks.

"It is for us to seek guidance of the White Christ, who was without sin or stain," announced Brother Giselberht, his eyes turned toward the clear, wind-buffed sky. "It is fitting that we come to Him when sin is done, for He alone can cleanse us of it, and He alone will keep us from the perils of Hell. He is the light of Salvation; He has redeemed us through His death." He Signed himself and waited while all the rest did the same. "And when the sin is great, being made of the Great Sin of lust and the treason of dishonoring a husband, it must be twice-damned, in this world and the next," he went on with fervor. "We who serve Him must not permit our souls to waver in their devotion to His rule."

Ranegonda listened with distress, and wished Saint-Germanius were sitting beside her so that she could take comfort in his presence. But that, she realized, would be reckless and hazardous, especially with Brother Giselberht in so vehement a mood; it was always possible he would retaliate by turning his judgment on her. There was gossip enough about her and the enigmatic foreigner, and to create more, in this place and on this occasion, was a risk she could not endure. She folded her hands and lowered her head; she could not bring herself to look at Captain Jouarre or his wife.

"We will pray now for the White Christ to be with us in all that we do and say here, that we may do His will. We ask Him for a sign of His will in this, and the omens to show us the right." Brother Giselberht Signed himself again, and all the rest echoed his gesture except Captain Jouarre, who placed himself between his wife and the monks seated at the table.

Margerefa Oelrih rose from his place on the front bench. "I wish to say now that it is my belief that this is not a correct trial, and that the question of Captain Jouarre's wife has already been settled. Brother Andoche has stated already that she has not sinned, and is not guilty of betrayal of her husband or the laws of the White Christ. There was no question he had not asked that had not been answered to his satisfaction." He met Brother Giselberht's gaze steadily. "I am satisfied, as well, with Brother Andoche's decision, and I repose my trust in his judgment." As he said this, the unwelcome recollection of Berengar remaining behind at Leosan Fortress with Pentacoste thrust itself forward. He did his best to banish it.

Brother Giselberht was not impressed with the Margerefa's words. "This is not a matter that you can decide, that is evident. You are not in Orders and Captain Jouarre is your officer. It is to be expected that you would share his beliefs, as these monks share mine. But I will have Brother Desidir note what you have said, Margerefa Oelrih, so that it will not be claimed that you were not heeded." He lowered his head over his hands, remained silent for a brief while, and then Signed himself once more. "We will begin."

The monks at once stopped shuffling in their places and sat very still; the men with Margerefa Oelrih were not so cooperative, and some of them continued to comment in undervoices to their fellows. Seeing this, Brother Giselberht rapped the flat of his hand on the table. "You will all be silent."

It was a poor start to the proceeding, thought Saint-Germanius as he watched from the rear bench. He could see the determination in Captain's Jouarre's stance and the implacable light in Brother Giselberht's eyes. He sighed once, thinking back to Tunis and the son of the Emir, and his relentless hatred.

"Have the woman answer," said Brother Erchboge loudly. "Hear her Confession for yourselves."

"Yes," said Brother Giselberht. "She will answer." He turned toward Captain Jouarre and his wife. "She must face us, Captain. You may not stand between her and us, for then she could lie with impunity."

"She does not lie," said Captain Jouarre, now more desperate than defiant. "I will answer for anything she says that is not true."

"You will have to," said Brother Giselberht bluntly. "By standing with her you have sworn to uphold her name."

"Then I say again, she does not lie," Captain Jouarre repeated, his jaw so tense that the muscles stood out.

"Many women lie. It is their nature because of Eve." Brother Erchboge waited a moment, and then said, "Move aside, Captain. You may stand behind her."

For an instant it appeared that Captain Jouarre would defy the order, and then he moved back, behind Milo, deliberately standing close enough to her that she could easily lean on him. "Ask her your questions, then, if you must." He put his arm across her, as if to extend his protection.

Brother Andoche spoke quickly, before either Brother Erchboge or Brother Giselberht had the chance. "Do not be frightened, child. The White Christ forgives poor sinners, and knows where the sin is found. Tell them the truth, as you told it to me nine days ago. Tell them simply, child."

Although Milo faced him, her eyes were distant, and she moved awkwardly, as if her limbs had been fastened to her by apprentice carpenters. "I will answer. The White Christ have mercy on me." She

Signed herself as well as she could with Captain Jouarre's arm impeding her.

"You are Milo, the so-called wife of Captain Jouarre?" asked Brother Giselberht. "Where were you born?"

"I don't know. I was found near Lauenburh when I was a child, or so I was told. A merchant bought me from the carter who found me. I was about six or seven." She stared down at the ground and saw Captain Jouarre's arm.

"And how long did you live with him?" asked Brother Giselberht.

"He turned me over to his wife, who baked. I assisted her. They had no living children and they needed the help. While I was there they bought another child like me. They kept me until the city was sacked, and they fled."

"Do you know what became of them?" asked Brother Andoche.

"No; I never saw them again, nor heard of them." Her stare grew more distant. "I sometimes wonder if they are still alive."

"And you met Captain Jouarre when?" inquired Brother Giselberht.

"During the battle for the city. He found me. I have been with him since then. He married me later, because I was young." She tried to meet his eyes and failed.

"Have you any other husbands?" Brother Erchboge's question was explosive.

"No," said Captain Jouarre's wife. "I have had no man willingly but my husband, not now or ever."

"And you have fallen into harlotry only since you were taken captive?" Brother Erchboge pursued.

"I have been faithful to my husband," Milo answered. "I have not sinned by lust. Brother Andoche said so."

"She gave her Confession as soon as her ransom had been paid," Brother Andoche added.

"This capture took place earlier this year, while you and the company of Margerefa Oelrih were going to Hamburh, is that true?" asked Brother Giselberht.

"Yes. We thought we were safe, but we were not," she said, her voice starting to sound strained. "There were men-at-arms, and the horses were rested. We were more concerned about outlaws than Danes."

"There was a fight?" Brother Giselberht went on.

Margerefa Oelrih answered for her. "It was a hard battle. Men on both sides were killed."

"You were taken captive by outlaws, or Danes?" said Brother Giselberht, ignoring the Margerefa.

"By Danes," she said, her voice soft and remote. "There were thirty or so in the raiding party. They had other captives."

"Was this at the beginning or end of the battle?" Brother Erchboge asked, his tone making it clear he put no stock in any answer she had to offer.

"Toward the end. The Danes split our men-at-arms into two groups. They surrounded the two groups and pressed their attack. I was with the smaller," said Milo, her voice eerie and serene at once.

"And they took you into Denmark," said Brother Andoche, encouraging her.

"Yes." She fixed her eyes on the sea. "Into Denmark."

"They made you a slave," said Brother Giselberht. "That is the reason you are branded."

She shuddered but her maimed face remained blank. "Yes."

"And what work did they give you to do?" asked Brother Andoche. "As a slave you had tasks to perform."

For a moment the wind faltered and the None Choir rose above the combined roar of sea and air, praising God for hearing their cry.

"They set me to cleaning the hearth and scrubbing grease," she said. "There were other slaves who did it as well, about five of them." Her voice was growing softer, less confident. "The other things were not part of the work, they were demanded when it was suitable."

"And what else did they do?" demanded Brother Erchboge. "Why is there that second brand?"

Color mounted in her cheeks but she remained expressionless. "I was part of their spoils of battle, one of their prizes to keep," she said after a short hesitation. "So were the other women."

"And they used you carnally?" asked Brother Giselberht in a flat, hard tone.

"Yes," she said. "They said I was theirs to do with as they pleased. They said if I resisted they would beat me."

"And did they ever beat you?" Brother Andoche asked.

"Eight times," she replied. "Twice I was senseless for a day."

"For a day? Are you certain it was not a shorter time? Who can we ask how long you lay thus? And who can say it was not deserved? You tell us it was because you resisted, but you may have been beaten for insubordination or some vice." He looked around as if he might expect one of the men-at-arms to answer his challenge. "Was that the extent of it, or were you used more times than that?" Brother Erchboge demanded.

Her answer was very soft. "More."

Brother Erchboge pounced. "Then you found it pleasurable?"

"I did not want the pain, so I—" She stopped, craning her head to look at Captain Jouarre. "They would have killed me sooner or later; I accepted them."

"I know, I know," said Captain Jouarre.

Brother Erchboge had heard enough. "There! She did not remain chaste. She has betrayed her husband and the White Christ."

Brother Andoche held up his hand. "She did not have the opportunity to remain chaste. It was the decision of her captors to make such use of her, she did not offer herself to them. They beat her into a swoon when she fought them. She told me that she had tried to be put to other tasks, even tending the midden, rather than be available to the men."

"Any woman would make such a claim," said Brother Erchboge, and turned once to glare at Ranegonda. "Women are the cause of man's fall."

This was more than Captain Jouarre would tolerate. "She is no more to blame than the slaves at the fortress. They are not held accountable for what we demand of them. They are ours to use as we wish, and when we have used them we do not drown the slave women afterward."

"They are not married women, those who are slaves at the fortress; marriage for a slave is ridiculous," said Brother Giselberht. "This woman is married. She is more than a concubine, she is a wife."

Saint-Germanius shook his head sorrowfully; the monks would prevail today, he knew. Brother Erchboge would have the victory he sought. There was the sting of vengeance on the air already. He watched Ranegonda, noticing how she sat, how straight she was, and how bent her head, as if she carried a heavy yoke. Her hood was thrown back and fall of her braids left the center of the nape of her neck bare; he thought again of her vulnerability, and her strength.

"How many of the men used you?" Brother Erchboge rapped out.

"I don't know," Milo answered without emotion.

"Surely you have a notion," prodded Brother Erchboge. "Two? Three? More?"

"I don't remember," she said.

Again the None Choir could be heard over the wind.

Brother Giselberht shook his head, his manner grave as he regarded the parchment sheets in front of Brother Desidir as if he could read what was written on them. "You must tell us, or we will not be able to judge you."

"I don't know," said Milo, a little louder.

Again Brother Andoche intervened, his tone gently reproving, persuasive. "She gave me the same answer, good Brothers. She told me as much as she could, but I believe that she did not number the times she was used by the Danish men."

Margerefa Oelrih was getting restive as this impasse deepened. He rose to his feet, pacing in front of the long table. "You have heard her say she does not know, or does not remember. She has done all she could to preserve herself, and setting her soul apart from the use she was put to was part of it. She can have no answer for you but the one she has given because she conducted herself like a good Saxon, Christian wife and salvaged her soul when she could not save her body. Surely that is the more important issue here."

"She has not said she preserved her soul, only that she does not remember the number of men who took her," said Brother Giselberht. "It may be that she was pleasured by the men."

"No," said Milo quietly.

"And it may be that she sought them out, no matter what she tells us here. She is a soldier's wife and she knows that she must have a man to protect her." Brother Erchboge pointed an accusing finger at Milo. "I say that you decided to give yourself to the Danes, because you wanted one of them to make you his concubine. You had no reason to hope for ransom, and so you did as all women do: you looked for a man to claim you."

"No," Milo said again.

"It is obvious to me," Brother Erchboge continued, paying no heed to her response, "that you have the duplicity of all women. It is inherent in your nature to deceive, as did Adam's wife. You have used the wiles of your sex to try to blind our eyes to your shame. You have been able to convince Captain Jouarre because he wants to believe you, because you have beguiled him. But I see through your lies, and I know that you are—"

"My wife does not lie," said Captain Jouarre. "And you are a false monk if you say otherwise."

There was a sudden stillness; only the wind moved as the enormity of Captain Jouarre's condemnation was realized.

"That is a deadly challenge," said Brother Giselberht at last.

Captain Jouarre had his hand on his sword once more. "I tell you that I know my wife, and if I believed she had dishonored me, I would not have given money to ransom her. The brands are nothing to me. If you want to drown someone, good Brothers, drown that pagan harlot at Leosan Fortress who amuses herself with captivating men and makes offering to the old gods in defiance of your White Christ." As soon as he spoke he knew he had gone too far. He stood straighter, prepared to take on the lot of them. "My wife is my wife, and I am the only one with power over her. She is chaste, and she is faithful. I swear on my life that she never betrayed me, and I will answer her falseness with my death. The White Christ witness my vow." He laid his hands on Milo's shoulders. "She is my wife." Then he moved so swiftly that no one could have stopped him, had they known what he was going to do. There was a loud crack, like the breaking of a tree limb, and then Milo dropped to the ground, her neck angled, her eyes vacant. "She is my wife," Captain Jouarre repeated.

The monks all Signed themselves, as did most of the men-at-arms. Margerefa Oelrih stood dumbfounded. "Why?" he demanded. "You have just paid—"

"She is my wife. I will defend her unto death. I will not permit her to be disgraced," said Captain Jouarre. "It is my right to kill her. I will not surrender that right to the monks." He knelt down beside Milo's body, Signed himself at last, and began to weep.

Ranegonda was on her feet beside Margerefa Oelrih. She held out one hand to her brother. "Say that she was blameless, Giselberht; I beseech you."

Brother Giselberht was pale but his face was set. He rose from his place at the table and came around the end of it toward her. "How can I when her husband has so eloquently condemned her."

"But he hasn't condemned her," said Ranegonda, trying to keep her voice low. "He has done all that he can to save her, and in the face of Brother Erchboge's determination to have his sacrifice." She watched him out of the tail of her eye, her expression wary, for she was treading on uncertain ground.

"He made accusations against my wife," said Brother Giselberht darkly. "He did that to try to lessen his woman's shame by calumny—"

"Pentacoste does have men who would be suitors but for you," said Ranegonda, giddy with apprehension at making so direct an accusation. "And I have heard that she knows how to leave the fortress so that she can leave offerings for the old gods in the night. But I have not seen her do it, and you would not want me to bear false witness against her." She paused. "And there is no way to leave the fortress but the gate, and that remains closed; the slaves and the men-at-arms on watch have said so. But in the village they declare she offers to the old gods, and some say she flies through the air to do it."

It was a short moment before Brother Giselberht spoke. "There is a way out of the fortress, a narrow passage, enough for one soldier at a time." He sighed. "And Pentacoste knows where it is. I told her in case she would ever have to show it to our sons." He stared at the cross over the chapel.

Ranegonda could not conceal her shock. "Yet you said nothing of it to me? You have left the fortress in my keeping and have said nothing to me about this secret?" She was not certain if she was more angry or horrified. "Why would you not? What is your—?" She broke off. "Giselberht, it was wrong."

He shrugged. "You are a woman, Ranegonda, and you are moved by your womanliness. How could I be certain you would not betray the fortress to our enemies if you were worked upon?"

"You doubted me?" she asked, her voice soft because she wanted so desperately to scream. "You told Pentacoste, but you had no faith in *me?*"

"She might have had our sons to protect," he said, and moved away from her toward the knot of men gathered around Captain Jouarre, bent over the pathetic body of his wife.

Ranegonda moved blindly away from the table and the men. There were unshed tears standing in her eyes and her face was expressionless with outrage. She walked a short distance away, limping heavily, and stood looking toward the vast, steel-green sea. No matter how she tried, she could not take it all in: that her brother should tell his feckless wife of the secret and not trust her with the knowledge. That was a double treason, for it left her unprepared to defend the fortress as it might need to be defended and it put knowledge into the hands of Pentacoste, who would use it against her if she could.

"It was an act of desolation," said Saint-Germanius gently.

She turned abruptly and nearly lost her footing; he was standing slightly more than an arm's length away from her. "What?"

"Captain Jouarre," he said. "He could not watch her drown."

"No," she agreed, her voice remote.

He realized that something more than Milo's death had stricken her. "What did your brother say?" His tone was kindly, reassuring, and for that reason she could not arm herself against it, and at last her tears came.

Saint-Germanius knew it was dangerous to be seen talking to her: to comfort her would expose both of them to the confusion and thwarted rage that roiled among the men-at-arms and monks. So he kept his distance and offered the anodyne of words. "Whatever your brother did, or said, Ranegonda, you will endure. Nothing he could do or say will lessen your strength, because it is within you. He has lost the right to your loyalty; I can see that in your eyes. And you feel that you have been cast off."

"He has—" She could not go on. She put her hands to her face.

"Listen to me, love. You have been determined and able from the time Brother Giselberht put the world behind him. You have shown prudence and capability and restraint, more than your brother has it in him to do. You are the one who has made Leosan Fortress the haven it is; Giselberht could not do that. You have made the decisions and put them into motion far better than he could."

"He told Pentacoste," she whispered, trying not to sob.

Saint-Germanius stood very still. "What did he tell her?"

She turned around to him, and fought her need to hold him. "There is a secret entrance to the fortress." The tears shone on her face, marking the scars. "He told her where."

"And you do not know," he said, nodding once.

"He should have *told* me," she insisted.

"Yes; and he should have said nothing to his wife." He was about to say more when he noticed that Margerefa Oelrih was approaching. His voice and manner changed at once. "I will ask what arrangements are to be made for her burial, and if she can be laid in consecrated ground, Gerefa."

Margerefa Oelrih's color was high and his beard jutted with indignation. "They are saying they cannot let her lie here. We would take her to the fortress, but Brother Erchboge has already announced he will not permit her to be put into the graveyard in the village. He wants her thrown into the sea, as if she drowned. It is the fate she deserves. Captain Jouarre almost went for him when he said that."

"Did Brother Giselberht agree?" asked Saint-Germanius, with a quick glance at Ranegonda.

"He said that she must be buried at a crossroad," the Margerefa answered.

"With felons and witches," said Saint-Germanius in disgust.

Margerefa Oelrih gestured obscenely to show his contempt for the idea. "Brother Andoche told me he was grateful to the White Christ for the omen that told him to leave his mace at home, or he would have been tempted to raise it to his Brothers."

"Perhaps he should have," said Saint-Germanius, and went back toward the gathering of men, hoping that there would be no worse things done this day.

The voices of the None Choir soared over the wind, with paeans to God and the White Christ for mercy and justice.

Text of a letter from Brother Andoche to Bishop Gerht of Hamburh. Carried by men-at-arms and delivered in thirteen days.

To the Excellent Bishop Gerht of the Cathedral of the Nativity, my greeting on this twenty-eighth day of November in the Year of Grace 938.

I write to you from Luneburh, where the Margerefa Oelrih has decided we will winter, for there has been no madness here, may the White Christ be thanked for it, and no enemy threatens the town. When the snows are past, we will come to Hamburh, and I pray you will receive me then for the benefit of your wisdom and guidance.

There is a second purpose to this letter, and that is to inform you of events that took place at the Monastery of the Holy Cross some four weeks since. My soul has been burdened by the memory of these tragic deaths, and I believe it is best to inform you of how I witnessed the trial of Captain Jouarre's wife, and what happened afterward.

Your Excellency must understand that I was the first to hear Captain Jouarre's wife confess after she was ransomed, and I was fully satisfied that she had not sinned but had been used as a slave is used because to the Danes that was all she was. Her life before she became their booty was nothing to them, and therefore it was not important that she was a married woman. I saw and heard no indication in her Confession that she had taken pleasure in what was done, that she invited it, or that she sought it for other reasons. I believed then and believe now that she was truly penitent, and I share the conviction of the Margerefa Oelrih that she could not be cast off as a wife. Captain Jouarre paid the ransom with the understanding that as a slave she might have been dishonored, and still he was willing to give the money they asked for her. This, too, had bearing on my certainty that she was not dishonored.

But at Leosan Fortress, Brother Erchboge challenged my judgment and claimed that Captain Jouarre's wife was a harlot. He insisted that she be tried, and sought out the new superior of Holy Cross to enforce his demand. As the superior at the monastery was once Gerefa at the fortress, his decision was not protested, and the trial, such as it was, was held at the monastery.

The questions put to the woman distressed Captain Jouarre, and when he felt that she would not prevail, he exercised his right as her husband to take her life rather than permit them to order her drowned as a harlot. At that, Brother Erchboge demanded that Captain Jouarre be held for apostasy, which the Margerefa said that he would not allow. He gave his word to Brother Giselberht of Holy Cross that Captain Jouarre would be punished for interfering with the trial and protecting a criminal, and to that end he was prepared to make the Captain his prisoner.

Captain Jouarre, however, declared that he would not be parted from his wife and said that she was no criminal, whereupon he used his own sword to open the veins of his neck, and died before he could repent his action.

So both Captain Jouarre and his wife were buried at the crossroad leading to Oeldenburh, with their faces turned downward toward Hell, where it is said they must go. Holly has been placed on their backs to prevent them rising, even at the Last Trumpet. Although Brother Erchboge objected vehemently, I said the prayers for the dead over the two of them as the graves were filled.

I truly believe that the woman was not a harlot and that her sin was small. I would not have upheld her as I did if I was not convinced that she had not fallen into error while she was a slave. While I deplore the death of Captain Jouarre, I am certain he took his life because he was unwilling to be dishonored. Many fighting men are thus in their conduct. I also believe that it was a mistake to bury them at the crossroad, because if there has been an injustice, as I fear there has, their ghosts will torment travelers until they are vindicated. I have so informed Brother Giselberht, who has not seen the matter as I have.

For that reason alone, I have sought to inform you of the events, so that if there is any future disruption brought about by the deaths of Captain Jouarre and his wife, you will know what part I have played in them, and will know that the condemnation of the two was not universal or undisputed. I pray for guidance every day, and I ask the White Christ to show me the path of wisdom. He is the source of our understanding, and He is a mystery.

May you read this with kindness, Excellency, and find it worthy of your meditations and prayers. If anything terrible comes from these deaths, I beg you to look to Brother Erchboge and Brother Giselberht for the cause of it, and bring them to your court to answer for what they have done. It was wrong for Captain Jouarre's wife to be subjected to the trial when she had already received her penance for her acts. Those who ordered the trial will have to answer for it to the White Christ. If it is His will, they will also answer for it in this world.

In faithful service and with my prayers, I ask your blessing and the blessing of the White Christ before Whom all bow.

Brother Andoche
scribe to Margerefa Oelrih

5

During the night sleet became snow, riding on the north-eastern wind in silent ferocity. Leosan Fortress wailed as the wind sought out the cracks and crannies, turning them into hoots and whistles as it passed.

Pentacoste sat in the cloth room, working her loom with steady determination, humming with the wind. Two oil lamps provided her the light she needed as she sent the shuttle back and forth. She smiled as she worked, and occasionally stopped to finger the taut fabric she wove; the knots created a pattern that pleased her and, she knew, would bring delight to the old gods, those who whipped the storm across the sea and brought life to the land when the snows were gone. Her mantel was lined with fox fur, and it kept her shoulders and arms warm. But her fingers were so cold that they felt like twigs, and as the night wore on, her weaving slowed; her hands grew stiff and sore. She kept at her task, for the spell she made with the knots in the wool would fail if she faltered before dawn.

It was so obvious, she told herself as she paused to stretch and warm her hands inside her mantel. The foreigner had wanted her from the first, but had not dared to approach her, fearing reprisals for compromising a married woman. There was no doubt of it. She had seen it in his stance, in his eyes. She heard it in his voice, and recognized it in his continuing residence at the fortress, for what reason could he have to remain but to be near her? She was not deceived by his apparent attentiveness to Ranegonda: no man would prefer a lame woman with a scarred face to her, the daughter of Dux Pol, the most beautiful woman in all of Saxony. That was only a ploy, clever in its simplicity. Without Ranegonda's approval, he would be confined to his quarters. No, she realized that Saint-Germanius needed Ranegonda's favor if he was to be permitted to live as he did. She saw at once his strategy, and approved; it pleased her that he would be so careful in his approach to her. Respect was not often encountered in suitors.

As she returned to her weaving, she repeated his name over and over as she worked the charmed wool into a length of cloth, imbued with the power of her spell. Once she presented this to Saint-Germanius, she knew that he would no longer hesitate. At last she would have a worthy lover, of wealth and position, someone who would not be afraid of Dux Pol or Pranz Balduin or King Otto himself. Saint-Germanius would carry her off to his country, and there she would be esteemed by everyone.

She deliberately pricked her finger and let the blood run into the dark wool, calling him to her while she kept working, knowing that her desires filled her blood and the old gods would honor it. Her fancies were clouded with fatigue, but not so much that she could not maintain her purpose; if she lost sight of that there could be dire consequences. It would be worth the loss of a night's sleep, she decided, and would bring her more sleepless nights once she was bedded by the foreigner. That prospect filled her with warm delight. It would be so wonderful, so thrilling. What pleasure they would have together! How she would captivate him then! He would be wholly in her sway, and she would learn things from him that other men could not even imagine. Such was the power of her spinning and weaving that he would not be able to escape her, even in dreams.

The parchment screens over the windows had just begun to fade when Genovefe appeared in the doorway, her face still puffy from sleep and her mantel hastily thrown over her woolen bliaut. "I went to your quarters and you were not there," she said, making it almost an accusation and an affront, though she dared not voice the fears that possessed her. "Your bed was cold."

"I couldn't sleep," Pentacoste said dreamily, not wanting to come out of her reverie. "So I thought I would do something useful with my wakefulness and weave."

"And you came here?" asked Genovefe, looking toward the loom in alarm. "Black wool, worked in the night?"

"Only a coward thinks that it is ill-omened," said Pentacoste as she slid her stool back from her work. "It was only that I could not sleep. It was a shame to waste the night."

Genovefe Signed herself as she looked at the loom more closely, then regarded Pentacoste with shock. "What mischief are you up to now, Hohdama?"

Pentacoste laughed. "You only use my title when you are angry with me, Mädchen," she observed, enjoying Genovefe's discomfort tremendously. What a simpleton she was, and how easily frightened. "Why should you be angry?"

"When I wakened and you were not there, I searched all of the landward tower, looking for you. I came here only when I could not discover you . . ." Her words trailed off. "Berengar's quarters are in this tower. He is sleeping immediately below this chamber. What are you thinking of, to come here in the night?"

"Berengar's servant sleeps at the foot of his bed, and he would know if anything transpired there. Ask him if there has been any dalliance tonight," said Pentacoste, growing tired of the game. "Ingvalt will tell you that his master has slept undisturbed."

"He is a servant, and he will uphold anything his master requires," said Genovefe, her eyes filled with distress. "To do less would dishonor his master."

"How can I convince you that nothing unacceptable has happened? Do you want to ask whoever is guarding the light? He will know if anything took place; he would hear it." Pentacoste rose from the stool. "The work has been good. Now I am ready to sleep, and may the White Christ guard me from all envy." She Signed herself and gave Genovefe her best captivating smile.

"I will have to speak to the guardian," said Genovefe without apology. "And if you bring further disgrace to this fortress, you may find yourself on your way back to your father in Lorraria, by the order of your husband." It was a threat she was not in any position to realize, but she could not accept Pentacoste's cool assumption that she was untouchable. "And if you return to your family disgraced, your father will not be pleased with you."

"That could never happen," said Pentacoste in a burst of spite. "My husband has renounced me, and he cannot send me back to my father. It would be useless. My father has my sisters to tend to him. He would not have me with him again, for I am not debauched, and no one will make me go back to that. Besides, I would rather be a slave to the Danes than live again with my father. He is a worshiper of Satan and he defames the White Christ. Giselberht would not send me back to that, for fear of my damnation, and his." She tossed her head and moved by Genovefe with such haughtiness that her cold apprehension was successfully concealed. "I am going to my quarters now, to rest, and you may set a guard over me if you think it is necessary." She hoped that her waiting-woman would do that, so that she would have the excuse to sleep all day; then she could dance for the old gods again that night, and show them the fabric she had woven in their honor.

As she reached the ground level, she paused to glance toward the closed door of Saint-Germanius's quarters. It was tempting, so tempting, to imagine him lying behind that door, waiting for her, longing for her, ready for her. That time was almost come, and it gave her a great sense of accomplishment. To have that dark-clad stranger to do her bidding: her foreign lover, who would take her far beyond the reach of King Otto and her father, and would lavish wealth and service on her. Not yet, she told herself, but soon. It was only a matter of days until the full moon, and then she would see her spell fulfilled. There would be no more hesitation, no more deception with Ranegonda. She would triumph at last. That door would open to her and she would revel in his embraces and his enthrallment.

When Pentacoste left the cloth room, Genovefe remained behind, determined to discover what Pentacoste had been doing with her weaving, for surely she had had some intention beyond filling sleepless hours, and Genovefe knew that anything done in secret was malign. She searched the place carefully, looking for tokens that would reveal what powers Pentacoste had invoked at her work. She found the last of the newly spun black wool, and noticed that there was a pattern of knots worked into it. At this she frowned, and pulled a length of the yarn from the spindle, for she knew the old ways as well as the new. What she saw turned her pale, and she dropped the spindle as if it had burned her hands, Signing herself twice in the hope that she had taken no contamination from the purpose of the knots. She fled the cloth room, rushing down the stairs, afraid to look back for fear of what she might see there, caught in the warp and woof of the loom.

She rushed across the icy court to the landward tower and stumbled inside, her heart racing for more reason than haste and freezing air. She steadied herself against the wooden door before she shoved it closed and started up to the third level where Ranegonda slept. With every step she reminded herself that what she was doing was necessary, and that appalling as it was, Ranegonda had to be warned or the spell would continue.

Duart was there before her, standing by the door, his face set in lines of strong disapproval. "I believe that it would be a mistake to refuse to send grain to the monks. They have had a poor harvest, and their need is great."

"As ours may be, come the New Year," said Ranegonda without apology; she had taken Saint-Germanius's advice to withhold the summer rye, since she would not destroy it, until he could show her that the grain held madness in it. His suggestion had not bothered her earlier, when they had more flour and fewer mouths to feed. Now, with stores getting low, she doubted she would be able to continue to keep it in reserve. Still, she told herself, if she waited a while longer, what was the harm?

"They are dependent on us," Duart reminded her. Since he had taken the madness, he had been left with a tic on the side of his face. It made his cheek and eyebrow jump, and he knew it was a bad omen. "We fail the White Christ if we fail to see that His servants are fed."

"They have fields of their own, and they brought in a harvest, as we did. Their grain was less plentiful, and for that we will aid them if we must. But there are now thirty-nine new villagers to consider, sent to us by mandate of King Otto. My sworn duty is to this fortress and the village, not to the White Christ. My brother attends to that." She was putting the wrappings on her braids, shivering a little in the dank morning cold.

Genovefe held her place at the door of the room, her attitude deferential, as if she was intruding. Finally she could wait no longer; she lowered her head. "Gerefa," she said quietly.

"Yes, Genovefe," said Ranegonda with a nod in her direction. "I will hear you in a moment." She looked back at Duart. "If the monks must have something of ours, there are extra cheeses in the village. Send a sack of them to the monks, and some of the turnips as well. And take one of the goats, a nanny, so that they can have her milk or her meat, as they like."

"Your brother will not be pleased to have such treatment from you," Duart warned her. "You have his honor to maintain, as well as the honor of Leosan Fortress."

"If my brother believes I am failing to do my duty here, then let him come and tell me himself," she responded with asperity. "Then let him show me how I may improve, given what there is to do here, and what King Otto has commanded of us." She shook her head once, settling her braids down her back.

"Cheeses and turnips, and a goat," said Duart, his eyebrow twitching.

"And if there is any more honey from Jennes's wife's hives, send that as well. Giselberht likes honey, or he used to," she added as she recalled the austerities he had embraced.

"I will tell him it was your order," said Duart at his most depressing.

"Certainly; he would do the same were he in my position." Ranegonda met Duart's gaze without visible sign of doubt, though inwardly she quailed.

Duart capitulated, stepping back and touching his forehead. "What are your instructions for the journey? I will require an escort, or the outlaws will take the food."

"That they will: have Geraint and Faxon ride with you, and Severic, too." She hesitated. "Carry spears as well as swords, go armed. The outlaws have been restive, and there have been bands of strangers seen in the forest; you will need to travel fast. Saint-Germanius has reshod the horses in the stable; they are all ready to ride. Choose the mounts you prefer."

"Yes, Gerefa," said Duart, and turned away from her with a contemptuous smirk caused by the tic.

When he was gone, Genovefe approached Ranegonda with trepidation. "May you forgive me for what I have to say. I am frightened to tell you this, Gerefa," she began, lowering her head once more. "If it were less terrible, I would not speak at all."

"What is it?" Ranegonda asked, noticing how pale Genovefe was, and the glint of dread in her eyes.

"I have seen a thing. I do not like to speak of it, but I must. You should know of it. It is an omen." She Signed herself, hoping that it would again protect her from what was in the wool.

"What thing is it?" Ranegonda spoke gently, as if to a child. "Why does it trouble you so?"

For a moment Genovefe could not answer, and when she did, she spoke very quickly. "In the cloth room, the big loom is webbed in black, and the wool in the shuttle is black and knotted." She Signed herself once more. "It was knotted on the spindle."

"Pentacoste?" said Ranegonda, not needing to be told it was she. "What has she done?"

Not understanding, Genovefe began again. "She has webbed the big loom with black wool and—"

"Yes," said Ranegonda, cutting her off. "What is she bringing upon us." She looked toward the door as if she thought they might be spied upon. "Get Hrosia, and see that you or she is with Pentacoste through the day. I will find one of the village women to watch her at night." She looked toward the parchment-covered window. "At least it is snowing. She will not want to go far." Even as she spoke the words, she thought of the hidden entrance to the fortress and she was shaken.

"Hrosia, all right," said Genovefe. "And Winolda?"

Ranegonda made a sharp gesture of dismissal. "No; Pentacoste wants the herbs Winolda has. Ask Juste to be with you when Hrosia cannot. Each can look after the other's children." She put her hands together, but not in prayer. "Tell me everything she does. I will visit the cloth room later, to see the loom for myself."

Genovefe Signed herself in gratitude. "What woman in the village are you going to ask to guard her?"

"I suppose Osyth would do it. She is newly arrived and she will not be afraid of Pentacoste as some of the women are." It would require some persuasion; Ruel's wife was pregnant and would deliver late in spring. "She could watch in the afternoon, in the cloth room."

"They know what she does in the night," said Genovefe just above a whisper. "Both Hrosia and Juste."

"Or they pretend they know," corrected Ranegonda. "I have yet to see her fly through the air as some of them claim she does." She drew her fur-lined mantel around her shoulders and fixed it with a large pin fashioned in the Roman style. Her fingers caressed the metal, for the pin was a gift from Saint-Germanius.

"They do not know how she leaves the fortress," said Genovefe. "It must be by some power she possesses."

"Yes; she has knowledge of a hidden door. And I have not yet found her way out." It rankled with her that Giselberht still refused to tell her where the passage was, or how it could be reached. At first she had thought he was being cautious; now she was convinced he was obdurate.

"She says nothing of it," Genovefe assured Ranegonda. "I listen when she sings, in case there is something in her songs that might reveal how she escapes, but I have heard nothing."

Ranegonda shook her head. "No; she is too clever to make so simple a mistake. We will have to watch her until she gives herself away." She stood straighter. "The woodcutters will stay in the village today, and I must speak to them. We do not have the number of logs King Otto requires of us."

Genovefe looked aghast. "There are outlaws and wolves in the forest when the snow comes."

"They are there all the year," said Ranegonda. "But in winter they are hungry."

This time Genovefe permitted herself to shudder. "If I were a village wife I would not want my husband venturing beyond the stockade in winter." She looked toward the covered window. "It will be colder tomorrow."

Ranegonda said nothing in response as she left her quarters and made her way down the narrow stairs. She did not want Genovefe to see how much the information about Pentacoste vexed her; now that she was alone, she let her gloom settle on her features. What could she do about Pentacoste without making matters worse? She could not oppose her openly, for Giselberht would not tolerate that. Yet Pentacoste was determined to bring ruin on them all, for no reason other than she wished for amusement. She would have to talk to Saint-Germanius, but after she saw what was in the cloth room. The thought of him troubled and comforted her as she hurried down the last few stairs.

Reaching the ground floor, she was struck with the chill that filled the place. She would have to order braziers set here, to provide a little warmth. She decided to order a slave to stay in the Common Hall through the night, to keep the fire lit, and one in the kitchens, as well, so that the hearths would not go cold. As she pulled the door open the bone-gnawing cold took hold of her, and she shivered, watching the ghost of her breath cloud her face as she started out into the snow.

It was her intention to go directly to the Common Hall to join the others at their morning meal, but on impulse she continued past it to the seaward tower. She decided she might as well look into the cloth room now. And then she could seek out Saint-Germanius.

On the stairs she met Ingvalt, who stared at her suspiciously. "My master has not yet risen," he said.

"Let him rise as he wishes; he is a guest here and need not wake with the rest of us," said Ranegonda, and realized that Ingvalt supposed she had come to the tower to seek Berengar out. "But warn him it is snowing."

Ingvalt stared down his nose at her. "You were here earlier. I could hear the loom working."

"Then you should know it was not me," said Ranegonda with asperity, making Ingvalt give way to her. "I am no weaver, as anyone in this fortress may tell you. If someone was at the loom, it was one of the other women."

"If you tell me so, Gerefa, then it is surely true," he said in patent disbelief. "Some other woman must have been abroad in this fortress at night."

Had Ingvalt been the servant of a less high-ranking master than Berengar, Ranegonda would have ordered him to leave Leosan Fortress, in spite of the weather. As it was, she gave him a hard stare. "If you speak untruths against me, you will regret it. I tell you I do not weave. You heard some other woman."

"I am not a fool, Gerefa," said Ingvalt, and lowered his head to her.

Ranegonda's temper was still seething by the time she reached the cloth room, and she took a brief time to stand by herself in the cold without looking at the big loom; she needed to rid herself of the wrath that coursed through her, and she could not think of any way. Ingvalt was just a piece of it, yet she had been ready to throw him down the stairs. She felt her breath quicken as her ire increased. She steadied herself against the small loom and tried to concentrate on it, on the simple white wool that was being woven there.

A figure appeared in the door, black-clad and composed. "Ranegonda," he said softly.

At the sound of her name she lifted her head, prepared to defend herself. When she recognized Saint-Germanius, she was relieved and wary at once. "I didn't hear you come."

"You have other things on your mind," he said, and added, "Pentacoste was here last night. All night."

She was not surprised that Saint-Germanius should come to her, and that startled her as she realized it. "So Genovefe warned me," she said, and was shocked to hear how tight her voice was.

He stepped inside the cloth room and pointed out the two oil lamps. "There. She used those for her light. She was chanting as she worked, but I could not make out the words."

"A waste of oil," said Ranegonda. Then she motioned toward him. "This is for women. You shouldn't be in here."

"All right," he said, and went back to the door.

It annoyed her that he was so willing to cooperate, and challenged him. "You are glad to be rid of my company, aren't you?"

"No," he said steadily. "And you know it." He went on, his demeanor firm, kindness in his dark, compelling eyes. "But because you are worried you are trying to drive me away. You want me to go now, at your order, rather than desert you later when you have come to trust me."

Ranegonda was dumbfounded. "That's not so," she said, knowing her protest was a lie. She felt her anger increase again, and then lessen.

"You cannot send me away, Ranegonda: I will not go." He smiled faintly. "And that is not because of the snow."

"So you have told me." She could not allow herself to reveal how much she needed his help. "You are bound to me through blood." At least, she reminded herself, she was not without an ally. Whatever the danger was, Saint-Germanius was not afraid.

"It is not fear or the lack of it, Ranegonda," he said quietly, sensing her emotions. "It is lack of action that is contemptible. Only the mad do not fear where there is danger."

"And only cowards flee," she added.

His expression changed; wry humor briefly replaced his somber concern. "Not always, my life; not always."

"You say that as if you have run away," she said, but was unprepared for his single crack of laughter.

"More times than I can easily remember," he told her, not moving from the door. "Because to hold on was the true death, or folly, or worse. There are times when the bravest course is to retreat so that you can fight again, and have men to fight with."

"What can have made you retreat?" she asked, welcoming the distraction he provided.

"Superior force, most of the time; a few times, an indefensible position; serious damage to men and equipment; fire." He ticked them off readily enough, but the memories stirred and brought back the slaughter he had come to loathe.

"I don't believe it," she said, knowing that she did.

He inclined his head to her. "I am grateful for your high esteem, Ranegonda."

"I would not retreat," she declared, hands on her hips.

"No; not from this place. This fortress is built to be the last position, the final outpost." He could still feel her wrath, but it was softened now, and diffuse. "This is where the rest would come, if driven by the enemy, and this is where you would prevail or come to ruin."

She shuddered, and cold had little to do with it. "Don't say that," she told him quietly, and could not bring herself to admonish him when he once again crossed the threshold of the cloth room to come to her side. Without considering the consequences she reached out to him and was heartened when his arms went around her. As she leaned on his shoulder, she said, "There is danger to us both in this room."

He said nothing for a short while, and when he did speak, he held her more closely. "What is it you fear Pentacoste will do?"

"I don't know," she answered after a moment. "And that may be the worst of it. If I knew, I would be able to do something to counter her, perhaps. But I know she spins, and works spells with her spinning. And I know the cloth she weaves has her purpose in it." She sighed unevenly. "Sometimes I suppose she wants the fortress destroyed, sometimes she seems to want to shame my brother." Reluctantly she broke away from him. "That's why I came here. To see what she has been doing."

"Would you know her intent if you look at the cloth?" he asked, not attempting to restrain her.

"I might," she said. "I know some of the old traditions, and recognize the tokens. Everyone does, even the monks." She Signed herself as a precaution as long-hidden memories niggled at her. "Most of us have vowed to the White Christ, but we have learned the ways of the old gods, as well."

"Such as the seedling trees planted at the crest of the roof-thatching in the village?" Saint-Germanius guessed.

"That is to protect the house, to bring it to the World Tree," said Ranegonda. "That is why serpents are painted on the central beams, as well. And when children are born there are rites done with the cord and the afterbirth to be sure that the child does not go mad or fall prey to the Stealers of Breath."

"Before they are baptized by the monks?" Saint-Germanius said.

"Yes." She had moved toward the big loom and now she stared at it, and the knots worked into the wool. "Wolves and Ravens," she whispered.

"What is it?" Saint-Germanius asked without allowing his apprehension to color the question.

"There is something . . ." She touched the wool, her face set with repugnance. "This is ensorcellment; it is not a simple thing." She stepped back, Signing herself. "There is power in this."

"How do you mean?" Saint-Germanius came to her side.

"This is a binding. I have seen nothing so powerful from Pentacoste's hand before. This cloth will make the one who wears it Pentacoste's willing slave." She put her hand to her throat. "His ghost would follow her after death."

"You mean it is her intention that he should do this," Saint-Germanius corrected her gently. "There are those who do not succumb readily to spells and sorcery."

Ranegonda was only half-listening to him. "I thought she was like the rest of the women here. I thought she knew those spells everyone learns. But this is the work of someone who has been a student of forbidden things."

"Are you certain of that?" he asked, aware that this was part of the secrets she kept from him.

"Yes," she answered quickly, and then added, "I have never done such things. I would not do them. But I have . . . seen them."

Saint-Germanius took her hand. "Then will you tell me how is it you recognize it? How can you know what it intends?"

She turned to him abruptly. "What?"

"If you know what this weaving is supposed to do, and you say it takes special knowledge to do it, how do you know what it is? When did you see it?" He spoke lightly, sensibly, but Ranegonda flushed and drew away from him.

"It is reprehensible," she said slowly. "It weighs upon me like sin."

Outwardly nothing about him changed, but his presence was different, as if his strength surrounded and protected her. "Tell me, Ranegonda," he said.

To her astonishment, she did. "Before the Great Pox came, and this"—she indicated her scarred cheeks—"happened to me, there were two brothers, twins, who came to aid my father. They were said to be scholars, and they surely knew many things. The villagers went in fear of them, because they looked alike and because they were always writing things. And it was learned that they were powerful sorcerers."

"Because they were twins who could read and write?" Saint-Ger-

manius said, remembering other places, other times when he had encountered the same prejudice, and others more extreme.

"Not entirely. They had great skills, and they provided them to my
father. They were the ones who most fortified this place. But they made
demands, also, and my father permitted them to be met. He allowed
them to work their arts." She grew agitated, pacing away from him,
unable to face him as she went on. "I used to hide in their quarters and
watch them. I saw the things they did." She swung back toward him,
her face pale. She spoke defiantly, as if she expected recriminations at
every word. "That was why I knew you were not a sorcerer, even when
you built your athanor, as you call it. I have seen sorcerers. I know what
it is they do, and how they work their sorcery, and you are not one
such." Her face was haunted. "I was wrong to watch them. It endan-
gered my soul to see them ply their craft. Only my father knew of what
I did, and he made me swear an oath that I would never reveal it, for
fear of what the monks would do." She Signed herself. "But my audacity was noted and its price set. And the White Christ marked me for
what I had seen, and the Bishop bound me by the marks."

"What happened to these sorcerers?" asked Saint-Germanius, both
hands extended to her.

"They were taken by Margerefa Carwic, and were stoned to death in
Bremen. And the Great Pox came here. My father knew I brought it,
and that I survived to remind him of the vileness I witnessed, when it
was done here." Her voice was hushed, her childhood dread summoned
up in full might; her grey eyes were restless, fever-bright. "I kept my
oath until now. On the honor of my father's memory, I have never said
anything, not afterward to Giselberht, not to Brother Erchboge."

"They will hear nothing from me," said Saint-Germanius at once,
trying to lessen her growing terror. He regarded her compassionately.
"And your brother? Did he keep the same silence?"

"No; he knows nothing. He never said anything, but to curse them
once, for bringing bad cess to this place. He forbade me to speak their
names when our father died." She looked about as if she expected the
stones to speak. "And he must never learn of what I saw, never."

"I have no reason to mention it, to anyone," said Saint-Germanius
calmly. "And I will not."

"Swear it," she demanded, for now that she had spoken she was
trembling. She Signed herself once again. "Swear it, Saint-Germanius."

"You have my word," he said, then, seeing her dejection, added,
"But if you prefer, I will swear it. On my life I will not reveal anything
you have told me about the sorcerers: believe this."

At last she put her hands into his. "You do not despise me for what

I learned? How can you not despise me?" Her doubt was turning to wonder.

"I? despise you?" He bowed over her hands, kissing them both on the palm. "I know you, Ranegonda. There is nothing in you to despise."

"But I have knowledge of damned things," she whispered. "I have seen the Devil's work."

He knew it would be cruel to laugh but he could not conceal a sardonic smile. "According to the monks, I am one of those damned things."

She pressed her lips together and met his eyes with hers. "No."

He heard movement on the steps above and he swiftly stepped back to the door, leaning in, one hand on the stone frame. "I only noticed a voice, Gerefa. I cannot say whose it was, other than it was a woman's."

Ranegonda blinked and stared, then realized what he was doing. "Well, I will have to find out who was here. Someone must have seen something. Perhaps the keeper of the light noticed who was here in the night."

Saint-Germanius gave her a quick, covert signal of approval, then gestured a greeting to Captain Amalric as he descended from the fifth level of the tower. "Did you pass a good night?"

"I passed a confoundedly cold one," grumbled the Captain as he paused beside Saint-Germanius. "Tonight I will bring both my mantels and wear them both, and my pelican as well." He nodded in the direction of the cloth room. "What is the matter here?"

"It appears that someone was weaving in the cloth room last night," said Saint-Germanius. "The Margerefa would like to discover who was at the loom."

"Um," said Captain Amalric, making it clear he would keep his opinion to himself. "I had the storm to watch."

"It was very loud until the snow came," Saint-Germanius agreed. "But you were awake. Isn't it possible that you noticed something?"

"I don't recall anything," said Captain Amalric as he fumbled to remove his gloves.

"Did you see anyone in this tower during the night, Captain Amalric?" asked Ranegonda, her composure almost restored. "I have been examining the cloth here, and it appears that something untoward was done."

"I thought I heard singing once or twice," Captain Amalric admitted after a short silence. "That was all."

"You never saw anyone?" Ranegonda asked, doing her best to remain self-possessed.

"I would have had to leave the light to do that, Gerefa, and leaving the light is forbidden. Besides, who would be about in the middle of a stormy night?" He squared his shoulders. "I need hot cider and toasted cheese."

"The cooks will provide it," said Ranegonda, dismissing Captain Amalric, and then, so the Captain could hear it, she added, "And I will want to have a word with you later this morning, foreigner, when I return from the village. Come to the muniment room."

"I am always at your service, Gerefa," said Saint-Germanius at once. He touched his forehead to her and followed Captain Amalric down the stairs.

Ranegonda stayed in the cloth room; it was cold beyond the cold of winter. She stared at the big loom and then the spindle, her mind harkening back to the days when she was a child, hidden, watching the sorcerers at their work. It had been exciting then, and now she quivered at the memories as much as she did at the evil pattern of knots in the wool. Now that she had revealed her secret to Saint-Germanius she felt curiously light-hearted in spite of the abiding shame that accompanied it. She glanced once more at the big loom, and some of her anxiety resurged. Carefully she Signed herself, and wished that her gesture of faith in the White Christ would lessen the pall of apprehension that enveloped her as she considered the omens surrounding her.

Text of a will dictated by Karal on December 21, 938.

In the name of the White Christ and to the honor of King Otto, I, Karal, formerly merchants' factor of Bremen, put down my wishes for the disposal of my worldly goods and chattel against the hour of my death. My wishes are being written by Sister Colestine at the Most Holy Grace Priory where I have been since we found the gates of Luneburh closed against us.

Let me recount how I come to be at this place now that my life is ending. At the time of our arrival here, we were informed that we could not remain, and we determined to strike north in search of a monastery that would take us in. Less than a day on the road and I collapsed from a vast pain in my guts. So great was my suffering that I could not hold bread in me, nor water. I was brought back to the Priory in the hope that the nuns would know a remedy for me.

I have been cared for and tended with charity, but the pain has increased and though I was starved before, now I am wasted, within and without, and I know that my time is near, for which I am grateful.

Though my city has been sacked and is now in ruins, I still have title

to a house in the Stonecutters' District of the city, next to the Church
of the Martyrs of Agaunum. This I leave to my nephew who bears my
name, if he is still living and can be found. If he cannot, then title
should pass to the Church of the Martyrs of Agaunum for a place to
provide shelter and food for those who have lost their homes, as I have.
I also leave the sum of three golden Francian Arks, which were left
with much of my wealth, in the care of the Brothers of the church.
Should ten years pass and my nephew not make a claim on the house,
it will pass to the Brothers, to remain theirs for all time.

As my wife and children are all dead, I have no direct line left to me.
Because I have lost my livelihood and my city at once, I do not grieve as
I might have had they died in happier times. Yet there are a few things I
would want done so that our name will not entirely be forgotten. First, I
ask that my grave be marked, and that the names of my family be included
with mine. The Prioress has a record of them and will make them available to the stonecutter. Let there be a serpent twined around the cross that
stands over my grave, and let the grave be planted with yarrow. Second,
I ask that word be sent to my uncle in Goslar, with a copy of this will, so
that one of my blood will know what became of me and mine. Third, I ask
that those of my blood who are able to donate money to this Priory, and
to the Sisters who work here to save those without home or food, in
memory of the ministrations they have given to me in these final days.

My strength is gone and I cannot hold a stylus or pen to write. The pain
in my gut increases every hour; my faith alone sustains me. The White
Christ will take me to His bosom in Heaven before many more days pass,
and I will go to Him willingly. It is fitting that I depart this earth at the
dark of the year, and take it not as an omen of evil, but of hope, for as
the year darkens, surely it will lighten again. Thus, our death is the
doorway to light, where those we have lost here will be restored to us in
perfect joy, for all in Heaven is perfect, as all in earth is flawed.

Karal, once of Bremen
at the Most Holy Grace Priory
by the hand of Sister Colestine

6

Berengar glared at Saint-Germanius and held up his kithre. "If you can do better, then do it."

Saint-Germanius rose from his place near the hearth and touched his forehead as he bowed. "It would be most gracious of you to permit me to play. I haven't touched an instrument in over a year, and I've missed it." The thought of music was almost painful, so acutely did he long to play; there were few consolations in his life and music was one of the most treasured.

Berengar's smile was mocking. "Fingers forget, in a year," he said, holding out the kithre.

"I trust mine will not," said Saint-Germanius as he made his way toward Berengar with quiet composure that hid his excitement.

The cavernous room smelled of wet wool and sweat. Most of the people of Leosan Fortress were gathered in the Common Hall, lingering there after their evening meal to take advantage of the warmth of the fire and the fellowship they could have, for their own quarters were colder, and in the depth of winter it was known to be a dangerous thing to be too much alone.

Beside Berengar, Pentacoste beamed at Saint-Germanius as he took the short-necked instrument from its owner and found a place at the end of the next table, where he could half-sit on the planks; Pentacoste watched him hungrily, the tip of her tongue showing between her lips. "Play us something we have never heard, foreigner," Pentacoste called to him.

"If that is what you would like to hear," he said, and glanced toward Ranegonda. "Is that what you want, Gerefa?"

"Play whatever you choose." Then she added, "We know all Berengar's songs now. Let us have some new ones."

Saint-Germanius fiddled with the tuning pegs until he brought the strings into better agreement, and he tried a few experimental chords, listening closely to the sound they made, for the strings were old. Before he began, he said to Berengar as he strummed the twelve strings, "These are showing their age. Let me make new strings for you, especially these seven drone strings. They will hold their temper and their pitch better. These five fretted melody strings are getting fragile."

"In this place there are no strings," said Berengar, as if speaking to a dull-witted child.

"True enough. But I can make them for you," said Saint-Germanius with unruffled cordiality. "To thank you for being allowed to play," he added, certain that Berengar would not now refuse.

"If you can make them, well and good," said Berengar petulantly.

"Thank you," Saint-Germanius responded, and fingered a melody on the frets. The kithre was set in the Lydian mode, and he thought over the melodies he knew that could be played in it as he practiced, listening closely to the quality of the sound; he was vaguely aware of the jealousy that flamed in Berengar's eyes. Finally he braced the kithre on his thigh, holding it expertly. "There is a song I learned many years ago, in Italia," he said, thinking back more than eight centuries to Comum and the eloquence of Gaius Plinius Caecilius Secundus, who had improvised it one night as they sat together on the terrace of Saint-Germanius's villa overlooking the magnificent lake on the orator's last visit to his birthplace. He lifted the kithre, and sang in Latin, his voice clear and rich:

> *There is special wisdom in the night,*
> *Unknown to the day.*
> *The wheeling stars dance to a harmony*
> *The sun cannot hear.*
> *The moon bears the burden of time*
> *In her changing face.*
> *I know my mortality and my love*
> *Better in the dark.*

Berengar was outraged at what he heard, at the masterful playing and Saint-Germanius's mellifluous voice; he folded his arms and lowered his head to show that every aspect of Saint-Germanius's performance was an ordeal for him, the more so because Pentacoste was listening in rapt fascination. He wanted to reach out to take the instrument away from this foreign interloper, but hesitated, not wanting to incur Pentacoste's displeasure or to draw attention to Saint-Germanius's superior playing by making him stop. It was galling to realize that the foreigner was so fine a musician. He wanted not to listen to any part of the song, yet he was intrigued; he knew just enough Latin to realize that the words were scandalous and beautiful.

> *In the night there is deep solace*
> *Unfelt in noon's brilliance.*
> *The rhythm of the stars rocks me*
> *In the ocean of the sky.*
> *The moon veils herself in daylight*

And glories in the night.
I find my secrets and my passions
Better in the dark.

Night is a more trustworthy confidante
Than the bustle of day.
The revelations of the myriad stars
Quiet my restlessness.
In moonlight the arcane knowledge
Of the senses flourishes.
Enigma and rapture are exalted
Better in the dark.

Darkness is friendlier to lovers
Than the splendor of the sun.
Stars lend a kinder light to—

"This is blasphemous!" bellowed Brother Erchboge. He rose unsteadily to his feet, pointing at Saint-Germanius in rage, his mouth square. "It is the work of the ungodly! Heresy! It invites laxness lasciviousness and obscenity! Let no follower of the White Christ listen to it, for the sake of his salvation. This is loathsome. It exalts sin and the wiles of the Devil."

"What does it say?" asked Winolda, who, like most of those living at Leosan Fortress, could not understand the words.

"Yes," said Pentacoste with a provocative smile. "Tell us."

"Sinful things. Damnable things," said Brother Erchboge. "It is not good for anyone to hear words of such intent, not if they seek to come to Heaven and the White Christ. Those words are unclean."

There was a buzz of whispered words in the Common Hall, no one else daring to raise an objection to the monk's condemnation.

Saint-Germanius regarded Brother Erchboge evenly. "It was sung by my friend, and he was an honorable man, revered for his scholarship and famed for his oratory."

"It is shameful," the monk insisted. "I tell you again: those who follow the White Christ should not listen to such music."

"Let him finish it, good Brother," said Ranegonda quietly. "The words are Latin, and you and he alone know what they say. He is not one of us, and the song is foreign. It cannot be like ours. Its foreignness protects us." She motioned to Saint-Germanius to continue, realizing that in spite of his ordinary bliaut and chanise, he was more elegant and commanding than Berengar in all his finery would ever be.

"Yes," said Pentacoste, for once agreeing with the Gerefa. "I want to hear all of it, all of it."

"It is the work of one who has not come to the White Christ. Those who serve Him know that the night is the time of demons and the dead, and that work done in the night is malign work." Brother Erchboge Signed himself. "But, as you say, the man is foreign." He pointed directly at Saint-Germanius. "If you have such a friend as the author of these words, then bring him to the White Christ, or he is lost to the Devil."

"Sadly," Saint-Germanius said, "he is dead, long ago."

This revelation mollified Brother Erchboge, who nodded his head with satisfaction before he Signed himself. "You may be sure that he serves in the fires of Hell, for such a song would not admit him to Heaven. If he was eloquent, so much the worse that he turned his talent to such usage. Night is dangerous and vile. Those who praise the powers of the night are praising the heart of sin, which is done most freely in the dark of the night and the soul."

Saint-Germanius deliberately Signed himself also, but in the Greek manner. "Gerefa? Shall I go on?"

Ranegonda made a decisive gesture. "Yes."

> *Darkness is friendlier to lovers*
> *Than the splendor of the sun.*
> *Stars lend a kinder light to embraces*
> *Making kisses on the sky.*
> *An eternal lantern, the moon reveals*
> *Paths unseen in the day.*
> *Love's mysteries transform me*
> *Better in the dark.*

There was silence when Saint-Germanius finished, for some did not want to appear to approve something which offended Brother Erchboge, and others wanted the song to continue. Genovefe was weeping, and Hrosia, sitting beside her, blushed deeply as the flower she was named for.

Saint-Germanius could see how puzzled Captain Amalric and the men-at-arms were, and he said, "I have another song. You will like it better. It is a soldiers' song. A much-loved Emperor wrote it, many years ago." And with that he launched into Nero's great tribute to the Legions of Rome, playing it as the Emperor himself had, accompanying himself in parallel fifths at a steady march tempo against the cantering cadence of the song.

As far as any eagle flies, the might of Rome will go.
From out of steaming Africa to Hyperboric snow.
Oh, hear the awesome marching beat
The steady tread of Legions' feet
Advancing as the foes retreat;
Advancing on the foe!

The sands of Egypt know the sound, and so does three-part Gaul
The Legions stand to guard us all, and never Rome will fall
Oh, hear the awesome marching beat
The steady tread of Legions' feet
Advancing as the foes retreat;
Advancing on them all!

There were thirteen more verses to the song, and Saint-Germanius doubted he could remember the whole, or would want to, given the audience he had. He settled for six of them, and was pleased as the men began to join in the refrain, some of them keeping the beat by pounding the tables with their tankards, just as the Legionaries themselves had done, nine hundred years before. This time when he was done the men of the fortress cheered.

Brother Erchboge regarded Saint-Germanius in open disapproval, his face rigid and his eyes hard as granite.

"I don't know what it means," said Geraint, his cheeks hectic with drink and enthusiasm, "but it is stirring. It would be a pleasure to march to such a tune."

That, thought Saint-Germanius, was what Nero had intended. With a sudden pang he recalled the night at the Golden House when Nero had sung that anthem, performing the octave jumps on *advancing* with musical flair, a night when he and Olivia had met under a laurel tree and had dared to love each other in spite of her terror of her husband. He realized that Captain Amalric had said something to him. "I'm sorry; would you repeat?"

Captain Amalric looked quizzical. "I wondered if you would translate the words so that the men here could sing it. They want to know what they're saying."

Saint-Germanius hesitated. "Yes, I suppose I could," he said after a moment. How delighted Nero would have been, he thought, to know that his songs would be sung so long after his death. "If you will give me a few days." He would need little more than an hour to fulfill Captain Amalric's request, but realized he would have to take longer if he was to avoid greater suspicion than he had already incurred by singing in Latin.

"Of course," said Captain Amalric with enthusiasm. "The way the men were singing, it is the kind of song they would use for marshaling, if it is appropriate in its text: Brother Erchboge will have to approve of the words. A song like that could encourage them, give them heart when they need it. But it will be for Brother Erchboge to decide." He clapped Saint-Germanius on the shoulder. "You are a surprising fellow, foreigner."

Saint-Germanius inclined his head. "As long as the surprises are welcome, what can I be but pleased?"

"Surely," Captain Amalric said, chuckling, and went on more seriously, "It's a shame more of the men do not like you. I reckon that they could learn a thing or two from you. But they like no stranger; you must not be slighted by their manner, for they have that way with all who are not Saxons."

"Yes," said Saint-Germanius. "I know." He turned and handed the kithre back to Berengar. "I'm grateful for this opportunity to play once more. It was kind of you to allow it."

Berengar took the kithre in thunderous silence.

"I will provide you new strings as soon as possible, to show my thanks," said Saint-Germanius as if he were unaware of Berengar's wrath.

Berengar said nothing as he glanced at Pentacoste, who stood smiling at Saint-Germanius in dreamy concentration.

"I did not know you could sing," she said to him, her eyes wide with implied promise. "You have an unusual voice. I would like to hear more."

Saint-Germanius touched his forehead deferentially. "If the Gerefa wishes and Berengar will lend me his instrument, perhaps you will, some other time."

Pentacoste frowned a little, distaste in her expression at being put off. Then she favored Berengar with a dazzling smile and looked back at Saint-Germanius. "I will wait to hear you—some other time," she said, and moved back toward the hearth, earning a condemning stare from Brother Erchboge, who deliberately remained near the door in the coldest place in the Common Hall, to show his contempt for earthly comforts.

"The White Christ have mercy on me, but I want to throttle her," murmured Ranegonda as she accepted Saint-Germanius's bow.

"She may well feel the same toward you," said Saint-Germanius equally softly. "Be careful of her, my life. She will not hesitate to act against you if she believes she can get away with it."

Ranegonda raised her voice so that the others would hear. "Saint-Germanius does have other songs to offer us if we wish him to sing for us again, or so he tells me. One evening he will perform those Brother Erchboge approves."

"Well done," said Saint-Germanius to her in an undervoice as the conversation grew louder.

"I hope so," she replied, her grey eyes flicking toward Brother Erchboge and then toward Pentacoste. "Everything is uncertain."

Saint-Germanius bowed again and stepped back from her, then left the Common Hall at once, ahead of most of the people of the fortress. No one attempted to stop him, or to say anything more about his music.

It was snowing, the flakes coming in stark ranks out of a blank sky. The air was so cold that it stung the nostrils; Saint-Germanius pulled his pluvial more tightly around himself and walked steadily toward the seaward tower, taking care to tread firmly. Underfoot the snow crinkled, and at the back of the wall where the bakehouse and kitchens had their ovens, there was a puddle of ice-rimed water, black as pitch in the night, which he avoided, knowing how dangerous such footing could be. Little as he wanted to admit it, Saint-Germanius found Captain Amalric's observation disturbing: he was disliked and distrusted by most of the people at the fortress, and would always be. As he stepped into the shelter of the seaward tower, Saint-Germanius thought of Osbern, who kept the light on the highest level of the tower just now. He often avoided all conversation with Saint-Germanius and, when he had to speak with the foreigner, Signed himself at the conclusion in order to prevent acquiring any contagion the stranger might carry.

His quarters were cold, and in spite of the parchment covering the narrow windows the wind insinuated itself everywhere, making the room nearly as cold as the night outside. He paused to put wood onto the brazier near the western window, watching the first red eyes of flame appear in the oak burl. A thousand years ago in Rome, he thought, this would have been the most prized part of the wood, not the least, and it would have been cut and polished to panel the walls of a rich man's villa instead of serving as fuel for the brazier.

Saint-Germanius went to one of his banded chests and opened it, frowning at what he knew he would see. Beyond what he had here, there were only two chests of his native earth left, and they were smaller than the rest. At most he would have another six months before he would require more, or face lassitude in the daylight hours, agony in the direct sun, crippling nausea when crossing running water, and abiding, esurient thirst. He sat on the edge of his bed and removed his heuse, then pulled out the leather inner soles and dumped the thin lining of earth into a sack. He rose and went back to the open chest, measured two handfuls of earth into each sole, then replaced the leather inner soles once again before he closed the chest and fixed its lock with his eclipse sigil inscribed on it in place. Satisfied, he set the laced boots at the foot of his bed, then drew up his stool to his writing table and put a few sticks of charcoal into the little mortar that stood next to his quill pens, grinding them with a drop of rabbit-skin glue to make ink.

Osbern had been replaced on duty in the light room by Reginhart and the last sounds of labor had faded from the kitchens when Saint-Germanius at last heard the faint knock he expected.

He opened the door quickly and brought Ranegonda inside as swiftly as possible. "Ingvalt has been watching me again," he explained as he took care to close the heavy door as soundlessly as possible.

"Why?" she asked as she put her arms around him. "What does he suspect?"

"I am foreign; that is enough for him," said Saint-Germanius, surprised at his own bitterness. He looked at her and smiled. "This is not the first time someone has watched me, love; it has happened before, nor is this the last time it will happen." The years he had spent just two centuries ago, wandering in the Polish marshes, had taught him once again how hazardous being a foreigner could be. "I am more thankful than you know that you are not like the rest, that you do not fear me for being a stranger."

"And you are not like the rest, either, and for that I am grateful." She tossed her head, casting back her hood. "If you were like the rest, you would fawn over Pentacoste, as Berengar does, and Margerefa Oelrih, and most of the men-at-arms of the fortress." Her cheeks reddened, and not from cold alone. "When I see her looking at you I want to scream at her that she cannot have you, that you are mine already."

"For the time we have, yes, I am yours," he said gently, sadness in his eyes.

"Bound to me," she added.

"Yes." He kissed the corner of her mouth, the touch of his lips so light that she could barely feel it, though the kiss went through her like fire. "Your lover until you come to my life: bound to you until the true death."

She stopped the words with her fingers. "No, foreigner." Her eyes were fixed on his. "Say nothing of death. It is an ill omen to speak of it when you are performing acts of life."

Saint-Germanius regarded her in concern. "You know what we do is not what other men and women do, Ranegonda. You will take no life from me, nor would I do anything that would cause you that danger; I've told you I cannot be as other men."

"But you said that blood is life. Surely something can spring from it?" she protested, and was suddenly shy. "Have I misunderstood? Saint-Germanius?"

The irony faded from his features. "No, no; you have not misunderstood." He took her face in his small hands and kissed her eyes. "I was mistaken." He paused, his thoughts racing. "Children are got in only one way, Ranegonda, and that is what those of my blood cannot do. When we escape death we lose our tears and the . . . ability to spark new life."

"But you say there are those of your blood—" she protested.

"As you are of my blood. That is our only propagation, my life." He touched her face once more, his fingers light.

"How?" she asked anxiously. "Have I offended you? Is there something I have done that you dislike? You say you are not able to—Are you withholding your seed from me because you are afraid of what could happen to me? I don't want to offend you, but I must know."

"No," he said, drawing her close to him. "You cannot offend me." He smoothed the tendrils of hair back from her forehead. "I thought you meant that a child could come from what we do, and that is impossible."

Her face was somber. "Truly? But great heroes have been born without men and women doing Eve's act. The White Christ was not from union of man and woman, and there are others . . . Can you never have a child? Not with any woman? Never?"

"I can bring those I love to my life," he said patiently as he unfastened the pin he had given her from her mantel. "They are the family of my blood, not the children of my body."

"But you have no children," she persisted, struck with the magnitude of his misfortune; she Signed herself quickly. "How terrible, to leave nothing behind, no heritage, nothing to let your name live on."

He took her by the shoulders and looked deeply into her eyes. "I have already lived for longer than you can imagine; I was old when your White Christ walked the earth. For valor or dishonor, my name lives in me." He knew that his explanations were useless, that for Ranegonda and every well-born Saxon the only real worth was continuation, and that meant children.

"Doesn't that trouble you?" she asked, bewildered; yet beneath her question was a plea, asking him to grant her solace in her imposed childlessness. "Haven't you failed your House if you have no heirs? You say that you do not mind, but how can that be? What man does not want healthy children?"

"It is not possible, Ranegonda. Since I woke to this life I have been impotent." He smoothed the mantel back from her shoulders, sheltering her from the cold with his arms. "But there are more ways to make love than penetration, and ecstasy is not only found in one act. I have long reconciled myself to my life."

"And you can never have them?" She trembled as she asked the question, knowing it was from distress rather than cold. "How can you bear it?"

"None of my blood can have children, Ranegonda: you must understand that. I have told you before, and I do not lie to you. When you come to my life you will discover it for yourself; it is one of the many things you will learn to accept, in time. And you will have time. I cannot give you children, but I can give you time." His kiss was lingering, soft, and compelling, and she came away from it with regret that it had to end.

"But you will not tire of me?" she asked, growing more anxious. "There is nothing to hold you to me, not lands or contract. Without children, you could renounce me, abjure your promise."

That was the heart of it, he realized, her dread of being cast aside by him, and her family as well. "No, Ranegonda, I cannot, and I would not," he said, so directly and simply that she began to believe him at last.

"You will come for me at the end of my life, as you promised?" She started to Sign herself, then stopped. "You will?"

"If I am able, I will," he said.

"And I will be like you," she said with apprehension and satisfaction.

"Not quite," he said, his voice calm, low with tenderness. "Remember what else I have told you: you will be able to have men love you fully, as I cannot."

"But there will be no children," she said, sighing as she touched his face and his dark, loosely curling hair. "I have been considering all you told me, about lovers and the blood and its bond."

Saint-Germanius was very still, and his words filled with quiet strength. "For us, love must suffice; so it must be genuine or we are nothing."

In answer to this she held him more fiercely, every muscle and sinew taut with desire. She pressed herself against him, shivering in her need. "Show me," she whispered. "Show me how you are bound. Renew the bond."

He moved back from her but only to open her bliaut, taking care to shield her from the worst of the draughts. "You will be cold," he said softly as he bent to kiss her breast through her heavy woolen chanise. "Here, Ranegonda," he said, brushing the back of his hand lightly over her nipples. "Feel this."

She reveled in his touch, and put her hand over his as he caressed her. "On my skin. Take off my chanise."

He shook his head, both hands motionless. "Ranegonda, you won't enjoy it. You'll freeze."

"Not in your bed," she countered, urgent and playful as she shrugged out of her bliaut and let it drop to the floor. "Take me there. Warm me."

"You know the way; you lead me," he said softly.

She looked at him in amazement. "But . . ." Then she took his hand. "Yes, come with me," she said with decision.

As she pulled him toward his bed, Saint-Germanius smiled at the way she moved, uncertainly at first and then with increasing confidence. As she reached the bed, she bent at the waist and shed her chanise, then reached for one of the fur rugs and wrapped it around herself as she lay back. "Find me. You say you always will. Find me, Saint-Germanius."

He put one knee on his bed, standing on the other leg as he watched her snuggle into the soft grey wolf-fur rug; it had been made of six pelts and was the largest and warmest of the three he owned. He reached out, his hand brushing the opulent fur as he sought her. "I will start with your eyes," he said, and bent to kiss her brow.

She reached out and caught her hands behind his neck. "I have you," she exulted. "In spite of everything, I have you."

His chuckle was nearly a purr. "That is what I have been trying to convince you of for a year." He stretched out beside her, moving without haste, letting her accommodate her body to his on the narrow bed so that she would have all the freedom of movement she might want. When she had at last become comfortable, he opened her rug enough to give him access to her; he bent his head, hands and lips seeking all the pleasure she had so long been denied. "Feel this," he whispered as he began his journey at her lips. He took time on his quest, lavishing attention everywhere she indicated sweet ease or increased excitement, drawing out her joy to a pitch she had never attained.

Ranegonda arched, stretched, and arched again under his generous, expert ministrations. Gradually she gave herself over to him, trusting his ardor at last.

"Feel this," he murmured to her as his veneration of her became more intense; no nuance of fervor was neglected as he called forth her entirety.

Her passion became his own; he felt himself shaken by the frenzy of her release. To her very core he plumbed her as they achieved fulfillment, and when he cradled her as her delirium subsided, she was transported again as she pressed against his side, her legs around his. Tired and triumphant, she drifted into sleep.

He wakened her at the end of the night, leaning over and kissing her as she opened her eyes.

"It's still dark," she protested.

"The cooks will be awake soon, and the watch in the light room will change," he reminded her. "You will want to be in your quarters before then, and I doubt you want the men-at-arms on duty to see you cross the courtyard."

"No," she agreed, then looked more closely at him. "You're already up," she said, noticing he had changed from the bliaut he had been wearing to the dark wool roc he had persuaded Enolda to make for him four months earlier: like the Roman tunica circula he had worn six hundred years before, the shoulders were pleated to take up the fabric, and the sleeves of his heavy woolen chanise were revealed, and his dark braies below the knees. "You are planning to ride today?" she asked, for these were the garments he favored for hours in the saddle.

"Perhaps, if the weather is clear enough later," he said, and went to his writing table. There, on the writing table was something he had labored for over a month to make. He lifted it and examined it in the faint light of the oil lamp.

"What are you holding?" she asked, propping herself on her elbow.

"Something for you, Gerefa," he said with a formal, old-fashioned, Byzantine reverence. "Wear it to remember my pledge to you."

"What is it?" she asked, unable to see more than the portion of his face the lamp lit. "Show me."

He took the lamp in one hand and his gift in the other, then returned to the bed, holding out his right hand to her so that she could see what he offered by the wavering lamp-flame.

The pectoral was a dark, luminous stone surmounted by displayed silver wings. The whole was slightly larger than his small palm, and the workmanship exceeded any she had ever seen outside of the Church of the Nativity in Hamburh. She could not bring herself to touch it. "Your sigil?" she asked, fascinated by the object.

"Yes," he told her.

"And it is for me?" Her wonder was so great that she could hardly breathe. "You made this for me?"

"Yes." He indicated the braided leather thongs that held it. "This should be silver, but there wasn't enough to make a chain for it. I will make one for it." He hung the oil lamp from the bracket over his bed and unknotted the thongs. "May I put it on you?"

She could only nod, her eyes brilliant with tears. She sat up, the fur rug close around her, but her shoulders bare. "Is it cold?"

"I've warmed it," he said, indicating his hand as he leaned toward her.

The silver was cool on her skin, and the braided leather rough. She fingered the pectoral as Saint-Germanius knotted the thongs at the back of her neck. "What is the stone."

"A black sapphire," he said. "I made it in the athanor, with a few other jewels: a dark topaz, an amethyst, and two emeralds. They're not as large as the sapphire, and not as fine." He stood back from her.

"You are able to do that? You can make jewels in that oven of yours?" She regarded him with awe.

"I told you it was possible. I have made some gold, as well, and the silver you see. It will be silver, the chain I am going to make. If you want the gold, you may have it." He started to reach for a leather pouch that lay at the far end of his writing table.

She Signed herself, and tried not to weep. "To pay your ransom? Is that what the gold is for?"

Saint-Germanius regarded her steadily. "No, Ranegonda, that is not what it is for."

"You are leaving," she said in sudden desolation, the elation of their night now as insubstantial as a dream. "You have given me this as your parting gift."

He folded his arms and shook his head. "It is February, my life. I would have to be more of a fool than I am to try to leave here in the dead of winter, unless the danger here was greater than the danger in the forest, and on the roads." He smiled at her to reassure her. "I thought you might want the gold. It means little to me; I can make more."

She was watching him closely, her jaw tightening against the despair that was fast possessing her. "When you say more, you mean you could make enough gold to pay your ransom, don't you?"

"Certainly," he said, aware that she was upset by what he had told her. "It would take a little time, but—" He shrugged to show this was not an important consideration.

"And you have known this from the time you came here?" she demanded, her face stark with shock. "You could make gold?"

"From the time I built the athanor, not before," he corrected her gently. "I work no magic, Ranegonda, only the Great Art. I cannot conjure things out of nothing on the instant. I need my supplies as much as any smith does, and the skill to put them to good use."

She covered the pectoral with her hands and the fur rug fell away to her waist; gooseflesh raised on her exposed body. "No one must see this," she said emphatically. "There are too many who suspect us already. If they see this, it will be regarded as an admission of our—" She stopped, her face flushing so that the scars were sharply visible.

"Our what, Ranegonda?" Saint-Germanius asked.

She met his eyes. "Our bond."

"Ah." He nodded. "Wear it or not, as you like, love," he said to her, compassion in his dark eyes. "This is not meant as a display or a hazard, it is a gift. It is yours."

"I will wear it," she said with resolve as she cast the wolf-fur rug aside and stood naked and shivering. "Next to my skin. Under my chanise and bliaut, but I will wear it."

"It pleases me that it will touch you," said Saint-Germanius with deep warmth in his voice.

She gave a single, shaky laugh and wrapped her arms across her chest as she tried to rub the cold out. "I have to get dressed. I'm freezing." She looked around for the clothes she had discarded the night before, and was startled when Saint-Germanius brought them to her, warm to the touch.

"I put them next to the brazier when I got up," he explained as he held out the chanise. "The old Romans always used to warm their clothes before donning them in winter."

"And you learned this from them?" she asked as she drew the chanise over her head; it was welcome as a hug.

"Among other things," he answered, offering the bliaut to her. "Here. Put it on before it cools."

She scrambled into it with alacrity and set about buckling her belt around her hips, her leather wallet and ring of keys secured by a knot. As she straightened up, she grew still, looking at Saint-Germanius. "I feel the jewel, and the silver."

"Good," he said.

"Saint-Germanius," she said as she came up to him, "I know you will not stay here forever."

He indicated his chests. "My supply of earth is running low. It would not be wise for me to remain here if I run out of it." He put his arm around her waist. "My strangeness will be much greater once my earth is gone."

She sighed. "I guessed it was something like that." Her face was sad but her eyes were resolute. "I don't want you to go, but when you must, I will not try to keep you here."

He wanted to offer her some consolation beyond the pectoral. "You could come with me when I leave," he said as he went with her toward the door.

She moved against him, turning so that she pressed against him. "No, I can't."

"Because you are Gerefa here," he said, knowing it was the answer.

"Because I am Gerefa," she echoed, and kissed him one time before opening the door.

Text of a letter from Hrotiger in Rome to Atta Olivia Clemens in Avlona. Delivered in thirty-four days.

To the most distinguished Roman noblewoman, Atta Olivia Clemens, the greetings of Hrotiger the bondsman in Rome on March 4, 939.

I have had word from my master, who is in the north-eastern part of Saxony, on the Baltic Sea, at a place called Leosan Fortress. He is being held for ransom, which he has asked me to pay. He is well.

It is my intention to set out in two weeks. I have been told that by the time we reach the Alps two of the passes will be open and we will be able to make our way into Francia or Germania. I have arranged to travel with armed escort from Rome to Saxony, since the gold I will carry will be a great temptation to those who steal from travelers. Those I have engaged to guard me have said it will take at least sixty days to reach the fortress, and perhaps more, depending on the conditions of the roads and any regional fighting. They say that since Bremen was sacked last year groups of people from that city have taken to robbery and marauding. Those in Bavaria and Franconia who have rebelled against Otto may well be in arms still, but they are not inclined to waste their lances and arrows on foreigners. A few golden Angels should clear the road for us.

You need not remind me to carry several chests of my master's native earth as well as his ransom. I will take four, and with good fortune three will arrive with us. He has requested his red Roman chest as well, and its contents, for the disease that comes from blighted rye has struck there as well as in Francia.

If there are no obstructions encountered, I presume that Saint-Germanius will be in Rome again before the end of July, and if the barbarians will leave the city in peace for a while, it might be possible to bring crops

*in once again. Your villa has received some damage, but it is being
repaired and expanded against the time of your return. While I am gone
from Rome the major domo, Marzius, will be in charge here. He has
instructions regarding your villa as well as Villa Ragoczy.*

*Be comforted, Madama, knowing that Saint-Germanius will return,
and be encouraged that he has lived with some protection for these many
months.*

In highest regard and on behalf of my master, by my own hand.

*Hrotiger
Bondsman to Franzin Ragoczy
Comites Saint-Germanius*

7

His mule was bleeding from many injuries and the monk himself was
badly bruised, his knuckles cut, when he tumbled out of the saddle
inside the stockade gates.

Burhin the cobbler and Udo the thatcher admitted him and quickly
set the long horizontal brace to hold the gates closed. Udo grabbed the
mule's bridle and Burhin reached to keep the monk from falling.

"Bands of men," gasped the monk, one hand pressed to his side, his
eyes anguished. "Wild and starving." He stared around. "Don't let—"
He stopped. "Where am I?"

"The village at Leosan Fortress," said Udo, noticing some of the
others approaching from the newly planted fields and the cluster of
houses. "You are safe here." He cast a quick glance over the mule and
suspected that the animal was lamed for life: a lame mule was worse
than useless, but it would be for the monk or the Gerefa to rule on what
was to be done with it.

The monk needed time to consider this, making an effort to master
himself and the growing pain in his chest, then said, "Leosan Fortress.
How far is Holy Cross Monastery?"

"Half a day's ride, south-east," said Burhin, feeling blood on his
hands where it had soaked through the monk's habit; he was shocked
to discover that some of it was still wet. "You are in no condition to—"

The monk made a weak lunge, as if to break free of Burhin's support,
then staggered back, his face contorted with every breath he took. "I
vowed I . . . would warn them. The band . . . will go there . . . the omens

were bad." He turned his head to stare at the cobbler. "There were . . . two rats dead under the crucifix. I have . . . to warn them."

"You're hurt," said Burhin. "Someone will have to carry the message for you." He looked toward the fortress, wondering what the Gerefa would do now, for she was obliged to aid the monastery.

"No, no, the White Christ protects . . ." said the monk as he Signed himself, his tone distracted. "But they must be warned. The men might well . . ." He staggered again and would have fallen if Burhin had not held him up. "Warning. They need warning," he gasped, his hands fixed in Burhin's mantel.

Ormanrih was at the head of the villagers as they reached the gate, and he made a gesture for the others to stop as he saw the injuries on the mule. "What is going on?" he asked sharply. "Who is he?"

"We don't know," Udo admitted. "He has just come. Look at him. He's been given quite a drubbing." He nodded toward the mule. "And the animal as well. That off rear leg is wrecked."

"I reckon he was trying to get word to Holy Cross," Burhin said, working to keep the monk on his feet. "That's what he says."

"And where is he from?" asked Ormanrih, already anticipating the questions he would have to answer as soon as he reported to the Gerefa.

"He hasn't said," Burhin answered.

"They are hungry," said the monk. "They wanted the mule for food." Again he Signed himself.

"Who are they?" asked Ormanrih, fearing that the outlaws had at last banded together to make little wars on isolated places like this.

The monk blinked several times before he answered, and he set his jaw against the growing agony of breathing. "From Bremen. The city is gone. They are . . . without homes or food." He panted. "That fall . . . just now. My side."

Ormanrih was appalled. "What became of Bremen? It is a great place, with more than a thousand houses." Although he had never seen the place himself, he knew, as all Saxons knew, of the great cities of Hamburh and Bremen. That it was gone was unthinkable, and he regarded the monk with sudden suspicion. "Who could have brought it down?"

"Men from the east," muttered the monk, trying to put his hand against the pain in the side of his chest; he could not bear to do it.

"The Margerefa said there had been trouble at Bremen," Udo reminded Ormanrih. "Before the harlot was taken to trial at Holy Cross."

"He said the King won the battle," added Keredih, who skinned and tanned hides for the village and the fortress.

"He did not say that the city was gone," Ormanrih objected. "Great cities have trouble, but they endure." He Signed himself.

"The people who escaped," the monk said, and coughed blood, "they are the danger now."

Burhin almost dropped the monk as he saw the foamy red spittle at the corner of his mouth. "It is the death!" he exclaimed.

"He is a monk," Ormanrih reminded them all. "We must care for him or the White Christ will curse us. Take him to the Gerefa."

"She will decide what can be done," said Udo, relieved that that responsibility should fall to someone else.

Ormanrih signaled Keredih. "Help Burhin. Carry the monk to the fortress. And you"—he pointed to Udo—"bring the mule along."

"He's on his last legs," warned Udo, but gave the bridle a commanding tug. "If he falls, it is none of my doing."

"Well enough," said Ormanrih, and started back along the road between the fields, waving his arms to encourage the others to keep up with him as well as to fend off the villagers who pressed toward them.

Keredih regarded the monk with the same apprehension Burhin displayed, but he knew better than to refuse a direct order from the village headman. He got on the other side of the monk, and half-dragging, half-carrying him between them, Keredih and Burhin straggled after the rest, both of them too frightened to curse. Behind them Udo pulled the lame mule.

The wooden horn sounded as the villagers approached the fortress gates; almost at once the gates swung open, the chain of the device that Saint-Germanius had installed screeching and clanking. From the ramparts Ulfrid shouted down, "What is your cause, headman?"

"A monk!" bellowed Ormanrih. "A stranger! Hurt." He swung his arm to show the monk as Burhin and Keredih made their way up the slope, their burden hanging between them.

"Enter!" Ulfrid yelled back.

The slaves operating the winch cranks stared impassively at the villagers and the newcomer. One of them made a gesture with his hand to ward off evil.

Kynr was the first of the men-at-arms to reach Ormanrih, and as soon as he saw the monk, he came to a halt. "What is wrong with him?"

"He says he was in a fight," answered Ormanrih. "He was trying to get warning to Holy Cross." He Signed himself automatically. "Where is the Gerefa?"

"I'll fetch her," said Kynr at once, and hurried into the landward tower, grateful for the excuse to put distance between himself and the stricken monk. He Signed himself, and then made the gesture of the old gods, in case the White Christ could not protect him against His monks.

Ulfrid came down the stairs from the parapet and faced the villagers. "Who is the monk?"

"I don't know who he is," said Ormanrih heavily. "Or where he comes from. But he is in the habit of a servant of the White Christ, so—" He opened his hands to show he had little choice about helping the stranger.

"He does not look well," said Ulfrid, watching the stranger from a little distance in order to protect himself. "He may have a miasma about him."

"It seems more likely that he was beaten," said Ormanrih. "His mule certainly was." He pointed to the miserable animal.

Delwin leaned down from his guard post, staring openly at the little party. His youthful features were hard with fear, and he quickly retreated to the section of the wall above the chapel, Signing himself and praying that nearness to the altar would provide him greater protection than he might have otherwise. He hoped that Brother Erchboge was inside, tending to his prayers.

Chlodwic and Ewarht had left off honing the blades of their spears and set their whetstones aside to watch the village group. They were curious but not willing to expose themselves to the danger of the unknown monk.

Duart appeared at the door of the Common Hall, Signed himself, and withdrew, hovering just out of sight in the shadows.

There was a bustle of activity at the door to the landward tower, and then Ranegonda pushed through the people gathered there. "All right," she said as she came toward the villagers, her manner brisk. "What has happened." She was limping as she advanced on the newcomer, and her expression combined distrust of foreigners, exasperation, and increasing apprehension. She saw the discomfort in Burhin's demeanor as well as the dismay in Keredih's.

"He just arrived," said Ormanrih. "He fell off the mule. He is hurt, from that and from wounds."

"Then we must tend to him at once." Ranegonda glanced over her shoulder at Winolda, who had just hurried up to the growing crowd of villagers. "Bring your herbs and fetch Saint-Germanius. This monk is in need of help. Now," she said, and did not wait to see if her orders were obeyed; her attention was already focused on the injured man. She went directly to the monk. "Brother. Who are you?"

The monk was only half-conscious, but his eyes fluttered open as he attempted to answer. "Brother Curtise," he muttered. "Of the . . . the Monastery of the Redeemer." He tried to Sign himself, but could not as coughing seized him and more pink-tinted spittle flew.

"You were attacked coming here?" Ranegonda persisted, knowing how distressing the omens were and trying to put a brave face on it. "Who attacked you?"

"Bands of men. They overran the monastery, and . . ." He could not continue. He shuddered in the grasp of the villagers.

Udo and Ormanrih exchanged uneasy glances, for both knew it would be a very bad omen if the monk should die in their charge, just as it was a bad omen that he should come here to die of such hurts. Burhin looked miserable as he held onto the stranger's arm and tried to keep him upright without permitting any of the man's blood to get onto his clothes.

"Where is the Monastery of the Redeemer?" asked Ranegonda, hoping the man would answer.

"On the other side of the road to Hamburh, four, five days' steady ride," he answered in a rush, and then gave way to more coughing; this time he turned an ashen hue while the lines in his face grew rust-colored. Each breath was labored. "I fled. The Prior ordered me to go. But I could not reach Hamburh. There were more bands on the road. Other travelers said so."

"You minister to travelers?" asked Ranegonda, anticipating his answer.

"And those in need," said the monk, his voice fading. "Those starving. Those mad." More blood had soaked through the side of his habit. "We could not help the men from Bremen. They were too many. And they took . . . everything."

Ranegonda looked about her. "Well?" she demanded. "Get a pallet for him, and summon Brother Erchboge." She saw that Pentacoste had come out of the landward tower, Berengar trailing behind her. "You, Chlodwic, get Brother Erchboge. We need our monk here. Hurry. Brother Curtise is failing."

Chlodwic obeyed with unseemly speed.

"He fell off the mule as soon as he was through the gate," said Ormanrih, reminding Ranegonda of that mishap in order to prevent any blame for the man's condition lighting on him. "The mule . . . well, there is no doubt that he has been ill-treated. The monk must have ridden hard after his fight. And you can see from the mule that he was struck with heavy weapons and—"

"Yes, the creature has been in a fight, beyond question; the omen is clear. Take him to the stable and have someone care for him, so that the omen will not hold against us," said Ranegonda with asperity. "Monk. Brother Curtise," she said to the wounded man, speaking slowly and distinctly. "We are going to do everything that we can to ease your hurts and to restore your health, and with the favor of the White Christ we will succeed."

Brother Curtise blinked at her, no recognition in his eyes. His head lolled back and he gasped. There was more blood, fresh blood, spreading over his habit, seeping through what had already dried.

"Shall we lay him on the ground?" asked Keredih, a shade too eagerly. "He is breathing so heavily, it might be best."

"We'll see what Saint-Germanius and Winolda decide between them," Ranegonda declared, allowing no contradiction. "Hold him up until they come, and see that he doesn't choke. You're right. He does not breathe well."

More of the people of the fortress had come to see this strange monk, though most of them kept their distance, afraid of being touched by the miasma of suffering or being subjected to the omens. Of those who dared to approach, most Signed themselves when they saw the color of the newcomer's skin and heard his ragged breathing, and a few of them risked offending the White Christ by invoking the old gods by gesture and whispered words. Pentacoste vanished into the landward tower.

Then Winolda was making her way through the throng, Saint-Germanius directly behind her. She wore her apron with its array of pockets containing packets of herbs over her bliaut, and he carried a small wooden case. As she saw the monk, Winolda faltered and Signed herself, then looked back at Saint-Germanius, her cheeks suddenly pale. "I cannot touch him. I cannot. He is . . . Look at him. The shadow is on his face."

Hearing those dreaded words, many of the people gathered drew back, for to be where the shadow was invited death to the ones who saw it. If the woman who tended them in their illnesses was afraid to approach the man, then so were they.

"Let me." Saint-Germanius moved past her to the villagers and their distressing burden. "How long has he been bleeding at the mouth? Hold him upright," he said to the men carrying Brother Curtise. "Has there been foam in the blood like this for long?"

Keredih was afraid to speak, saying only, "Not long."

"It . . . it started when he rose from his fall, I guess," said Burhin. "He is bleeding from the side, and the back."

Saint-Germanius nodded, then, to the appalled astonishment of everyone, leaned forward and rested his ear against the monk's chest, listening carefully for a short while, as if fear of the shadow was nothing to him. Then he gently probed the bloodied habit, testing the wounds beneath, noting when the monk groaned and when he winced. Finally he stood back, his expression grave. Turning toward Ranegonda, he rubbed his face with his hands and gave a hard sigh. "There is nothing we can do, Gerefa," he told her in a low voice, shielding their exchange with his shoulder. "The wound on his side appears to have been caused by a blow with a heavy weapon that broke a rib, possibly two. Since he came this far, the injury must have worsened recently. When he fell, the rib must have punctured his lung." He glanced back at Brother Curtise. "If I had all my medicaments with me, I might be able to ease his pain, but I don't think I could save him, not now."

She Signed herself. "His hurts are mortal?"

"I'm afraid so," he answered, and tried to prepare her. "I have no wish to give you false hopes, Ranegonda. The monk is dying."

"But the White Christ grants miracul—" she began.

"The miracle was needed before his lung was punctured," said Saint-Germanius bluntly. "Now that it has happened, I doubt the archangels could save him if they tried. He's lost too much blood to be saved."

"How can you tell?" she asked, and felt the pectoral against her skin.

"The look of him, the smell, the way his heart sounds," he answered, and added, "I have seen death like this countless times, Gerefa. He has reached the point where he cannot be recalled."

She ignored the attention the people directed at her. "Is it possible you are wrong?"

"Yes, about the specific wound," he said at once. "He may have been hurt in some other way, and the blow might have done more damage than break ribs, damage that needed the fall to be made apparent. And it could be that he is not telling you the truth of where he came from, and he was hurt not days but hours ago. But I doubt it would make any difference in the monk's case: he is mortally wounded, no matter how or when the wound was made." He looked into her eyes, his own deep with old grief. "I would not say this if it were not true, and if it were not necessary."

"No, you would not," she agreed distantly, then felt a new alarm. "There is a miasma?"

"Not from broken ribs," said Saint-Germanius, and looked back at the monk. "If we make him comfortable we will have done all we can for him."

She plucked at his sleeve as he was about to turn away, saying in an urgent undervoice, "And you cannot help him? With what you have told me of your powers, is there nothing you can do?"

This time hidden pain hovered in his dark eyes. "Nothing that he would accept, Gerefa." He took a long breath. "He would damn me if I tried."

She motioned him to turn away with her. "But you told me, didn't you? your blood could restore—" She broke off.

"It could, but he would not welcome it, and he would not want to live my life," said Saint-Germanius quietly, his eyes directly on hers. "And Brother Erchboge would not tolerate such a restoration, not as Brother Curtise would be after he changed."

Ranegonda nodded. "You would guide him," she said, and added at once, "No. I realize that it would be foolish. But the omens of his death are so dire."

"For him, death will be kind," said Saint-Germanius gently. "He will go to it with thanks."

Signing herself, Ranegonda sighed. "Perhaps," she said, and indicated to him with a gesture to return to the monk; then she addressed the villagers. "You had better bathe, to be rid of the shadow," she said to them, signaling for one of the slaves to heat the men's bathhouse. "You have done good service to the fortress today, and to the White Christ by caring for His servant."

"You will come to bathe at the end of the day," said Ormanrih, who could not release the men from all their labors for the rest of the afternoon. "It will be in good time by then."

"That is satisfactory," said Ranegonda, knowing that the bathhouse would hold heat well into the evening.

The villagers looked relieved, but Ormanrih was not entirely satisfied. He strove to make it clear that he and his villagers had no part in this event. "He spoke of bands of men in the woods; remember that. He said they attacked him."

"He said they overran his monastery," said Burhin. "Men from Bremen. He said Bremen was gone."

A low moan of dismay rose from those who heard this, and Duart, who had retreated a safe distance, said loudly that he did not believe it. "I have been there, ten years ago, and its walls, I tell you, cannot be broken. No city as great as Bremen could fall. It is too mighty."

"There was a battle," Ranegonda reminded them. "The Margerefa Oelrih said that King Otto was the victor, but there was a battle for the city, fiercely fought on both sides."

"And some of the city must have suffered, as any city will when enemies come against it," said Saint-Germanius. "No matter how well the people defended their walls, if there was a battle . . ." He did not finish.

"If there are men from Bremen, surely King Otto will provide for them," said Culfre, who was still favoring his mangled hand. "It is the vow of the King to provide for his vassals."

"The Margerefa said that the Magyars attacked the city," Saint-Germanius reminded the Gerefa. "They are relentless fighters."

She stared at him. "You have seen them?"

"Oh, yes," he answered, precisely and remotely, thinking of all the battles he had fought, and those he had witnessed, and the waste of them. He realized that many of the people of the fortress were staring at him now, and a few of them wore the hard look of suspicion.

Then there was a loud cry and Brother Erchboge burst through the gathering, rushing toward Brother Curtise, one hand extending a crucifix to the stranger as he shouted Latin prayers.

Burhin held onto Brother Curtise, but Keredih moved back, too overcome by fear and the sense of approaching death.

"The White Christ will lift you up, Brother, and He will save you though all the world deserts you and detests you," Brother Erchboge declaimed as he embraced Brother Curtise, unaware of the raging pain he caused.

Brother Curtise groaned and coughed with such wracking force that he threw Brother Erchboge back from him, raving in agony. He shuddered, and coughed again so that more foamy blood rose in his mouth.

Brother Erchboge held up his hands in horror. "The Devil!" he exclaimed. "The Devil!"

The small crowd went silent with dread before Signing themselves against the new danger Brother Erchboge announced.

Ranegonda glanced over at Saint-Germanius. "Is it possible?"

"No," answered Saint-Germanius with a decisive shake of his head, though he saw the people of the fortress shrink back from the newcomer, and the villagers exchange appalled glances.

"He is possessed. The Devil has brought him his pain! He suffers for his denial of the White Christ!" Brother Erchboge clasped his crucifix more tightly, and began once more to chant in Latin.

Burhin looked around the courtyard in distress. "Let us put him down, Brother, so that he—"

"Yes," declared Brother Erchboge. "Put him down. Put him down." He gestured quickly, frantically. "And pray for the salvation of your souls, that God does not send you suffering such as his."

Brother Curtise was growing more pale, and he was no longer quite conscious. He muttered bits of words that might have been prayers as the villagers laid him on the paving stones with as much dispatch as possible. Aside from the rapid prayers of Brother Erchboge everyone remained silent.

Saint-Germanius touched Ranegonda's shoulder. "You can't let him lie here, Ranegonda. He's suffered so much already. You're leaving him to die alone," he said quietly.

She had caught her lower lip in her teeth, but she made herself answer him. "What else can I do? Brother Erchboge would not permit anyone to shelter the man, not now: the monk is a stranger and in a habit. Brother Erchboge speaks for the Brothers here. If I contradict him, who will obey me?"

A number of sharp words crowded in Saint-Germanius's mind, but he bit them all back. Then he said, just above a whisper, "Would you forbid me to help him?"

"I should," she answered after a moment's hesitation. "But I will not."

He nodded once, and pushed his way through the staring people of the fortress to the side of Brother Curtise. Paying no heed to the Latin prayers Brother Erchboge continued to recite, he dropped to one knee beside the stranger, who had huddled onto his side and was spasming with every cough.

"The White Christ will curse those who fail to honor His servants," Brother Erchboge shouted suddenly. "You are already suspect, foreigner, as this so-called monk is suspect. You show your true affiliation when you aid that Devil-filled miscreant. Hear his blasphemy! What true monk would fail to pray in the hour of his death? If you protect one who is possessed, I will know you for an enemy of the White Christ!" He held up his crucifix toward Saint-Germanius, his eyes bright with zeal. "You are not one of His servants, and you will fall to His might."

Saint-Germanius had not listened to this vitriolic attack, and when it was finished, he spoke without turning his attention from Brother Curtise. "It was your White Christ Who cast out devils from those possessed, and it was He Who promised to forgive your sins. If the White Christ can do this, surely you can succor one of His followers." He had felt the monk's pulse and noted the increasing bright stain on the side of his habit. "Your White Christ also said that whatever you did for the least of His creatures you did for Him also."

"Those are disputed texts, and true followers of the White Christ are not bound by them," Brother Erchboge shouted, insulted that the foreigner should question his grasp of doctrine. "That man is cursed, and we must cast him out to cast out the Devil who possesses him." Brother Erchboge rounded on Ranegonda. "You must order him to stop, or the White Christ will hold us all accountable for giving sanctuary to evil."

Ranegonda looked from Brother Erchboge to Saint-Germanius, her eyes wide with turmoil. "Saint-Germanius, if—"

"Don't ask me to abandon the dying, Gerefa," said Saint-Germanius clearly. "He is suffering for no reason but the fear of Brother Erchboge. That is not sufficient reason for me." He leaned over Brother Curtise and lifted one eyelid, seeing how the eyes had rolled back. "It will not be much longer."

"All the more reason to keep away from him!" Brother Erchboge shouted. "The Cross will not protect you when the vile spirit departs that body and seeks another to possess, and I will not be able to—"

Saint-Germanius held up his hand. "If there is any risk it is mine, not yours. You will have nothing to fear for yourself or the people of this fortress."

Ranegonda touched the pectoral she could feel through her bliaut and chanise, and found its omen comforting.

"Then do not come to me for Confession," ordered Brother Erchboge. "I will not permit you to carry the Devil to me."

"You have my word I will not," said Saint-Germanius, and continued to watch over Brother Curtise, his slight frown increasing as the stranger convulsed; it was almost over.

Brother Curtise gave an incoherent cry that ended on choking; more bloody foam ran from his mouth, and he flung his head back once again, a slight, gurgling cry coming from his lips, then shivered as a quantity of dark blood with very little foam welled from his mouth and ears. All those watching Signed themselves as the monk died, and several turned away so as not to be touched by the death.

"He cannot remain here!" Brother Erchboge screamed into the silence that followed Brother Curtise's death. "The Devil will find another vessel!"

Saint-Germanius bent down and lifted the lifeless monk in his arm. "You have nothing to fear, Brother Erchboge," he said evenly. "I will see to his burial." He hesitated. "I am correct, am I not? you do not wish to bury him yourself. And you will not let him lie in consecrated ground?"

"Away with him!" Brother Erchboge yelled, pointing toward the gate and holding his crucifix in both hands. "Before any of us is taken by the Devil!"

The villagers moved out of Saint-Germanius's way, their expressions awed and afraid. Udo Signed himself repeatedly as Saint-Germanius went by him toward the gates.

"Let no one impede him!" Brother Erchboge ordered. "And close the gates after him. Keep him without! Do not let him return with that death on him!"

Ranegonda, who had watched this transpire in a daze, now suddenly was alert once more. "No." She pointed toward the slaves who were starting to crank the winch. "No, you will not do that. When Saint-Germanius returns you will admit him. If there is any attempt to keep him out, you will answer to me, and I will have you flogged. I will have anyone flogged who acts against Saint-Germanius." She swung around to face Brother Erchboge. "You may see to the souls of the people here, but I am Gerefa, and I am responsible for the fortress and the village. I need that foreigner, and I will not allow you to bar him from this place."

Brother Erchboge stared at Ranegonda in disbelief. "The Devil," he said at last, "seeks women, for they are always his servants, and they are worse than the demons of Hell."

"I do not speak as a woman, but as Gerefa," she countered. "I would fall in my duty to the King if I kept that man outside these walls. He is our only smith, and he has saved four of the people here from death. The fortress needs him."

"And you will keep him once his ransom is paid?" Brother Erchboge challenged. "Will he be needed at this place then?"

"Yes, he will be needed, but I will not keep him. Not in honor, no. But I will keep him as long as honor allows." She raised her head defiantly. "You are to say nothing more against him, not in regard to the death of that monk."

"He was not a monk, he was a servant of the Devil sent in disguise to bring damnation to this place," Brother Erchboge insisted. "But if you forbid me from giving the protection of the White Christ, I will submit."

There was a low muttering among those who watched this exchange, and the villagers took advantage of the moment to leave, only Orman-rih remaining to hear any orders the Gerefa might have for him.

"Good," said Ranegonda. She gave a sweeping motion with her arm. "The rest of you, there is nothing more to look at. Go back to your tasks." She saw Duart put his hands on his hips, and she singled him out. "You, monitor, will see that everyone is about their business. Now."

Duart glowered, but did not oppose her. "The men-at-arms will need orders from Captain Amalric," he reminded Ranegonda with a hint of condemnation.

"Then tell him to look to his men," said Ranegonda, and looked around the courtyard. "All of you. Pray for your souls and for the soul of that poor stranger. Brother Erchboge is afraid that he was the Devil, but do not forget the tales we have all heard when it was not the Devil who came in humble guise, but angels of the White Christ." There were similar legends of the old gods, as well, and she knew that everyone at the fortress had heard them as children and recounted them now to their own families. "The baths will be ready tonight, and those who fear the shadow may wash themselves clean of it."

Brother Erchboge gave Ranegonda a measuring stare of disapproval. "You will remember this day, and your betrayal, when vengeance is visited upon us."

"Let us hope that the White Christ will show us mercy, as you have said He will," Ranegonda told him, and walked away from him into the landward tower.

Pentacoste was waiting for her. "That monk died," she said breathlessly. "He came here to die."

"He came here for help," said Ranegonda will unconcealed distaste. "But we could not help him."

"He was in agony, wasn't he?" she asked. "Terrible agony."

"I fear so," said Ranegonda, wanting to get away from her sister-in-law.

"And there was nothing to do to stop that. He had to suffer," Pentacoste went on, the tip of her tongue moistening her lips. She fingered the embroidery on her wide belt, patterns emphasized with knots. "It was for the White Christ he suffered."

"Brother Erchboge says so," Ranegonda said quietly, and attempted again to put distance between Pentacoste and herself.

"The White Christ will have him then," said Pentacoste with sudden venom. "And welcome to him, eunuch that he was." She turned away abruptly. "At least Berengar isn't a eunuch. Or Oelrih."

It was all Ranegonda could do to keep from demanding of Pentacoste that she explain herself. She watched as her sister-in-law climbed the stairs that led to her apartments, on the level above Ranegonda's own, or the women's quarters, on the level below; once she could no longer see Pentacoste, she listened, hoping to discover where she had gone, and what she was doing there.

Dusk was over the fortress by the time Pentacoste descended the stairs again. She had changed clothing, wearing now her wine-red bliaut over her blue chanise, and she had wound her long braids on her head and held them in place with a fretted gold chaplet. Before going to the Common Hall to eat she paused in the door of the muniment room where Ranegonda still labored. She stopped just inside and watched for a short while and then said, "Are you going to send word to my husband? About the monk who died?"

"I have already," said Ranegonda distantly, not bothering to look up from her records to speak to Pentacoste. "Culfre and Severic left with the message shortly after you went—" She pointed upward. "Wherever it was you went. Had you remained with the women, or gone to the cloth room to weave, you would have heard of it."

"I was in my own quarters," said Pentacoste, but with a look that was eloquently mendacious. "A death like that is shocking, isn't it?"

"For the monk, most certainly," said Ranegonda, setting her quill aside. "What do you want, Pentacoste?"

She shrugged gracefully. "I merely wondered if you informed my husband. Now that he is a monk, he must hear of everything that pertains to monks, mustn't he?" Her lips curved in a sweet smile but there was a hardness in her eyes that was not found in iron.

"It is my duty to inform him," said Ranegonda in careful neutrality. "So you were overcome, seeing the monk?"

Pentacoste put her hand to her bosom. "I am not like you, Ranegonda. I cannot look on death and remain unmoved. I was reared more gently than you, in a grander place by kinder hands, and I do not see the dying without requiring time to compose myself. I could not watch from outside." She recalled afresh the hurried rush she had made to the cove, knowing it was foolish to go there in daylight but unable to wait until moonrise. She had made offerings to the old gods, and danced to thank them for the dreadful death Brother Curtise had suffered. There was sand in the hem of her bliaut when she returned, and she had realized she must not let that be seen. "I put on these clothes to be rid of the presence of death. It clings to what I was wearing."

Ranegonda did her best to appear solicitous. "And are you strong enough yet to take a meal with the rest of the people of the fortress? Or do you need Genovefe to bring you porridge and bread?"

"I am able to eat," said Pentacoste sharply.

"That is fortunate," said Ranegonda. "It might be seen as a bad omen if you were to keep away from the Common Room. There are those who are already certain that there was a miasma with the injuries the monk suffered, and they might believe that your absence confirms their worst fears."

"The monk was wounded. I saw the blood," said Pentacoste with passion.

Ranegonda did not respond for a moment. "How? You were not in the courtyard."

"I watched from inside this tower," said Pentacoste. "I saw him fall and I saw the blood run from his mouth."

Ranegonda Signed herself. "May the White Christ welcome him to Heaven."

Pentacoste's laughter was derisive and musical, and Ranegonda could hear it long after Pentacoste left the landward tower.

Text of a letter from the Comites Pacal to King Otto, delivered under armed guard in twenty-three days.

To the most powerful ruler of Germania, Otto, the dutiful greetings of his Comites at Hedaby and Slieswic, who is always devoted to Otto's cause and the power of Germania, and the protection of the northern borders and this port, on March 29, 939.

Now that the worst of the winter storms are over and there has been no snow for a fortnight, shipping has once again become active in this place, and merchants from many ports are coming here with their goods and their slaves and their gold. In accordance with your wishes, I have expanded the customs house and have found two more clerks to assess the cargoes being carried in the ships that land here, and to inspect the goods waiting to be shipped to other places from our harbor. I have also put more guards on the gates of Slieswic in order to protect those merchants carrying their goods overland to the ships in this place, as well as a scribe to record the extent of the merchandise. From these activities I have gained more than forty pieces of gold which I will entrust to your officers when you wish to send them hither to claim this tribute.

It has been necessary to ransom five fighting men from the Danes, who had captured them and announced their intention to make the men their slaves if the ransom could not be paid before the Equinox. Had there been more time I would have waited for your decision in the matter, but as the Danes demanded immediate payment, I have acted as I pray you would want me to act, and I have chosen to ransom the men rather than permit them to be branded, in the belief that these men are needed here, and that those men-at-arms who serve here will be increasingly loyal to you because they have seen that you will not permit them to be abandoned. If I have erred, I submit myself to your judgment and accept your ruling.

Unfortunately, the Danes are not the worst of our troubles in this place. Many of the merchants coming from Hamburh and other cities to the south tell of gangs of men from Bremen who have become more rapacious than the outlaws who live in the forest. They have attacked many of the merchants' trains, taking food and any gold and silver they can lay their hands on. Unlike the outlaws, they do not bother to sell any of their captives to the Danes, and it is said that anyone who falls into their hands is eaten by them, so great is their hunger. Men arriving here have told me of these men tearing their victims apart and leaving the arms and legs on the road as a warning. Whether that is the case, most of them are said to be near starving, and with the first crops still two months away, they must be in great need. It is urgent that the merchants be protected on the road, and I ask you, great King, to dispatch men-at-arms to guard those travelers who stand to lose all their goods and food at the hands of these desperate bands.

But there is another danger that threatens us, and it is more ghastly than the depredations of the men from Bremen. Of the madness that was seen last year, it is my duty to tell you that it has returned in some parts of this place. For the last month the monasteries on the roads south of here have sent reports showing that the madness has struck once again. It is possible that the madness will grow worse as spring comes on, for so the omens suggest. From this there is no protection but the White Christ, and He has not seen fit to spare us. Two merchants have died here, their feet rotted and their minds blasted. I fear there will be more as spring comes on, and if that is the case, I ask that you permit me to bar the harbor and keep ships away so that others will not be touched by the miasma and come to curse Hedaby and Slieswic. What is lost in revenue will be made later, when it is safe to come here. If we let the madness reach abroad, this harbor will be cursed and no ship will land here for fear of the miasma. I will be guided by the priest at the Church of the Holy Sacraments. Father Mayne has said already that he will advise me if his prayers reveal a greater danger.

I have given orders that the monks at the Monastery of the Savior admit no traveler with any sign of illness, and that the inns where the foreigners stay at the waterfront turn away anyone who appears to be subject to fits, or shows other signs of bringing the miasma. I have also ordered all slaves to be inspected, so that they cannot be the agents of the Devil or the Danes in bringing us to disaster. I have required that the guards report to me in the morning and the evening and account for anything suspicious.

Also I have issued orders that salt pork and salt beef are to be laid down in the event of siege, and I will confiscate grain, onions, cheeses, and apples that are brought here to be sold to the men from the ships, so that the city, if it must be closed off, will not be at the mercy of the Danes for lack of food. Those who are not Saxons or Germanians and have their goods taken will be compensated for their seizure; those who are your subjects and vassals will have their goods entered as provided in lieu of taxation or customs charges. This is acceptable to the Margerefa Oelrih, who has sent word already approving these precautions.

If it is necessary for us to ask for the assistance of your troops, I will be at pains to protect them from the miasma. If the miasma is too great, then I pray you will send monks as well as men-at-arms when the miasma is past, so that the sacrifice of the people of Slieswic and Hedaby will be recorded in the annals of Heaven as well as those at your royal court.

With the assurance of my fealty and the continuing loyalty of the Saxons on the border, I pray that the White Christ will guide all you do and give you the victory over all who come against you.

Comites Pacal
of Slieswic and Hedaby
(his sign)
by the hand of Brother Friedolht
merchants' scribe at Hedaby

8

New blossoms filled the air with their faint perfume; from the orchard and the fields, newly turned, came the first promise of summer bounty. Ranegonda leaned over the crenelations of the parapet and looked down into the village. "In two months, we will do well, if nothing blights the crops."

"And if the new rye is not still tainted," added Saint-Germanius beside her.

"You persist in saying that the madness stems from the rye," she said, turning to look at him. "You do not change."

"Because it does," he said. "You need not believe me, but it does." He was aware that nothing but acrimony was to be gained by renewing this debate, so he deliberately changed the subject. He pointed toward the stockade gates where two youngsters had been set on guard duty. "How young they are; hardly more than children. They are farmers and woodcutters, not men-at-arms. Do you think they are going to be ready, if this place is attacked?"

"It will not happen," she said lightly, her mind on other things.

"But if it did," he persisted.

"Why should it? This is a remote fortress. And it is not wealthy, nor does it have a harbor. It is of small use to the Danes, or the outlaws. You have said so yourself, Saint-Germanius: only King Otto has use for it," she reminded him with a slight smile. "And as for the men from Bremen, if they are truly as numerous as we have been told, why should they come here, any of them? There is more food to be had elsewhere. Besides, they probably know nothing of our existence."

"That is a dangerous assumption to make, Gerefa," he said. "You cannot afford to be unprepared."

The mid-morning activities in the village held their attention for a short while; Jennes had yoked his oxen and was preparing to finish the plowing in the field that would be planted with grain. Men worked on the new houses and from the cutting shed came the sound of sawing as the woodcutters labored with the first logs of the spring.

Ranegonda laughed. "You're so grave. You might succeed in worrying me if there was any way those bands of men could find us. But they don't know we're here." She indicated the vast forest. "We are hidden better than the young of foxes."

He remained somber. "That might have been true last year, but not this one. If they have survived through the winter, they will have learned of every place where they might find food. They will have made it their business to learn such things. They will have to go where there is food or die." His dark eyes were distant and grief-filled as he recalled other starving men, in Nineveh, in Tunis, outside Baghdad. "You think that you are in no danger except from the outlaws."

"And the Danes," she reminded him. "And," she went on, Signing herself, "the Danes have not raided here for more than a year. They have given up on this place, because the fortress is too strong. Not even the chance for plunder and slaves is enough to make them challenge our walls. All we have had to fight are the outlaws, and they are poorly armed, unlike the Danes, so they are less likely to prevail against us, if they are foolish enough to attack at all. They have no ships, and they fight with clubs and swords and spears. The stockade will keep them out; even the village is safe from them."

"And why do you suppose the Danes have not come?" Saint-Germanius asked her in a level tone. "Is it your fortifications, or something else?"

"Because the White Christ guards us," she answered at once, lifting her head and staring over the top of his head.

"Not Brother Erchboge's answer, if you please," he responded gently. "Let Brother Erchboge rule you and you will be overrun more quickly than Bremen was. Use your sense, Ranegonda. The Danes are not vassals of the White Christ, and His protection can mean nothing to them."

"But He has power over all the world, at least Brother Erchboge say He has, and my brother as well," she said, and then shrugged. "The omens are good for our protection, whatever the cause." She saw he was not satisfied. "Very well. There may be opposition from another quarter. And if the Danes do not come here, they may have found better pickings elsewhere."

"Or perhaps they have found the outlaws too numerous. Perhaps the men from Bremen have stood against them, or joined with the outlaws." He hesitated, reluctant to alarm her but convinced that she had underestimated the danger the outcasts could be. "And perhaps the men from Bremen have filled their need for slaves, so that there is no reason for them to raid here."

She cocked her head to the side. "Do you believe that?"

"I think it is possible," said Saint-Germanius in a steady tone. "So do you, because whatever Brother Erchboge says, you have ordered more spear-points and arrow-heads." The severity of his expression softened. "I think it is wise to prepare against raids."

She regarded him in silence for a short while. "Very well," she told him at last. "You are sure that there will be trouble, and I am willing to be ruled by you in this. If nothing else, the Margerefa Oelrih will report the preparations favorably to King Otto when he sends word of his return. If we are to have more peasants to work the land, it would be wise to show King Otto that we will guard them well."

"If the precaution is not merely show," added Saint-Germanius. "There is another thing to consider: the outlaws could become more desperate themselves if these hungry gangs of men prey upon the same travelers as they do. They may decide that it would be worth the risk to attack this fortress."

Ranegonda laughed once more. "Why deplete their weapons so uselessly? The stockade is strong and the fortress is made of stone. They could not prevail, and what would be their purpose?" She put her hand over the place where his pectoral lay against her skin. "If there are men from Bremen in the forest, why should the outlaws attack another enemy?"

"To take the fortress for themselves," said Saint-Germanius. "This place would give them a stronghold they do not have now, and if they controlled this fortress, they might well control the coast."

"There is no harbor here," she reminded him, looking over her shoulder to the courts of the fortress and the Baltic Sea. "How could they control the coast?"

"They could use many small boats. Your nearest stream is only a short distance away. With a dozen open craft they could turn sea raiders very quickly, and with the merchants coming from the east to Hedaby, they would do well. They might be stopped by King Otto, but that would take time, and they could find new places to hide in the meanwhile. They could continue their raids for years without serious hindrance." He regarded her with increasing concern as he spoke his thoughts. "There have been others who have done such things." He had seen outlaws on the seas from Greece and Egypt to Burma to the coast of Spain. It was all too easy to see such outlaws at Leosan Fortress.

"It will not happen," she said with confidence, and held out her hand again, not quite touching him. "The Margerefa Oelrih would learn of it, and he would bring his soldiers here."

Saint-Germanius wished he could share her certainty, but he could not convince himself that the fortress would be reclaimed by King Otto's men if it fell to the outlaws, as long as the outlaws kept their depredations to Danes and foreigners. He gave Ranegonda an honest response. "I hope you are right, Gerefa."

Stung, she lifted her chin. "Why should I not be? This is my home, and I know it. You are a foreigner, and you admit yourself that your land is lost. You have forgot what it is to have a home."

"I know the pull of my native earth, Ranegonda, never fear," he said quietly.

She colored. "I did not mean that. I meant that you are far from your people and your country, and that this place is not like that was."

He saw how upset she was and relented. "My land was gone long ago. In that you are right. But those of my blood are bound to our native earth as we are bound to those who give us life." He wanted to embrace her but knew it would be unwise; too many people would see and Ranegonda would be compromised. "When you come to my life, you will know it for yourself."

She tossed her head, and walked a short distance away from him, then looked down at the village again. "I believe that this is the hardest time of year, with winter just over and the first traces of spring coming, but the hardships of winter still imposing their demands, so that the spring seems a cruel lie. There is all promise and no sureness. The supplies have dwindled down to the last remnants and there is not yet enough growth to ensure that we will be able to bring in a good harvest;

when there is the greatest reason to hope there is also the greatest reason to doubt."

For a brief while Saint-Germanius said nothing, thinking only that she needed to learn how her life would be when she rose from the grave, and yet she consistently refused to discuss it. He went to her side, saying, "Better there should be some promise than none at all; spring would be a mockery then."

She Signed herself. "May the White Christ never send such to us."

He echoed her gesture, then looked away toward the forest. "The men in the forest must feel the same way. And with no fields to plant, their needs are great."

"You are warning me?" she asked distantly.

"Or reminding you," he said, and added, "The secret entrance to the fortress could be a problem."

Ranegonda shot him a single hard look. "It is in the landward tower. That much we know. It is not in my quarters, or the muniment room, or the nursery, or with the weapons on the sixth level. For that alone I am grateful. The hidden entrance does not also expose our weapons. But it is in this tower. So it must be in Pentacoste's suite or in the women's quarters."

"I am inclined to think that it must be the women's quarters," said Saint-Germanius. "It is below the level of the parapet, and there must be a tunnel in the walls." He looked down at his feet. "We may be standing over it now."

"Don't say that," Ranegonda said, her voice cutting. "It is a bad thing that the entrance exists at all, but that we cannot find it is . . . a rebuke, if it is not a bad omen for the fortress."

"All right, I'll remain silent, if that is truly your wish," said Saint-Germanius.

She motioned him away from her, then called to him, "Perhaps we will discuss it later."

"Whenever you decide, Gerefa; I am willing," he answered as he descended the stairs and crossed the Marshaling Court to the smithy, considering as he went that now the winter storms were over the chance of some action against the fortress grew hourly. It was not a reassuring notion, and he did what he could to banish it as he pounded out new spear-points and arrow-heads for Captain Amalric and his men-at-arms, using the labor to mask his apprehension. When he was finished he left the smithy, pausing long enough in the men's bath to wash the soot off before returning to the seaward tower.

He had stepped inside the tower when he saw movement on the stair above, and came to a halt. "Who's there?" he called out, expecting

Ingvalt to answer as he kept to his self-appointed task of watching Saint-Germanius.

Pentacoste came down from the next level, so graceful she seemed to float down the rough stone stairs. She was dressed in a new bliaut, of soft amber wool edged in a pattern of green leaves that matched the woven chaplet around her brow. Her chanise was new as well, good white linen that showed her dark auburn plaits to advantage. She paused two steps from the bottom and stared at Saint-Germanius. "Give you good day, foreigner," she said to him with a greater display of courteous recognition than she had ever accorded him before.

"And to you, Hohdama," he responded in form, all his senses on the alert. There was something in her sudden graciousness that bothered him.

"I have been hoping you would come." Her melting smile could not mitigate the voracity in her eyes. "In fact, I have been waiting for you, because I knew you must return here."

"Yes," he said. "My quarters are here."

"It has nothing to do with that. You have answered me at last." She gestured to indicate the seaward tower. "The place does not matter, nor the time. We could be in the farthest reaches of the Danish lands or in the center of Rome, and you would come when you heard me. Your place, your will does not matter. My call does. My call must be answered, no matter how far away you are." She regarded him in pretty petulance. "It has been more difficult than I thought it would be. I have called to you and called to you."

"Apparently I did not hear you," said Saint-Germanius, politely distant. He could sense something in her like a fever, and it made him more circumspect than he usually was with Pentacoste.

"You did." She came one step lower. "You heard me because you could not help yourself. You heard me because it is what you want most, to answer my call, yet you have not let yourself hear." This time her smile was openly predatory; she stroked her thighs through her new bliaut, making sure that Saint-Germanius saw. "That is over now. There is no need for you to resist the desire you have for me, because it is what I have wanted. I have made you want me. The sands of the sea and the birds in the air all speak of your longing to possess me. Every omen tells of your devotion to me. You have been mine from the first because you were brought to me. You came because you long for me, because your body aches for mine."

Saint-Germanius did his best to divert her. "Were you not a married woman, Berengar would rejoice to provide you with the love you seek. He is willing to adore you."

"He is nothing but a puppy. He is not worthy of my love. He is a foolish boy who cannot know the whole of my love. But you are a man of power, and you are going to do those things you have dreamed of because I have shared your dream. I will be everything you desire in a woman, and you will be a lover who fills me and brings me pleasure and children."

"Hohdama," said Saint-Germanius firmly, "it isn't fitting for you to speak this way." He needed more to convince her. "It is wrong for me to listen to you. If anyone heard you, they would assume things that could endanger you and I would not be able to prevent harm coming to you. As a foreigner in this place, I cannot allow you to put yourself in such hazard for no reason. It would offend you and the fortress, which is inexcusable in such a guest as I am."

He might as well have remained silent for all the attention she paid. "I have known from the first how you have desired me, how the omens showed your desire," she said, her hand to her throat. "I have seen it in your eyes, that need of me. I know you long for me, and that you have remained here for the delight of being near me."

Saint-Germanius realized that this encounter was more than an awkward moment; he could not let her go on without bringing shame on her and condemnation on himself. He looked directly at Pentacoste, his expression enigmatic. "It is an honor you do me, Hohdama, but it is, sadly, a mistaken one."

Again Pentacoste ignored him. "I saw how you pretended to favor Ranegonda, so that you would be protected, and could remain near me instead of made to live with the slaves. You flattered her and lent her your assistance as if you honored her. At first this vexed me, and then I understood your purpose, and I decided you were very clever. I have watched how you are with her, and the regard she has for you, and I applaud your wisdom." She held out her hand to him. "I knew it was your love of me that led you to court Ranegonda, to make yourself useful to her so that you might remain near me."

Now Saint-Germanius was growing inwardly alarmed. "Hohdama, believe me, I would not disgrace you so much. I have never wanted anything from you, and I want nothing now. You are married, and you are the daughter of a Dux. You are beyond the reach of any suitor. I would offend King Otto and the White Christ as well as your husband and this fortress if I hoped for anything from you." He bowed in the Byzantine manner and stepped back.

"Yes, yes, say that when others can hear you, of course. I have noticed how prudent you are, and that is a fine thing in a lover when it is necessary to be as careful as we must." She pursued him, walking directly to him, standing less than an arm's length away. "I am glad you are so wise, that you do not make your love for me apparent to those who would make evil assumptions."

"But, Hohdama, I am not your lover, and I do not seek to be," he said in a level tone.

She made an impatient gesture. "Yes, it is good of you to keep your yearning to yourself when there are others about. It shows how great your regard is, how highly you esteem me. But we are alone now. You need not say such cautious things here, not now. No one can see." This time she rested her hand on his arm. "You can take me in your arms; we will be safe. No one else is in the tower. Berengar is out netting birds, and Ingvalt is with him. Culfre is in the light room and he cannot leave his post, even if he suspected that you and I were together. There is a chance for you to have the reward you want."

It was dangerous to anger Pentacoste; Saint-Germanius was well-aware of it. But it was more dangerous to permit her to continue to court him. "Hohdama, I am not your lover," he repeated, going on forcefully, "It has never been my wish to be your lover. I do not seek to be your lover now. And for the sake of your husband and this fortress, I ask you to say nothing more." He looked for some flicker of doubt in her eyes and saw none. "I cannot permit you to address me this way."

"That is not for you to say," she snapped, and then she was languorous again. "You want to guard me, and that is to your credit; I am grateful that you want to keep me from harm," she whispered. "I am pleased it is so important to you to keep me from any suspicion. But you need not hesitate now. I am willing to risk all for you."

"But I am not willing for you to take such risk; I have no reason to want that from you, and I will not take on more danger than is already my portion, not for your amusement," Saint-Germanius said, and now his voice was commanding. "I must tell you, Hohdama, that you have erred. You may think you do me honor with your . . . affection. But you only place yourself and me at a great disadvantage. I cannot be your lover. I will not be your lover. And I ask you to cease this—"

She took the last step to him and pressed against him. "You are mine, foreigner. I have you now, as my promised reward for what I have done; the old gods know it. Let yourself reveal your love at last. I am ready to receive you. The old gods have given you to me, in reward for my service. They brought you to me, and now I am claiming what is mine. I have waited, so that you could come to me, but I will wait no longer. It is time you—"

His small hands closed on her arms just above the elbows; firmly and with strength Pentacoste did not know he possessed, he moved her back from him. "Listen to me, Hohdama. I am not yours. There is nothing between us. Nothing you can do will make me yours. I do not seek you, and I do not want you to seek me: to attempt to . . . claim me. I have no bond with you, and you have none for me. You cannot change this, not with your rituals and not with your spinning. No gods shape my will, and no omens."

"You want me," she said, and this time she offered no smile, no compliant manner to lure him. "I know it. The old gods gave you to me. And I have secured you with the power in the wool."

"No," he said bluntly.

"You are mine!" she demanded, all but shouting at him. "You love me and you will carry me away from here because it is what I want, and you will do only what I want!"

"No, Hohdama." He moved further away from her, his demeanor remote. "Put those desires from your mind. I will not be wooed by you, or ordered."

Her face was rigid with disbelieving wrath. "How dare you!"

"Hohdama," he said, his features sardonic. He started toward the door to the courtyard.

"How dare you!" she shouted again. "You will do what I am entitled to have of you! I have paid for your love, and I will not be cheated of it." As she started toward him, he moved aside. "You cannot deny me what is mine."

Saint-Germanius paused, turned, and bowed once more; he spoke with quiet authority and as much kindness as he could muster. "Hohdama, for your sake, this conversation never took place. It is forgotten. You have said nothing, and I have not heard anything."

"You are not able to do that," she said with pride. "I am fixed in you like a barbed and festering arrow, and you cannot be rid of me without bringing death." She made a sound that was supposed to be laughter. "Die or love me, foreigner."

"You ask, Hohdama, something I cannot do," said Saint-Germanius, the curve of his mouth ironic though his voice was flat.

"You will," said Pentacoste. "Because I will it."

Saint-Germanius shook his head once, and this time did not bow; his tone was cool. "I regret your necessary disappointment, Hohdama."

"I will have you," Pentacoste vowed, and watched in fury as Saint-Germanius strode away from her out of the seaward tower toward the Common Hall. "You are mine and I will have you."

Left ignominiously alone, Pentacoste gave way to outraged weeping. Then, as suddenly as her tears had come, they stopped, and she had mastery of herself once again. She wiped her eyes with the wide hem of her sleeve and glanced up into the tower. This was a test; she recognized that. The old gods sought to be sure she was theirs and would not flee them for the White Christ at the first disappointment. Gradually she understood how she had failed to captivate Saint-Germanius when she had done so much to make him hers. He was not prepared. He had not let himself hope to have her, and he had been taken unaware by her availability; of course he had been reluctant to act, since she had been unattainable. He would need time to accept her desire. She realized now she had approached him too soon. The moon was not yet full and the great spells she had worked would not reach their full might until then. But it had been such a good opportunity, for her women for once had not been with her, and she could speak with the foreigner alone. Yes, she told herself, she had been precipitous. "You have always been a hasty child," she said aloud, admitting that she deserved this chiding. For a short while she remained on the ground level of the seaward tower, and then she mounted to the third level, where her loom stood waiting. There were still a few days left before the moon was full, and in that time she could strengthen the spells she had woven into the fabric. She sat down and reached for the shuttle, noticing with pride that the wool she had spun was meticulously knotted. Let him try to break free of these, she told herself. Let any of them, strive as they might, attempt to be free of her power; they would realize then how potent her spells were. None of them would escape. The old gods could not fail to respond to all she had done. It was fortunate, she thought, that Juste and Osyth were busy tending to their ailing children: she could weave alone and in peace.

Once out of the seaward tower, Saint-Germanius paused, his thoughts in more turmoil than he liked to admit. He had not realized the depth of Pentacoste's obsessions: that was a dangerous error already. But what might happen now that he had rebuffed her? He flinched at the images that rose in his mind, memories from other times when obsession took the place of observation. He knew all too well that Pentacoste could turn on him for refusing her; she could also turn on Ranegonda for claiming what Pentacoste regarded as hers. He started toward the Common Hall, hoping to find Ranegonda, for no matter how awkward it might be to speak of what Pentacoste had done, Ranegonda needed to be warned.

Geraint was in the Common Hall, overseeing the three slaves who were engaged in cleaning the winter's accumulation of ashes from the hearth. "Save the best for soap," he reminded them as they worked.

"The Gerefa is not here?" Saint-Germanius called from the door.

"No," Geraint answered, directing a frown at the foreigner. "She might be in the village."

"Thank you," said Saint-Germanius in spite of the suspicious glare Geraint gave him at this courtesy; he went to the gate where he was informed that she had not left the fortress at all that day.

Saint-Germanius found Ranegonda in the muniment room, frowning over a parchment sheet of inventories. He left the door open as he came toward her, acknowledging her in good form. "May I have a little of your time, Gerefa?"

Since he rarely sought her out this way, Ranegonda was curious to learn why he had come. "Certainly." She laid the parchment aside, explaining as she did what was troubling her. "I know I said we would not use any of the rye from the last harvest, but our supplies are so low that I fear we may have to, after all. It is that or go without bread."

"I pray you will not use the rye," he said, and did not offer her further argument.

"Because the grain is the source of the madness," she said for him.

"Little as you believe it, it is," he said with the air of someone repeating a lesson learned by rote.

"And you will tell me again in a day or two, and again after that." She smiled wearily and then became aware of his ill-concealed distress. "What is it?"

Now that he had her attention, Saint-Germanius faltered. "It is what may be a minor thing, a momentary lapse that means little. It may be. You must understand, Gerefa, that I would not ordinarily speak of this. But it impinges upon you as much as on me."

She swung around on her stool. "Mädchen Mairia, you sound as if you had been forced to open the gates to the outlaws."

"It feels not unlike that," Saint-Germanius admitted, and went on with difficulty. "Your sister-in-law has just now had words with me."

"And what words were those?" The amusement had gone from her voice and she refused to meet his eyes. "What does Pentacoste want with you?"

He knew it was folly to try to lessen Pentacoste's demands. "She claims to want me. I gather she has done spells to insure I will be hers."

Ranegonda sat very still, her face unreadable. "And when did she inform you of this? How long have you known?"

"She spoke to me a short while ago. It would seem she has a right to my love, or so she claims," said Saint-Germanius directly. "She seeks to have a lover who will carry her away from here, in any case. I suspect she has hit upon me because I am foreign; she hopes I will not be bound by the rules of Saxony and King Otto."

"And will you be?" asked Ranegonda quietly.

"Where she is concerned I will be as correct as a Bishop." He came a step nearer to her. "She is determined, and she does not like to be refused."

"As Berengar and Margerefa Oelrih and my brother all know," Ranegonda said with bitterness. "She has set her mind on these men and they have succumbed to her. Now she wants the same of you." Her grey eyes challenged him. "She is a woman who does not rest until she has what she wants."

"Then my denial will be a unique experience for her," Saint-Germanius said with brittle humor, as much to alleviate the anguish he saw in Ranegonda's eyes as to indicate how he felt about Pentacoste's demands.

Ranegonda shook her head slowly. "She will have what she wants."

"She will not have me," Saint-Germanius said gently.

"She hasn't started to work on you yet, not as she can. Her spells are nothing compared to her courtship," Ranegonda said with the certainty of one who has seen the pattern before. "Once she does, she will bend you to her will."

"I am not so malleable," he assured her. "She will not change me."

"Won't she?" Ranegonda asked forlornly. "She is a beautiful woman, and you have said that beauty is important. Therefore I suppose you will go to her, to be restored by her."

"I have said that she is lovely," Saint-Germanius corrected her gently, his dark eyes on hers. "I have said that you are beautiful."

"And I have been foolish enough to listen," she responded, and for the first time there was anger in her voice. "I have let you convince me."

"You have been willing to listen, which I hope you will now," he said, and went on in a steady, reasonable manner, "Ranegonda, consider: I have told you of this as soon as it happened. I tell you so that you may be warned and we may be on guard against whatever she may attempt. If I wanted to be one of Pentacoste's court, why should I bother to seek you out? You have made it plain from the first that you are not convinced of my bond to you, and my love. What purpose could such an avowal have if I sought another?"

"To win me over so that I would not suspect you, or your purpose," she countered, setting her work aside. "And now you have achieved what you want, and you wish to tell me so that I will not be embarrassed at the laughter of the people of the fortress."

There was exasperation mixed with his concern. "No," he said. "I have told you of this in order to warn you, and to ask your help."

"Why should you need my help? You are strong. You are clever, very clever. And you have said that you could leave this place at any time." She waved her hand to show how quickly she feared he could vanish. "You have more than enough gold made to pay your ransom. You could leave in honor and I would not be able to complain of it."

"But if I were intending to possess Pentacoste, those things would mean little. And they would mean still less if I left you to face danger alone," he added, his voice low. "I need your help, Ranegonda, and you need mine. Do not thrust me away because you are afraid I will desert you."

"And when you do, what then?" she demanded.

"But I will not desert you. How often do I have to tell you before you are persuaded?" His dark eyes fixed on her grey ones. "What do I have to do in order to convince you?"

Her hands were trembling; she clenched them, knuckles pressed against knuckles on the table. "I don't know."

He came nearer, his abiding concern exacerbated by aggravation. "I will tell you again, Ranegonda, that I love you, that in the gift of your blood, which is my life, I am bound to you. No oath of fealty is more binding than the bond I have with you, for it will endure until the true death. When your people tell you that no man will want you and no man can seek you, that is a lie. When they tell you that you can receive nothing but in your brother's stead, that is a lie. I know the truth in our bond. It is a bond of knowledge, for I know you, I know the deepest part of you, and the most trivial, and all the scope of you is precious to me. It is nothing to me that others cannot appreciate you, except that their neglect causes you pain." He put his hands over hers. "If Pentacoste were the most beautiful woman in the world—and I promise you she is not—I would never seek any tie to her."

Ranegonda was staring at his hands laid over hers, his small hands, as steady and easy as if he held wild birds. Quite unexpectedly she realized that Saint-Germanius's hands were beautiful, and that revelation shocked her as much as his declaration. She moistened her lips. "You said there was danger."

"Yes. Pentacoste does not strike me as a woman who retires gracefully," he said, the irony back in his words once again. "She may try to lash out at me, and perhaps at you as well. If you should come to hurt on my account—"

"Surely that will not happen," said Ranegonda. "I am Gerefa, and not even Pentacoste would be so reckless."

"But she well may be," Saint-Germanius corrected her. "She hates being thwarted." He lifted his hands, but only to take hers again, so that he could bend to kiss them. "I wish I could guard you day and night."

"Truly?" Her tone was disbelieving; she put her attention on their hands.

"Yes." He released her and took a prudent two steps back from her, for with the muniment door still open he knew they risked being observed. "Set a woman to sleep in your apartments, to ease my mind if nothing else."

Ranegonda sighed. "But it would be remarked. There are those who would be offended if I did such a thing."

"Then say it is to guard the tower itself," Saint-Germanius suggested.

She pressed her lips together, then said, "It would offend Pentacoste to do that, for it would be taken as a sign that her women were not trusted." As she got off the stool she added, "But you may be right, and something ought to be done."

"Think about the risks, Ranegonda," Saint-Germanius said, urgency making him press her. "And decide soon."

"Yes," she said after a short silence. "Yes, all right." She Signed herself automatically. "The White Christ protect us all."

"He is more apt to do that if you provide Him some help," added Saint-Germanius with a tinge of asperity. "The White Christ is no substitute for a man-at-arms with a sword."

Ranegonda nearly smiled. "No wonder Brother Erchboge mistrusts you, foreigner. If he heard such things he would ask Heaven to strike you with lightning; he wants you gone from here."

"No doubt," said Saint-Germanius, who had been the recipient of religious condemnation many times in his long life.

Ranegonda's demeanor changed a bit, and she made herself stand straighter. "I might as well start tending to the problem. Where is Pentacoste now, do you know?"

"No," Saint-Germanius admitted.

She clapped her hands in exasperation. "Then she had better be found." Her brow creased with a frown, and she folded her arms. "You are certain that her desire is unwelcome to you?"

"As running water in full sunlight," he said.

She nodded once more as if satisfied, but the skepticism remained at the back of her grey eyes.

Text of an official dispatch from Pranz Balduin at Goslar to Dux Pol in Luitich, carried under armed escort from Germania to Lorraria in twenty-four days.

To the noble Dux Pol who rules from Luitich, the greetings of Pranz Balduin on this fourth day of April in the Lord's Year 939.

It is my wish that you, Dux, consider well what I say to you in these leaves, and that you make no hasty decisions but bend your will to the service of your judgment so that no rash action will bring disgrace on either of us.

You are certainly aware that I have a son called Berengar. He is a young man still, and one who is the brightest hope of this House. Therefore you can understand how I, as a father and the head of the House, despair when I reflect on the manner in which my son lives his life, and the ways in which he passes his hours, for neither brings honor to himself or the House.

Because it is your daughter who has captivated my son, I appeal to you to cause her to release him from the sorcery she has worked upon him. For it must be sorcery that keeps him in Saxony, attending a married woman. He has been besotted with her for more than a year, and the monks here have prayed that he will come to his senses every day since he went to that forsaken place. If my son is not mad then he is possessed, and the fault is your daughter's.

It is known that you have other daughters, so the behavior of this one is not as damning to your House as it would be if she were the only living daughter of your flesh. You may command her as none other. She is obliged to obey you in all things now that her husband has sworn himself to the service of the White Christ. I ask that you tell her to release my son so that he may once again return to his House and fulfill his duties to it.

It would cause me great distress to have to act against you, Dux, or against your daughter as a means of bringing my son back to me, but if that is what must be done I will not hesitate, and I will pay the wergeld on your daughter with a penitent but glad heart. If it is your wish to preserve her life, then be sure she gives up my son, or she will not live to see the New Year.

I have no desire to battle you, or to feud with your House. I am sending this to you so that you may exercise your authority as the father of Pentacoste. Once my son has come back, I will have no argument with you or any of yours, but what King Otto imposes upon me. But if you will not require your daughter to act in duty and honor, then I will see that her life is ended so that my son may be free of her spell.

There are servants of the White Christ who are willing to do whatever

I require of them to bring about the salvation of my son. They abhor sorcery because it denies the White Christ; they will do whatever is within their power to bring about its end. They will serve the White Christ and me to the end of their lives, and if they fall in this cause they will know themselves blessed. If you seek to stop them in their mission, you will have to settle the matter with the Church as well as with my House. Be guided by those who seek to preserve peace. What is the worth of fighting over a daughter when you have others? It is in your hands now, whether or not your daughter lives or dies by the hands of these holy men.

Your messenger will be received here at any time, and his answer from you will be accorded the respect a man of your position deserves. I give you my word that your response will be given my immediate attention. Whatever you decide, it will be my obligation to act with you or against you to rescue my son from your daughter's toils. If you are willing to put your interests with mine, my House will be grateful to your House for three generations, and aside from the service owed to the King, I and mine will be first to your defense until the death of Berengar's youngest son.

In proof of my word, I affix my mark to this, and my seal.

Pranz Balduin of Goslar
(his sign and seal)
by the hand of Prior Hovarht
of the Monastery of the Resurrection

9

As the Compline Choir began to chant the Ninety-third Psalm Brother Giselberht felt a tingling in his hands that excited him. He Signed himself and went on with his own prayers, stretching out prostrate to show his piety and humility. The sensation grew stronger, a feeling that was not unpleasant, but one that began to alarm him as it increased. His prayers faltered and he strove to sit upright, only to discover that his cell had tipped somehow, and become infused with brilliant, dancing light.

In the brightness there were faces, and a sound like the sea at high tide, or the rushing of wings. Brother Giselberht grabbed the floor and clung to it as the walls wheeled and the faces in the light grew more numerous and glorious. He saw into the very mansions of Heaven, and was exalted. There was the White Christ, dancing in the midst of angels and seraphim, His wounded hands outstretched to leave the seal of His blood on all those who came to Him. Brother Giselberht felt the world tremble, and in the vindication of his faith he rose to his feet, his hands lifted as he saw those of the White Christ lifted, and with the same steady grace, he, too, danced as Heaven and earth joined in worship.

The Compline Choir was not chanting as it usually did, but for Brother Giselberht this was nothing more than the result of the extraordinary transformation going on around him, and for this the Psalms would have to share in the glory, becoming more than they had been. The ordinary chanting of the Psalms would not do now, when he was offering to the rapture of Heaven. He danced, his movements simple and graceful, and he heard the monks accompany him, their melodies changing and twisting as he turned in circles, as he saw the bright wings of the angels turning in the fading light.

Several loud blows on his outer door distracted him, and with resentment seething in every fiber of his being, he went to answer the summons, disgusted that any Brother should compromise his adoration of the White Christ. Wrath was not only a Deadly Sin, it was the righteous power of God. Angels hung in the air around him, and as he opened the door, he could see the hosts of Heaven massed in the south where clouds usually were at the end of the day. He looked directly upward into the violet sky where every new star wore an angel's face and the last ruddy glow of the sun revealed the nimbus of the Throne of God.

"Brother Giselberht," said Brother Olafr, leaning heavily on his crutch. "Brother Gailharht . . . he needs your help. Urgently." He was panting and the lines of his face were scored as if with a harrow. "He was reading the lesson at the evening meal when there—"

"What is the matter?" Brother Giselberht demanded, fearing now that the Devil had sent his servants to corrupt the monks just when Heaven was welcoming them, giving a sign at last that they had achieved the blessings they had sought so long.

"It is Brother Dionnys: he is stricken with madness. Just now, as he sat with the rest of us at the table." Brother Olafr stared at Brother Giselberht, and paused as if he expected some change in his superior. "It is . . . that madness, as there was madness before, with visions and omens known only to him. The miasma has returned." Doubt deepened the lines by his mouth; he spoke as if he feared to be misunderstood or misjudged. "It is as it was before. Madness has come to Holy Cross Monastery again."

"No, this is not what you fear. This is triumph. This time the White Christ shows us His mercy. It is not madness. Not madness. Never madness, Brother. There can never be madness again, only sacred rapture. Only worship as the angels worship. Exaltation," Brother Giselberht corrected with a sudden gesture as he raised both hands aloft. "This is not madness, Brother Olafr. You may tell Brother Gailharht that only the Devil would seek to confuse us in this regard. There is no madness here. If Brother Dionnys appears mad, Brother Gailharht should look to his own soul for the cause of it." He threw back his head and laughed.

For the first time Brother Olafr let himself hear the sound of the Choir, and he opened his eyes in dismay, for the strong, simple melody he had expected was now a confused conflict of sounds, the words lost. "They, too."

"It is the music of Heaven," cried Brother Giselberht, and began to chant a harsh, monotone recitation of the text of the Ninety-sixth Psalm with the Choir. He broke off after three verses, his hands clasped and extended to Heaven to show his delight. "Hear the rejoicing, the paeans to the White Christ."

To Brother Olafr it sounded more like the discordant howling of wolves, but he dared not speak against his superior, especially not now, when he, too, was in the throes of madness. "Brother Giselberht . . ."

"Listen to them. They are echoing the anthems of Heaven. This is the song of the angels," Brother Giselberht assured him. "It has been sung since the first day of creation, and we have not been privileged to hear it, because sin has closed our hearts to it." He began to dance again. "If you throw away your crutch, Brother Olafr, the White Christ will give you the strength to dance with Him."

In response to this, Brother Olafr hung onto his crutch with both hands. "If the White Christ wishes me to dance, He will take the crutch Himself. Until then, I will bear it with humility."

The defiance in Brother Olafr's eyes did not unduly upset Brother Giselberht, who left his cell and began to dance on the grass and the earthen path, continuing to turn and bend and sway, his arms out, his palms up, his head thrown back so that he could see the splendor of Heaven in the coming night. It was much better here, in the open, he thought, where the massing forces of the White Christ could witness this lifting up of the devout.

Brother Olafr let go of his crutch long enough to Sign himself. He was supposed to have his supper now, as sunset faded over the forest. It was time for those who had spent the afternoon chanting the Psalms to eat and then to pray. But he was too upset for any food, and he began to draw back from Brother Giselberht. "Brother Gailharht is concerned. He and the others are watching him, to see that he causes no injury to himself or the rest . . . Brother Dionnys has become . . . unlike a proper monk."

"He is giving his thanks to the White Christ," said Brother Giselberht serenely as he continued to sway and turn, the angel-riven sky wheeling around him. "Be glad for him, and pray that the White Christ sends the same revelation to you."

"But Brother Dionnys has cut himself with knives," said Brother Olafr desperately. "He has used them to score his flesh and he . . . he has tried to hurt the others. He says that demons are in his body and he must cut them out. For his safety he must be stopped until the trouble is past and he is able to supplicate for forgiveness. It is those who follow the old gods who make such sacrifices, not we who are the servants of the White Christ."

Brother Giselberht was untroubled; the smile he offered Brother Olafr was suffused with good-will and serenity. "He is protected by Heaven, and if he wishes to suffer for the love of the White Christ, then you must not stop him in his devotion. It is the vision of Heaven that fills him and he is seeking to know the sacrifice that was made for us. Let him embrace the White Christ in blood, if that is what his visions reveal to him."

"Brother Giselberht," protested Brother Olafr. "He could kill us. And if more madness comes, who is to stop him?"

"Why should he be stopped? What cause is there to keep a follower of the White Christ from sharing in His joy?" Brother Giselberht was feeling quite dizzy now, and his feet were starting to ache from his dancing, but he continued. Such demands of the flesh were sent by the Devil, and those who served the White Christ were given the power to rise above pain and suffering. He sang a few more verses of the Ninety-seventh Psalm, no longer attempting to stay with the Compline Choir. "This is the ecstasy that we have been promised from the saving of our souls. Why should we refuse it when it is what we have sought?"

"Brother Giselberht," said Brother Olafr, "it is the madness. Truly. I beseech you, let me confine Brother Dionnys, and any other who shows madness."

"How will you know the others are mad?" Brother Giselberht asked in a distant voice. The angels seemed to be in greater number but farther away now. He strove to reach out to them once more, and increased the frenzy of his dancing. If his legs ached, so much the better, for he could then more fully despise the flesh and its weakness. "See?" he called into the darkening sky. "See? I want to dance as you do, in the air. I want to turn and wheel with clouds and cherubim. But for sin we are confined to the ground. So guide and help me, Heavenly Guardians!"

Brother Olafr Signed himself and moved back from the erratic gyrations of his superior. "I will . . . tell Brother Gailharht what you have said," he assured Brother Giselberht. "He will decide how we can best serve you and—" He saw there was no response; it was useless to speak to Brother Giselberht anymore, for he had taken the madness as well. The miasma was on the monastery, and it might claim any one of them. Looking over his shoulder as if he expected to see a hovering vapor, he hastened back toward the refectory, where the evening meal had been abandoned.

Brother Dionnys was lying on the floor, his face down, blood spreading beyond the shape of his habit. He twitched and howled from time to time, but it was obvious that he would not last long. None of the monks in the chamber wanted to approach him, for fear that the madness would light on them.

Brother Gailharht was near the door, forcing the monks to remain inside, though most of them clearly wished to leave. "What did Brother Giselberht say?"

"He said that he was dancing with angels and that we should permit Brother Dionnys to bleed, in honor of the White Christ. The Compline Choir is no better, and they have not yet begun to dance, as Brother Giselberht has; when they do they will be . . ." He shook his head and indicated Brother Dionnys where he lay. "What did he do? Did he cut himself too much? Was it deliberate?"

"He tried to make himself a eunuch, and fainted while he cut, but the damage was done," said Brother Gailharht bluntly, Signing himself. "He said that he would be rid of the flesh, that we all should be rid of the flesh. And then he pulled his clothes open and struck."

Again Brother Olafr Signed himself, this time with greater emotion. "What is to be done about him?"

"As soon as he is dead he will be carried outside, to lie for the night. But he will not rise in the morning." Brother Gailharht turned grave eyes on Brother Olafr. "And others may be mad by then, as well." He rubbed his beard. "Can you stay on the mule well enough to ride to the fortress?"

"Leosan Fortress?" asked Brother Olafr in horror.

"It must be that or Oeldenburh, and we know that there is no help for monks in Oeldenburh." Brother Gailharht folded his hands and bent his head over them. "When Brother Dionnys served the meal, he said that the bread was better, and the fish was fresh, and for that we should be more thankful than usual."

"We must pray that he and Brother Giselberht are the only ones the miasma has touched." Brother Olafr looked doubtful as he said it.

On the floor Brother Dionnys buckled and twitched, and then the shadow of death fell on him.

All the monks in the refectory Signed themselves, and all of them knelt warily to pray.

Brother Gailharht looked over the men. "Two of you will have to carry our Brother Dionnys outside. Brother Thorbjorn, you and Brother Aranolht, you tend to that. See that he is properly laid out and remember to put the seals on his hands and feet as well as his eyes and mouth, to protect him from the miasma. If anyone attempts to disturb him, they must be prevented. Since he has been taken with madness, he must be completely tended if he is not to become one of those creatures given false life by the Devil so that they may prey on good servants of the White Christ, or marked for the old gods."

Neither Brother Thorbjorn nor Brother Aranolht seemed pleased at this instruction, but both of them were unwilling to resist the orders of Brother Gailharht. Someone had to instruct them, and better this monk than their superior, if Brother Olafr spoke the truth.

"Take one of the mules and ride to Leosan Fortress," said Brother Gailharht, for now that he had been obeyed he found it was easier to give orders. "Inform the Gerefa of what has happened, and tell her that her brother is in danger for his body and his soul."

"But Brother Gailhart, it is Brother Giselberht's sister who will . . ." Brother Olafr ended with a gesture to his crutch. "How can she fight?"

"That cannot be helped; the fortress is to be notified," said Brother Gailharht. "Ask the White Christ to lend you His strength, and you will prevail through Him. All the world may desert you, but if you are His true servant, He never will." He turned back into the room. "The rest of you will fast tonight, and the meal will be given to the animals to eat, in tribute to Brother Dionnys and in submission to His will, to show that we hold the body in contempt, as we hold the animals who cannot worship the White Christ. Our hunger will be our praise. And tomorrow we will fast on bread and water, and we will pray for Brother Dionnys and Brother Giselberht as we sing the Psalms."

A few of the monks looked annoyed, but most of them accepted this gladly, seeking something to do that would not entail risking their lives and souls.

"But it is nearly dark," protested Brother Olafr, seeking to shore up his argument. "Let me go at first light. Tomorrow will be better. I will cover the distance faster, and the mule will not have to find his way in the fullness of night. The forest is dark enough when the sun is high. Why venture there now?"

Brother Gailharht shook his head slowly. "It must be now, before any greater misfortune comes. We will need the help of the Gerefa and the might of the men who serve her if we are stricken with madness."

"If madness comes here, the Gerefa may not," Brother Olafr predicted. "The King does not want those who might bring a miasma to touch others with it, and has instructed his officers to deny aid where there is miasma. Therefore, she would exceed her authority to come here. Why should she risk harming her men or taking the madness herself?"

"Because it is her duty," said Brother Gailharht, looking askance. "Because Brother Giselberht is her brother and she rules in his stead."

Brother Olafr sighed in concession, realizing it was useless. "All right. I will take the largest mule. I will carry two lanthorns, and pray that one will remain lit throughout the journey so that I will not become lost. I thank the White Christ that the mule knows the way. He will get me there quickly and he is a strengthy beast. As soon as I am able, I will return, and if the White Christ wills it, I will bring the Gerefa and her forces to guard us."

"May the White Christ light your way and preserve you from harm," said Brother Gailharht as he Signed himself, and then turned his attention once more to the two monks given the task of laying out Brother Dionnys.

Muttering words that in a less religious man might have been curses, Brother Olafr made his way across the monastery compound toward the far end of the stockade where they kept their animals. He was not pleased that Brother Gailharht had assigned him the task, and the more he dwelled on the risks he was being required to take, the more he wished he had the courage to refuse to do it. He kept his eyes down so that he would not have to see Brother Giselberht, who was swooping and turning between the rows of cells. He was less successful in closing his ears to the cries of the Compline Choir; he had sung those verses himself too many times not to cringe when they were incorrect.

Brother Avalir was asleep in one of the stalls at the end of the little stable, his maniple pulled over his head. In the feeble flame of the rushlight the simple-minded monk looked more like an overgrown child than a servant of the White Christ. When Brother Olafr spoke his name he turned and rubbed his eyes with his fists, as a five-year-old might do, and peered into the darkness. "Who's there?"

"Brother Olafr," he answered, as always feeling uncomfortable in the presence of the dull-witted Brother Avalir. "I am ordered to take the biggest mule."

Brother Avalir blinked twice. "It is dark, isn't it?"

"Yes. And riding into the night is folly, but that is the order of Brother Gailharht, and I am bound by my oath to the White Christ to obey him."

"Brother Giselberht is ruler here," said Brother Avalir, smiling at his correctness. "He has been ruler since Brother Haganrih died of rot."

"Yes," said Brother Olafr, doing his best to keep them from getting lost in the maze of notions that claimed the attention of Brother Avalir. "Yes, Brother Giselberht is superior here; but he is taken with the madness that gave rot to Brother Haganrih, and so it falls to Brother Gailharht to decide what we must do."

Brother Avalic Signed himself. "May the White Christ put His mantel around Brother Giselberht and preserve him."

"Yes," said Brother Olafr, Signing himself again. "And in the meantime, I have been told I must go to Leosan Fortress."

Brother Avalir's face brightened. "I have a brother at Leosan Fortress, don't I?"

Very patiently Brother Olafr answered, "Yes, you do. And it is my duty to warn him, don't you agree? And everyone else who lives at the fortress and in the village. The people of the fortress need to know that the madness has come, that they may prepare their defenses. And they will have to guard us against the outlaws and the Danes until the madness is past."

"Will they?" He Signed himself automatically. "But what if they take the madness, too?"

It was the very question Brother Olafr wished most to avoid, and so he snapped, "They won't."

"Because the White Christ protects them?" Brother Avalir frowned. "Why should He protect them more than us? What have they done more deserving of His mercy than what we have done?" He took hold of his habit and twisted it, becoming more dismayed. "We are His servants, and we are asking for help from the fortress, aren't we?"

"Yes," Brother Olafr allowed. "But they will not give it if I do not ride there and ask for it." He indicated the stall where the largest mule was confined. "Where is the saddle?"

"There is one at the end of the row, and another in the room beyond," said Brother Avalir. "But . . . should not another monk go? You are one who walks with a crutch and you have shown that your legs are weak. I pray to the White Christ and His Father that we find our protection in their salvation. But resting such faith in you, good Brother . . . Should not one with better legs make the ride?"

"I wondered that myself," answered Brother Olafr as he went for the saddle. "But Brother Gailharht believes that I must make the journey, and I agree it is my duty to submit myself to his rule until Brother Giselberht is restored to wholeness."

Brother Avalir was tagging after Brother Olafr. "What does Brother Giselberht do that Brother Gailharht must act for him? What has the madness done to him?"

That was a question he did not want to answer. Brother Olafr took up the saddle and a rough, large blanket along with the girths, balanced them over his free arm, then started back toward the largest mule's stall. "What's his name again?"

"Harniewic," said Brother Avalir at once. "Because he is stubborn."

"I'll remember that," said Brother Olafr grimly.

"He'll go where he has to go, but he won't do it faster than a trot," Brother Avalir explained as he did his best to keep up with Brother Olafr. "If he gallops, it will be because he has been injured or there is a fire in the forest. Otherwise, he will trot, and trot all night if you must have it, but he will go no faster."

"Yes," said Brother Olafr as he put the blanket on the mule's angular back. "I grasp that." What was it about the simple-minded, he wondered, that made them so tenacious about certain things? He had had a sister with no more wit than this mule he was saddling, yet once she had determined upon a thing, would not be deterred from her course for any reason, no matter how persuasive the argument against her.

Brother Avalir leaned in the end of the stall. "He won't need much water, but you will have to give him a bucket of it when you reach the fortress. He will drink then, but not on the trail. That's a good thing, because outlaws attack while mounts are drinking, don't they?" He cocked his head. "The Choir is singing new songs tonight."

"They are," Brother Olafr agreed through clenched teeth. "Where is the bridle."

"I'll get it," Brother Avalir offered with a broad smile, and hurried off before Brother Olafr could stop him. He was back shortly with a good military bridle on his arm. "Brother Giselberht brought this when he came here."

"And I will take it back to the fortress," said Brother Olafr as he continued at his work, fastening the girths and reaching for the breast-collar.

"He has left orders at the fortress, and if there is trouble there, his will has been established, and those who serve the fortress will also serve the White Christ," said Brother Avalir.

"He has done all that he can," said Brother Olafr as he made a last check of the girths, and then buckled the bridle into place on the mule's head. "When I have reached my destiny, I will see that word is sent back to this place at once, and you will honor what has been done."

"Certainly," said Brother Avalir, turning to look at the other animals in the stable. "The White Christ has said that those who knelt to Him first would receive His mercy before all the rest. Therefore those who were in the stall when the White Christ was a babe will know His salvation. There are animals in Heaven, aren't there? Brother Giselberht says there are."

"Amen to it," said Brother Olafr, and with a sigh hauled himself into the high-fronted saddle as he dropped his crutch to the earthen floor. "I am off for Leosan Fortress. Because it is so dark, I will need to carry two lanthorns to see my way in the night."

Brother Avalir accommodated him at once, handing him an oil lamp with a fresh wick. "Carry this, Brother Olafr, and you will find your way through the night. It has enough oil to burn all night if you need it to," he promised. "You will not need a second. Before dawn the gates of the fortress will open to you, and the lanthorn will seem to be nothing more than a burden you have carried with you." He smiled at Brother Olafr as if he had said something amusing. "Ask anyone at Leosan Fortress and they will tell you the same thing. All of them are subject to the omens that we are, for they, too, bow to the White Christ."

"Do you have a second lanthorn?" asked Brother Olafr as he dragged on the reins.

"No," Brother Avalir answered, suddenly downcast to make such an admission. "I had one, but Brother Aranolht took it."

"To keep watch over Brother Dionnys," said Brother Olafr, half to himself.

"But that will be enough," Brother Avalir said, trying to sound confident of it. "Ride with the White Christ and the Wild Hunt will not find you."

Brother Olafr scowled at that as he dug his heels into the mule's sides. He no longer believed in the Wild Hunt, he assured himself as he rode for the rear gate and asked the warder to open it for him. The Wild Hunt was the sport of the old gods, and since he vowed to serve the White Christ, he was protected from the Wild Hunt. But when the storm raged and the trees bent and broke, when the sea scoured the coast and the wind shouted and wailed, then it was hard to forget that the Wild Hunt was out, and that their prey was the souls and the lives of men. He stared up into the sky, seeing no angels there. He was glad that the wind was mild. As he held up his lanthorn he felt terribly small, and the little puddle of light it cast made the night seem more vast, more dense than it had been before; even the shadow of the mule appeared unnatural as it blotted out much of the flickering brightness. He tugged the reins so that the mule faced the line of trees, and with a long, unsteady sigh, he set out for Leosan Fortress.

Once into the forest, Brother Olafr became badly frightened. There was always so much noise in the forest, the sound of twigs breaking, of stealthy footfalls, the crash of fleeing deer, the silent flutter of owls' wings. At least there was a trail, one he had walked not six weeks ago. He drummed his heels to press the mule forward but Brother Avalir had been right: Harniewic would not go faster than a steady trot.

As he neared the ancient hollow tree where the old gods were still venerated, Brother Olafr thought he heard voices, and this terrified him. He saw the mule put his long ears forward, nostrils flaring to catch the new scents. As he drew closer, he saw a snip of light, and smelled burning oil. Yes! He could not question his senses, not now. He Signed himself and clung to the mule with all his strength. The worshipers of the old gods were there, making their hideous offerings to them. He wanted to flee, to escape the taint that was surely as deadly as the miasma at the monastery. Perhaps the old gods were the cause of the miasma, an effort to stop the worship of the White Christ in their stead! He wanted to ask Brother Giselberht or Brother Gailharht, and he had to struggle with himself to keep from turning back to the monastery. But he had been ordered to reach Leosan Fortress, and he had vowed obedience to the superior. He Signed himself three times for the Trinity and nudged the mule onward.

There was a flurry of sounds ahead on the trail, and hasty whispers, and then the light was gone and there were cracklings and rustlings as the servants of the old gods vanished into the dark woods, leaving behind swaying limbs and leaves, and the sharp scents of sweat and smoke. The mule brought his head up, snorting, and plunged past the hollow tree at a pace that galloped in front and trotted behind.

Brother Olafr had one arm around the mule's neck and his legs pressed so tightly to Harniewic's flanks that he was certain he would leave indentations in the mule's ribs. He dared not to look at the hollow tree for fear of what he might see there and the damage it could do to his soul. There were some omens better left unseen, he decided, as the mule hurried onward.

It was not long after midnight that Brother Olafr reached Leosan Fortress. The village stockade was not guarded at night, and so the monk made his way around the perimeter, searching for a place he might be able to enter, or, barring that, where he would be near enough to the houses to call for help. He was on the west side of the village when one of the men on the fortress parapets high above saw him and raised the alarm.

"To the west! A man and a horse!" Ewarht shouted, and his shout was taken up by Faxon.

Four blasts on the wooden horn brought men out of their houses, all carrying weapons. But the gate was not opened, and the men who shouted at Brother Olafr did so in accusations and with soldiers' oaths.

"I am Brother Olafr, from Holy Cross Monastery," he called back when the din subsided. "I am alone. I was ordered to come here, to warn you."

There was a brief period of discussion, and then one of the villagers shouted, "How do we know that?"

"I tell you so. I came here on orders of Brother Gailharht because Brother Giselberht, your true Gerefa, is stricken with madness." He realized that he was very hungry and thirsty, and his throat ached when he shouted. "For charity, open the gate and give me something to eat."

From the fortress came the groaning clanks of chains as the winch opened the gates; another blast on the wooden horn accompanied it.

Ormanrih had just reached the gate, only half-dressed and grumpy. He glared at the bolt holding the gate shut. "It is the middle of the night."

"Yes. I was told at dusk to ride for this place, and I obeyed," said Brother Olafr. "I am lame. I am hungry. I am cold. Let me in. And give water to my mule." He rubbed his face with both hands.

There was another hurried discussion among the village men, and then Ormanrih said, "I will ask the Gerefa."

Brother Olafr sighed. "My mule is thirsty. And so am I. At least let us have some water."

"There is a stream sixty paces to the west. You can drink there," came the answer. "I will fetch the Gerefa. At this hour we cannot open the gates without her authority."

Brother Olafr did not relish going back into the forest again, but he sighed and accepted the order. "I will return shortly."

"If the old gods don't get you," shouted one of the villagers. "Or the Danes."

The notion of either chilled Brother Olafr, but he gave no response. He took the reins and caught one hand in the mule's mane to act as his crutch; he made his way unsteadily toward the stream. There was a wide path used by the woodcutters that led to a bridge. Not far from the bridge the stream widened and the bank sloped more gently to the water. The mule took his time drinking, and then stopped twice on the return to graze. Both times Brother Olafr listened for the disaster he was certain would befall him, but aside from a glimpse of a pregnant fox bitch, he encountered nothing but the mule.

"What omen is a fox bitch?" he asked through the gate as he returned, by way of announcing himself.

"Ask your superior," Ormanrih answered, and would have gone on, but there was the approaching clatter of hooves, and a moment later Captain Amalric called out, "Honor the Gerefa!"

There was a bustle on the inside of the gate and then Ranegonda called out, "You are here from Holy Cross?"

"Yes, Gerefa," answered Brother Olafr. He was getting colder now, and his arms ached, and his head. "I must speak to you."

Ranegonda heard this with the nasty feeling that the news would be unwelcome. Why, she asked herself, did such news always come at night? The omen was warning enough, she thought. The words were hardly required. "Open the gate. Captain Amalric, you and Geraint stand on either side, and if anyone besides the monk and his mount comes through, kill them."

Captain Amalric grinned and slapped his left shoulder with his right hand. "I will, Gerefa."

Two of the villagers were already drawing the bolt back, struggling with its weight as it slid from the iron guards. Her two men-at-arms took up their positions, holding their horses on tight reins so they could spring to the fight if one came. Ormanrih came as close to Ranegonda's horse as he dared and he looked up at her apprehensively. "Do you think the man is alone?"

"Probably," she answered, and felt for the sword hung from her saddle scabbard. She had fought with it only twice but she found it comforting now. "If he is not, we are ready."

The gate was opened carefully, the entrance just wide enough for the mule to pass through with Brother Olafr leaning on him. As soon as he was inside, the gate was shoved closed again and the bolt laboriously set once more.

"Just the monk," said Captain Amalric with a trace of disappointment. He rounded on Brother Olafr as if to make the best of it. "And what are you doing here?"

"I . . . I've come to . . ." His words trailed off. "May I have something to eat? And a mantel? I'm cold and hungry."

"Tend to it," said Ranegonda to Captain Amalric and Geraint. "Take him up, one of you," she went on, "and the other lead the mule."

Ormanrih was annoyed by this sudden change, and said, "We in the village need to know what news he brings. It will be important to us, too."

"Yes, it will," said Ranegonda. "At first light come to the gates and you will be admitted at once. Then I will tell you whatever I have learned." She yawned suddenly. "In the meantime, get some sleep. If the news is bad, rest will be in short supply."

Captain Amalric had caught the mule's bridle and Geraint was hauling Brother Olafr onto the rump of his bay. A moment later they were headed down the road between the fields toward the long sloping road to the fortress gates. Again the wooden horn sounded, and as soon as Ranegonda was inside with her two men and the monk and his mule, the chains once again crumped as the winch closed the gates.

"See that he has something hot to eat, and then bring him to the muniment room," said Ranegonda as she climbed out of the saddle.

"Gerefa?" said Captain Amalric. "Why not wait until first light?"

"Because we may not have until first light," she answered, and started toward the landward tower, letting the two men sort out settling the monk. As she entered the muniment room she put her hands to her head and pressed hard against her temples. "Wolves and Ravens! what now?"

She expected no answer and was startled when she heard a voice in the darkness. "There's no danger, my life," said Saint-Germanius, coming into the circle of light cast by her lamp. "At least, none from me."

Ranegonda Signed herself. "My heart leaped into my throat," she said, half in relief and half in accusation.

For a moment Saint-Germanius said nothing and then he spoke in his most matter-of-fact manner. "I was worried about you. Pentacoste was in this room earlier in the evening, while you were with Brother Erchboge. I saw her enter, but I did not see what she did."

"Pentacoste," said Ranegonda with disgust. "Another token, I suppose. She has been putting lengths of knotted yarn in my quarters."

"This time she did a bit more," said Saint-Germanius carefully, his voice level and his eyes darker than the night. "This time she put dried wolfsbane in your water ewer."

"Wolfsbane?" Ranegonda repeated incredulously.

"Had you drunk the water it would have made you very ill at the least." He had intended to soften the blow; the amounts he had discovered would undoubtedly have been fatal. "She is no longer content with invoking the old gods to deal with you." He put his small hands on her shoulders. "Now she is determined to deal with you herself."

"But that's . . . foolish?" She looked at him. "It is foolish, isn't it?"

"It's malicious," Saint-Germanius corrected her as kindly as he could. "Ranegonda, don't assume she will not harm you. If she has the opportunity she will."

She put her fingers to her lips so that she could not speak until she had framed her words. "It is a reckless thing to do. And it is senseless." With a sigh that bordered on a yawn she sat down on her stool. "And I have no time for her pettiness. According to the monk who just arrived, the madness has come again to Holy Cross Monastery. My brother has been taken with it." She Signed herself and waited for Saint-Germanius to speak. When he remained silent, she went on. "Aren't you going to tell me that they have eaten tainted flour?"

His smile was not very successful. "You've heard me say it before. You have yet to believe me."

She conceded his point with a gesture. "If you are right, then it could return here. Ormanrih has asked for permission to use the stores of rye and barley." She regarded him for a short while. "If I permit him to use the grain and the madness returns, what then? It could be that the miasma has reached us. And perhaps it means you are right. You will not give the flour to one of the slaves, and we have not yet captured an outlaw."

"Therefore we have reached an impasse?" Saint-Germanius suggested, and added with intensity, "Indulge me a few days yet if you can, Ranegonda."

She looked at him for a moment, then said, "It is probably wrong to let you persuade me, but I will hold off releasing the grain if it is possible. But if the miasma comes, there will be little I can do."

"If the miasma comes," Saint-Germanius appended as he offered her a small silver chain, "it may not matter what you do with the grain."

She touched the pectoral through her clothes as she accepted his gift in silence.

Text of a letter from Hrotiger in Valence to the merchant Everart of Paris. Carried by courier, delivered in twelve days.

To the distinguished merchant of furs and jewels who resides on the Street of Pale Scarves in Paris, the greetings of Hrotiger, bondsman to the Excellent Comites Saint-Germanius, on the 29th day of April in the Year of Grace 939, from the Inn of the Laughing Ferret in Valence.

This is to inform you that I have secured proper escort from this city to Trier, and will leave at dawn tomorrow with the men-at-arms I have engaged for this journey. I am grateful to you for recommending them and giving them your praise, for many of those who purport to guard and protect the traveler turn on those they are supposed to have in their care. Men have been sold as slaves and worse through such misplaced trust. Without your recommendation I would be in despair.

I will, of course, dispatch a message to King Otto so that there will be no other delays in releasing the cargoes which my master seeks. I, too, bring things of value to him, things he has sought. Your kindness on behalf of my master will be rewarded, you have my word on it, and should any mishap befall any of the men you recommended, the necessary wergeld will be sent to you with a commission for attending to the matter.

While it is a welcome thing to know that my master is safe, I know that it will be an arduous journey to bring him to Rome again. The roads, as you and many others have warned me, are often nothing more than rutted tracks. Some that cross the mountains are fallen away or so narrow as to be unpassable except for goats. But we have come this far and we will reach Saxony if we have to be on the road a year. And we will return to Rome in good time. The mules and the horses you arranged for us to buy are sound and they have good wind and endurance for the distances we must travel to reach Saxony; for these, too, I am grateful.

When my master is again in Rome, arrangements will be made for new ventures, and you will be one of the four merchants and factors my master will seek out, to show his gratitude for the assistance you have provided. You are to rest assured that the service you have done will be honored for more than three generations.

I will dispatch word to you once my master has been found. Until then, unless there should be some great peril as yet undiscovered waiting ahead, you will have no other news from me.

May the White Christ answer your prayers and may your family prosper and thrive. May your daughters all find rich husbands and your sons marry handsome women of fortune. May they all have many healthy children. And may your business prosper so that your dignity may grow greater.

With my thanks,

Hrotiger
Bondsman to the Excellent
Comites Saint-Germanius
by my own hand.

10

"In the village they are already saying I am mad, that the miasma has touched me and caused me to destroy food." Ranegonda limped as she paced; she refused to face Saint-Germanius. "Duart has complained to Brother Erchboge."

"You had to destroy the rye; you showed great courage doing it, and I know it was difficult for you to do, because you did it for my word, not because you are convinced of what I have told you so many times," said Saint-Germanius patiently. "You were right to destroy it, Ranegonda. If you had not, the madness would have you all. Destroying the rye, grain, and flour, stopped it." The door to the muniment room was ajar, open enough that someone in the entry beyond might overhear what they said; he wanted to close it, but knew that would be more damning than leaving it as it was, and would serve only to call attention to their meeting.

"So you keep saying to me," she accused him as she lengthened her stride. "I pray that you are right, and that I have done . . . But if it comes again, then what will happen? What else will you say must be destroyed before the madness is gone? The apples? Or the water in the cisterns? There are those who say followers of the old gods poison wells and cisterns to bring madness to the servants of the White Christ." She stopped pacing and stared at him. "In the village, they would hold you to blame, and they would make you pay dearly." Her voice dropped. "I couldn't bear that."

"Possibly they would," said Saint-Germanius gently. "And if the madness comes again, perhaps I will deserve their hatred, and whatever else they do. You, however, deserve their gratitude, though I doubt you will have it." He had seen many times before how quickly suspicion could turn to rancor and odium; his situation at Leosan Fortress was less hazardous than many others, for at least he had the confidence of the Gerefa. In Burma no one had trusted him when he tried to warn them about their diseased water; the Emir's son had trusted him, but only for treachery, and held him responsible for his father's death. "Their hatred means little to me," he said, though it was not quite true, "but yours, Ranegonda, your hatred is the thing I could not bear."

She bent down and felt her leg where the new brace was, an odd contraption like a small cage of metal and horn and leather that gave her ankle strength. "I am wrong to speak to you this way when you have done this for me. I owe you . . . so much, more than I can ever return, and yet, when I realize what could become of us, I am vexed with you."

"One has little to do with the other," he reminded her, smiling slightly. He was pleased to see her walk without limping; the brace changed so much about her—her stance, her carriage, her demeanor—and it changed the way the people of the fortress saw her. She was no longer obviously impaired, and even her pox scars seemed less apparent now that her limp was gone. "You can be angry with me for the grain and pleased to have the brace at the same time."

"Saint-Germanius," she said, shaking her head and trying not to laugh. "It is very annoying of you to understand me so well." Then she straightened up and came directly to him. There was a light, metallic *cling* when her brace came down, but it was so minor that it could be ignored. "I hope I have done the right thing in destroying the rye. But I had to do something, and you have said all along that it is a pestilence in the rye . . . I cannot hold the anger of the villagers against them. They are afraid of starving. We have no new grain yet, and now that the rye is gone, we have less than before in our barrels, and it decreases every day."

"If the grain sickens, maddens, and kills, you have done well in being rid of it," he said, facing her squarely. He put his small hands to her waist. "Well. Where am I in balance? in your favor or out of it."

"The brace and the pectoral argue for you eloquently," she said, smiling more openly. "And you, yourself, are held in high regard by the Gerefa."

"I am fortunate," he said, his dark eyes somber.

"But if there is more madness here . . ." She held up her hands to show how helpless she would be in that event.

"There will be madness only where there is rye flour made from tainted grain, where the madness has lodged. That is where the madness comes from, the tainted grain; there is no miasma. Believe this." He touched her face, loving the strength he saw there. "I doubted that was the truth, too, at first, but I learned otherwise, many, many years ago."

Ranegonda stepped up to him and put her arms around him. "And what if you are wrong? What then? I will have to answer to Margerefa Oelrih for what I have done, and he may decide that it was treasonous. He will not believe that madness comes from tainted rye, Saint-Germanius."

She could not see the distant, ancient pain in his eyes, but she heard a little of it in his quiet answer, "If I am wrong, more than two thousand years of study have been in vain."

Her arms tightened around him. "I believe you, Saint-Germanius. It is the rye."

He kissed the line of her brow. "Thank you for that, love," he murmured, and stood with her in silence a short while.

At last she said, "You have made my life . . . rich." She continued to lean against him, as if taking strength from his presence. "I never realized that it was possible to have so much; not when I was scarred and . . ." She shivered.

"If you can bear my scars, Ranegonda, I can bear yours, and gladly," he said with a wry smile, and went on before she could question him, "More than the wrath of the villagers I am worried at the thought of what Pentacoste might do."

"Has she approached you again?" asked Ranegonda; although she did not retreat from him, she stiffened against him.

"Yes," he said with an aggravation that hid his apprehension. "This time to give me a length of wool, to make a garment for winter, or so she claims. I suspect it is the cloth that we found on her loom, for it is made of black wool and there are knots in it."

"She is fixed on you, and she will have you," said Ranegonda sadly.

Saint-Germanius shook his head. "She is fixed on me because I will not come to her, because I do not want her and she knows it. She cannot abide that. As long as I am not her devoted slave, she will respect me, and that is intolerable to her. So she is determined that I will be what she wants, which is not possible."

"But she offered you that cloth," Ranegonda protested.

"Very courteously," he agreed, stroking her back, letting her long braids fall against his hand. "With flattering praise that made it awkward to refuse."

She gripped him tightly. "Did you take it?"

"Of course," he answered with faint amusement. "It may cause her to leave me alone for a while, or so I hope. She assumes that the spell worked in the cloth will bend me to her will, and therefore she will not have to speak to me until I come to her. At least that is what I think will happen."

Ranegonda's voice was small and tight. "And if the spell works? What then?" She turned her head enough to see more of his face; she kissed the line of his jaw and the corner of his mouth. "I don't want to give you up, not to her."

Saint-Germanius knew that he could not dismiss her dread of the spell, that it would be cruel to laugh at her fears, and so he said, "If such magic works at all, it works on the living, not on those who have broken the seal of death. A living man might succumb to such a spell, if he knew what it portends, but a vampire: never."

She shivered at the word. "Is that what I will be? A vampire?"

"Yes, when you die, if your spine is not broken or your body destroyed; sever our spines, burn us, and we die as surely as any of the living," he told her with the same steady gentleness he had used to speak of these things from the first. "But without that, you will rise from your grave and live again, in my life, and you will live as I live. You will seek life as the devout seek Heaven, and those you touch you will know to the core of them. That knowing is the bond, and until the true death, it will hold you."

"I try to imagine it, and I can't. I have looked at the men of the fortress and none of them stirred me as you do." She nuzzled his neck experimentally. "I have no longing, not as you describe."

He smoothed her hair back. "No; not until you come to my life." He kissed her again, this time with slow passion that reached her soul. "This is not wise," he whispered as they broke apart. "Too many might see us." He angled his chin toward the door.

"Too many are watching," she agreed, her cheeks flushed and heat smoldering in her grey eyes like hot steel. "Ingvalt and Duart and half the men-at-arms."

"And Brother Erchboge," added Saint-Germanius. "And Pentacoste."

Ranegonda Signed herself. "How can we be safe?"

"We will be cautious; that is the best we can do. Stay in your quarters tonight. I will come to you there." He moved two steps back from her. "Be careful, my life, and do not let anyone frighten you into folly."

Ranegonda nodded. "Tonight, then?"

"Late, after the watch changes," he promised her, starting toward the door.

She stopped him with one last question. "Does Berengar know Pentacoste gave that cloth to you?"

Saint-Germanius met her gaze levelly. "I don't know."

There was more she wanted to say, but prudence kept her from speaking. She waved him out of the muniment room, and went back to pondering how she would explain to Margerefa Oelrih how she came to have all the rye in the fortress and the village buried in the midden. Try as she would, she could find no words to account for her actions; she decided she would have to remain at her writing table until she had hit upon a suitable way to account for what she had ordered. She was still there when the gong was sounded for the mid-day meal. Dazed, she rose from her writing table and mentally shook herself, admonishing herself to be more alert. She had been too lost in her problem and half the morning had slipped away from her. She reached for her casula to throw around her shoulders and started for the door, only to be startled by two blasts on the wooden horn.

There were shouts from the ramparts and the creaking of the winch as the slaves strove to open the gates. The people of the fortress who a moment ago had been hurrying toward the Common Hall now gathered at the gate to see what brought the villagers to them this time.

As soon as the gates were open far enough, Ormanrih barreled through, with Ruel, Kalifranht, and Glevic in his wake. He put his hand to his forehead as Ranegonda hurried up to him. "Gerefa," he said urgently, fear straining his voice. "You must listen to these woodcutters."

"The White Christ show you favor," Ranegonda said by way of perfunctory greeting; she saw that the dread in Ormanrih's face was also in the other three men's. "What's the matter?" she asked them bluntly as they touched their foreheads.

The three exchanged uneasy looks, and Glevic Signed himself, but none of them was able to speak; all of them wore the taut expression of contained fright, and Kalifranht looked as if he might vomit.

"Tell me," Ranegonda commanded. "At once." She saw that the people of the fortress were all moving closer, determined to hear as much as they could. "Why have you come to me?"

"In the woods," said Kalifranht at last. "In the woods we found—" He stopped, his weathered features going pale.

Ranegonda felt an echo of their horror. "What did you find in the woods?"

At last Glevic answered. "We came upon a place. It had been a place for outlaws and robbers. But someone else had been there." Under his sun-darkened skin he was grey.

"The old gods," whispered Kalifranht. "Or their monsters."

There were whispers among the people of Leosan Fortress, and a few of them made gestures that were not Signing themselves.

"Monsters?" called out one of the women of the fortress.

"How do you mean?" Ranegonda asked, remembering the hollow trees and their offerings. "What happened?"

"Something came for them," said Ruel. "They were dead. Some of them had been hung from branches, like sheep in the slaughterhouse. Their guts . . . were hanging out. The rest were . . . broken."

"Broken?" Ranegonda repeated as if she did not know the word.

"A giant might have done it," muttered Kalifranht. "A giant with a club or a maul."

"A giant." Ranegonda looked from one woodcutter to the other two. She was having difficulty understanding what they said to her, and as she listened, she found it increasingly hard to hear at all. It was if a wind was rushing at her ears, distorting sound and turning everything to garble. "Go on."

"There were fourteen or fifteen men, probably," said Ruel. "If there were more, we could not find them." Belatedly he Signed himself.

"How many?" Ranegonda asked, aghast.

"Fourteen or fifteen," said Glevic. "That we found."

"There could be more," said Ruel, and pressed his lips together tightly.

"Hanging from trees like slaughtered sheep?" she persisted, and wished that Saint-Germanius were with her to help her make sense of what they were telling her. "Outlaws, you say?"

"Outlaws, almost certainly," said Kalifranht.

"There were huts. In ruins," said Glevic. "It was a camp."

"Some of the men were . . . in pieces," said Ruel. "Beaten to bits." He made a high sound that was not laughter and there were tears on his face.

As she Signed herself, Ranegonda issued an inward order for composure and to pay attention to the woodcutters' story. "When did you find this?" she asked, determined to sort it all out.

"This morning," said Kalifranht. "We came here as soon as we . . . finished counting."

"We ran most of the way," Glevic added.

Again the words slipped away from her like fish and it was an effort to question the three men. "Could the Danes have done it?"

Ormanrih answered for the woodcutters. "Danes take prisoners to be slaves, Gerefa. They do not slaughter. In all my years, I have never heard of Danes doing a thing like this."

"Unless there is opposition," Ranegonda added. "Then they kill as readily as anyone. If the men fought them, couldn't they have wanted vengeance?"

"Outlaws fight the Danes as much as we do," said Faxon from the edge of the gathering people. "Danes know that."

"Danes take prisoners!" shouted another of the men-at-arms.

"And they may have!" Ruel shouted back. "Who knows how many men were there at the start."

"No Danes. A giant," Kalifranht insisted. "Or something worse."

Ranegonda held her lower lip between her teeth as she forced herself to make a decision. "Captain Amalric," she called.

"Here, Gerefa!" he yelled down from the parapets above the gates. She had the beginnings of a plan, and that was enough. "Take a dozen men, armed, on horseback. Go with these men. See that the . . . dead are buried."

"They are outlaws!" shouted one of the women.

"And we are sworn to the White Christ," Ranegonda snapped. "We do not leave the dead unburied." She Signed herself. "Go on."

"I cannot . . . I cannot," said Kalifranht, cringing.

Ranegonda looked at him and realized that he was trembling. "What now?"

"I cannot go back there," he said more loudly. "No!" And then, without warning, he fainted.

Ormanrih kicked him. "Get up, you turd," he muttered.

"Leave him," Ranegonda said, holding out her hand to prevent the village headman from inflicting more punishment. "Someone fetch Winolda if she isn't here, to tend to him." Without watching to see her order carried out, she turned back to the other woodcutters. "It is mid-day and you will have to set out at once if the work is to be done before sundown. Prepare yourselves. The men-at-arms will need guides. It would be best if both of you will go with them."

Ruel Signed himself twice, swallowing hard before he could speak. "I . . . If I must."

Glevic stared up at the sky, as if hoping to find an omen there. "It was a terrible thing to see. To look at it again . . ." He Signed himself, and added another gesture to older, more dangerous gods.

"The omen is bad," shouted Ewarht from his place on guard. "It is bad."

There were more whispers, growing urgent, and some of the people drew back from the villagers, wanting to get away from their horror. Two of the women bustled the staring children away, and another ran to get Brother Erchboge.

Ranegonda wondered where Saint-Germanius was, and at the same time was relieved that he was not among those watching. The villagers were against him as it was and she saw no reason to give them more reason to distrust him, as they might, hearing such a tale as these men recounted. She motioned to the nearest staircase. "Captain Amalric. Come down. You, Culfre, Osbern, Severic, you come too." She clapped her hands to add emphasis to her words. "We will want more. Captain Amalric will select who is to ride with him." As she said this, she realized that Saint-Germanius was in the smithy. Perhaps, she guessed, he was working and had not heard the outcry.

Winolda appeared at the edge of the crowd, her pregnancy making her awkward. She Signed herself as she caught sight of the fallen woodcutter. "Is he ill? Is it madness?"

"He is sick," said Ranegonda. "Hartshorn will bring him around." Hearing her own voice she was astonished at how calm she sounded. "He will need beer and something to eat when he is himself again, or he will faint a second time."

Winolda nodded warily, and started toward Kalifranht.

Her husband Culfre stepped between her and the unconscious man. "No. Not if your child may be touched by his fear," he said.

Winolda stood still, looking toward Ranegonda. "I am his wife," she said, allowing Culfre to propel her back through the gathering.

As if this were a signal, many of the people of the fortress moved away from the villagers; those who remained kept an even greater distance from Ranegonda and Ormanrih.

Captain Amalric was descending the stairs quickly. He carried his spear at the ready and kept his stance without seeming to be upset by what he had heard. As he came up to Ranegonda, he said, "We will take three mules as well as our mounts, in case there is anything we have to carry back."

"What would that be?" asked Ranegonda, concealing a shudder.

"Who knows?" the Captain shrugged. "But we don't want to weigh down our horses, and . . ." He let the words trail off.

"All right," she said, "take mules, and your weapons, and go in armor. It may not be necessary, but if it is—" She stopped.

"Yes," Captain Amalric agreed. "We'll take cheeses and water for food. We will leave as quickly as we can be ready." He coughed once, and then barked an order. "Those not riding with us will stand watch until we return. No change of watch until we are back, except in the light room." He glanced at Ranegonda. "Is that acceptable?"

"It must be, unless the watch is to be kept by children and women," Ranegonda answered. She folded her arms. "And I will ride with you. Duart will be my deputy in my absence."

"Gerefa," Captain Amalric warned, "you are not prepared to fight."

"I could be," she said with determination. "As Gerefa, this is what I must do."

"No," said Captain Amalric. "If you were your brother it would be different. He was a good fighter in his day. But you can barely use a sword and you have no skill with a spear. If you ride with us, you would have to be guarded constantly, and that would keep us from the work you have ordered we do. Your men won't permit you to do it. You are not trained for battle, and you do not know what we will find. If the woodcutters have told us truly, it may be that there will be more to fight off than men."

"Bears," said Ormanrih, Signing himself. "Wolves. Boars."

"And other beasts." Captain Amalric nodded. "They will not stay long from such a feast as these villagers describe. Leave the task to us, Gerefa."

She hesitated, torn between her duty and the Captain's suggestions. "I should go with you," she said at last. "But if there are the dangers you describe I would hamper you, and that would be ill for all of us."

"And if there are Danes," Captain Amalric went on, determined to make his point, "you would be a treasure for them. They would use you as their whore and demand ransom. No matter what happened then, you would be lost."

For an instant the memory of Captain Jouarre killing Milo was before her, and then it vanished, and she said, "Yes, I would be lost." She smoothed her bliaut with her hands. "All right. Select your men and get your mounts. If you have not returned by dark, we will have to close the gates against you until morning."

Captain Amalric Signed himself, and the woodcutters followed his example. "If we are not back before dark, you will know it will take Margerefa Oelrih's company of armed men to fight whatever is in the forest." He touched his forehead again, and then hurried across the Marshaling Court, calling aloud to his men as he went.

Ormanrih watched him go in consternation. "He is a worthy soldier, no doubt, but he—"

"He will take care of your men well enough," said Ranegonda, nodding toward Ruel and Glevic. She noticed that Kalifranht was beginning to stir. "One of you had better help him to his feet. I want no more weakness from him."

"He will stand," said Ormanrih in a tone that made it clear he would not tolerate anything else.

Ruel had bent down to Kalifranht, and he held out his arm. "Better get up," he said as the fallen man opened his muzzy eyes.

Kalifranht blinked twice in puzzlement, and then sat up abruptly. "How . . . The men in the forest!"

"You will not have to go there," said Ranegonda quickly, and noticed that most of the people of the fortress had left them alone now; it was time for the mid-day meal, and they were hungry.

As Kalifranht got to his feet, he ducked his head in shame. "It was wrong to do that."

"Then do not do it again," said Ranegonda, and added, "You will want to go to your house. Tell your wife to bind your head."

"Put your feet in pig's blood, to strengthen you, and tie red yarn to the beams of your house," Ormanrih advised, and shook his head as he watched Kalifranht trudge out of the gate. "This is troublesome. He's not as strong as he looks, they say. He's big enough, but there's no stamina to him. At the end of the day he is weak and trembling."

"He does his work," said Ruel, wanting to defend his companion. "We do well together, the three of us."

"Yes," Ormanrih agreed, and added in another tone, "Perhaps we should do something to ease his burden. Perhaps he should be put with the men who fish."

"They are injured or old!" exclaimed Glevic. "Kalifranht is too young, and he is whole."

Ormanrih looked to Ranegonda. "What should I do, Gerefa? You saw him faint. He has done it before. And he is often too tired to join in village feasts. He says there is pain in his shoulder when he is tired, and his hand is cold."

"Has Winolda seen him?" asked Ranegonda, wishing she could have Saint-Germanius treat the woodcutter.

"His wife tends him," said Ruel. "It is what he wants."

"But his shoulder pains him, and his hand becomes cold," said Ormanrih stubbornly. "He should do other work."

This was more than Ranegonda wanted to deal with, and so she said, "When this matter of the dead men in the forest is settled, then you will decide what is to be done with Kalifranht. There is too much needing attention now to worry about him." One more thing occurred to her. "Brother Erchboge!" she said. "They will need a monk to bury those men properly." She turned away from Ormanrih and the woodcutters without another word and hurried through the line of soldiers' housing to the little chapel, hoping that the monk was not lost in his prayers.

Her insistent pounding on the plank door brought a quick response: Brother Erchboge pulled it open and snarled a blessing. "Why do you disturb me, Gerefa?"

Ranegonda quickly recounted what the woodcutters had reported. "Captain Amalric is preparing to leave now. He is taking armed men with him. They are to find these dead men, discover who they are if they can, and see that they are buried. For that, you will be needed."

Brother Erchboge Signed himself at once. "Yes. They cannot be left for the old gods or demons to inhabit. Such bodies are the booty of devils." He gave her a hard, narrow glance. "You have done well to come to me," he admitted grudgingly.

"I am thankful to the White Christ that one of His servants is here to minister to the dead," she said, deliberately complimenting him.

"Yes. Yes. The White Christ protects this place and its people," he said before he ducked back into the chapel, only to emerge a moment later with a small case in his hand. "To anoint the dead," he explained, and pulled the chapel door shut. "Where is Captain Amalric?"

"At the stable, with his men." She wondered whom he had selected to ride with him; she would find out soon enough, she supposed.

"I will go with them," he said, and started off in the direction of the stable in long, jerky strides.

Ranegonda hurried after him, almost running to keep up with him. "If it is possible, find out who the dead men were. Margerefa Oelrih will want to know that."

Brother Erchboge stopped and swung round on her. "You believe I do not know!" he accused her in a vehement whisper. "You run as if you were healed, but that is a lie! A lie!"

Of all the responses Ranegonda might have anticipated, this baffled her the most. "What?"

He pointed to her foot. "You believe I do not notice that you walk and run without halting? You believe that I pay no heed to what that foreigner does? You have made yourself his creature for a cure that is not a cure. You are not truly healed. Do you suppose I cannot see the cage he has made for you? Do you imagine that I cannot hear the sound of it, or see it? You believe I do not know you wear his sign? There. Under your clothes." He spat at her. "I will tend to the dead men because it is what the White Christ asks of me, not because you order it. You have no right to speak to me at all. If you were not still chaste I would ask that you be drowned. You have put yourself beyond the White Christ in following that foreigner. So be it." He turned away from her and continued on toward the stable.

Ranegonda stared after the monk, aghast. She wanted to protest, to tell him that she knew she was not healed, only helped. She wanted to defend Saint-Germanius and the brace he had built for her. But she was trembling with a fear she did not know she possessed. She stood in the narrow strip of sunlight between the family quarters of the men-at-arms and felt a cold go over her.

Not long after, Captain Amalric and a dozen men clattered out of Leosan Fortress with Brother Erchboge bringing up the rear on a mule, a second one attached to his saddle by a lead. Ruel and Glevic shared a big horse, a massive red roan with a head like a bucket. Ranegonda stood by the gates and watched them go, her emotions in conflict. It was not right that she should remain while they ventured out. And it was not right for her to go with them. They were already compromised by the two woodcutters and the priest. If the men in the forest had been killed by Danes, having a woman with them would be a greater risk, for Danes were known to hunt for Saxon women.

Geraint, who had been left in charge of the remaining sixteen men-at-arms, came to her side. "Your decision is a good one, Gerefa. It is best you stay here, in case those who attacked the men in the forest come here. You will be needed here."

She Signed herself and glanced toward the slaves waiting by the winch for orders to open the gate. "I pray it will not come to that."

"As do we all," Geraint agreed at once. "But we are ready if they do."

"I hope we may be," said Ranegonda with an uncertain look at the fortification. "If they are many, or they are well-armed, it could be a hard fight. And if they destroy the village in trying to reach us, we could starve before autumn." She Signed herself for protection.

Geraint had little consolation to offer her, and wisely remained silent.

The afternoon dragged on; work in the fortress and the village below was desultory, and though women tended the small flock of sheep and goats in the village, and Udo and four of his thatchers climbed ladders to mend roofs, most of the woodcutters confined themselves to the sheds where they worked with planes and saws to prepare logs for shipping.

As the kennels and the coops fell into shadow, Saint-Germanius completed his work at the smithy and went to wash in the men's bath-house. By the time he emerged, his dark hair damp and curling, most of the people of the fortress had climbed to the parapet to watch for the return of Captain Amalric and his company.

Ranegonda was waiting for him at the entrance to the seaward tower. "I thought you'd be up there," he said, indicating the ramparts. "Looking for Captain Amalric."

"I want to be," she answered. "But it would cause trouble, having the Gerefa watch. The omen would be bad."

He smiled a little. "Would it."

"The people of the fortress are afraid. They fear the old gods." She looked at him in confusion. "Don't you fear them?"

He was still for a moment, and then shook his head. "No."

"Because of what you are?" Whatever his answer might have been was prevented by the sudden shout from many of those on the ramparts, followed at once by two blasts on the wooden horn. Ranegonda looked from him to the walls and back at him again. "They're coming back."

Saint-Germanius saw the gates start to open, his winch clanking as the slaves worked the cranks. "You'd better go to the gate. They will want you there."

"Yes." She stared at him. "Will you still come? Later?"

"After midnight," he promised, and went into the seaward tower.

Ranegonda hurried past the bake-house, kitchens, and Common Hall, and pride at her speed and grace flickered through her. She reached the gate as the slaves stopped their efforts, and she called up to Geraint, "What can you see?"

"They are through the stockade, all of them," he shouted back as he shaded his eyes and leaned against the stones to see better. "And there is a body on one of the mules."

"One of our men?" she asked, hoping it would not be.

"No," Geraint answered. "It must be one of those they found." He looked down at her. "The stockade gates are closed."

"Good," she said with a relief that startled her. "Ormanrih did well."

Geraint was coming down the narrow stairs, a few of the people of the fortress behind him. "Shall I tell the cooks to prepare the evening meal?"

"Yes," she said. "Then return here." She was about to take up her proper position when something occurred to her. "Have them order an extra measure of beer for everyone."

"Yes, Gerefa," said Geraint with enthusiasm.

Ranegonda had just taken the correct position when Pentacoste emerged from the landward tower and came across the gate-court to her side. "I've been watching from my quarters," she said breathlessly. "Are they truly bringing a body with them?"

"So I suppose," said Ranegonda with distaste.

"One who was gutted? Didn't the woodcutters say that some of the men were gutted?" Her lips were open and moist.

"They said it," Ranegonda answered curtly. She wished her sister-in-law had remained in her quarters.

There were shouts in the village as Captain Amalric and his men made their way along the single road to the approach to Leosan Fortress. One of the villagers was banging a drum in celebration.

"Will they bring the body here?" asked Pentacoste anxiously.

"I don't know," answered Ranegonda. "If it comes from the village, or is a relative of one of the villagers, it will be left there."

"But if it comes from here? If it is one of ours?" Her enormous eyes were bright with fervid excitement. "They say that gutting is an agonizing death."

Ranegonda recalled the terrible scars on Saint-Germanius's body, and what little he had said of his death. "It must be."

The horses of Captain Amalric's company could be heard now, their iron-shod hooves loudly marking their progress up the slope; a cheer went up from the men-at-arms on watch. And then they were through the gates, passing from the brilliant orange glow of sunset outside to the shadow of the parapets within.

Captain Amalric was the first off his horse. "The White Christ guide and keep you, Gerefa," he said as he tugged off his heaum.

"I thank Him for bringing you all safely home," she answered, reaching out to take the reins of his horse, and those of the big roan the woodcutters had ridden, for they had dismounted in the village.

"Amen," he said with uncharacteristic piety, Signing himself.

"What did you discover, Captain?" Ranegonda asked.

A few of the others were out of the saddle now, all of them looking worn and blank, as if they had seen more than they could endure.

"The woodcutters were right. Someone killed them. They were outlaws, by the way. The killers took all their food and some of their clothes." He rubbed his head and then his eyes. "The work is done. We buried what we could find."

"Yes," said Osbern. "They were in pieces, some of them. Not hacked, not with a sword. Smashed with clubs." He took a long breath.

"He's right," said Captain Amalric heavily. "They were purple, some of those wretches."

"And what killed them?" asked Pentacoste eagerly.

"Other men," said Captain Amalric in disbelief. "Brother Erchboge was sure it was demons at first. But you could see it was men. Their footprints were everywhere in the blood."

"How many?" asked Ranegonda, feeling her bones chill.

"A lot," said Captain Amalric. "Far more than there were outlaws to fight them."

Pentacoste was staring at the body slung over the back of the mule. "Why did you bring him here? So that you could show us what was done?"

"No," said Captain Amalric heavily. "He belongs here." He went to the mule and reached out to the body, grabbing a handful of hair to reveal the face. "It's hard to recognize him with the bruises," he said.

Ranegonda stared. "Karagern?" she said. "He became an outlaw?"

Captain Amalric did not give a direct answer; he Signed himself. "We cut him down when we buried the others. We'll put him out for tonight and bury him in the morning."

An entry in the records of Holy Cross Monastery, made by the scribe Brother Desidir, on the Feast of Saint Monica.

In the Name of the White Christ on the feast of the mother of Saint Augustine, Amen.

Too long has this monastery been filled with the miasma of visions and rot. All our prayers and fasting have been for naught. All the Brothers have been on bread and water for two weeks, and the madness continues to claim them.

Fourteen monks have died of the miasma since it has returned to this monastery. Another five have made a first recovery from the worst of its predations. Two others are caught in its throes and it is not possible that they will survive the rot that has taken hold of them. What curse or malign action brought it to us we have yet to discover, or what secret sin has kept it here.

Most vilely stricken is the superior, Brother Giselberht, who has suffered the torment of the Devil and all the old gods from this mania. He is filled with fever from the rot of his legs, and he is caught up in visions that will not cease. Of those still alive, his is the greatest torment. Were it not a sin to do it, I would pray that the White Christ let him die to end the agony he now endures.

With the miasma upon us, no one will bring us succor, and we have been reduced to the fish we catch and the last of our bread. Neither the village of Leosan Fortress nor the merchants of Oeldenburh will bring food here, for fear that if the monks cannot escape this miasma, what man in the world can?

Some have said that we should slaughter our sheep and our goats, and eat flesh to restore our strength. But that would be the abjuration of our vows. Our faith will sustain us, even as the White Christ promised us when He lived on the earth. If we must still be taken by this madness, then it is for the glory of the White Christ, who was crucified for us. Let the ravages of the miasma expiate the wrongs we have done and bring us closer to Heaven.

On the order of Brother Giselberht, a party of monks was sent to the forest two days ago, charged with destroying the hollow trees where the old gods are worshiped. But they have not returned; some say that they were frightened, lost their faith, and fled. I pray that is what became of them, for anthing else is more terrible, and I cannot put word of it to the page without endangering my soul.

When our food is gone we will be entirely in the hands of the White Christ. If it pleases Him to bring us to Him, then we will go with thanks and prayers. If He desires that we remain on earth, help will be provided so that starvation will not do what the miasma has failed to accomplish. In humility and with the sureness of faith, I commend myself to those monks who will follow me and to the mercy of Heaven.

Brother Desidir, scribe
Holy Cross Monastery

11

"They say I will soon be a widow," Pentacoste whispered as she came through the door of Saint-Germanius's chamber. "Word from the monastery is that he is filled with rot. They say he shrieks from the pain of it."

"What are you doing here?" Saint-Germanius asked flatly, as if speaking to a willful child whose pranks no longer amused him.

"I shouldn't have to come here," she said, pretty and petulant. "You should have come to me days ago. I wanted you."

Through the narrow window the sky over the Baltic Sea was an odd, opaque blue-white, as flat as if it were a painted ceiling. Beneath it the sea was sullen and quiet. Throughout the fortress and the village people were bracing for the first of the summer squalls; Ranegonda was below in the village supervising the strengthening of the stockade, in case the men who slaughtered the outlaws should come to the fortress.

He went and pointedly opened the door of his quarters. "Because of the cloth you gave me?" He bowed to her in the Byzantine manner. "You must excuse me, Hohdama, but I am in the middle of something I cannot easily leave."

She squinted and then opened her eyes deliberately wide. "Are you afraid of me? Do I frighten you?"

"No, I am not, and no, you don't." He went back to his trestle table and continued to assemble the bits of sand and crushed, colored rocks, measuring them out with care as she prowled through the big stone room. "Pray, touch nothing."

She stopped where she was and lowered the lid of the chest. "It is only dirt in here."

"As this sand and these stones have virtue in them, so does that earth," he said very seriously. "You, of all people, should understand that."

Her laughter was delicious, the sound of clear water in an open stream, and would have been more winning if it had been less practiced. "You seek to teach me lessons? Me? I have no need of that oven you have built, or for sand. Those are trivial, the things you make like a baker. I have skills no one in this place possesses. Not even you. No one in Saxony can best me."

He did not respond to this challenge as she wanted; he continued to concentrate on his work and said rather distantly, "Then I am surprised you would waste your time with me. Surely there must be others who can offer you more than I can, either in knowledge or in wealth. Why be limited by a baker?"

Now her eyes were bright with offense. "I will be where I like. You have no right to say such things to me."

"On the contrary," he said, still working on combining sand and powdered rock, "you gave me the right when you put that cloth of yours in my hands."

She looked startled and did her best to shame him. "Do you suppose I would need cloth to bind you? You are more ignorant than I guessed."

Saint-Germanius let her scathing remark pass. "You gave me that cloth for some purpose. And for having done that, now you will listen to me."

Pentacoste tossed her head: a wasted gesture since Saint-Germanius did not bother to look at her. "I am the Gerefa's wife. The true Gerefa, that is. I am entitled to your respect and obedience."

"You said you are about to be his widow," Saint-Germanius corrected her in the same remote way. "If that is the case, it would be wise for you to gain the protection of Ranegonda, or at least her good-will. As I understand it, once your husband dies, his authority transfers to her, along with the responsibility he gave her as his deputy."

"She would not dare to go against his wishes," said Pentacoste hotly. "I would complain to the Margerefa and King Otto."

"She will honor his orders while he lives; you know that. When he is dead, she will answer entirely to the Margerefa Oelrih and King Otto, and they will have greater regard for the memory of your husband than you do. Your complaints may not gain the things you wish. Your custom, as I understand it, is for the widow of a man in Holy Orders to follow him into the cloister while he lives, for he is dead to the world. Since you did not become a nun, it could now be required of you." He set the small cup of measured sand aside and at last turned to look at her. "You have been at pains to vex the Gerefa, Hohdama."

"She can command me nothing! She is nothing!" said Pentacoste, her expression haughty. "Her father was no one. My father is Dux Pol of Luitich in Lorraria."

"A valiant man, and a debauched one," said Saint-Germanius. "If what is said of him is true."

Pentacoste was furious now. "True! You told Ranegonda you are a Comites. That must be true, because you say it." Everything about her indicated she did not believe him.

"It is one of my titles," said Saint-Germanius with unchanged calm. "Though my rank has nothing to do with your predicament here, or mine." He turned back to his work. "Leave Ranegonda alone. And leave me alone, Hohdama. My time here grows short and I do not want to have it . . . cluttered." He made no mention of the dwindling supply of his native earth, or the peril they all faced from the new and ruthless men in the forest, but there was a finality in him and she saw it.

She stared at him in incredulous wrath. "Cluttered?" Her anger flared more hotly. "You think I am *clutter?*" She rushed toward him, her fists raised. "I am *not* a rag! You cannot cast me aside! You cannot do this to me! You are mine! *You are mine!"*

He permitted her to strike him once, then turned with a speed that startled her; he caught her hands in his own and held them aloft easily, though she pressed and struggled with all her strength. Her face was ruddy now, and her mouth square; little of her loveliness remained. "That is enough, Hohdama," he said firmly, never raising his voice. "No more."

"You cannot do this!" she shouted at him, her fury increasing because he would not be ruled by her.

"I can, you know," he responded evenly, and fixed her with his compelling gaze. "I want no more of this from you, Hohdama. You bring disgrace upon yourself and you humiliate me. No more of it."

"I will have you" she screamed.

"No."

In her ire there was a sudden craftiness. "No? The cloth will—"

"The cloth is only wool, Hohdama, for all it touches me. There is nothing you can do to make me what you want: no spinning, no weaving, no offerings left at the cove during the night." He lowered her hands with his own but held her away from him. "You have two men who would go to the ends of the earth for you: Berengar and Margerefa Oelrih. Be content with them."

Her single laugh was scornful. "Content myself? How could I? They are nothing!"

"Because they are devoted to you," he finished for her. "And you would have the same contempt for me if I succumbed to your spells, as you would for any man. But that will not happen. You are not what I seek and cannot be." His manner changed again, becoming marginally more friendly. "Either Berengar or Margerefa Oelrih would pay a high bride-price for you, when you are a widow. You would do well to decide which of them you want, and quickly, before the decision is out of your hands entirely."

"Why should I have either of them?" she demanded. She tried to wrench free and failed.

"Because it is not amusing to be a widow, Hohdama," he answered her. "Especially in this place." His grip moved from her hands to her wrists, but he continued to keep her at arm's length.

"I would not have to remain here," she said with the certainty of one who has worked out the future to her satisfaction and done all that she could to insure its coming. "I will leave. I will go to Francia or Italia or anywhere, and I will live better than my father lives," she went on grandly, confident that the offerings she had left for the old gods would release her from the constraints that would bind others.

"You will remain where King Otto or your father orders you to be," he reminded her.

"Then I will surely go elsewhere. They will not leave me in the charge of a woman!" She smiled, her triumph fierce. "The King may bring me to his court. Margerefa Oelrih would escort me."

"Are you so certain of that? of any of it?" Then he was severe once more. "What you decide to do is nothing to me. But whatever your decision, leave Ranegonda alone. You have put wolfsbane in her water and antimony in her food; you have half-cut the girths of her saddle. All such will stop; I guard her and you cannot do anything to her. No more defiance, no more attempts to harm her."

Her eyes heated afresh. "You care so much for her? You? She is lame and she is scarred and she is ugly and she is *old!*" Pentacoste cried out.

"I am far older than she," Saint-Germanius responded.

Pentacoste pulled away from him, her voice raised to a shriek. "I despise you! You disgust me. I loathe you!"

"Then leave me and be glad," he said, releasing her wrists.

Impulsively she started toward the door, and then halted. "You cannot tell me what I am to do. You are not Gerefa here, or my husband."

"We're agreed on that," said Saint-Germanius in a flat tone.

"I am the wife of the Gerefa. You will have to do as I wish or you will be turned out from the fortress." She raised her chin. "You could suffer the same fate as those outlaws, if you were sent into the forest."

He said nothing, for the memory of the knives that had disemboweled him three thousand years before still summoned up the ghost of pain for what was done to him and repugnance for what he had done in retaliation. Finally he said, "And that would please you."

She slammed the door as she left him. She was in seething furor, needing to do something destructive to vent her passion. Weeping with fury, she ran up the two levels to the cloth room, not knowing what she would do when she got there, but set on exacting a price for her rejection.

Osyth was at the smaller of the two looms, her hands busy as she hummed. She started to rise in order to lift her skirt in expected courtesy when Pentacoste shoved her aside and reached for the big loom, hooking her hands into the webbing and pulling with the full might of her temper; the threads began to break.

"Hohdama!" Osyth exclaimed, reaching out to grasp her shoulders and restrain her. "Hohdama, no!"

Pentacoste threw her off and, as she staggered, kicked her knee hard. As Osyth fell there was the sharp sound of a breaking bone, which made Pentacoste laugh loudly as she continued to pull the wool out of the loom, using the shuttle to poke holes in the woven fabric. Her strength astounded her, and her speed; it might be over too quickly, before she had time to relish what she had done. She cried to the old gods and recited parts of the spell she had worked into her wool, but there was only emptiness in her and that increased her wrath.

The pain in Osyth's shoulder was immediate and intense. She cried out once; the last thing she saw before she lost consciousness was Pentacoste smashing the shuttle on the frame of the loom.

At least the village woman understood her power, Pentacoste gloated as she stood back to see what she had accomplished. Only then did she realize that someone was standing behind her in the doorway of the cloth room. She turned around, unaware of how disordered her appearance was, her bliaut hanging askew on her shoulders, her chaplet displaced, her long braids no longer even and smooth. The broken shuttle was still in her hand and she was raising it to strike when she realized that it was Berengar who stared at her in abiding horror, and that recognition brought her back to a sense of where she was and the danger around her.

"My treasure," he said tentatively, one hand out to her but unable by the power of custom to enter this room reserved to women. "What . . . what is the matter?" From his expression it was apparent he feared that the madness had taken her.

She answered in a distracted way, "There is a spell on me." It was the first thing that occurred to her, and only after she said it did she realize the opportunity she had made for herself. "It . . . it is leaving me now. It must be your presence that ends it." She looked around as if dazed. "How do I come to be here?"

Berengar was staring at Osyth, aware that she was injured, and he goggled at the woman with an emotion like panic growing in him as he observed the chaos of the cloth room. The loom was bad enough, but the unconscious Osyth troubled him deeply. "That woman. Look at her. How did she . . . fall?"

Pentacoste was ready to respond. "I don't know. She was supposed to watch me. But she could not, not from . . . There was something here, in the spell. Something very powerful and . . . filled with evil."

At once Berengar Signed himself, and told himself that the reason Pentacoste did not do the same was that she was still being controlled in part by the spell. "May the White Christ protect us."

"Oh, yes," said Pentacoste, turning to him at last, making her eyes huge and shiny with tears. "It was so terrible." She was already coming to believe part of her story, and she concentrated on enumerating those details that would be most likely to shock Pranz Balduin's son. She dropped her voice so that it was hardly more than a whisper, making it necessary for Berengar to strain to hear her. "It was . . . unspeakable. The tower yawned open and showed the way to Hell. It was a mouth of flames. I had come here to weave. You know that I spin and weave?"

"Yes, Pentacoste," said Berengar, shocked that she could forget that.

"Yes," she said vaguely. She put her hand to her throat. "Osyth was working at the other loom. You can see that she was. And I was about to begin when . . ." She put her hands to her face. "There was a sound, oh, worse than the keening of storm winds. It howled like the Angel of Death and it came to darken the cloth room."

Again Berengar Signed himself. "What did you do?"

"What could we do?" she countered. "It was more powerful than anything I have ever seen but the might of the King's army in battle. It mastered both of us and set us to such hideous deeds in the frenzy of the spell that . . ." Again she trailed off. "I have ruined the cloth, haven't I?" She said it as if she were a child who had been caught disobeying her mother. "I never meant to. I was going to weave, and then the spell began, and I could not keep from . . . what I have done."

"Pentacoste, come to me," Berengar pleaded, holding his arm out to her. "Let me care for you."

"There is . . . danger," she whispered.

On the floor Osyth stirred, moaning once.

Pentacoste stepped back as if to keep herself from further hazard. She could not remain here any longer, for if the village woman should speak, her tale might be very different than Pentacoste's own. She turned to Berengar and let a sob catch in her throat. "Oh, yes. Please take me away from this place. I fear the spell could come again. Take me to the landward tower."

In spite of the horror that lingered around him, Berengar could not conceal his pleasure at Pentacoste's decision. For more than a year he had longed for her to put herself in his protection, and now it appeared she would do just that. He felt mightier than King Otto himself when Pentacoste put her hand into his, came to his side, and leaned her head against his shoulder. "Be comforted, my treasure," he said to her in what he hoped was a calm voice.

"I have never known anything so appalling," she whispered, and let her tears spill down her face. "I was frightened and the weight of it was on me, possessing me. It was worse than the Devil singing to the damned." She faltered at the stairs, looking down as if she saw hideous things in the shadows. "The spell. It is still here."

"It is fading," said Berengar, trying to make himself believe it. "You are more yourself already."

Osyth groaned again, and Pentacoste could hear her move; it was time to leave. "If you will guard me, I will try not to be afraid," she said faintly, and turned her eyes toward his. "You are my defender, Berengar. I can place myself in your keeping and know I am safe." It was so easy to win him to her will, she told herself as she watched him flush with pleasure. Even without her spells this one would never have the will to resist her.

They made their way down the stairs carefully, Pentacoste remembering to shiver from time to time as they went. At last, as they reached the ground floor, she leaned heavily again Berengar and sighed, "It came from here, making the floor seem to open and the flames of Hell lapped at me like the sea. I could feel it well up from this place."

"From here?" Berengar asked, and took care not to glance in the direction of the door to Saint-Germanius's quarters.

"It . . . it is possible," she said in an undervoice. "Oh, Berengar, take me away from this place. Let me go to the women's quarters where none of this vileness can touch me."

"The women's quarters?" he repeated, wanting to object, for he would not be permitted to accompany her there. "Why not stop at the kitchens? Have something to revive you so that you will not grow weak from what you have been through?" He did not like the notion of giving up her dependence on him even for something so sensible as food, but he reminded himself that she would be grateful for his concern. At least in the kitchens he would not have to relinquish his control of her.

"The kitchens?" She pretended to be troubled by his suggestion. "How can I do that? I cannot conceal my terror from any of them. They will see how I have been used. They will know that a dreadful thing has taken place." It was exactly what she wanted to happen, but she was aware that she must not appear eager if Berengar was to remain her supporter.

He smoothed her hand and stopped walking long enough to adjust her chaplet. "I will explain. You need not say anything."

"How good you are to me," she murmured, and let him rest her head on his shoulder again as they walked to the rear entrance of the kitchens.

Laus, the senior cook, was in the village inspecting the fields and the livestock; his assistant Iforr was in charge of the four scullery slaves and the three bakers. Even better, Brother Erchboge was seated near the main hearth, hunched over a wedge of cheese and a tankard of beer. One of the bakers was churning butter, the other two were sifting what little flour they were allowed for the evening meal, and Iforr was supervising the cutting up of two goats as Berengar stepped into the kitchens with Pentacoste clinging to him.

"What in the name of Fire Ships—" he exclaimed as he saw the two of them. "What do you mean coming here?"

"Hohdama!" one of the bakers exclaimed as he caught sight of Pentacoste.

Brother Erchboge was on his feet at once, Signing himself and staring in affronted outrage at the new arrivals.

Berengar was ready for that question, and he answered promptly. "You must give your help. There has been a terrible spell worked in the cloth room, a great sorcery. The Gerefa's wife has barely escaped it. She must have something to eat to sustain her. And your blessing, Brother, to guard her against the spell."

"Sorcery!" Brother Erchboge repeated, aghast.

The announcement had precisely the impact Pentacoste had planned: everyone in the kitchens stopped their various tasks to listen.

Saint-Germanius had heard Berengar and Pentacoste depart, and for a short while had continued his work; but he became aware that there was still a sound coming from above him. At first he thought that the man-at-arms assigned to watch the light might be singing one of the repetitious melodies many of the soldiers preferred. Then he heard a cry of pain, high and keening. He set his work aside at once and hurried to the door, flinging it open, half-expecting to find an injured child waiting for him. But the entry was empty, though the sound came again. He realized that it originated above him, and he hurried up the winding stairs two at a time, calling out once, "I will help you." As he approached the third level he knew what he sought was in the cloth room. Osyth had managed to pull herself away from the wreckage of the loom, but now she was bleeding where her broken collar-bone had pushed through the skin. Her face was the color of whey and she was breathing quickly, shallowly, cold sweat on her brow. She did not hear Saint-Germanius climbing the stairs and she was unaware he had found her until he gently picked her up, holding her with an ease that revealed his great strength. As he got to his feet his movement accidentally caused her weight to shift in his arms. Only then did she stare at him. "This is the cloth room. You cannot be here, not here," she muttered, and lost consciousness again.

Saint-Germanius had come down half a level when he saw Ingvalt standing outside Berengar's quarters, arms folded, his crucifix clasped in one hand, his expression intractable. For a brief moment Saint-Germanius hesitated, then said, "This woman is hurt and needs immediate care. I pray you will move aside so I may pass. Whatever I have done that troubles you, let us deal with it later."

Ingvalt looked more obdurate. "If anything has happened to that woman, you are the cause, foreigner."

It was pointless to argue and he was not willing to lose precious time in posturing. "This woman is in pain. Stand aside or I will force you to move," said Saint-Germanius in quiet, commanding tones; there was a sureness in him that was utterly convincing. "Now."

Too long had Ingvalt lived by the habit of obedience; at the sound of Saint-Germanius's crisp order, the habit won, and he grudgingly stepped back enough to allow him to pass. "You are without virtue or honor," he muttered as Saint-Germanius carried Osyth by. "And I will proclaim your use of that woman to everyone."

Saint-Germanius paused long enough to look back at Ingvalt. "If you are afraid I am going to rape her, come with me and watch what I do." He could not keep the impatience from his voice. "But whatever you decide, do it quickly, before she loses more blood." With that he resumed his climb down the stairs, carrying Osyth into his quarters and leaving the door open.

There had been many times since he arrived at Leosan Fortress that Saint-Germanius had longed for syrup of poppies and tincture of pansies to relieve the agony of those who had been hurt; he had never wished for it as he did now, for he knew that in setting the bone he would add to Osyth's pain. He did not have the time to talk her into that other sleep where he could mask the hurt with other visions. As he put the woman on his bed, he said, "I regret that you will have to suffer more. But once I have done what is necessary your bone will knit properly."

Osyth, drifting at the edge of consciousness, uttered the fragments of words and then lay back.

It was a task that ordinarily would require two men, but Saint-Germanius's strength was greater than that, and his centuries of experience at the Temple of Imhotep had given him a skill no other possessed. He braced his knee against her side, took her hand in his, stretching her arm out and attempting to ignore her fainting moan as he did. Then, in a single, concentrated movement, so swift it could not clearly be seen, he set her collar-bone; he was relieved that the bone had not splintered, and that she had not screamed. He straightened up, but only so that he could reposition her so that he could bind her arm and shoulder with strips of selvage and linen rags.

"How did you do that?" demanded Ingvalt from the door.

"Do what?" asked Saint-Germanius, his attention on Osyth as he formed a pad of woolen scraps against her shoulder.

"You made a gesture and the bone was right," said Ingvalt, Signing himself in growing distress. "That is sorcery."

"It was more than a gesture, much more," said Saint-Germanius, looking once at Ingvalt. "It was not sorcery."

Berengar's servant shook his head. "I saw. You bent over her and gestured." He started to back away now.

"No one sets bones with a gesture," said Saint-Germanius bluntly as he went back to his task.

"You are a magician, a sorcerer." Ingvalt withdrew still further. "Magicians are damned. You are damned."

It was useless to describe what he had done; Saint-Germanius recognized the superstitious dread in Ingvalt's manner at once. There was no explanation he could offer that would not confirm Ingvalt's conviction that the bone setting was a work of magic; most of those who called themselves physicians at this time would agree with the servant, and would add their fear to his. He heard Ingvalt run from the seaward tower and sighed. "When you wake you will be sore and stiff," he said to Osyth. "And it will be a few days before you can move without pain. But it will end, I promise you, and you will heal." He put his small hand on her head. "If I could have lessened the hurt, I would have, but it had to be set or your shoulder and arm might have been useless to you." He thought back again to the priests of Imhotep in his long, long centuries out of the House of Life; they would be appalled by this place.

Some while later, as the first winds of the squall buffeted the fortress, Osyth stirred, cried out softly, and came awake. She blinked slowly several times, and started to move, only to be stopped by the pain. "Where am I?" she asked at last.

"In the seaward tower. In my quarters," he answered from his table where he was working. "The door is open. It has been open for the whole time you have been here. You are not disgraced. No one can question your chastity."

"We are alone?" she asked.

"Yes, but we have been observed." He knew she feared compromise as she shrank from the threat of Hell. "You need not worry that any will speak against you."

She nodded as if she were very tired. "My shoulder—"

"Your collar-bone is broken. I've set and bound it. With a little care it will knit well." He came to her side. "When you like I will help you to sit up."

Osyth closed her eyes. "How did this happen?"

Saint-Germanius smiled faintly. "I hoped you would tell me. I found you lying on the floor of the cloth room, the larger loom wrecked and the cloth on it ruined. I do not know how it happened."

She would have Signed herself but could not, so he made the gesture for her. "I do not remember," she admitted after a brief silence, and did her best to recall how she came to be hurt. "I was weaving, at the smaller loom; there was a sound at the door, and then—nothing. I opened my eyes here."

Saint-Germanius did his best to reassure her. "It is often thus when there has been sudden hurt. Wait a day or two and you may recall what happened."

"The White Christ protect me," she said quietly. "I ache."

"Yes," said Saint-Germanius. "And you will for a while. But it will end, given time and care." He came closer, deliberately gentle in his demeanor. "If you like, I will help you to sit up. I will help raise you from behind, so that you do not have to lever yourself with your arms."

She looked drawn at his offer but nodded resolutely. "It is wrong for me to lie here? Yes. Help me sit up."

He made a point of moving slowly, of taking what time was needed to brace her and to reduce the pressure on her upper body. As he propped her up with two rough pillows at her back, she sighed.

"Are you all right?" he asked.

"Your bed is very hard. Like a peasant's bed." She turned her head gingerly in order to look at him. "I thought the likes of you slept on soft beds."

"Some may," said Saint-Germanius, whose thin, straw-filled mattress lay over the few remaining chests of his native earth. "I never developed the taste for it." He waited while she oriented herself. "You need not hurry to move, but when you do, let me know so I can give you help in rising to your feet. Do not try to do it on your own, not yet."

"Not yet," she agreed. She could not conceal the shudder that went through her at the mention of the prospect. "Shortly."

"Whenever you wish," he said in his calm way, and went on in the same quiet tone, "You will need help for the summer while the bone heals. Your children will have to be tended with the help of the other village women. And you will have to deny your husband until the hurt is no longer painful at all."

"He will beat me if I refuse him," she said. "Ruel is a good man, but he is not one to give up such comforts."

"I will tell him," said Saint-Germanius, hoping he could come up with some way to convince the woodcutter that he would be damaging his wife to his later disadvantage if he demanded her body before her bone healed.

"He has a right to me," said Ruel's wife.

"Not just now," Saint-Germanius corrected her. He continued to study her, to look for signs of new pain or other distress. "How are you feeling?"

"Well enough," she said after a moment.

"Has the room stopped spinning? Do you want to stand?" He asked as if he were inquiring about the color of her bliaut or the sort of cattle kept for milk; there was no urgency and little apparent interest.

"Not yet," she answered with more clarity. "Shortly. I am supposed to sit with the Gerefa's wife."

"Not today, and not for a while," Saint-Germanius told her. "When your arm is better."

Osyth looked at him in disbelief. "I must do it. The Gerefa has ordered it."

"I will explain it to her," Saint-Germanius promised. "You will have all you can do to heal. When your shoulder is sound again you may return to your duties."

She stared at him as if he had run mad. "But—"

"You may do less through the summer, or you may do less for the rest of your life," he said firmly. "Better to rest for the summer and be strong before winter; if you do not you could lose the strength in your arm."

For a moment she was again silent. "I am ready to stand now," she announced. "But you must be certain I do not fall."

"Of course." It was not difficult to get her to her feet, and he stood next to her while she mastered the dizziness that came over her. "As soon as you wish I will send for Duart. And Genovefe as well if you need her. Duart can escort you back to your house in the village when you are ready."

She shook her head. "I want to come with you to find him. I have to know if I can walk on my own." She straightened up as best she could, her features very white. "I will be myself shortly."

Privately he doubted that, but he said to her, "Why not save your strength? The way from the fortress to the village is steep. You will need to prepare yourself to walk down it." He took her unharmed hand in his and led her a few steps. "As you can tell, it is a difficult thing to walk without help."

"I can't balance," she complained, gripping his hand tightly.

He brought her to his trestle table and offered his stool. "Sit here and sit with the table at your back. It will hold you up."

She accepted his offer quickly, but again protested when he suggested he leave her to fetch Duart. "I wish to come with you. If I remain here my husband would have reason to complain of me."

"With a broken bone and bruises on your face?" asked Saint-Germanius.

"He could assume many things from it." She lowered her eyes and then stared at him. "If you were not a foreigner . . ."

He understood her meaning: she was under more suspicion because he was not one of the people of the fortress or the village. "We will go to find Duart together. Shortly."

"Yes," she said, and strove to master her weakness; she closed her eyes and her face grew taut. In a bit she said, "It is just that I have been hurt, very just; I will not ask the White Christ for vengeance. What I have suffered I have brought upon myself. I was entrusted with the task of waiting upon the Gerefa's wife and I failed to serve her. My husband and I could be cast out from the village for that, and at a time when madmen are pillaging."

"You will not be cast out," said Saint-Germanius with the intention of easing Osyth's mind. "Ranegonda will not allow it."

"She can do nothing if her brother does not permit it." She sighed. "If Genovefe had been in the cloth room, perhaps—"

Saint-Germanius interrupted her. "You cannot be hampered by what could have happened." He regarded her curiously, and continued. "You tell me you cannot remember what happened; there is no reason to concern yourself with everything that did not happen, as well." His wry half-smile softened his words.

Osyth flushed deeply. "Pentacoste fought me. She was ruining the loom and I tried to stop her." Now that she had said it, she put her hand to her mouth.

"So you do remember," said Saint-Germanius without making his observation an accusation.

"Just now. It came back in a rush. She was furious." Osyth paled. "I have never seen a woman so angry." She made another attempt to Sign herself.

"Perhaps I had better find Genovefe for you," said Saint-Germanius. But Osyth stopped him before he could move. "No. No. The omen is terrible already. Genovefe must not know of it." She was becoming agitated, her eyes moving quickly because her body could not. "If I were of the fortress, it might be different, but Genovefe would not permit me to speak against the Gerefa's wife, not as a village woman."

As irrational as these distinctions seemed to him, Saint-Germanius knew that they had great significance to the people who lived here and they were obligated to live by them. "Very well," he said after a short, thoughtful moment. "But in turn I ask you to tell the Gerefa what you remember. She deserves to know so that the wrong people will not be punished."

Osyth gave this careful consideration. "The Gerefa's wife will not like it."

"While that is unfortunate," said Saint-Germanius dryly, "it was her action that brought your injury about."

It took Osyth longer to answer this time, but at last she said, "Yes, all right. I will tell Gerefa Ranegonda what the Gerefa Giselberht's wife did."

Text of an introduction and safe-conduct dispatch issued to Hrotiger at Verden.

To the distinguished Margerefa Oelrih, resident of Hamburh and commissioner for King Otto, the greetings of Brother Brodicar, scribe to the Dux at Verden on this fourth day of May in the Year of the White Christ 939.

This is being carried by Hrotiger of Rome, bondsman to the Excellent Comites Saint-Germanius, Franzin Ragoczy. The man is of goodly years. His hair is cut in the Roman manner and is a light, dusty color. His eyes are blue and clear. His Germanian is passable, his Latin expert, and he knows Greek and Francian as well. He will identify himself with a phrase from The Story of Roland *which he will speak in Francian. The phrase has special meaning to your House, and you will know him by it.*

His reason for coming into Germania is the desire to visit Leosan

Fortress where he says his master, the Excellent Comites Saint-Germanius, is held for ransom which he wishes to pay. He has sufficient gold with him and other goods as well to satisfy the Gerefa at the fortress.

He describes the Excellent Comites thus: a man of somewhat more than middle height, appearing to be between thirty-five and forty, although he is, in fact, older than that. The Excellent Comites has dark hair that curls loosely, eyes that are of so dark a blue they appear black. The Excellent Comites is badly scarred at the middle of his body from a severe injury in youth.

You are requested to take this bondsman Hrotiger with you when you return to Leosan Fortress. Your men-at-arms will be augmented by the escort this Hrotiger has employed to bring him safely to his master; they will be no expense to you, and will offer compensation for the trouble of feeding them and finding appropriate places to sleep for a larger company.

Any Elder, Prior, Comites, Dux, or other vassal of King Otto is asked to render what aid he can to this Hrotiger, and to impede him in no way. If any should refuse him shelter or attempt to hold him, know that it will be an act of treason against King Otto and treated as such. It is the wish of King Otto that this bondsman be given the respect that is due his master, the Excellent Comites Saint-Germanius, and that his efforts to ransom the Excellent Comites be assisted in any way possible.

By the authority of Dux Giralht of Verden, and fixed with his seal.

Brother Brodicar
scribe to Dux Giralht
(his sign and seal)

12

"Brother Erchboge has again asked me to send you away from here," said Ranegonda with a look of frustration as she and Saint-Germanius rode down from Leosan Fortress side by side.

"For sorcery?" Saint-Germanius asked, doing his best to keep the irritation out of his voice; it was not she who annoyed him.

"Primarily," she answered, and shielded her eyes to look toward the walls of the stockade. "He cares nothing for the honor of the fortress; he claimed that it would be sinful to claim a ransom for you." She shook her head. "It is all Pentacoste's doing, saying that what she did in the cloth room was caused by your spells. Brother Erchboge believes her."

"So do many of the others," said Saint-Germanius as neutrally as he could.

"Because they listen to her. Because they long for excitement." Ranegonda pointed toward the forest. "Do you suppose they will come, those men who killed the outlaws? Do you believe Ormanrih is right to warn us? After all, the woodcutters didn't actually see anyone. They claim they heard men, but it could have been animals, or the men could be monks or other travelers."

The sun had not yet reached midheaven and already the day was growing warm for May; the fields below were at last showing the promise of a bountiful harvest to come, and in the orchard the apple trees were still in blossom. It seemed impossible that anything could disturb the pleasant tranquillity of the place.

"I think it is wise to be cautious, and if the woodcutters say that there are men coming in this direction, you had better be prepared to fight them. If they turn out to be humble travelers, they will welcome the protection you offer." They were just above the village now, where the fortress road turned.

"Yes. It would be best to be ready," she said, convincing herself, then glanced at him. "But if they have only clubs and cudgels, as we have been told, surely the stockade as it is will be proof against them. Why should we brace the walls a second time, and mount a bigger guard as well."

"And if they set fire to the stockade, what then?" Saint-Germanius asked, disliking himself for putting the question to her; he did not want to frighten her, or to give her reason to mistrust him.

She considered what he said. "We will have to keep buckets of water, and what barrels we can spare, to be sure they do not. A pity we haven't enough chain to install an opener on the stockade gate like the one you have made for the fortress." Then she indicated the crops. "The villagers will not like having to give up a day like this to watch their walls."

"They can watch their walls or lose them altogether, and their crops with them," Saint-Germanius warned her.

"Are you so certain of the danger?" They were passing between the first pair of houses now, and half-a-dozen young children shouted merrily at them before returning to their play. "Don't you suppose they will seek other prey?"

"You saw Karagern," Saint-Germanius answered. "What do you think?"

Her grey eyes were earnest as they met his. "The men who did that would stop at nothing."

"So it seems to me," he agreed as they stopped by the main house which served as a meeting place for all the villagers.

Udo and Keredih were waiting for her. They touched their foreheads as she dismounted and did their best not to look at Saint-Germanius at all. "We have gathered fourteen men to guard the stockade," Udo announced with pride.

"You will need more than that," Ranegonda told him. "Call all the men, and the women, too. And send your children to the fortress until the danger is over."

"There is work to be done here," protested Keredih. "The fields and the orchards need our care, and the livestock—"

"It will all wait," said Ranegonda, and started into the village house. "Summon everyone, at once. We must prepare ourselves, and quickly." She motioned to Saint-Germanius to follow her; when Udo Signed himself, she stopped and fixed her clear gaze on him. "Don't do that. You waste the White Christ's good-will when you invoke Him for no good reason."

Udo glared, not quite at Saint-Germanius. "He is a sorcerer."

"He is a foreigner, not a sorcerer. Only a fool would fear him for that, for he is our ally. If he were not here, none of our horses would have shoes, and your carpenters would be without metal bolts, and there would be no points for the lances and spears." She continued her way into the village house, not looking to see if the others were coming behind her.

Outside a loud, unmelodic bell was sounding.

"You did not need to do that," Saint-Germanius said to her softly. "But I thank you for it."

"This is no time to have them doubting you," she said. "It will add to their doubts of me."

"Unfortunately that may be true," said Saint-Germanius, and saw the first of the villagers hurry into the village house. He drew back from Ranegonda so that it would not appear that they were conspiring in any way.

The villagers were troubled at this summons, and many of them asked sharp questions as they took their places on the benches that provided seating for most of them. Ranegonda did not answer any of these but waited until Ormanrih himself arrived and acknowledged her. Then she went to the center of the village house. "Your woodcutters went out at dawn," she said, beginning to pace. "They came back quickly, for a number of them heard the sounds of men in the forest. Your headman reported that to me as soon as he learned of it, and I have come to you with my decision." She nodded toward Ormanrih.

"Your headman has your safety and preservation at heart. Therefore we have agreed that you must send your children to the fortress at once."

"Our children have tasks to do," one woman called out.

"The first one is to live long enough to grow up," Ranegonda countered. "If the village is attacked, they will be the most helpless."

"How can we know that will happen?" demanded another man.

"How can we know that it will not?" Ranegonda answered promptly. "You will have to put extra men on the stockade, day and night. Your work will be less, but the watch is necessary."

"You have men on the ramparts of the fortress. Why do we need men at the stockade when you already have men-at-arms on watch?" asked Nisse. "My pigs need my attention, not the stockade."

"The men-at-arms at the fortress," said Saint-Germanius, moving out of the shadows, "cannot see what is going on next to the stockade. To know that you must have someone directly above, in the little platform towers, looking down. Had the stockade been built further from the edge of the forest it would be possible to guard it from the fortress, but as it is you must do that." He did not stand too near Ranegonda, but he looked at her once, then gave his attention to the villagers. "The stockade was built to protect your fields and your crops and your livestock."

"Have him put a spell on it," shouted one of the villagers near the door.

Saint-Germanius paid no heed to this. "If you lose the fields and the animals and the orchards to these men, you could face starvation, though the fortress protects you. The men-at-arms know that."

Ormanrih came forward, addressing Ranegonda. "There are apprentice-aged boys who could be put on watch," he suggested.

"The oldest of them would be useful, but not the youngest," said Ranegonda. "The guards need sound judgment, and youngsters do not always have it. Guards need to be prudent." She faced Ormanrih. "I would not object if the women of the village kept watch."

Her proposal was met with outrage and shock. "What man would let his wife do such a thing?" cried Jennes. "What sort of husband would he be?"

"You trust the women to guard your children and cook your food," said Ranegonda persuasively. "Why do you not trust them to guard your walls? They would not have to fight, just watch."

"We strengthened the walls already," shouted Kalifranht, fear in his voice. "Isn't that enough? Why do we need more?"

"Possibly the strengthening is sufficient," said Ranegonda. "It may be that the men who killed the outlaws may never come, nor the Danes. We could live here at peace for ten generations. But why take an unnecessary chance?" She was about to explain more when a loud alarm sounded from the fortress, and a moment later from the village.

There was quick-spreading fright among the villagers; many of them hurried out of the village house only to mill at the front of it, no one certain of what to do next.

Ranegonda acted quickly and effectively, striding out and raising her voice in order to be heard over the nervous babble. "If you have weapons, or tools that can be used as weapons, get them, then go to the walls. Women, fill all the buckets and barrels and pots with water and have them ready to put out fires. If the children have not been taken into the fortress, let Burhin's wife take them at once. Now!" Her order was sharp and clear, and most of the villagers obeyed her. Those few who faltered, she rallied. "The village needs your help. Get your weapons. Do you want the stockade to fall?" she demanded.

All but Kalifranht hurried off; the woodcutter sat quivering, leaning against the side of the village house, his eyes set at a distant point only he could see.

Saint-Germanius approached him. "You cannot remain here," he said gently to the terrified man. "If there is to be fighting, you could be hurt." At Kalifranht's quiet, desperate cry, he said, "Go to the cutting shed. Busy yourself sharpening the blades of your axes. The other men will have use for them." He bent down and helped Kalifranht get to his feet; the woodcutter moved slowly, as if he were an invalid, unlike the rest of the villagers who rushed to their tasks.

Ranegonda had already mounted her horse and started down the road toward the gate. She was shouting to the men of the village, pointing to places on the wall where they would have to fight. She did not wait to see if anyone obeyed her, but kept moving, assigning the men as they hurried out with axes and mallets and cudgels. Some she ordered to bring ladders, pointing out where they should be placed.

From his post on the ramparts above the fortress gates, where he had been watching this sudden out-break of activity, Captain Amalric turned to Geraint. "Mount two dozen men. Now."

"That's most of our men," said Geraint.

"Get them," Captain Amalric said briskly. "I want the first dozen in the field as quickly as possible, the second dozen behind them."

Geraint hesitated. "We have not yet seen—"

"That's why we are going," he declared. "Sound the horn and get the men moving. Tell the slaves to start saddling while the men arm." As Geraint hastened to carry out these instructions Captain Amalric swung around, shouting for Culfre. "Come here! Take my place. I leave you in charge." He was about to descend the narrow stairs when he asked, "Who is guarding the fire? Severic or Kynr?"

"Kynr," answered Culfre.

"I'll need him," he decided aloud. "I'll put Duart to the task," he announced. "See that he is relieved by mid-afternoon if we have not yet come back. Have Severic take charge of the second troop."

Culfre looked baffled. "But why? There cannot be much danger."

"We don't know that yet; we don't know who we are fighting, or how many of them there are," shouted Captain Amalric, and bolted down the stairs, watching as his men came running in answer to the blasts on the wooden horn.

"The children from the village are being brought up the road," said Brother Erchboge as Captain Amalric hurried around the bulk of the landward tower.

"Good. Put the wives to caring for them." He shouted to the slaves to open the gates wide. "And keep them open until we are back or until the village is destroyed and the enemy is advancing up the hill."

Brother Erchboge listened to this in horror, Signing himself for protection. "It is impossible," he said. "The gates must be closed as soon as you and your men leave."

Captain Amalric stopped and turned back toward the monk. "And how are we to retreat if the gates are closed? And who will defend you if we are outside?" He came directly up to Brother Erchboge without deference. "Close those gates and you make dead men of us."

"But—"

"And if you say that the White Christ demands sacrifices like His sacrifice, I will forget the habit you wear and order you onto a horse with the rest of the men, in case we need your prayers," said Captain Amalric decisively. "Remember, the Gerefa is in the village, not in the fortress."

Brother Erchboge was prepared to continue the dispute, but Captain Amalric shoved past him, yelling to Rupoerht and Osbern to don their heaums and broignes and bring swords and lances. He crossed the Marshaling Court quickly and entered the stable as the slaves who served as grooms were leading out the horses for the fight. "Heavy breastcollars for all of them, if we have enough," he shouted, then pulled the youngest of the slaves aside and said, "Go to my quarters and fetch my heaum and broigne. And my cuisses. I don't want my shins broken." The slave headed off at once, leaving Captain Amalric to go to the armory to bring out the new weapons Saint-Germanius had made for the fortress.

Four of the horses were saddled and bridled by the time the last of the children entered the fortress. Several of them were crying and many sought the comfort of the first friendly woman they saw.

Geraint was the first to be fully armed, and as he buckled his spurs on, he grumbled, "I gave your orders to Severic. He will begin mounting his men as soon as you have left with yours." He ran his finger along his forehead where the heaum rested. "I wish they had chosen a cooler day for this."

"I wish they had not come here at all," said Captain Amalric, hitching his thumb in the direction of the village. "Listen to that. They're trying to beat down the stockade." He indicated the headstrong bay in the Marshaling Court. "You take that one. I want the roan."

"Well enough," said Geraint, who liked high-mettled horses.

"Where is Berengar? And Pentacoste, for that matter?" Captain Amalric demanded, looking over his shoulder as if he expected to see them approaching.

"In the common hall, I think. Berengar was playing the kithre there a while ago," said Geraint. "The women were listening until the horn sounded."

Captain Amalric sighed. "A pity he is not a fighter." He saw Ewarht and Ulfrid hurrying up; Ewarht was buckling his scabbard onto his belt. "One of you tell the slaves to make sure the bathhouse is heated. The other find Duart and be certain he knows he is to guard the light. Get back here as fast as you can. We must be out of here quickly."

The two men rushed off on their assignments.

"It's getting worse," said Geraint after a moment of listening. "How many of them are there?"

"Too many," said Captain Amalric. "That's why we're going down to help." He hefted his lance and slung it into the sheath hanging on the right side of his saddle; the roan whickered in excitement.

Kynr arrived next, and Walderih came after with Chlodwic. "Reginharht is almost ready," Chlodwic said, pulling on his studded leather gauntels.

"I don't like those," Captain Amalric remarked as he prepared to mount. "I don't like anything that impedes my hands."

"Better than getting knuckles smashed," said Chlodwic, looking at the horses. "Which one should I take?"

"The spotted one," said Captain Amalric. "And you, Walderih, take the light bay. Kynr can have the chestnut. Get mounted." He was more restive than his mount. "They need help in the village." He rode to the gate, shouting up to Culfre, "What do you see?"

"Trouble," answered his deputy. "The Gerefa is on the west side of the wall. There's something wrong."

"A breakthrough?" Captain Amalric asked; in the Marshaling Court another three men-at-arms had arrived, and Geraint was urging them on, saying something to Osbern as he came up, his heaum still in his hands.

"Not yet. There's another bad spot to the east of the gate." He shaded his eyes. "Ten, eleven villagers are there, some on ladders."

Captain Amalric bellowed toward the men in the Marshaling Court, "Hurry! On single line! Now!" He waited long enough for eight of the men to fall in behind him, and then he started through the gates, trusting that the rest of his men-at-arms would follow. "When we reach level ground!" he yelled over his shoulder. "The first half of you, go to the Gerefa. The other half, come with me. Severic and the rest will be along shortly."

Above them on the ramparts Culfre cheered.

Ranegonda's horse was sweating, trying to pull away from the section of the wall the attackers had set afire. She had drawn her sword and was holding it at the ready as she chided the villagers who faltered at the sight of the burning stockade. "They can't come through the fire any more than you can. Be ready and let none of them in."

Beside her Saint-Germanius held his horse facing the flames, an ax in his left hand; Kalifranht had given it to him in an attempt to make up for his cowardice. He pointed to the fortress. "Your men are coming," he said to Ranegonda.

She glanced away from the fire and was pleased at what she saw from the fortress. "Good. We need them." Then she rallied the villagers again, riding up to them and wheeling her horse as she wanted them to wheel. "Each of you prepare yourselves. You know what these creatures can do. It is up to you to join with my men to stop them."

From the other side of the stockade there came a sudden cry of dismay, and suddenly a huge section of the stockade wall collapsed inward, carrying one of the watchtowers with it, pinning five of the villagers beneath it and smashing part of the field planted in grain.

The men who surged in over the log wall were gaunt and frenzied, dressed in rags and animal skins. They were already swinging their clubs and striking at any defender they could reach. They made almost no noise, no shouting or cries, and if one of them fell none of his companions stopped to aid him.

"Wolves and Ravens!" Ranegonda exclaimed. "How many of them are there?"

Saint-Germanius's dark eyes were grim. "Sixty or more," he said, certain that the count was higher.

Udo Signed himself as he saw the first of the invading men rush forward. "What are they?" he asked in terrified awe.

"Madmen. They have the madness," Burhin declared, and turned away in horror. "Kalifranht is right. They are monsters."

"All the more reason to stop them," Ranegonda commanded, and spurred toward the attackers.

Saint-Germanius was with her, hefting the ax he carried. "By the look of them, there is no leader," he warned her.

"Then we must stop them all," she answered grimly, and gave a wolfish smile as she saw Captain Amalric and five of his men galloping toward her.

The villagers fell back as the men-at-arms surged in, ready to join the battle.

More of the attackers crowded through the break in the walls, their clubs at the ready, swinging at the horses' legs as the soldiers drew near, trampling the fields as they came.

"Keep back!" Saint-Germanius warned Ranegonda sharply. "If your horse goes down—"

She nodded to show she heard, and swung her sword at the nearest of the men, then shouted to the villagers, "Be ready!"

A few of the village men had fled, but most stood their ground, holding their tools ready to strike. Jennes had a long pruning hook in his hands, and thrust with it as if with a spear. Not far from him, Glevic held his stripping saw, the toothed blade toward the advancing men.

From the other side of the stockade where the fire was burning, a hideous shout went up as twenty of the invaders forced their way through the charred opening. Ewarht led the second group of soldiers toward them at the trot.

The silent, dire men were as inexorable as the tide, pushing into the fields relentlessly; as they bludgeoned their way forward they began to chant, "Bremen! Bremen! Bremen! Bremen!" as the villagers began to fall back, leaving the men-at-arms exposed to the assault of the clubs.

Two horses were down almost at once, legs shattered, and then skulls crushed by the attackers' clubs. Ulfrid escaped, leaping from the saddle before his mount could fall, but Osbern was not so fortunate; he was battered, screaming, to death.

Ranegonda saw this out of the corner of her eye and it horrified her. She started toward the attackers who were still drubbing Osbern's corpse, and felt her horse dragged back by a firm hand on the reins.

"It's useless, Gerefa," Saint-Germanius said with rough kindness. "There will be worse today, and you must get through it."

She stared at him, angry at first and then determined. "Yes. Oh, yes. I will exact wergeld from their bodies. Every one of them I can reach."

"Not at the cost of your own men, or yourself," he warned her, having seen that fighting rapture too many times; he recognized blood-lust in others from the capacity within himself, and it sickened him even in the midst of battle. "Master yourself, Ranegonda. Do not let the battle rule you."

For an instant she opposed him, and then something in her grey eyes changed and she gestured assent. "They need help, by the other wall."

He followed her, protecting her back.

At the burning section of stockade the ground was already growing soggy with blood. More than a dozen of the attackers had fallen, some still living but most of them dead. Eight of the villagers were down; Saint-Germanius recognized Nisse among them. More men were coming through the wall, but this was surely the last of them, for these men were maimed from other battles, unwanted at the front of the force.

A blast on the wooden horn announced that the second troop of men-at-arms had left the fortress.

The numbers of the attackers were sufficient to overwhelm many of the villagers, and some of them broke away, rushing toward their houses in the hope that they would be safe.

"Craven!" one of the men-at-arms cried, and was echoed by a few others who jeered more angrily.

The villagers continued to bolt.

"You must fight!" Ranegonda shouted after them, swinging her sword and spotting her horse with the blood of the man she had killed.

Beside her, Saint-Germanius called to her, "Fall back! Reform your lines. You can't hold them like this!"

She rounded on him. "They are killing my men!"

"And they will kill more of them if you don't reform your lines, where they can hold!" He turned suddenly in the saddle and swung his ax back-handed, the flat of the head striking one of the invading men in the center of his chest; he went down at once. "Ranegonda!"

The last of the invaders stopped at the bodies found and began to hack them apart with butchers' cleavers.

"All right," she decided. "Back. And all the men-at-arms will stand together."

From the ramparts Culfre watched with horror as the tremendous host of invaders continued their steady advance, leaving their dead behind them with the broken bodies of villagers and men-at-arms alike.

"What are they doing?" demanded Brother Erchboge, who had climbed up beside Culfre and was staring at the battle in consternation. "They must stand! Stand!"

"They can't, not in the field, not against so many," said Culfre as the men-at-arms fell back to the edge of the buildings, forming a line facing the enemy. "They need Severic and his men."

"But it is dishonorable to turn!" Brother Erchboge insisted. "For the White Christ they must not be made to turn."

"Look what happened to Osbern and Rupoerht," said Culfre, pointing in turn to the two fallen men-at-arms. "And Chlodwic is unhorsed." He was about to order the monk to return to his chapel when he saw two more figures climbing the stairs to the parapets, and realized they were Berengar and Pentacoste.

The chanting men fanned out and moved steadily across the fields, only the men in the rear slowing to hack at the bodies of the defenders.

Ranegonda was at the center of her men-at-arms, feeling more restless and more exhausted than she could remember having been at any time in her life. Immediately behind her Severic had drawn his dozen men up in a line, weapons at the ready. Her arm ached from the weight of the sword and her eyes were burning. She sensed the others were as strained as she, but more trained for it. Sitting erect in the saddle, she ordered her men to hold their position. "Let them come to you. Be ready to take them," she said hoarsely. She looked to her left where Captain Amalric was, and to her right, where Saint-Germanius waited, and thought that if she had to face death, she could not do it in better company.

A few of the villagers stood with them, keeping their weapons poised to strike. Others had begun the work of barricading their houses and carrying what they could of their food up the hill into the fortress; the women had left the village when the walls were broken and were gathered inside the stone walls.

The invaders at the rear were gathering a pile of heads they had struck off; it was not very large but its intent was clear: the men intended it as their victory monument.

"It is going badly, isn't it?" Berengar said as he surveyed the fields.

Culfre bit back a sharp answer. "It isn't going well."

"What are they going to do?" Pentacoste whispered to Culfre, leaning close to the parapet. "You're a soldier. You know."

Culfre would not let himself look away from the village below. "Fight," he answered.

Pentacoste nodded and ran her tongue over her lips.

"Hold steady," Ranegonda told her soldiers quietly. "When they get here, fight. Fight hard."

The men-at-arms heard her and gathered themselves for the fight; the steady chanting of the invaders was irksome, but they had not yet reached the stage of fighting when it was intolerable.

"Not yet, not yet," Ranegonda warned them as a strange and unexpected calm came over her. "Let them get too close to break and run."

But four of Severic's men, eager to be at the invaders, jolted forward from the line and plunged their horses into the midst of the advancing men. In an instant they were surrounded and their mounts chopped out from under them.

Shocked, Ranegonda could do nothing for a moment, and then shouted, "Forward! Surround them! Get around them! Now!"

More than a dozen of the attacking men were busy with killing the over-hasty soldiers, but those who were not battling the soldiers gathered into an ominous circle, facing the men-at-arms, a living stockade.

The men-at-arms went forward, no longer skirmishing, and the battle began in earnest, the invaders going toward the men-at-arms in that steady, irresistible way that made them the more frightening.

"Get around them!" Ranegonda yelled again, spurring her horse to hurry around the men, before they were so scattered through the village that there was no hope of so small a force as hers containing them; the ring around them was almost complete when the invaders rushed forward, using the clubs on the horses.

"Back! Get back!" shouted Severic, and the men-at-arms strove to move them out of range, but not all of them could escape the furious blows the fanatical men rained on them. Another four went down, their horses screaming and kicking futilely, and then a fifth; the enemy was on them at once, their clubs rising and falling steadily, lethally.

"Look," whispered Pentacoste as she leaned as far over the parapet as she could. "Look."

Culfre was hardly able to breathe, so great was his horror as he watched the battle erupt. He stared in disbelief as the defenders fell, transfixed by the disaster. He was not aware he had Signed himself, or that he had spoken a prayer to the old gods to protect and honor the men of Leosan Fortress.

Now the invaders were at the village houses, and some of them began to drub the doors while others sought out the pens and the storage sheds, seizing any food or livestock they found.

"Are they drawing back?" asked Pentacoste after a short while. "Why should they do that?"

"They . . . they have to," muttered Culfre, and finally shook off the numbness that held him. "If they don't they'll all be killed." It was an unbearable admission, and he spoke it as if he expected his mouth to burn.

"Could they do that?" Pentacoste asked, her voice strangely soft. Before Culfre could bring himself to answer, she moved away from the parapet and shouted down to the slaves, "Close the gates!"

Brother Erchboge, who was standing a short distance away, goggled at this. "Hohdama! What are you saying!"

The winch groaned and clanked as the slaves hastened to obey.

Culfre turned, filled with shock. "You must not do that," he protested.

"Close them!" Pentacoste insisted, and then faced Culfre. "You said yourself they could get killed. That means we could get killed as well. We must close the gates." She glanced toward Brother Erchboge. "Do you want all of us to be martyrs to your White Christ? Close the gates."

"You can't," Culfre said. "Hohdama, those men will die. The Gerefa will die."

"Better to lose them than all of us as well," said Pentacoste, and added, "They are supposed to guard us with their lives, aren't they? Close the gates."

"I cannot permit you to—" Culfre began.

"You cannot forbid me to give orders. I am the wife of the Gerefa and my father is Dux Pol. Defy me and I will have you thrown over the wall." Rarely had Pentacoste felt such intoxicating power, and so great a reward. She turned to watch the gates swing shut. "Now, bolt them!" she told the slaves. "If anyone but me tells you to open them, refuse, or you will die."

Culfre stared at her in stupefaction, so appalled that he could find no way to express the enormity of what he felt. He backed away from her, then turned on his heel and left her where she stood, Berengar watching her from a short distance away, his face rapt.

The fighting had become chaos, every man-at-arms battling on his own, surrounded by the invading, chanting men. The combat churned between the houses and through the orchard, it scoured the fields of their promised bounty and brought ruin to the buildings.

Somewhere during the confusion Saint-Germanius was separated from Ranegonda. At first he was too busy protecting himself and his mount to look for her, and then he saw her, holding the approach to the fortress with Geraint at her side. He kicked his horse to a bucking canter, clearing his way with broad sweeps of his ax, calling her name as he rode toward her.

Then his horse staggered, half-reared, and fell, with Saint-Germanius still on his back. Around him the invaders converged, their clubs raised. For one hideous instant Saint-Germanius longed for the true death those blows would surely bring. And then he dragged himself from under his horse and caught the nearest of the enemy, swinging him up with such force that the man rose as if he were a little child; a moment later he fell among his companions, flailing and shouting. As he landed, Saint-Germanius hefted a second invader into the air.

Nine of the invaders had been tossed among their own number before Saint-Germanius was able to get clear of them enough to make himself run, weaponless, to aid Ranegonda; his speed was a gift of his blood, and he moved more swiftly than most wolves could run. As he reached her side, she grinned at him. "I was afraid I lost you."

"Not yet," he responded, and swung the thatching hook he had seized on the way into the side of the nearest invader.

"I have a short sword," offered Geraint, indicating the scabbard on his back.

Saint-Germanius nodded. "If I need it."

Ranegonda pointed suddenly to the middle of the destruction of the fields: there was Captain Amalric with five men, and they were gathering for a charge. "He might have a chance this time," she said, and thrust out at another attacker.

"Where are the rest of the fortress's men?" asked Saint-Germanius, and grabbed another man, lifting him and then slamming him into his fellows' ranks.

"I don't know," said Ranegonda in a strangely emotionless tone. "The gates are closed."

"What?" Saint-Germanius was revolted; fueled by his abhorrence of what had been done to them, he cast himself forward among the attackers, and seizing one, used him to hammer at the others, holding them off with the ferocity of his resistance and their dread of anyone who could perform such feats. He could feel his extraordinary strength begin to ebb, and he shoved his human maul into those who were still coming for them. He held out his hand for the short sword and Geraint slapped the hilt into his palm.

The attackers were massed below them, and now they widened their attack, forcing the three defenders to move apart.

"Captain Amalric!" shouted Ranegonda. "Can you see him? Is he still—"

"He's coming," Geraint cried out a moment before a club caught him on the side of the head just above his ear; he fell soundlessly, dead before he dropped.

Now there were just the two of them on the approach to the fortress, and both of them were tired. Ranegonda gave Saint-Germanius one quick gesture of triumph, then struck again at the men who faced her. Saint-Germanius dragged a club from one of the fallen men's hands, and wielding the sword with his left and the club with his right, he stood and fought single-mindedly until one of the cudgels bludgeoned him on the side of the leg. His knee buckled. The next blow, aimed for his head, caught his shoulder, and in the next instant he fell from the roadway leading to the fortress and rolled down the long slope to the place behind the slaughterhouse. Dazed, he lay there while he tried to bring himself to his feet. He could not lie here, he told himself. Ranegonda needed his help.

The fighting above him became more intense and he strove to rise. He heard horses and the incoherent howl of battle; when he finally got to his feet he saw only a tangle of men and horses on the approach.

As he tried to make his way up the incline he lost his footing; this time when he fell he could not force himself to his feet for some while; a gash had opened along his thigh and the combination of pain and weakness was too much for him to overcome. A coldness went through him, and he persuaded himself that it was exhaustion and the end of the heat of battle. He sat down and methodically tore at his chanise, making strips to bind his wound closed. He tried not to think of what could happen to Ranegonda and he could think of nothing else.

Then, without warning, the attackers broke and ran, just a few at first, and then in larger numbers, until every one of their number who could flee was gone.

Bloodied and filthy, Saint-Germanius made his way toward the destruction of the village, where he collapsed. Ewarht found him a short while later, himself nursing a swollen arm.

"They're gone," he said when Saint-Germanius opened his eyes. "I saw what you did. We could not have driven them off without you."

At another time this unexpected praise might have pleased him, but now Saint-Germanius had only one thing he wanted. "Ranegonda. The Gerefa?"

Ewarht averted his eyes; he Signed himself with his injured arm and told Saint-Germanius what he already knew. "No."

Text of an official letter to Pentacoste from her father, Dux Pol of Luitich, carried by escorted messenger to Hamburh and given to Margerefa Oelrih for delivery.

To the wife of the monk-Gerefa Giselberht of Leosan Fortress and Holy cross Monastery in Saxony, this greeting on the 9th day of May in the Year of Grace 939.

It is through your machinations that my honor is impugned. I have been informed by Pranz Balduin of Goslar that you have made his son Berengar your waiting-man, to court you although you are still a wife, and to serve you although you are not permitted such a protector.

Because of what you have done, my House is compromised, and Pranz Balduin is wholly within his rights to demand that I charge you to release his son. As my last command as your father, I tell you to turn that young man away from you and to conduct yourself as it is proper for a wife to do. If you fail to do this, I will instruct your monk-husband to turn you off from him as I, with this letter, turn you off from me.

You are no longer my daughter. You are entitled to nothing that is mine but my curse, and your name is to be stricken from the records of this House. If your husband will have you still, that is his concern. If he will not protect you, I charge no one to care for you and I will do nothing to provide that care. Any who open their doors to you will do so without the hope of reward from me or any of mine. Any child of your body will have no claim upon me and no place in my House.

King Otto and Pranz Balduin will receive copies of this letter, with my request that they honor what I have done. They will not take you as wife or concubine and will allow none of theirs to take you as wife or concubine. They will grant you no charity.

The Church of the White Christ may receive you as a penitent, if you appeal to the Sisters. But if you go there you will not enter the world again, although you will be safe from calumny in the cloister. No Order has agreed to refuse you, but if you seek advancement through piety, you will discover that your way is blocked. If you become a nun, a nun you will remain to the end of your days, and nothing more.

Make your way in the world however you can, Hohdama, but do not come here, or I will treat you as the traitor you are and chain you in a cell for the rest of your days.

Dux Pol
by the hand of Brother Luprician

13

Most of Captain Amalric's wounds had begun to heal, although there was still an angry red welt across his forehead where one of the invaders' clubs had grazed his heaum. "Brother Olafr has come from the monastery." He stood in the middle of Saint-Germanius's quarters, looking around at the chests and sacks. "You are still determined to leave with Margerefa Oelrih."

"Yes," said Saint-Germanius; he had almost left a week ago, the day after the battle: only the wound in his thigh prevented it, and as the gash healed he had reconsidered. Now the deep cut was nothing more than a faint, raspberry-colored line on his skin, as if the injury were years instead of days old. He was lying back supine atop the fur blankets on his bed, his neat, dark linen bliaut over a saffron-colored chanise and black leather braies looking more appropriate for Berengar than the foreigner he was; he regarded Captain Amalric without raising his head. "When he leaves, I will go with him."

Captain Amalric sighed, shifting his weight into his hip. "I know the people of the village and the fortress are not . . . grateful for what you did, not while you've lived here, and not during the battle. But some of us know what we owe you. Some of us do not want to lose you." He looked over at Saint-Germanius with embarrassment. "And we've lost so much."

"Ranegonda," said Saint-Germanius with a world of unspoken grief in her name.

"And Osbern, and Rupoerht, and Walderih, and Kynr. And Geraint. And the others. In the village they lost seventeen men and women. Seventeen." He Signed himself out of respect for the dead. "Ten houses destroyed, the stockade useless, and not enough woodcutters to rebuild it by winter."

"They lost most of the crops, as well," said Saint-Germanius with little apparent concern.

"Yes," said Captain Amalric slowly. "If the Danes come now, we will be at their mercy."

"You could hold them off. Gather in the fortress and . . ." He found it difficult to say the words aloud. "Close the gates."

"I hope it will not come to that. I hope we will have a chance to recover from the fight. Once we have crops growing things will be better." Captain Amalric cocked his head to the side. "It will be difficult without a smith."

"The Margerefa will arrange for you to have one," said Saint-Germanius.

Captain Amalric tried another tack. "All but two of my injured men are recovering well, their wounds healing. The two that are not, well, there was not much hope for them, in any case. Severic will have to live with his blindness, and as for the smashed knee, no one could—" He stared at Saint-Germanius. "You treated the wounds. If you had not been here, five or six more of my men would be dead or dying by now."

"Winolda can treat them as well as I can from this point, given what's available," said Saint-Germanius, and sat up, his mourning, enigmatic eyes on his visitor's. "There was one thing that kept me here, Captain, and she is gone."

Captain Amalric clapped his big hands together. "But it is for her, don't you see? There are things we need urgently, and if she were here—"

Saint-Germanius's look stilled the plea in the Captain's throat. After a short silence, Saint-Germanius said, "All right. While I remain here, I will do what she would expect of me."

Again Captain Amalric was somewhat relieved. "Good," he said. "Yes."

Before the Captain could launch into a new petition, Saint-Germanius forestalled him. "Is all the news bad, or is there some good?"

"Oh, there is good," said Captain Amalric. "None of the children were hurt, but a boy who skinned his knee. The attackers carried off only two of the goats and none of the pigs. If Nisse were alive, he would be happy to know that." He cleared his throat. "The hives you built were untouched, so there is honey, and half the apple trees can be saved. Four dozen cheeses are left in the village, and most of the ducks have come back. And Brother Olafr says that the monks will share what they have with us if we will lend them people to work their fields. They haven't enough monks left who are strong enough for the tasks; the miasma sapped their strength too much." He lowered his eyes and his voice. "Brother Olafr also says that Brother Giselberht was buried under the altar in their church. He says that Brother Giselberht had visions at the end that foresaw all that happened here."

"Ah." Saint-Germanius achieved a faint, ironic smile as he stood up, his leg aching distantly with the effort. "Brother Giselberht. You know, in a century or so they will forget that there was tainted rye here, and that madness came, and they will remember only that he had visions, and they will call him a saint, and they will make the monastery a shrine to his holiness." He saw disbelief in Captain Amalric's face. "I surmise you think not."

"Brother Giselberht took the madness. He died of rot," said Captain Amalric. "He was no saint."

Saint-Germanius shook his head very slightly once. "They'll forget that in a hundred years. They will not want to know it. They might remember he had been ill, but they will think he prayed for relief from his suffering and the White Christ granted him visions instead."

"No one could believe that," said Captain Amalric.

"No?" Saint-Germanius left his question unanswered. He crossed the room to the narrow window and looked out over the sparkling May afternoon. "How long, do you think, until the Margerefa arrives?"

"Five, ten days," said Captain Amalric. "If our messenger reaches him, perhaps a day or so earlier."

There was another brief silence between them. "And Pentacoste? What about Pentacoste."

Captain Amalric frowned and pulled at his lower lip. "That is more difficult. She is the daughter of a Dux, and if he forbids any punishment, there is nothing the Margerefa can order without the approval of the King, and the King could decide . . . oh, anything, or nothing." He swallowed hard. "She is being kept in her apartment and the women's quarters, with two women to guard her night and day. She is not permitted to go anywhere outside the landward tower, not even to the Common Hall. And she is not permitted to see or speak with Berengar."

This last surprised Saint-Germanius and he turned to Captain Amalric. "How is that."

Now Captain Amalric looked embarrassed. "It is difficult," he said. "But you see, Brother Erchboge has set himself the task of breaking the hold Pentacoste has on Berengar. He prays with Berengar, and exhorts him to confess. Berengar can go nowhere without the monk."

"Has he had any success?" asked Saint-Germanius with slight amusement.

"Not yet. But he glories in opposition." He rocked back on his heels. "So Pentacoste cannot spin or weave, and she is kept confined."

Saint-Germanius considered this. "Perhaps," he said, remembering the fruitless search Ranegonda had made for the secret way out of the fortress. He ran his small hand through his hair. "What more?"

Captain Amalric pursed his mouth, then looked away from Saint-Germanius. "You're right. There is another . . . problem. Berengar is saying that Pentacoste did not give the order to close the gates. He claims that Culfre did it. He has told everyone that Culfre became frightened and thought the battle was lost, so he ordered the gates closed. He says that the order came after Ranegonda fell, and that Pentacoste went along with him."

Saint-Germanius could not speak for a short while. "Ranegonda was alive when the gates closed. I saw it. Anyone watching from above would have seen her clearly; she was alive then." It was astonishing how much pain the mention of her name could bring him, how it stilled his body and voice.

"That is what I've told anyone who asks me. I saw her, though I did not see the gates close until after it was done. You're right. Ranegonda was alive afterward: closing the gate was treasonous. But you know how it is: people hear a thing they want to hear, and they believe it. It is easier to believe that Culfre panicked than that Pentacoste deliberately betrayed the fortress." He opened his hands and stared down at them as if he expected something to materialize in them. "I cannot change that. And some would rather execute Culfre than accuse Pentacoste."

"Berengar most of all, it seems," said Saint-Germanius, holding himself very straight.

Captain Amalric shrugged. "He is devoted to her. He cannot say what she has done, not and maintain his devotion."

"Certainly not," said Saint-Germanius after an instant's thought, so gently it was impossible for Captain Amalric to tell if he was being sarcastic. "What will become of Culfre if Berengar's version of the event prevails?"

"Culfre?" Captain Amalric was suddenly extremely uncomfortable. "Well, if it is decided that he countermanded the Gerefa's order, and that was done while the Gerefa was alive, he would be castrated and broken on the wheel. If it is decided that the Gerefa died because of what he did, he would be sawn apart by ropes. It is a . . . a slow death."

"Yes," said Saint-Germanius, then turned to face Captain Amalric. "I will say when the gates were closed, if that will help Culfre."

Captain Amalric shook his head several times. "I don't know," he confessed. "You are a foreigner, and the Margerefa might not let you speak, not against someone like Berengar."

"Because he is the son of Pranz Balduin," Saint-Germanius added for him. "I understand."

"But Culfre did nothing wrong. Once she gave the order, he was powerless against her. He could not oppose Pentacoste, not while Berengar was with her." He paced nervously, saying, "If he had tried to stop her, she would have ordered him killed on the spot. And it would have been done, especially with Berengar to support her. If Culfre had tried to stop her it would have made no difference, the gates would have closed. But . . . She had no right to give the order; if the Margerefa decides that she lacked the authority no matter who her father is or what Berengar said, then she will answer for the Gerefa's death and the loss of half of our men."

"And what would they do to her, if she is guilty?" Saint-Germanius asked as if inquiring about events that happened long ago.

"As a Dux's daughter she cannot be executed except by the order of her father. But she can be confined. There are dungeons, they say, where traitors are left to die, dungeons deep in the earth where no light falls and no door opens. The dungeon is like a bottle in the ground, and—"

"I know what such dungeons are like," Saint-Germanius said, cutting him short as memories of the centuries he had spent in the Babylonian oubliette filled him with profound self-loathing; the priests had called him a demon then, and had provided him victims at every full moon to appease him. In time he had come to despise the terror he fed on, and to yearn for the ephemeral durability of intimacy to end his unutterable loneliness.

"What is it?" asked Captain Amalric.

Saint-Germanius made a gesture of dismissal. "A thing from my past. It is over."

"Then may the White Christ be thanked for that. Your eyes were like charred sockets." He Signed himself and looked at Saint-Germanius with new respect and caution.

Saint-Germanius did his best to smile. "Tomorrow. I will be able to work tomorrow. Let me know what you need me to forge for you. I will go to the smithy, if the people of the fortress won't object. Have the children gather up any metal they can find where the fighting was." He had not been able to save Ranegonda; her body had been bludgeoned and pulled so badly that she had had to be buried in pieces. But she had given her life, and the life he offered her, to preserve this place, and for that he owed the fortress more than he had given it.

"Those who will object know to keep silent," said Captain Amalric in a tone that promised he would tend to the problem before it could arise.

Saint-Germanius nodded his acknowledgment. "She deserved better of me," he said, more to himself than the Captain.

Captain Amalric scoffed. "She had more of you than anyone. And without shame. Not many men would grant any woman so much." He touched his forehead, and was surprised when Saint-Germanius responded with a proper Byzantine reverence. "What was that for?" He waited, but Saint-Germanius gave him no answer.

As the Captain was about to leave the room, Saint-Germanius asked, "Who will be Gerefa here next? You?"

"I doubt it," said Captain Amalric without rancor. "I'm as common-born as any soldier. They don't make Gerefas of the likes of me, not when the King has cousins seeking advancement."

"That's unfortunate," said Saint-Germanius sincerely. "The fortress could not do better than you to protect it."

Over the next several days the damaged parts of the stockade were pulled down and new logs set in place. Those houses in the village which had been wrecked or damaged received their first repairs. Nine of the villagers and their wives followed Brother Olafr back to Holy Cross Monastery to work their fields. Gradually the usual rhythms of life were resumed, tentatively at first but with growing sureness as each day passed.

On the sixth day the precarious normality of fortress life was upset when Osyth came running from the landward tower shortly after dawn, screaming that Pentacoste was missing. She gave Genovefe and Captain Amalric a distraught account of going to the women's quarters in the landward tower where Pentacoste had retired late the night before to pray and meditate—or so she had assured Juste and Winolda, who tended her in the evening—and now was not there, or anywhere else in the landward tower that any of the women could discover.

"Search for her," ordered Captain Amalric. "Look everywhere in the tower, including the women's quarters and the Gerefa's rooms. Have the women out, and let the men-at-arms search."

Enolda objected as soon as she heard this. "It is not fitting for men to go to the women's quarters. The search must be made by women."

"Women have already searched," Captain Amalric pointed out with exaggerated patience. "And Pentacoste has not been found."

At the edge of the excited gathering, Saint-Germanius said, "Let me do it. I am a foreigner and I am leaving."

There was silence at his offer, and then Captain Amalric decided. "Yes. That will do it. And a woman will accompany you." He looked around to see if anyone would protest.

"It is irregular," said Delwin, doing his best to be more grown-up than he was.

"That it is, but what else can we do." He motioned to Enolda. "Have the women remove anything that men should not see, or look through. Hurry."

Enolda and four other women worked quickly, and in a short while Saint-Germanius and Osyth began their search of the women's quarters on the level above the muniment room.

"There is nothing in either room, nothing. The walls are stone," said Osyth after making a second careful circuit of them; her shoulder was paining her this morning and her temper was short. "She could not leave this place. There is no door, no stairs, no corridor. Perhaps she found a way to make her spells work without spinning and weaving."

"Perhaps," said Saint-Germanius as he inspected the irregularities in the walls. "But first I would rather exhaust simpler explanations." He went behind the screen in the smaller of the two rooms, ignoring the shocked warning from Osyth. A line of stones projected from the wall here, one of them more prominent than the rest. Saint-Germanius pushed and pressed each of them in turn, and was not surprised when a narrow section of the wall swung down making a bridge into a tunnel. He stood looking into the darkness, his features expressionless. "Tell Captain Amalric the passage has been found," he said softly.

Osyth hurried to his side, staring at the opening. "The White Christ preserve us!" she exclaimed, and Signed herself.

By afternoon both ends of the secret passage had been sealed, and Captain Amalric put his hands on his hips in satisfaction. "Of course, she won't be able to get back in with this closed." His chuckle was rich. "Then she'll have to come to the stockade gate like any traveler on the road, not being strong enough to knock down the new sections of the wall."

"And when do you think that will be?" Saint-Germanius asked him.

"Certainly before sunset. With those men still wandering, she would be a fool to remain outside." He hitched his thumb in the direction of the cove. "She won't find much protection there, not with the old gods."

"No, she won't," Saint-Germanius agreed.

But Pentacoste did not return that evening, nor the next day, nor the day after, and Berengar had gone from fretting to despair. He accosted Captain Amalric at the edge of the Marshaling Court to air his grievances.

"We must search for her. The madmen are still in the forest, killing. The man-at-arms in the light room said that there have been Danish ships at sea. They may have taken her." He Signed himself; he was Signing himself frequently now. "She is at their mercy."

"If the Danes have her, they will have to appeal to her father for ransom," said Captain Amalric with a gesture of resignation. "With Brother Giselberht in his grave they can obtain none here." He looked away from the distressed young man. "If the madmen got her, she will be dead by now, hanging from a branch if she was lucky."

Brother Erchboge, who had been listening with ill-disguised righteousness, Signed himself and whispered a prayer for the missing Pentacoste.

"I should have insisted she marry me," said Berengar, his emotion revealed in his taut features. "As soon as word came that Brother Giselberht was dead, I should have married her."

"Well, you didn't," said Captain Amalric, who was growing tired of this, for it had become Berengar's litany. "So you will have to deal with her father, if the Danes have her."

"But think what they will do to her!" exclaimed Berengar, flapping his arms in horror and dismay. "You know what they do to the women they take."

"They make them slaves and whores if they are not ransomed," said Captain Amalric, and signaled to Culfre, who was inspecting tack, looking for battle-inflicted damage; it was one of the few duties he could be assigned until the Margerefa Oelrih decided his fate. "How many of the saddles are usable?"

He answered promptly. "Ten so far, but most need new stirrup leathers."

"That's easily managed," said Captain Amalric, paying no attention to Berengar's outburst.

"She has to be saved," Berengar interrupted passionately. "She is suffering, and we must answer for it."

Captain Amalric swung around and faced Berengar. "Thanks to your beloved, our Gerefa was killed, and some of our men died who did not have to, because she ordered the gate closed—"

"That was Culfr—" Berengar began, only to be cut short.

"You and I know that is not true." Now that he had started, Captain Amalric could not contain the indignation he had pent up within him. "Pentacoste ordered the slaves to close the gates. Our men-at-arms within the fortress could not get out to help, and those fighting in the village could not retreat; those who died after the gates were closed were needlessly lost. Needlessly. And all because of the Gerefa's widow." He regarded Berengar with a look of pity and contempt. "And you stood there, you let her do it, because you could not say no to her, not even in that. What man permits a woman to make a poppet of him? She might as well have left you for an offering at that cove of hers."

Berengar was white with rage and something less defined. "You cannot say that to me."

"Because you are Pranz Balduin's son," Captain Amalric stated. "So be it."

Brother Erchboge laid his hand on Berengar's shoulder. "Come away from here, and pray. Pray for her salvation, and the salvation of all men."

As Berengar went off with the monk, Captain Amalric looked back at Culfre with a sheepish half-smile. "I probably should not have said those things."

"He is angry," said Culfre. "Deeply angry."

Berengar was still angry the next day when the wooden horn sounded from the parapet to announce an arrival.

"It is the Margerefa!" shouted Faxon from the post over the gates. "He has a large escort with him."

"Now something will be done!" bellowed Berengar as he came from the chapel, Brother Erchboge at his heels. "We'll see about these lies and deceptions."

By the time the gates clanked open, most of the people of the fortress had gathered to greet him, a few of them kneeling in gratitude as he dismounted and handed his reins to the waiting slave.

"There has been a fight here, I see," Margerefa Oelrih observed instead of going through the forms of greeting. "When was it?"

"Nine days since," said Captain Amalric. "There were seventy or eighty men, all bearing clubs." He hesitated. "The Gerefa is among the dead."

Margerefa Oelrih looked surprised. "Giselberht?"

"Ranegonda," said Captain Amalric. "There are others, as well."

"You will have to tell me the whole of it—a full and accurate account, mind. But after we have some beer or mead. It has been a long ride." He motioned to the others with him. "We would not have been here for another day or two, but the Roman kept urging us to travel."

"Roman?" asked one of the women.

Toward the rear of the Margerefa's company there were eight men in Francian armor surrounding a well-dressed, sandy-haired, blue-eyed, middle-aged man on a lanky dark-brown horse, leading five pack mules. "That Roman. His name is—"

"Hrotiger," said Saint-Germanius from the back of the crowd.

At the sound of that voice, Hrotiger turned, and in a single motion swung out of the saddle and went down on his knee. "My master," he said in Saxon Germanian, though his accent was even stranger than Saint-Germanius's.

The people of the fortress fell back as Saint-Germanius advanced, a few of them staring at him as if they had never seen him before.

Saint-Germanius touched Hrotiger's shoulder as signal for him to rise, and asked in Persian, "Aren't you being a . . . trifle extreme with this deference?" and added in Germanian, "It is good to see you, old friend."

Hrotiger answered first in Persian, "Having seen how these people treat foreigners, I don't think so." Then he added, again in Germanian, "I rejoice to have found you at last."

"And not an hour too soon," said Saint-Germanius as sudden desolation swept through him.

"From the look of the village I should have got here sooner," said Hrotiger as he rose to his feet.

Saint-Germanius shook his head, unable to speak of what happened where so many could hear. "Was it a long journey?"

"We came as quickly as we could," Hrotiger answered, and did his best not to notice the people who crowded around him. "This is May eighteenth. I left Rome in March, on the seventeenth."

"You made good time," said Saint-Germanius, and added with a quick half-smile, "You were determined." He put his hand on Hrotiger's shoulder again. "Thank you." Then he turned and went toward Margerefa Oelrih, giving him a Byzantine reverence. "If there is anything you need to know from me, I am at your disposal. I want to tell you about . . . the things that happened."

The Margerefa watched him, his manner critical, measuring. "Good." He narrowed his eyes, inspecting Saint-Germanius as if this was the first time he had seen him. "That bondsman of yours says you are an important man in Rome."

"For a foreigner," said Saint-Germanius honestly and sardonically.

"Certainly a wealthy man, if your bondsman is any indication." He nodded toward Hrotiger, who was better-dressed than anyone at the fortress, including the hollow-eyed Berengar.

"Yes. I am wealthy." His tone was carefully neutral as he gave the Margerefa a bow. "I will not keep you from your refreshment; do you excuse me? I would like to speak privately with my bondsman."

Brother Erchboge tugged at Berengar's sleeve, whispering, "There will be a better time, when the foreigner is out of the way. The Margerefa will listen to you then; now he will not."

"He has to listen," said Berengar in quiet certainty.

As if they had been given a signal, the people of the fortress began to speak loudly and to drift toward the Common Hall, a few of them making a clumsy escort for Margerefa Oelrih and his company. Captain Amalric was careful not to behave as if he were Gerefa, but did what he could to be certain that the Margerefa was properly received.

Hrotiger turned to the armed men who accompanied him. "Go with them. Have your meal. You can see to the horses after the slaves have tended them."

Saint-Germanius pointed to the seaward tower. "There." As he and Hrotiger went toward it, he added, "You brought the ransom with you?"

"That and more." He indicated the pack mules. "There are ninety gold coins in the sack, Angels and Crowns. From what the Margerefa says, you could purchase this entire fortress and village for that amount."

Saint-Germanius gestured his approval. "Have you had to pay many bribes?"

"A few, and once I had to give a donation to the monastery or be refused the right to use their bridge." Hrotiger glanced around, then said, "It isn't Rome."

"Rome is hardly Rome any longer," said Saint-Germanius as he led Hrotiger into the seaward tower. "It is not the way we knew it before."

"Sadly," Hrotiger agreed. He entered Saint-Germanius's quarters with an expression of misgiving. At last he said, "Well, you have lived in worse places."

"So I think, too," said Saint-Germanius, and sat on the stool at his trestle table. "I will arrange for you to have a bed here tonight."

"Only tonight? It was my understanding that the Margerefa plans to be here for several days." Hrotiger took care with his next observation. "Only that Captain seems to be in charge."

"He is," was Saint-Germanius's terse answer.

"Your letter said there was a Gerefa." Hrotiger watched Saint-Germanius, sensing the loss within him.

Saint-Germanius nodded, and longed for his lost capacity for weeping. "Ranegonda. The Gerefa? was killed."

"In the battle?" asked Hrotiger.

Again Saint-Germanius nodded. "I tried to prevent it. I tried to protect her. It was not enough." He rose from his stool and faced toward the narrow window and the sea. "There is nothing here for me now."

Eventually, Hrotiger knew, he would learn much more. Now he recognized the anguish in Saint-Germanius's eyes and was content to do the tasks set for him. "Tomorrow, then, we leave, if the Margerefa will consent to let us." He started toward the door. "I will bring your chests, and the other things you need."

"You are a wise man, Rogerian," said Saint-Germanius in the Latin of Imperial Rome. "I am more grateful for that than you know."

Hrotiger bowed and withdrew.

By midmorning the following day only the athanor and the trestle table remained in Saint-Germanius's quarters; the rest had already been moved to other rooms or was packed and loaded on the mules. Saint-Germanius stood in the stone chamber, a large jar in his hands. He felt restored by the new lining of his native earth in his soles. He looked very splendid now, and more foreign in his talaris tunica of black silk edged with tablions of silver in his device of the eclipse. Black goat-leather bamberges protected his legs and thick-soled brodequins shod him. On his left hand he wore a silver signet ring with his eclipse sigil incised on it. In Rome, where this finery was fashionable, he would still attract notice; in Saxony he was someone to gawk at.

Captain Amalric came to the open door and hesitated, awed by what he saw. Finally he touched his forehead and said, "Thank you for telling your part in the battle to the Margerefa. After what Berengar said, I thought it would be impossible to convince the Margerefa what—"

Saint-Germanius turned and looked at him. "I was honored to do it," he said with great sincerity.

"For the Gerefa." Captain Amalric could not take his eyes off this imposing figure, for although they were of the same height Saint-Germanius had a presence about him that the Captain had never experienced before.

"For Ranegonda," said Saint-Germanius.

The Captain stared at the leather bag in his hands. "Culfre will be grateful to you all of his days."

"There is no cause. I told the truth, no more." He put the jar on the table. "And this is given in her name." He looked back at Captain Amalric. "It is for open wounds. You do not need much of it. If you put it on open wounds, they will heal more quickly and take less pus. When the lungs are rotten, drink a little of it in mead and if the rot has not taken hold the lungs will clear."

"Is that what you made here?" asked Captain Amalric. "In that hive-shaped oven?"

"This is a better preparation, but they are similar." He stared at the jar for a short while. "It will last you for some time if it is used judiciously."

"In the name of the Gerefa," added Captain Amalric.

Saint-Germanius gave a short sigh. "Yes."

There was a strained silence between them, and then Captain Amalric lifted the leather bag he carried. "Osyth brought this to me." He unfastened the thongs but did not open it. "She . . . she found it while she and Genovefe were . . . were preparing the Gerefa . . . were preparing to bury her." He thrust the bag forward. "Here."

Puzzled, Saint-Germanius took the bag. "What is it?"

"It is yours," said Captain Amalric.

While Captain Amalric watched, Saint-Germanius opened the bag and drew out the silver pectoral set with a large black sapphire; one of the raised wings on the pectoral had been bent and it was still discolored with blood. The chain was broken, the links smashed. Saint-Germanius stared down at it, feeling as if a huge, icy wind blew through him. Carefully he returned the pectoral to the leather pouch, and only then did he look directly at Captain Amalric. "Thank you," he said, his voice barely above a whisper.

Captain Amalric lowered his eyes. "It is yours," he repeated.

Saint-Germanius did not speak; he took the leather bag and slipped it inside his talaris tunica. He could feel the pectoral as if it were hot, as if it were alive; in some strange way it assuaged his grief.

"Do not forget her," said Captain Amalric softly.

"No." Saint-Germanius would never forget, could not forget until the true death itself.

As he rode out from Leosan Fortress that morning with Hrotiger and his armed escort, of all that he carried with him Saint-Germanius treasured most this last token of Ranegonda.

Excerpt of a report from Margerefa Oelrih to King Otto, written by Brother Andoche. Carried by escorted messenger to King Otto at Ratisbon in seventeen days, on the 24th of August, 939.

. . . In regard to matters at Leosan Fortress, my King, it is my duty to tell you that the men who were cast out from Bremen have been there and brought much damage and suffering to the village and the fortress. It will be necessary to provide more men to work the land and the forest as well as send men-at-arms for the fortress if the fortress is to be the bastion you wish it to be. Before the end of the year they will need to be supplied food, as well, for the Bremen men, in their fighting, ruined the crops growing in the fields.

I would recommend two measures be taken at once in order to insure the safety of the fortress and the village. First, generous allocations of food should be provided at once, including barrels of salt pork and goat, along with flour, dried peas, and cheeses. That will do much to end the fears of these people, who are haunted by the spectre of starvation every time they look at their fields. If such foodstuffs are provided, I am certain that the work carried on by the people of the village and the fortress would increase, which will not only benefit these people and their settlement but the work you have mandated as well, my King.

Second, I would double the number of men-at-arms at this fortress. Given the number they have, they have done very well, but they have no one to spare, and should there be an injury or an illness their protection diminishes sharply. With more men-at-arms there is every reason to believe that they will not have to endure another such battle as the one against the men of Hamburh, that took the life of their Gerefa as well as many of the villagers and men-at-arms.

In regard to the Gerefa, she fell most valiantly in battle, and were it not for the actions of her sister-in-law, might have lived. Ranegonda led her forces well, according to Captain Amalric, who has served as her deputy here since her death. I have spoken to other men who were in the fight with her, and they have nothing but praise for her. The foreigner, the Excellent Comites Saint-Germanius, has written his account of the battle, much of which he fought at her side, and it is included in this dispatch. The men-at-arms who were on guard have confirmed most of what he said.

This brings me to a more difficult matter. There is an account of the battle from Berengar, son of Pranz Balduin, which differs markedly from what the others have said. He, too, observed the battle from the parapets, and he insists that the Gerefa fell some time before her soldiers say she did. It may be that he did not understand what he watched, for he is no soldier. But if he is correct, then there is a very difficult matter to solve, for he declares that the Gerefa was down when Pentacoste, the wife of the monk-Gerefa Giselberht, ordered that the gates be closed. At first he maintained that one of the men-at-arms gave the order, but later, when all the others denied this, he admitted that he might be mistaken.

If it is true that Pentacoste ordered the gates closed while the Gerefa was alive, she is a traitor to the fortress and subject to the fate of traitors. If the Gerefa had already fallen, then she may have had authority to give the order, but that is yet to be determined. If you conclude that the soldiers were right in their reports it will be necessary for me to send word of Pentacoste's treason to her father. I will need your decision on this point before I return to the fortress in order to put the record of it in the muniment room.

I must also inform you, my King, that Pentacoste herself is missing and that a demand for her ransom from the Danes has come. Had her father not disowned her I would, of course, deliver that demand to him. But as I was carrying his writ when I went to the fortress, there can be no possibility of appealing to him, so I must address you instead. The demand is for thirty gold pieces, which is a high price for a widow. But if you will not authorize the payment, she will remain the slave of the Danes and they will certainly make a whore of her.

Berengar, son of Pranz Balduin, has sworn that he will pay the ransom and then marry her, no matter what has been done to her. But the monk at the fortress, Brother Erchboge, has already declared that she is now an adulteress and upon her return must be drowned, for although her husband was a monk and died before she left the fortress, she did not know she was a widow when she went and therefore must be held accountable for the sin she supposes she committed. Again, I must ask you to make a decision and inform me of what you wish to be done before I return to Leosan Fortress in October.

The Excellent Comites Saint-Germanius, upon his departure, left a ransom of fifty gold pieces, a sum in excess of what was asked for him, and which he stated was for the cost of his maintenance while he was at the fortress. This money is currently in the muniment room of Leosan Fortress and will remain there as part of the fortress treasury unless you, my King, should require it. This brings the funds of the fortress to seventy-two gold pieces and ninety-eight silver pieces, which would pay for an extension of the fortifications to include part of the village without making a demand upon your purse. The work would require more stonemasons than are currently at the fortress, there being only one at this time. If you, my King, will authorize it, I will hire the stonemasons myself and take them with me on my next visit so that they may commence their work before the autumn storms come.

At the request of the monks of Holy Cross Monastery, the fortress's nearest neighbor, the villagers who have lost their crops are tending the fields for the monks, who have yet to recover from the madness and rotting that came over them. While this is worthy, it cannot long continue if Leosan Fortress is to thrive. Therefore I suggest that the Pope be asked to grant an enlargement of the monastery so that new monks may come to do the tasks that are now undertaken by villagers. The villagers will not be able to remain away from their own fields for very long without compromising their position more than they have already. It would be wrong to ask them to sacrifice more, no matter how much the monks say their souls will be improved.

In regard to the rebuilding of Oeldenburh, it is my duty to report to you, my King, that many of the houses are still in disrepair and it is not likely that they will be fit to live in before winter. The walls are also breached in many places, leaving the whole of the city open to any determined foe with weapons and a company of men. This is the fault of the Obodrites and

*Wagrians who have yet to submit to Saxon rule and continue to resist all
your efforts in their regions. I have no doubt that these people have aided
the unfortunate outcasts from Bremen who have so ravaged Saxony, and
will continue to do so until constrained to stop . . .*

14

Dellingr's hearth was crowded as his men gathered in the long room for
their evening meal, the first one in their own village since they went on
their raid to the south at the end of winter. Although it was now late
spring and turning warm, most of the Danes were dressed in fur garments, their untrimmed beards and unkempt hair making them look to
Pentacoste like animals instead of men. She decided that they acted like
animals as well, or the lowest foreign peasants, swilling down mead and
biting their food from knives instead of eating from trenchers with their
fingers and spoons; she expected better of fighting men. As she watched,
they drank mead from cups made of the skulls of their conquered foes
and boasted of the pillaging they had wrecked on the countryside that
was now in the hands of the Saxons—and that had been theirs until a
generation ago, and which they continued to regard as theirs.

"Do not listen to them," whispered one of the other new slaves, a
former potter from Bremen called Halvor; he had come to her side
while carrying a barrel of mead for the Danes. "They are liars, all of
them."

Pentacoste tossed her head and favored the man with a disdainful
look. "You are a foolish creature. How can you hope to best them if
you will not listen? Besides, most of them are half-drunk, in any case."
She smoothed the front of her bliaut, hating the stains that marred it,
and silently cursing the rents in the sleeves and the smuts on her
chanise. Yet she was determined to make her best appearance, as
befitted her heritage and her current position of relative favor, for
among the newly captured slaves, she alone was kept apart from the
others and treated with a modicum of respect, in anticipation of the
ransom she would fetch. She alone had not been regularly beaten. And
among the few women captured, she had not been raped.

"You are the one who is being foolish; you will need our help soon,"
Halvor said to her, and moved away before anyone noticed they had
been talking, for such contacts between slaves were forbidden, and the

punishment for defying the rule was severe. "Now that we are at the village, things will change. For all of us."

"That they will." Pentacoste moved out of her partial enclosure, shaking the straw from her clothes and doing her best to straighten her hair. She had asked for a comb several times but none had been given to her. Now, with a gesture of impatience, she took up her place near the corner where she would be fed when the Danes were finished with their meal; when she had first been captured she had not deigned to eat the leavings of these rough men, but now she waited for her portion of their scraps as eagerly as any of the slaves. This evening, as always, she was annoyed that the Danes would not speak Francian or Saxon Germanian, but insisted on conversing in their own guttural tongue, of which she could understand little.

Dellingr was laughing loudly now, his head thrown back and his eyes squinted almost closed. "What a time it was!"

The rest of the men roared their approval, and a few of them began to sing. Pentacoste believed that the song was worse than the howling of wolves, and she clapped her hands over her ears, wanting it to be over. She hated these Danes with an intensity that made her loathing of Giselberht and the White Christ seem insignificant. From the afternoon they had found her in the forest until this moment, she had been subjected to such humiliation that she could not recall any of it without chagrin. What made it worse was that the Danes expected her to be grateful to them for not doing more terrible things to her. It would please her to see each one of these men flayed and hanging from hooks over her father's gates. She did not like the men from Bremen who were captured with her much better than she liked the Danes, for they had become savage with living in the woods and raiding outposts and other places as they had attacked Leosan Fortress.

She was also coming to disapprove of Berengar, for surely he should have found her by now, and ransomed her, for all his avowals of passion; he was as feckless as all men, she supposed, and her contempt for him justified because of it. The Margerefa Oelrih was also lax in his responsibilities for not coming to her rescue, for he was an official of King Otto, with an obligation to protect his vassals; he claimed to have affection for her, but that was demonstrably untrue. Her father could not be expected to stir himself, but he could authorize men-at-arms to find her and bring her back to Saxony or Lorraria, although she had no wish to live in his household again. She rehearsed her many injuries at the hands of these men, relishing the vengeance she would have of them when she returned. Then she thought of the dark, scathing eyes of the foreigner, and she had to keep from cursing him aloud. If only he had taken her when she was prepared to accept him. But no, he had to stir her jealousy by his pretense with Ranegonda! How could he dare to treat her as if she were nothing more than a common trull, selling her flesh in the market-square? She glared at the backs of the Danes as they got down to the rambunctious business of eating, her wrath intended for them and for Saint-Germanius. What was it about these wild men that was so lost to conduct that they would treat her in this way? How could they not recognize her quality? And how could Saint-Germanius refuse her, when she had at last offered what she knew beyond any question he so clearly longed to have? He was worse than the Danes, for they knew no better, while he had the airs of one who has been at court, and claimed high position for himself. No doubt he was boasting, making more of himself than he was, much the same way these Danes were boasting about their exploits on their raids; how foolish of the others at the fortress to be taken in by his foreign accent and strange ways when anyone could see he was a charlatan.

Two of the slaves staggered toward the long plank tables, carrying a roasted boar slung on a pole between them. They hoisted this with some difficulty to the surface of the table and all but dropped it onto the bed of flat loaves that waited for it. The Danes roared their approval, waiting while Dellingr cut the first three slabs of meat for himself.

"Have at him," shouted Dellingr, reaching for one of the breads as he went back to his place at the head of the long table as his men surged forward, each determined to slice a portion for himself that was better than his fellows'. Their jostling was fairly amiable because there was more than enough to go around; had there not been, real contests would have been fought over the meal.

Pentacoste sat very still as she watched the melee that ensued. How disgusting they were, these great, hairy men with their big knives and roistering ways. She had long been offended by the manner of males, and never more than now, when the men who kept her treated her with less regard than they had for a good mare. She would not tolerate such degradation, even from marauding Danes. One day they would all pay for what she had been forced to endure here, she promised herself as she had done every hour she had spent in Danish hands. She would have recompense for her many indignities.

As the Danes settled back to devour their boar, Dellingr signaled for a harper to come toward the hearth and sing. "We haven't had any great stories but what we made up, not since we left, and most of them were lies," he said to the harper, chuckling with his men. "You are one of those we have missed; you and your harp and your stirring lays. You will tell us the adventures of heroes, Osred, so we may judge our own."

The harper was a man of middle-years and his voice was rough with over-use; he walked as if he were unsure of his footing until he reached his place by the hearth, where he twanged his seven-stringed instrument and began to recount the story of one of the heroes of the past, a red-caped scoundrel who kidnapped the children of a Christian Bishop and sold them to the Islamites, after carrying the children from the Baltic to the Black Sea and having a number of adventurous escapades on the way, all of which enriched him and made him the adored lover of beautiful women. Many of the verses were greeted with whoops and lewd gestures by the Danes, who appeared to know the tale well, for they fell silent as the harper played, listening attentively to the verses.

It was a repulsive myth to Pentacoste, for it made the Francians and Germanians appear foolish and venal, armored knights who were paid to kill peasants and burn keeps; she listened with growing ire as the harper sang the catalogue of adventures, his fingers moving restlessly over the strings, finding the mode of his song in their voices. For Pentacoste, she felt her sense of insult growing as he continued to play, recounting the desire his hero inspired in the breast of the Queen of the Greeks, a woman who claimed never to have known the caress of a man before the Danish hero arrived. As the Danes howled their approval and suggestions to the harper for the sake of his hero, Pentacoste plotted her revenge on these hideous men and their brutish pleasures.

The harper finally completed the story, and stood while the Danes bellowed their applause at him. Only then did Pentacoste realize the man was blind, and his skill at singing his sole means of making his way in the world, which served to increase her contempt for him. She watched him as he felt his way toward the large table, holding his harp very high in his left hand so that it would come to no harm. He took the place he was guided to and drank a long draught of mead.

"We will want another ballad," warned Dellingr, his high color revealing the quantity of food and drink he had consumed. "But take rest and feed yourself, good Osred. Fortify yourself for your next performance."

The Danes laughed and drank to Osred, who responded in kind, though with a certain prudent reserve which he claimed, when he was pressed to have more mead, was necessary if he were to remember all the words of his next tale. He was allowed to remain sober for that reason, and no other.

"Sing us a tale about willful women," Dellingr ordered a bit later when the harper had finished his meal; he had eaten hungrily and quickly, as if he feared the food would be snatched away from him. "Any woman will do, so long as her beauty matches her obstinance."

He glanced toward the corner where he knew Pentacoste waited, and nodded decisively. "Sing of how, through her willfulness, she came to grief."

Osred caught the hard intent in the humorous order, and bowed gravely. "If that will please you, then I will do it," he vowed.

"When supper is over," said Dellingr with a gesture to show he did not expect Osred to give up food to entertain them.

So the men continued their boasting, which grew more outrageous as the evening wore on; more dishes were brought, including a fish stew with fragrant herbs that made Pentacoste's mouth water. Toward the end of the meal a second barrel of mead was called for as Osred took his place near the fire once again and began to play, telling the story of a faithless woman who killed her bastard children and betrayed her noble lover for spite; when he was dead and her crimes discovered, she was charged for her cruelty and sentence was passed against her: her lips and breasts were cut off and her tongue slit so that she could never again work her heinous spells on men.

Around the table the Danes yelled approval for the judgment as Osred repeated the last stanzas of the song, his sightless eyes turned in the direction of Dellingr, who had requested such a story to amuse these men.

Pentacoste understood enough of the song to be furious. It was tempting to rail at the Danes, upbraiding them for their lack of proper reverence for high-born females of great power, but she knew it was useless, and imprudent. There would be time enough for that when she was ransomed and free of them. In the meantime, she decided she would give them a taste of her skill; she found several long straw stalks and began to knot them together, reciting certain conjurations as she did, calling upon the old gods to bring the Danes to a bitter and well-deserved end.

The fire had burned down to sullen embers by the time the Danes reeled out of the long house and made their ways to their own dwellings, some of them leaning on one another to keep from falling, others making their way from log building to log building, using the upright log walls for support. Only Dellingr was left behind, and as he signaled his slaves to come scavenge their meals from the remains of the feast, he approached Pentacoste, bowing a little toward her as his eyes grew large. "Come here. Sit. I have saved meat and stew for you, Hohdama," he said, in acceptable Germanian.

It would have been vastly satisfying to throw the food in his face to show how repellent he and his offer were, but Pentacoste was famished, and could not bring herself to do it. With her head high, she looked directly at him as if he were one of the lowest slaves in the compound. "It would compromise your ransom if I starve, would it not?"

He laughed, and Pentacoste realized that he was not so drunk as his men had been, which alarmed her; he would not be so sleepy as she hoped. "The ransom had better be more than your wergeld, to pay for all you have eaten and the trouble you have caused us, Hohdama." His use of her title seemed offensive to Pentacoste and she stiffened at the sound of it; Dellingr paid no notice to her umbrage and indicated a place near his chair at the end of the table. "Be seated and eat."

"From your plate?" she asked, affronted that he should suggest such a courtesy when he was nothing more than a Dane. Yet she sat and picked up the flat bread, now soggy with meat juices. It horrified her to find it delicious.

"You've gotten too thin," complained Dellingr, watching her eat with an intensity that troubled Pentacoste. "You're as lean as those men from Bremen. It will not please your husband or your father to find you in such a state." He straddled the bench beside her and stared at her profile as she did her best to continue to eat. "You miss your husband, I'd warrant."

"As would any wife," she responded between tiny bites of bread.

"There are things a woman needs when she has no husband by her." His eyes were fever-bright. "You are too much a woman, for all your temper, to live long without a man to . . . attend to you."

There was a thickness in his voice which she recognized with well-disguised scorn: the old gods had moved to assist her, and now this Dane was in her thrall. She turned her head to look at him. "How could any good woman seek the attendance of any man but her husband?"

Dellingr laughed. "Do you never feel heat in your womb, and the softness of your bones that—"

"How dare you speak of such things to me!" she cried out, and only a small portion of her indignation was false.

"You are my captive," he reminded her firmly, his courtly manner vanishing. "It is well you remember it. If we did not want ransom for you, I would have taken you the first night after we found you, and my men would have had you after that. But you are Hohdama, and you are worth gold for your return. That promise protects you. As long as you want it to protect you."

The food, which a moment ago had tasted fit for the gods, now had all the savor of dust. Pentacoste swallowed hard, wondering if her spell had been a bit too compelling. "If you defile me there will be no ransom; instead, you will owe my husband wergeld," she reminded

Dellingr, making an effort to keep from trembling. "And my father, as well."

"Let them come and fetch it, if they want it," said Dellingr. "They might thank me for teaching you to conduct yourself more properly. You are a difficult woman who has never been brought to obedience." He laughed again, the humor gone from the sound of it. "Tell me, what do you miss about your husband?"

Pentacoste bit back a scathing answer; if Dellingr knew Giselberht was now a monk of the White Christ he might decide it was useless to wait for a ransom. What would happen to her then filled her with dread. "He is my husband," she said. "What I miss is between him and me."

"Truly," said Dellingr, his implication lascivious; his smile ended as his tongue slid over his lips. "And you need not fear the loss of what is between you. If you would like to have it."

"I have no wish to drown," she said, her voice cold. "Nothing you can offer would save me from drowning. If you were to take me, drowning would be my punishment, whether or not my ransom was paid."

"A foolish waste of a woman," said Dellingr. "A good beating would suffice." He put his hand on her shoulder, reinforcing his threat. "If you said nothing about it, how could anyone know what you have done with me?"

Pentacoste deliberately moved the plate aside. "If I had a child, there could be no doubt."

"Say it is your husband's get. How would anyone know otherwise?" Dellingr challenged. "Or have one of the old women give you a potion to be rid of it before it fills your belly." His hand tightened and he leaned closer to her; she felt his hot breath on her cheek. "Don't you know that there are many other women who have done this thing? You are Hohdama, and surely you have learned of ways to be rid of such unwanted burdens."

Pentacoste shuddered, more from the weight of his hand than from his suggestion, though she pretended it was the latter and not the former which inspired her spasm. "And if the ransom does not come this summer? You would have to keep me until the next spring. Nothing would save me. And what if I have to carry a child through the winter? What then?"

"We will leave it in the forest when it is born," said Dellingr, and went on more forcefully. "Do not waste my time with these foolish disputes. You will not be allowed to oppose me here in my own house.

I have borne with your airs long enough; there will be an end to them. With or without your consent, I will have you, Hohdama. Now that I am with my people, I will make you my woman. You had best resign yourself. It is my right to have you."

"Not a married woman," she said, trying to pull away from him, without success.

"If you are still a married woman," Dellingr remarked lightly. "You escaped a battle, or so you claimed. Your husband might have fallen in that battle. You could be a widow. And that would mean only your father would have claim on you. Who knows if he is living still?" He moved his hand down her side. "Eat. Women were not meant to be sticks."

She chewed, working her jaw so that he could see it clearly. Her hands picked at the meat, tearing it into ever-smaller bits before she would put any more of it in her mouth. Perhaps, she told herself, he would feel the spell tonight, and by morning he would be as devoted to her as Berengar had claimed to be. Not that she wanted such a suitor as Dellingr, but the spell would bind him to her, and that would serve her purpose until the ransom arrived. There would be time to demand retribution when her father had paid for her release.

Dellingr touched her hair with his other hand, trying to loosen the long braid down her back. "How does a woman like you manage to cause such men as your husband to pay for her return? Why can he want you back, when you must treat him as haughtily as you do me? What sort of man is he, who would let his wife command him? Surely he will know you have been used by me, if not by my men. What lies will he be persuaded to believe?"

"I am the daughter of Dux Pol of Lorraria. My husband is Gerefa of Leosan Fortress," she said stiffly. "They know my worth."

"Your worth?" he jeered. "What is that? Are you made of precious stones or do you carry your husband's child, that you have worth beyond what any woman has?"

Her jaw lifted. "You are too ignorant to recognize—"

Dellingr stroked her braid. "I know a woman has the worth of her children and the value her husband has for her. How many children do you have, Hohdama? Living children?"

Her color heightened; she disguised her shock with an attack. "So that you can abduct them, and hold them for ransom, as well?"

He regarded her narrowly. "Remember where you are."

"In the country of the Danes," she shot back, making it an accusation. "Where I have been brought by despicable rogues who live like dogs, in kennels." She knew that Leosan Fortress was not much better a place than this Danish village, but she measured the place against her father's castle in Lorraria, and found the Danes wanting. "The ransom you demand is not going to come soon enough for me."

"You should be softer, and more compliant," said Dellingr. "It is not right that a woman should hold herself aloof from men." The hand that had caressed her side had moved; he covered her breast and sank his fingers into her flesh, smiling as she recoiled from the hurt he gave her. He pinched her nipple through the fabric. "Not much to hold onto."

Pentacoste was on her feet, hardly aware of getting there. "You will not speak to me this way! You will not touch me!"

Dellingr reached up and tugged hard on her arm, pulling her back down onto the bench, holding her there with iron determination. "I will speak to you in any way it suits me. I will use you as I wish in my own house. While I hold you, I will have you. You will listen and be grateful I do not knock out your teeth for defying me. Now, eat!" He grabbed his plate and shoved it toward her. "And drink."

She lashed out at the skull-cup in a single, hard movement. Her knuckles struck hard, and the cup rocked on its claw-footed base. "No!" In the next instant she had spilled the mead over herself; she shrieked in outrage as she lurched back against the bench, nearly falling.

"Be still!" Dellingr seized her around the waist, pressing his face against her breasts as she struggled in his grasp. "I will have you."

"No!" Pentacoste grappled for the cup, and raised it to smash it on Dellingr's head, but he anticipated her attack, and swiftly reached to stop her. His hand closed on her arm relentlessly as she made a futile attempt to get away. Her free hand flailed, found purchase against his beard, and she shoved as hard as she could, driving him back to the length of her arm. She felt more than heard the fabric of her bliaut tear, and she screamed at the affront, wrenching desperately in his grasp and stumbling back as he lost his grip on her body, though her bliaut remained fixed in his grip.

Aghast, Pentacoste pulled away from the ripped bliaut, standing in her chanise, her arms crossed protectively over her torso. She was about to scream her fury at this indignity when Dellingr surged across the space between them and fell upon her with all his weight, toppling them both to the floor.

The other slaves in the room took their food and moved aside, studiously avoiding giving the struggling figures any attention.

Pentacoste gasped as Dellingr landed on her; she could not get enough air into her lungs, and the only sound that came from her was a strangled mew as she strove to breathe.

Dellingr paid no heed to her suffering as he wrestled with their clothes. He kept his arm pressing on the base of her throat to keep her silent and still. He tugged at her chanise, and at last it tore from her neck to the hem. Quickly he bared her body and pushed onto his knees; he unfastened his belt, letting his braies slide to his ankles. Then he was on her again, her wrists secured in one hand as he pried her legs open with the other. She was not ready for him; he had to ram into her dryness four times before he reached full penetration. He cursed her with each thrust, pounding her with all his weight, slamming against her, making his invasion of her as much of a punishment as he could.

The only consolation she could find was that the whole unspeakable event was over quickly. He jerked, convulsed, and spilled into her, then collapsed on her, panting and exhausted, sweat gleaming on his forehead. He lay full length on her, recovering his breath and letting her bear the whole of him. As he levered himself off her, to kneel straddling her, he struck her hard in the face twice. "That's for resisting," he told her. "And to rid you of any burden of your husband's."

Pentacoste spat at him, and was struck again for her impudence.

Getting to his feet, Dellingr pulled his braies up and fastened them to his belt. Once it was secure, he kicked her. "You will not refuse me again." He left her lying where she was and went to retrieve his cup. When he had drained it, he came back to her side. "If you fight me again, I will break your legs."

"You are—" She could not find a word damning enough for what she thought him to be.

"You are mine, Hohdama," declared Dellingr, moving away from her. "Whenever I want to have you, you will comply, and with more willingness than this time, or you will regret it." He folded his arms and glared down at her. "Get out of my sight."

"You will forfeit my ransom if you touch me again." She had rolled onto her side and had drawn her knees up against her chest. She would not let him see her weep. "I will denounce you."

"When the ransom comes, you may make conditions. Until then, as long as you are in this village, you will do as I tell you." He picked up her bliaut where it had fallen. "This is ruined."

"Because of you," she said bluntly. In spite of her best intentions tears ran down her face.

He laughed unpleasantly. "You will have to earn more clothes if you are not to go naked."

This was too much for her to endure. She pushed herself into a crouch and glared up at him. "You would not!"

"Oh, but I would," said Dellingr, taking delight in her impotent wrath. "If you please me, I will give you clothes. If you do not, you will have none." He saw by the shock in her face that he had found her weakness. "Our women are fine weavers. You could be wrapped in new wool tomorrow, if you will comply tonight."

Pentacoste wanted to find his ax and sever his head from his body. But he was on guard against her, and would be watching for her to strike at him. She shivered, not from cold but from the plan that was burgeoning in her mind. Deliberately she made herself sink to the floor, her hands to her face to cover her sobs. Let him assume she would capitulate. Let him pride himself on besting her. That was the beginning. Galling though it was to grovel before this impudent Dane, Pentacoste realized that it was necessary for her schemes; she could make him dance to her tune in time. He had never known a woman of her quality before, she was certain of it. She would use this to her advantage, for she could make him yearn for her with dogged desire. He would come to hunger for her more than starving men hunger for food. Then she would tell him what he would and would not do. And then she would have cloth from far away, brought from the East by caravans to Starya Ladoga, and across the Baltic in merchant ships, which would land at Hedaby and Slieswic. This Dane would dress her in silks before she was done with him. The old gods would not desert her in her need, not after all she had done for them. She placed one hand on his foot. "All right. Tell me what I must do," she whimpered, noting with satisfaction that he preened at this supplication.

Dellingr reached down and took her by the hair. "You show good sense, Hohdama." He hauled her upward, forcing her to her feet. "You know where I sleep. Go there and wait for me."

She looked over at the captive slaves, huddled at the far end of the table. "It shames me to have them see me like this." She was testing him as well as telling him the truth.

He cuffed her ear. "You are one of them. What difference does it make if they see you naked?"

"They are . . . not high-born." She met his eyes directly. "They are beneath me. Can't you understand that?"

Dellingr scowled. "You may well be beneath them one day, if you continue to talk that way." His implication was unmistakable.

Pentacoste would not show her repugnance for fear of what the Dane might decide to do. She could feel the places where he had struck her growing painful and swollen; she would be badly bruised by morning, she had no doubt of it. She put her hand to her aching face. "I pray you, let me have a blanket at least."

"You may have one, when you go to my bed. If you please me." He nodded toward the slaves. "If she continues to disobey me, I will ask you to teach her to mind." He turned back to Pentacoste. "If she will not learn, she will be yours for as long as you want her."

"Never!" Pentacoste could not keep from crying out. "You would never give me to the likes of them."

"That is up to you," said Dellingr, then his expression went crafty. "Until your ransom offer is received, I will keep you by me, as my woman. What happens then will depend on how you have pleased me."

This was more in the line of what Pentacoste planned, and she lowered her head, as if in consent. "You do not need to threaten me so cruelly, Master, to have me serve you."

"Don't I?" asked Dellingr, dragging her close against him. "This is my promise to all of you. And the other slaves will bear witness. If you satisfy my demands and your ransom is sufficient, I will send you back to your father or your husband, if either wants to pay for your return. If they will not ransom you, then I will not keep you; you will serve these slaves as you serve me." His voice grew louder and deeper, and he leaned toward the slaves, leering at them as he turned Pentacoste in his grasp so that the captured men could see her. "My oath and honor upon it."

Pentacoste staggered as he suddenly released her and shoved her in the direction of the alcove where he slept. "They will pay, whatever the price; my father will not permit his daughter to endure you," she said, certain that by then Dellingr would not want to give her up to anyone, for any amount. Her father's men, or Berengar, would have to kill him for her to wrest her away from the Dane, so great would his passion be for her. She held her arms to conceal as much of her body as possible, and made her way to Dellingr's bed, pretending she did not hear the whispers of the slaves as she went past them.

There were calls and vows coming from the slaves; Halvor was among the loudest, claiming he would reduce Pentacoste to true humility. Dellingr encouraged them with rough laughter. For a time all Pentacoste could hear was the boasting of the slaves in ways they would bring about her degradation.

If only they would let her weave, she told herself as she sat on the bed and drew the covers around her. If she could weave, she could invoke the powers she needed to gain the control she wanted to have. Then Dellingr would kill those men for their lewd speculations, and would protect her from anyone who attempted to take her from him. She would ask in the morning if she could be allowed to weave with the others. If they would give her a spindle and some wool, she would be able to imbue the yarn itself with the spells that would give her the means to master her captor. With anticipation, she lay back, working out how she would snare Dellingr in the web of her weaving.

"I meant what I said," Dellingr announced a short while later when he returned to his alcove; his face was more flushed than before, and his Germanian slurred. He stared at her. "I will give you to them if there is no ransom."

She did her best to look frightened, but by now her plans were so well-developed she found it difficult to muster the necessary amount of horror. "I will do as you wish."

"Yes, you will, slave," said Dellingr, coming toward her unsteadily. He yanked her covers away and gloated down at her body. "My handiwork is coloring nicely," he told her as he began to loosen his clothes.

Pentacoste gritted her teeth, reminding herself that she would not have to put up with much more of this. It would not be long before her father paid her ransom, and then she would demand that the Danes be punished for their effrontery. As Dellingr mounted her, she forced herself not to struggle against him. If she could not work her full powers on him he might still make good on that threat to give her to his captured slaves. With that unbearable prospect to caution her, she tried to put her attention on other things than what Dellingr was doing to her; once she had him in her control, she would exact recompense for these humiliations.

Text of a letter from Gerefa Amalric on the 19th of November, 939, to Dux Pol of Luitich, carried by men-at-arms, and delivered on the 4th of January, 940.

To the most puissant Dux Pol, greetings from Leosan Fortress.

Although the Margerefa Oelrih has said that you wish to hear nothing more from this place, I have taken it upon myself to return to you the few items of jewelry belonging to your disavowed daughter, Pentacoste. It is the opinion of the Margerefa that these correctly belong to you, for she had no children to inherit them.

We have received no further word in regard to the fate of Pentacoste since messengers carried word to the Danes that no ransom would be paid; no wergeld has been sent to this fortress, so it must be assumed she is living still. The Danes do not want to go to war over a captured woman, so they will send the wergeld when she is dead.

In accordance with your wishes, her name has been removed from the fortress records in the muniment room; now it is as if Gerefa Giselberht had but one wife and became a monk of the White Christ after she died. Brother Andoche, the Margerefa's scribe, has inspected the records and will testify that your daughter's name does not appear anywhere.

The monks of Holy Cross Monastery have consented to remove Pentacoste's name from their records, as well. There is a new superior there who is of good family, and he understands these matters. He has vowed to make a full report to King Otto about what has been done and decided in regard to the daughter you have cast off. Any word of her eventual fate will be reported to him, of course, but he has given his word there would be no official record kept of this news.

As the sworn vassal of King Otto, champion of the White Christ, I commend myself to you. Should you ever require my service again, you have only to ask it, and it will be done.

Amalric
Gerefa, Leosan Fortress
by the hand of Brother Desidir
of Holy Cross Monastery

Epilogue

An exchange of letters between Atta Olivia Clemens at Aigües-Mortes in Francia to Ragoczy Sanct' Germain Franciscus in Rome, the first sent the 11th of September, 962; carried overland by messengers and delivered the 30th of October, 962: the second sent on the 24th of December, 962; sent by ship to Fraxinetum and carried overland by messenger to Aigües-Mortes and delivered the 12th of February, 963.

To my dearest and most vexatious friend, my greeting to you on this very warm afternoon of Saint Paphnutius's Feast.

He is the one who is supposed to have converted Thaïs, isn't he? Or was that another one of those dreary desert hermits? Never mind. I am sure it will not matter in another century or two.

I see that Otto has made good his oath and come to Rome at last. Very well, I admit you were right when you said that his ambitions would lead him south. I did not think he would be able to beat back the Magyars and the Slavs as well, to say nothing of holding the Danes in check and putting down the rebellions of his own vassals. Now if you will only explain to me what this Holy Roman Empire nonsense is, I shall think myself part of the world again. The Empire is centered in Germania, isn't it? And it is not an Empire as we knew when Nero reigned. And as for holy! What pressure did Otto use on Pope John XII to make him consent to this ludicrous fiction?

Niklos has finally found a villa that he deems suitable for raising horses, and in a short while we will be living there. We are currently posing as half-brother and -sister: same father, different mothers. This seems to forestall any awkward questions we would otherwise have to answer. Nevertheless, it does aggravate me that all the property must be in his name. In Rome, in my youth, laws were more sensible.

You will be pleased to know that I have found a lover at last, one who is not caught up in adoration of Christ, or seeking political advantages that are supposed to come attached to Romans. He is unaware of my true nature, but he has not reached the point where that is necessary. If it becomes necessary, I will tell him and trust that he will not be overcome with horror; as you warned me many centuries ago, I must be prepared for that eventuality, little though I want it.

Sanct' Germain, I miss you. I miss our long, pleasant conversations, and I miss our long, pleasant silences. I miss hearing you play the kithre and the liutus. I miss your smile and I wish it were not so rare. And once

in a while I miss the embraces we shared so long ago. But I do not miss
the grief that haunts you; I want to banish it from your thoughts and your
reveries. Yes, it is true that if you had had any choice in the matter you
would never have gone to Saxony. But I am grateful that you did, for to
have you face the long torture of death by water is more unthinkable than
the anguish Ranegonda's memory brings to you. And you have told me
that you treasure her and her memory, which sharpens your loss.

I know: if there were not this pain, there would not be the deep love, and
for that we would both be the poorer. You must pardon my desire to let
you have the passion and the cherishing and yet spare you the ache of
mourning. You have told me much the same thing from time to time, and
it has succeeded as well with me as this undoubtedly will succeed with you,
which is to say, not at all. Still, if you must grieve, will you let yourself
be truly comforted? Will you find another woman to love you more than
pragmatically? I can do nothing more than hope this for you, being of your
blood and your life. Do me the honor of loving again, with the fullness of
your love.

Enough of this. You will find a list enclosed of the merchants of this
area trading in Otto's enlarged Kingdom—or Empire. And you will find
a lock of my hair to give you happier memories than you have from that
silver-and-sapphire pectoral.

By my own hand and with my enduring, fondest love,

Olivia

My treasured, dearest Olivia,
You are exasperating when you are right.

Saint-Germain
(his seal, the eclipse)